Praise for Joshua Henkin

The World Without You

"Few American novelists, living or dead, have ever been as good as Henkin at drawing people."   —*Commentary Magazine*

"Intimate and insightful. . . . Reminds us that families are icebergs, with nine-tenths of their emotions just below the surface, capable of wreaking havoc when struck."   —*San Francisco Chronicle*

"Witty, poignant, and heartfelt."   —Gary Shteyngart, author of *Super Sad True Love Story*

"In the course of [a] long weekend, old and new tensions . . . bubble to the surface. It could be the plot of a Chekhov play or a Woody Allen movie. But on this classic narrative scaffolding, Joshua Henkin develops a painfully contemporary situation. . . . The skill with which Henkin explores the points of view and personae of his ensemble cast is masterful."   —*Newsday*

"Moving."   —*Vanity Fair*

"Henkin is a writer of voluminous heart, humanity, and talent."
—Julia Glass, author of *The Widower's Tale*

"Masterful. . . . Here are Tanglewood concerts overheard, fireflies, skinny-dipping, an intense tennis game, fireworks, jalapeno-lime corn on the cob and white gazpacho. Henkin gets all the details just right. Think *The Big Chill*, family style."   —*The New York Jewish Week*

"Pleasingly old-fashioned. . . . [A] warmhearted novel."
—*The Washington Post*

"A triumph and an important novel about America."
—Yiyun Li, author of *Gold Boy, Emerald Girl*

"In 2005, if a novelist had published a book that hinged on the murder of a Jewish American journalist by Islamic terrorists in Iraq, it would have been read as a political novel, a war novel, a post-9/11 novel—and, of course, a roman à clef about Daniel Pearl. . . . Yet the passage of time has made it possible for Henkin to turn this headline-news premise into a book that is quiet, inward-turning, and largely apolitical. . . . Henkin is a novelist of distinguished gifts." —*Tablet Magazine*

"An immeasurably moving masterpiece."

—Heidi Julavits, author of *The Vanishers*

"Henkin takes no sides in his novel. He simply presents his characters as they are, as they think, as they feel, how they interact, and lets it all reveal whatever it may. . . . A novel for mature readers—those who like fiction providing insight into how people actually live."

—*The Philadelphia Inquirer*

"[Resembles] Richard Ford's luminescent novel *The Sportswriter*. . . . Wonderful. . . . Powerful." —*The Rumpus*

"The American family in crisis has long represented rich source material for writers, from Hawthorne to Morrison. In his deeply felt new novel, Joshua Henkin offers his contemporary contribution. . . . [Characters] leap uncensored off the page as powerful and fully realized human beings, rather than types. . . . Heartfelt." —*The Miami Herald*

"Marvelous on the solitudes that exist even within the strongest and most compassionate of families."

—Jim Shepard, author of *You Think That's Bad*

"Gives us a welcome portrait of the repercussions of faraway wars on people who usually consider themselves to be spectators. . . . Compassionate and beguiling." —NPR

"Point this one out to contemporary fiction fans of Jonathan Franzen's *The Corrections*, or the works of Rick Moody, Richard Russo, Philip Roth, and John Updike." —*Library Journal*

Joshua Henkin

The World Without You

Joshua Henkin is the author of the novels *Swimming Across the Hudson* (a *Los Angeles Times* Notable Book) and *Matrimony* (a *New York Times* Notable Book). His stories have been published widely, cited for distinction in *Best American Short Stories*, and broadcast on NPR's *Selected Shorts*. He directs the MFA Program in Fiction Writing at Brooklyn College.

www.joshuahenkin.com

Also by Joshua Henkin

Matrimony

Swimming Across the Hudson

The World Without You

The World Without You

❁

Joshua Henkin

Vintage Contemporaries
Vintage Books
A Division of Random House, Inc.
New York

FIRST VINTAGE CONTEMPORARIES EDITION, APRIL 2013

Copyright © 2012 by Joshua Henkin

All rights reserved. Published in the United States by Vintage Books, a division
of Random House, Inc., New York, and in Canada by Random House of Canada
Limited, Toronto. Originally published in hardcover in the United States by
Pantheon Books, a division of Random House, Inc., New York, in 2012.

Vintage is a registered trademark and Vintage Contemporaries and colophon are
trademarks of Random House, Inc.

The Cataloging-in-Publication data is on file at the Library of Congress.

Vintage ISBN: 978-0-307-27718-3

Author photograph © Matthew Polis
Book design by M. Kristen Bearse

www.vintagebooks.com

Printed in the United States of America
10 9 8 7 6 5 4 3 2 1

In memory of my father, Louis Henkin
NOVEMBER 11, 1917–OCTOBER 14, 2010

Things seldom end in one event.

—RICHARD FORD, "Great Falls"

The World Without You

Prologue

"Here," she says, "I'll get you a sweater." She's barely done speaking before she's taking the stairs two at a time, her espadrilles clomping against the peeling wood, transporting her down the long hallway. It's July and twilight comes late, so even now, at nine o'clock, the last of the sun still colors the sky, but inside the house the corridors are dark and she's neglected to illuminate the antique standing lamp at the top of the stairs as if to reflect an inner austerity. It's their country house, but like their apartment in the city the hallway runs through it, an endless spine, which she traverses now, past the Kathe Kollwitz etchings and the street map of Paris and the photographs of her and David's grandparents staring down at them on opposite sides of the wall from another continent and century. She moves with such purpose (*dogged, implacable*: those are the words David uses to describe her) that when she reaches the lip of their bedroom and steps inside she's startled to discover she's forgotten what she came for.

She calls out to him, but he doesn't respond.

"Are you there?"

There's silence.

"David?" She'll turn seventy next spring, and David will, too (They were born a week apart. They've figured it out: she was emerging from the womb at the very hour he was circumcised, the first and last Jewish ritual he ever partook of, which places him, she thinks, one Jewish ritual ahead of her), and she's taken to saying her memory has begun to fail her, though she knows that's not true. Or no more true than for any sixty-nine-year-old—or for any adult human, for that matter. To have the memory of an infant, a toddler. She recalls Clarissa at ten months, those first stabs at language, how she resolved right then to teach her daughter French and German, to do it while it was still possible. She felt the same with Lily and Noelle, and again a few years later when Leo was born. She spent her junior year in Paris, at the Sorbonne, and

David spent his junior year in Düsseldorf. Her French was rusty by the time the children were born, and David's German was rusty, too, but it was worth a try, wasn't it, she said, and she still had her Berlitz tapes. And David, who in those days was still inclined to indulge her, allowed her to convince him to embark on a summer experiment; she would speak French to Clarissa and he would speak German. Two junior years abroad between them, one set of Berlitz tapes: the experiment lasted a week, the two of them speaking to baby Clarissa in their bad French and bad German until it became obvious to Marilyn what should have been obvious to her all along, that their daughter wasn't going to be trilingual; she was going to be mute, a wolf-child.

She remembers now. A sweater. She stands in front of their old closet, and there they are: David's shirts pressed and starched and evenly spaced, the shoes lined up in pairs, the sweaters folded in piles, next to them hanging a single brown cardigan. For a second she feels like a voyeur, looking in on a life that's no longer hers, and as she reaches out to grab the cardigan her hand shakes.

She heads back downstairs, and when she reaches the landing she calls out again, but he still doesn't respond. For an instant she panics: has he run off?

"I was calling you," she says. "Didn't you hear me?"

"I guess not." David is out on the porch, reading the *Times*, reclined on one of their old lawn chairs. His legs stick out in front of him; he taps his feet against the edge of the chair.

"I got you this." She hands him the cardigan, which he takes obediently, but now he's just laid it folded across his lap.

"You said you were cold."

"Did I?" His gaze is far off, tunneling past her.

He looks pale, she thinks. He's wearing a red button-down shirt with the sleeves rolled up, and he inhabits it so loosely that it billows around him like a pastry puff. He looks as if he's lost weight. He *has* lost weight. So has she. They haven't eaten much, either of them, this past year.

A mosquito lands on his neck. She swats at it, and he flinches. "A bug," she says.

He nods.

A firefly alights on one of her lilies, and another one, casting the garden in a sputter of light. "The girls will be arriving soon."

"Not for another twenty-four hours."

"That's soon enough."

Another mosquito lands on him.

"The bugs love you," she says. "Remember how we used to say that to the kids? Mornings before summer camp and we were coating them in Calamine? The mosquitoes loved Leo most of all."

She knows what he's thinking. That memory is selective, even in small matters like this one. But it's true, she thinks. Leo was the most bit-up of the kids. The bugs found him the sweetest, as did she.

He rises from his chair. "I need to get a haircut."

"David, it's nine o'clock at night."

"I mean tomorrow," he says, all impatience. "I'll go into town before the girls arrive." He checks his reflection in the porch window. He's patting down his hair, straightening out his shirt collar as if he has somewhere to go.

"You look good," she says. "Handsome." He still has a full head of hair, though it's grown silver over the years. When, she wonders, did this happen? It's taken place so slowly she hasn't noticed it at all.

She's sitting in a lawn chair, and she turns away from him. It's been a year since Leo died, and on the teak garden table, pressed beneath a mound of books, sits a pile of programs for the memorial. There will be a service at the Lenox Community Center; then they'll go to the cemetery for the unveiling.

"You changed into tennis shorts," he says.

"I was thinking of hitting some balls."

"Now?"

"The court is lit."

He shrugs, then goes back to the *Times*. He skims the editorial page, the letters, and now he's on to the arts. He folds the paper like origami, over and over on itself.

She steps off the porch and disappears into the garden. She continues along the stone path, which winds past the bushes to where their tennis court lies. The garage is next to it, and as she steps inside and flips on the court lights, the clay gets flooded in a pond of illumination.

She stands at the baseline with a bucket of balls, another bucket waiting in the garage behind her. She's in her shorts and an indigo tank top, her sneakers laced tightly, her hair tied back, though a few strands have come loose in the nighttime heat. She breathes slowly, in and out. She hits serve after serve into the empty opponent's court, taking something off the second serve, putting more spin on it, then returning to her first serve, hitting one ace after another. She serves into the deuce court and the ad court and the deuce court again. She empties one bucket of balls, and now she returns with the other bucket. Occasionally when she serves, her ball hits another ball lying on the clay, and they bounce off each other. There are a hundred and fifty tennis balls now, maybe two hundred, the court covered in fuzz the color of lime. Sweat drips down her forehead and singes her eyes. She simply leaves the balls lying there and returns to the house.

"Did you get it out of your system?"

She doesn't respond.

"So this is it," he says.

It is. After forty-two years of marriage, she's leaving him. At least that's how David puts it—how he *will* put it, no doubt, when they tell the girls. And it's true in a way: she was the one who finally decided she couldn't go on like this. A week ago she asked him for a trial separation. She hates that term. As if she's standing in front of a judge and lawyers, a jury of her peers. When she made her announcement, David said he wanted to give it another shot, but they've been giving it shot after shot for a year now and she has no more left in her. There are days when they don't talk at all. She has reminded him of the statistics, what happens to a marriage when you lose a child. Eighty percent, she's heard, maybe even ninety. Why should this surprise people? Already it's fifty percent when nothing obvious has gone wrong. But David doesn't want to hear statistics, and, truth be told, neither does she.

Another copy of the program lies forlornly on the porch. They're everywhere, it seems, strewn randomly about the house. She picks one up from the steps. Leo's photograph is across the cover, his curls corkscrewing out just like David's, and beneath the photo are the words APRIL 10, 1972–JULY 4, 2004. At the bottom of the page is a poem by William Butler Yeats.

When she told David of her plans, he wanted to call the girls immediately. He wanted to call Thisbe too. It seemed only fair, he said; Thisbe and Calder would be flying in from California. But she refused to let him call. She wanted to tell everyone in person, and to wait until after the memorial was over. But the real reason—she has only half admitted this, even to herself—is that she fears if David told the girls no one would come. It would serve them right, David says; she half suspects he wants to cancel himself. How can they have the memorial, David wants to know, when this is happening? But she disagrees. David thinks, How can they do this? and she thinks, How can they not?

Now, in the kitchen, she finds him on his hands and knees, taking a box cutter to four large packing boxes. He makes a single sharp motion down the center of each box. His back is to her; he looks as if he's searching for contraband. "Do you need help?" she asks, but he doesn't answer her.

The boxes are open now, gutted of their contents; a single Styrofoam peanut has flown out of the packing and skittered like a bug across the floor.

"The Williams Sonoma kosher special?"

He doesn't respond.

"What's the damage? A couple thousand dollars? More?"

David glances at the receipt, which is perched on the butcher-block table at the center of the room, lying in a bed of Styrofoam. "More or less."

"Oh, well," she says. "We can afford it."

"I suppose."

"You said you thought it was money well spent."

The contents of the boxes (plates and bowls, cutlery, serving dishes, pans and pots, a few extras that David insisted on, including a set of bowls for the children with famous sports figures on them—they're sports fiends, the grandchildren) have been purchased so that Noelle, Amram, and their four boys can eat in their house. Noelle won't eat off nonkosher dishes, even if those dishes belong to her parents. Especially, Marilyn sometimes thinks, if those dishes belong to her parents. Noelle and Amram live in Jerusalem and they visit at most once a year, so the dishes won't get much use. It's one of the many reasons Marilyn has been loath to buy them. But David has been lobbying for them for years; he thinks of them as a peace offering.

"A plate for me, a plate for you?" She's doing her best to make light of this.

He doesn't respond.

"Noelle will still come visit," she says. "Nothing has to change about that." Nothing has to change about anything, she wants to say, but she knows that's absurd.

She has found a rental on the Upper West Side, a two-bedroom in one of those all-services monstrosities, with a gym and a pool, a concierge, a playroom (it will be good for the grandchildren, she thinks), a party room, all the things she could want and a lot of things she couldn't. It's eleven blocks from David, which means they could run into each other grocery shopping, though in New York you can go for months without running into your own next-door neighbor. For a while, she thought it would be better to move to another neighborhood (she even considered moving to Brooklyn—Clarissa and Nathaniel live there, so she could be nearby), but except for those few years when the girls were in high school and the family decamped to Westchester, she has spent her whole adult life on the Upper West Side. It's hard to imagine living anywhere else. And the apartment opened up suddenly and the lease is month to month, so it will be a good place to figure out what comes next. It's the house in Lenox that makes her heart quicken. Will she be allowed to come back here? Will she allow herself? She and David have been coming to the Berkshires summer after summer for forty years now.

"You checked the food?"

David nods. "Everything's certified kosher."

"Are you sure?"

He is.

More Styrofoam peanuts are strewn across the floor, including one that has lodged itself under the fridge, which Marilyn stabs at with a fork. Now she's standing with David amidst the wreckage, and beside it all sits the bubble wrap unfurled like a runner across the length of the room. "We bought a whole kitchen," she says. "No spatula left unturned."

David gives her a tired smile.

"Are we supposed to bless them?" she says darkly. "Is that what you do?"

"Christen them?" David says.

She laughs, as she knows she's supposed to, and it feels good to laugh with David. For a moment there's a lightness between them, as if a screen has been lifted.

When David finds her a few minutes later, she's seated in the alcove that adjoins the living room, typing on the computer. "I know what you're thinking."

"What?" he says.

"There she goes again. Writing another op-ed about the war."

"What do you want me to say?"

"You could say you miss him."

"Of course I miss him."

"It's been a year since he died, for God's sake. And, yes, I know writing these things won't bring him back, but I don't care." She doesn't care, either, that she has become a mascot for the left and everyone thinks of her as the mother of the dead journalist. Because that's what she is. It's what David is, too: the father of the dead journalist. It's all they're ever going to be.

In the kitchen now, he prepares a citrus marinade for the chicken. He has chosen the menu: white gazpacho, caramelized leeks and endive, marinated chicken thighs, jalapeño-lime corn on the cob, pasta salad. They will also have watermelon slushies. At the moment, though, he's chopping vegetables. The year before Leo died, when he retired after thirty-nine years of teaching high school English, David took a course consecrated to the very subject, five Sundays running at the 92nd Street Y. Slicing and Dicing 101, Marilyn called it; it was evidence, she believed, that he had too much time on his hands.

Though there's certainly a technique, as he demonstrates now, the way he keeps his knife always on the cutting board, only his wrist moving. That's all there is these days, just the sound of David when she comes home from work, cutting vegetables in their kitchen on Riverside Drive, the sound of him here too, in Lenox, her husband chopping vegetables. She thinks how hard it's going to be, living on her own, how she has brought this on herself, the solitude, the silence, and now, when she's alone, as if in preparation for what's to come, she has begun to turn on the radio and she listens to music she doesn't care for, just to hear a sound in the room.

The phone rings, but when she goes to answer it, the person has hung up. She has a brief, paranoid thought that someone is following her. A trickle of sweat makes its way down her spine. She opens the kitchen window, but it's just as warm outside as it is in the house, so she closes the window again. Her heart still beats fast from hitting those tennis balls. She smacked one of the balls as hard as she could, clear over the fence and past the neighbor's property. She did it for the fun of it, but it wasn't fun. She feels the energy funnel out of her, wrung from her as if from a sponge. Sometimes she feels as if she could die, that she'd *like* to die; it would be better that way. "He used to walk around with his laces undone. Remember? It was like he was daring you to step on them."

"Who?"

"What do you mean who?" Because in her life there is nobody else. And because for David there has been somebody else (there have been their girls; there have been his hobbies—he has taken up running and become devoted to opera; he stays up late poring over librettos—there has been this relentless chopping of vegetables), because he's been trying to make the best of an unspeakable situation, she hasn't been able to abide him. Is that why she's leaving him? All she knows is she's so very very tired. She looks at him once more and feels the rage burble inside her.

Onions, scallions, leeks, endive, cucumbers, jalapeño: he chops them all. It looks like a trash heap, like volcanic ash. Always the reasonable one. For years she counted on him to be like that. Now it assails her.

"Did you call your mother?" she asks.

He nods.

"You didn't tell her, did you?" That was their agreement—the agreement, at least, that she extracted from him. No one is to know until after the memorial.

"No," he says sharply. "I didn't."

"Then what did you two talk about?"

"Nothing," he says. "She's a woman of few words, Marilyn."

"So what were her few words?"

"She's not coming."

"Are you serious?" And she thinks: You told her not to come, didn't you? Except, she realizes, she's actually said those words.

"My mother's been through a lot. Do you blame her for not wanting to go through it again? She's ninety-four years old."

"I know how old she is."

He's quiet.

"She's ninety-four, and she'll live to a hundred and forty. She has a stronger constitution than any of us."

She's washing the dishes now, going at them furiously, while David is still chopping behind her, the percussive sound of him. He presses down hard on a carrot, and the top comes flying off and sails across the room. "Jesus," he says. "Fuck! I cut myself."

"Is it bad?"

"Bad enough." There's a gash in his thumb. It looks shallow at first, but now, studying it beneath the sink light, Marilyn sees it's deeper than she realized. She takes a wad of paper towel and presses it to his hand. But the blood seeps through, so she goes to the pantry to get more paper towel, and when she returns his hands are shaking.

"Are you all right?"

"I don't know." He sits down on the stool and she's above him now, attending to him. She runs his hand under cold water. The blood drips off him and into the sink, down into the garbage disposal along with the vegetable peel and citrus rind, swirling around like beet juice. She comes back with tape and a gauze pad and bandages him up.

"Slicing and Dicing 101, huh? They should have flunked me out."

She presses her hands around his, wrapping him in gauze, as if she's taping up a fighter.

"How am I doing, doctor?"

She forces out a smile. She's an internist by training, but she did a second residency, in infectious disease. He has come to the wrong specialist. "You're lucky you don't need stitches."

"*Do* I need them?"

"I think I staunched the flow."

She guides him upstairs and into their old bedroom. She has him in their bathroom beneath the flickering lights, and David is saying, "We need to replace that bulb. And the mirror," he adds. "It has a crack in it. Hairline fracture."

But she's focused only on the task at hand, urging him to remain still. She takes off the bandage, which is shot through with blood, and wraps his hand again.

You're as good as new, she wants to say, but her breath catches on the words. They're out of the bathroom, and now David, in his white gym socks, is sitting on their old bed; tentatively, she settles herself beside him. One of his socks has a hole in it, and his big toe pokes out, white as a marshmallow nub. Through the window, she can see the tennis court still dotted with balls, lumpy as dough in the moonlight. Clean up, clean up. The girls will be coming soon, and they might want to play. "How are you feeling?"

"I'm all right."

She's quiet.

"Time to hit the hay."

She nods. At home in the city, they've been sleeping in separate bedrooms, but this is the first time they've been back here, up in Lenox, alone together. It seems that David has claimed their old bedroom. Squatter's rights. Though she, in fairness, is a squatter, too. She's also, she understands, the bad guy here. David's suitcase is on the floor at his feet; a shoe tree spills out of it, and a can of shaving cream.

"Good night," she says.

He gives her a quick nod.

She turns softly on her heels and heads down the hall. When she comes back a few minutes later, David is already asleep. There he is, her husband, and she feels a momentary heartbreak, knowing she's not supposed to be looking at him, that somehow she's not entitled. But she continues to stand there, tears falling down her face. She's back in their house in Larchmont, back in other houses and apartments, remembering hallways, portals, a domed ceiling high above the family dinner table, bedrooms whose configurations she can only dimly recall outside of which she used to stand at night quietly watching her children sleep—and later, listening to David breathe softly beside her, and she, a stealthy presence among the reposed, careful not to disturb the sleep of a loved one.

1

It's five-thirty in the morning and still dark out, but Clarissa lies awake, as she's been for the last hour, her feet thrumming against the bed, performing their solemn agitations. Nathaniel lies undisturbed beside her. At this hour, any reasonable person would be asleep, but especially Nathaniel, who considers waking up early an affront. If it were up to him, Nathaniel would keep the schedule of a college student, which, at forty-four, is what he still looks like, a lanky teenager all bone and sinew, with dark hair so straight you could measure something with it. He's beautiful, Clarissa thinks, and she loves him dearly, but watching him sleep makes her quietly enraged. It's a common feeling, she supposes—sleep to the sleepless can seem like taunting—though Nathaniel is no common sleeper. He lies flat on his back as if pinioned to the mattress, his arms raised above his head in a look of benevolent supplication. "Nathaniel," she whispers, trying to wake him without appearing to do so.

"Mmm . . ."

"It's morning," she says. "Sort of."

She waters the African violets, then tends to the cactus beside the bed. She's the family horticulturist—Nathaniel says he's indifferent to plants—but she can be lazy about watering them. Often she cheats, watering deeply but infrequently, letting the liquid pool at the bottom of the planters and hoping that, like cats, the plants will eat only when they're hungry. So far, at least, they don't seem to be suffering. She has chosen bulbs that don't require much attention, and thanks to the small garden she and Nathaniel have out back, she, a city girl, has found a new identity; she has become a grower of herbs and a puller of weeds.

She removes her suitcase from the closet and packs jeans, T-shirts, running shoes, underwear, then tosses several paperbacks into the bag, though they'll be gone for only a few days. Evelyn Wood, her sisters used to call her. When she was ten, she saw a speed-reading advertisement on TV in which a woman was reading as fast as she could turn pages, and though her parents wouldn't let her take the course, she gave herself her own speed-reading class, learning to move her forefinger diagonally down the page.

A couple of stray socks have landed on the chair, and she disposes of them.

"Tidying up for the housekeeper?" Nathaniel says.

"Not only."

"You keep that up, we should pay *you*."

If Brooklyn seceded from the other boroughs it would be the fourth-largest city in the United States; right now, though, it's as silent as a mausoleum. At the window, Clarissa stands sentinel over the row of brownstones, and presently she hears the sanitation workers collecting the garbage. A man crosses the street walking his collie; a FreshDirect truck drives by. Soon the rest of the neighborhood will be up, too, off to their holiday destinations, just as she and Nathaniel will be off to theirs, to her parents' country house in the Berkshires. Lily will be driving up from D.C.; Noelle and her family are flying in from Jerusalem. With all the children and luggage, it will take both Clarissa and Lily to transport everyone to Lenox, so they'll be meeting Noelle at Logan Airport. And there's her and Nathaniel's own business to attend to first.

Gwendolyn, their hundred-pound Bernese Mountain Dog, lumbers into the room. "Good morning, you," Clarissa says. "Have you come to say goodbye?" Gwendolyn will need to be kenneled for the holiday. Lily and Malcolm will have to kennel their dog, too, because one of Noelle's boys is allergic to dogs.

"You look pretty," Nathaniel says.

"It's six in the morning, Nathaniel. No one looks pretty at this hour." She's in her underwear, wearing a T-shirt that reads, WHAT IF THE HOKEY-POKEY REALLY IS WHAT IT'S ALL ABOUT?

"You do."

"You always say that."

"That's because it's true."

On the window ledge sits a plate of raisin scones, and she offers him one. Standing before him with the plate in her hand, she feels like a Girl Scout come to sell cookies.

Nathaniel obediently eats a scone, making noises of approval, but she can feel the effort in his response. More and more he's been doing things to please her, and though she's grateful for this, it also makes her think that he's mollifying her, that there's a tinge of appeasement to his kindness. "I made those myself."

"When?"

"Four in the morning?" she says. "Maybe three?"

It's not bad, she thinks, taking a bite of scone; maybe she has a talent she never recognized. When they were growing up, Noelle used to call her the Girl Voted Most Likely to Succeed. In her high school—it's been more than twenty years now—the students were too busy airlifting food to Nicaragua, helping organize the grape workers, spending their summers on farm collectives for anyone to have been voted most likely to succeed, and even if someone had been, it wouldn't have been her. She graduated from Yale, an entire college of students voted most likely to succeed: the pleasers and résumé padders. She's never been like that. Still, she isn't used to failure, and everything that's been happening these past months weighs heavily on her. It weighs heavily on Nathaniel too, but he expresses it differently.

She fills the toiletry kit with toothbrushes, deodorant, a razor, dental floss. There's gum disease in Nathaniel's family, so he flosses regularly, and Clarissa, who hates to floss, has tried to take this as inspiration. The family that flosses together stays together, she says. At the drugstore, she will stock up on floss, dropping ten rolls of it at the register. "Big family?" the cashier asked one time. "Eight kids," Clarissa said, back when she was able to joke about such things.

The forecast is for rain tonight, perhaps tomorrow as well, but on July Fourth itself it's supposed to be clear. It's the one-year anniversary of Leo's death, and with Noelle flying in for the memorial, it will be the first time since the funeral that the whole family will be together. Thisbe and Calder will be flying in, too. Calder is three now; Clarissa can hardly believe it.

She examines herself in the bathroom mirror. Her hair has turned strawberry blond, which is what happens every summer; the rest of the year she's a redhead. In one shade or another, all the sisters are. Leo was a redhead, too. When they were growing up, you could always recognize the Frankel children. Now, in Israel, Noelle covers her hair, and it pains Clarissa to think about her sister's lovely red hair, which no one is allowed to see except Amram. She has reminded Noelle how beautiful she used to be—she's *still* beautiful, of course—and how when Noelle first came to Israel the men called her *gingy* and trailed her on the streets, how they all thought she'd grown up on a kibbutz until they heard her speak Hebrew.

She allows herself to wonder whether Nathaniel is right and maybe she has become beautiful herself; he's so ardent and convincing. Her eyes are the green of freshly sliced cucumber, her face long like a mare's, with a birthmark on the right side going down to her neck. Mostly it just looks like she has a suntan, though it used to make her self-conscious. When she moves, it's as if she's walking in and out of shadows. "We'll need to have sex at my parents' place."

"It's been done before."

"The house will be overrun with grandchildren."

"All the better," he says. "No one will notice when we sneak off." He looks up at her from across the room. "What are you doing?"

"Checking my breasts," she says sheepishly. "I know. I must look like a porn star."

"No," he says. "Just like a compulsive."

Without even realizing it, she has developed a routine. She checks her breasts for bloating, then searches for headaches and other signs. She sticks her fingers inside her vagina to see if her cervix has gotten softer, and if it has opened a little. But it's hard to determine whether her cervix is harder or softer, further up or further back, more closed or more open. She's so focused on her body she can give herself pains she doesn't really have. Sometimes she feels a headache coming on; she almost wills herself to have one. *Oh, God, I have a headache*. It has become a joke between her and Nathaniel. It's the reverse of the old adage: headaches are now an aphrodisiac.

She puts half a dozen ovulation kits into her suitcase, though she knows that's more than she'll need. In their early months together, back when they were still using condoms, Nathaniel would stick ten, twelve condoms into his suitcase, even though they were going away for just the weekend; often they were visiting Clarissa's parents' country house itself. "Well, well, Mister Big Shot," Clarissa said.

"You don't want us to run out. Do they even have drugstores in that town your parents live in?"

Haughty, haughty Nathaniel. Transplanted to New York, and with the transplant's arrogance. He's the one, after all, who grew up in a small town.

For good measure, she throws in a couple of pregnancy tests. Her cycles are so irregular it's impossible to chart them: forty days, fifty days, but then it's nineteen, and she's spending her lunch hour in the office bathroom, her money squandered on an array of pee sticks, lurching from ovulation test to pregnancy test and back again. She buys her ovulation tests in bulk so she won't have to keep going back, and she rotates drugstores so the clerks won't recognize her. Sometimes she has Nathaniel buy the tests for her; it seems only fair. In her twenties, she used to buy condoms with a casualness that bordered on disdain, but this feels different to her. There's something more private about pregnancy than about sex, and although she understands the two are connected, it's the trying to conceive that feels personal to her.

In the bathroom, she removes the basal thermometer from its case and returns to bed. She's supposed to take her temperature as soon as she wakes up, since any activity at all can affect the reading. But she's been up most of the night; there's no changing that. So she lies in bed in compensatory stillness, hoping to fool the temperature gods. She even closes her eyes, pretending to be asleep, the way she used to when she was a girl on those weekend trips to the Berkshires when she didn't wish to play GHOST with Lily any longer and the only way to end the game was to feign sleep. She's looking for a subtle drop followed by a sustained rise. The drop has already occurred, and it's the rise she's waiting for, an increase of half a degree.

But her temperature is the same as it was yesterday. "Maybe I just don't ovulate."

"Come on," Nathaniel says. "The doctor says you do." He walks barefoot across the room and rests his hand on her.

"You must think I'm crazy."

"I don't."

"Sometimes *I* think I'm crazy."

"Well, you're not." There's an adamancy in Nathaniel's voice. He has always been protective of her, even when the person attacking her is herself. "It takes the average woman many months to get pregnant."

"It's been more than many months." Besides, she has never felt average, and even if she did, other people's difficulties don't make hers any easier. She's more impatient than average, she's finding out.

They've been trying for a year now; they started right after Leo died. She has gone to the doctor for some tests, and just last week she went in for more, but so far there have been no answers. The next step is to intervene medically. It's a journey she's willing to take, and Nathaniel is, too, though he's a more reluctant traveler than she is. He mistrusts the medical establishment; once you start something, it's hard to know where it will end. One place it might end is with twins, and there are already twins on Nathaniel's side of the family. As time has passed, Clarissa has come to think twins wouldn't be so bad, but Nathaniel believes it's hard enough when the children are spaced a few years apart. Clarissa doesn't disagree. It has become such a part of her family's lore that Noelle's difficulties were the result of being her and Lily's sister (to this day, her mother thinks that's why Noelle is in Jerusalem, married to Amram, mother of four) that no one can contradict it any longer. And maybe her mother is right. Clarissa doesn't care. She doesn't think her family should be a cautionary tale. "I'm thirty-nine," she reminds him. "That's one away from forty, in case you forgot."

"You just need to be patient."

"Please, Nathaniel. Stop it." Often his confidence seems cavalier, but she has come to rely on it just the same; she doesn't know what she'd do if they both were pessimistic. But then she asks herself how he can be so calm if they claim to want the same thing. It's not that she wishes he were more understanding. He's been hopelessly, infuriatingly understanding; it's his very understanding that assails her. What she wants is for him to be upset. She has begun to wonder whether he wants a baby as much as she does, whether, despite everything he says, he'd be as miserable as she would be if they couldn't have a child.

She removes an ovulation test from her suitcase and, squatting on the toilet, pees into the cup. She doubts she's ovulating—her temperature didn't rise—but measuring your basal temperature isn't foolproof. If the pee stick is positive, the second line is as dark as or darker than the first.

She hands the stick to Nathaniel. "What do you think?"

"The control is darker."

"Are you sure?"

He nods.

She breaks the stick in half and throws it against the wall.

"Clarissa . . ."

"Please," she says, "don't patronize me."

"I haven't even said anything."

She returns with another ovulation test and shreds the wrapper. "Here," she says, "*you* pee on it."

"What?"

It's a waste of a good pee stick, she understands, but she's been wasting these sticks for months now, and she wants him to feel what it's like.

And what will she do if Nathaniel tests positive? Sue the company?

Naked beside her, his penis flaccid, Nathaniel trundles to the toilet. He looks up at her as if hoping for a reprieve, then holds the stick beneath his urine stream, some of which bounces off the cup and trickles down his leg.

He lays the stick on top of the toilet and waits the required time. "There you have it."

"You're not ovulating," she says.

"No, I'm not."

She starts to cry. She knows what will come next. IVF. Big, painful injections every morning. She's terrified of needles. Divorce, she has read, is common among infertile couples. She jokes that what will split her and Nathaniel up won't be the infertility but the shots themselves. Standing in the bathroom, she decides that, if the time comes, she won't allow Nathaniel to administer the injections. She'll hire a professional IVF injector; she'll pay someone she hates to give her the shots, someone she never wanted to marry in the first place. "Oh,

God," she says, and she bends down with a wad of toilet paper to mop Nathaniel up, to wipe the pee off his ankles, his toes.

For years Clarissa thought she didn't want children, even into her thirties, after she and Nathaniel had gotten together. She had read the studies, about how childless couples were happier than couples with children, and though she wasn't someone to overemphasize happiness (she'd read her John Stuart Mill: "It is better to be a human being dissatisfied than a pig satisfied; better to be Socrates dissatisfied than a fool satisfied"), she didn't wish to underemphasize it, either. And she was happy with Nathaniel; she loved him. *It's us against the world*, she used to say.

They'd met in Boston, where Nathaniel had finished his doctorate and had decided on an impulse to do something different that summer and work at a mental hospital. Clarissa was working at the hospital, too, though in her case she thought she might want to be a psychologist; she was scouting out a possible career. It was a hospital for the wealthy, and everyone looked vaguely familiar to her, as if she'd alighted on a set of old B-movie actors. One time, somebody ran naked down the hall and had to be restrained by the nursing staff. "We should take photos and send them to *People*," Clarissa said.

"Or *Playboy*," said Nathaniel. "Girls of the mental ward."

It was the summer they discovered bad late-night TV. The cable hadn't been switched off by the previous tenants, so they would stay up until two in the morning in Nathaniel's Somerville apartment drinking beer and eating pizza while beneath them on Beacon Street teenagers were playing their boom boxes outside the Star Market. In the morning, they would haul themselves out of bed and into the shower and, with a doughnut in one hand, a cup of coffee in the other, they would negotiate the hazards of rush hour, descending into the bowels of the Porter Square station to take the T to work. Clarissa was always saying that the only difference between the patients and the staff was who had the keys. That as much as anything steered her away from psychology—she has taken another path entirely: she does foundation work, doling out money for international relief—because that summer she felt as if she and Nathaniel lived alone on a little island of mental health.

Through July and August, staying up late with their beer and pizza, they would talk about their respective life plans, making sure not to imply that the other was included; it was still early, after all. But it bothered Nathaniel, he later admitted, that Clarissa thought she didn't want to have children. It cast suspicion on her and made him realize there were things about her he didn't know.

That first year, they lived in separate apartments in Morningside Heights, a five-minute walk from Nathaniel's office. But it was Nathaniel who suggested they move to Brooklyn, to one of the child-friendly neighborhoods near Prospect Park. A couple of years later, when marriage came up, Nathaniel wanted to know whether Clarissa would consider having children with him. If she wouldn't, he wasn't sure he could marry her.

To hear it put so baldly startled Clarissa. If Nathaniel wanted a mother for his children, he should have chosen someone else; there were plenty of women who'd have been happy to bear his child. It felt crude and utilitarian, not to mention unromantic, as if their relationship had been driven by an ulterior motive she'd only now unearthed. It made her wonder whether she and Nathaniel should be getting married in the first place; for a time it seemed they would have to break up.

But they loved each other, and when Clarissa, despite holding no stock in biological clocks, began to see her friends have children; when she held a friend's baby and, to her surprise, was overcome by an almost visceral pull; when she turned thirty-one, and thirty-two, and she started to realize that although she wasn't a kids person, exactly, she wasn't exactly not a kids person either; when she began to think that if she never had a child she might someday regret it—when she felt all this, and saw how important it was to Nathaniel, she agreed to try.

But a year passed, and another, and they hadn't begun yet. She was thirty-five, she was thirty-six, she was thirty-seven, and it seemed they were in a holding pattern from which they couldn't emerge. Then Leo was killed, and she decided they couldn't wait any longer. Because she'd been planning her life and her brother went off and died, and there was no point, she realized, in planning things.

Something happened when it didn't work those first few months, and she panicked, realizing she'd waited so long to get pregnant that now she might not be able to. It wasn't supposed to happen, this savage, seemingly chemical urge to reproduce. Maybe it's the power of suggestion, living in Brooklyn, home to the world's greatest population explosion. Whatever the reason, this wish to have a baby has blindsided her, has blindsided Nathaniel too, who has found in the last year that he doesn't recognize the person he married.

She's dressed now, folding laundry in the alcove outside their bedroom, while Nathaniel is in the bathroom taking a shower. She removes her cello from its case and seats herself on the ottoman.

"Something to sing by?" Nathaniel calls out.

"I guess." Though it's hard to sing to Dvořák's Cello Concerto in B Minor: there are no words. "You can hum to it," she says, but Nathaniel can't hear her from beneath the shower water.

When he steps out of the bathroom, she's still moving the bow across the strings. He taps her lightly with his towel. "I thought you were in a rush to get going."

"Careful," she says, poking him. "You don't want to get water on the strings."

It's only in the last year that she has started to play again. For years—for decades, in fact—her cello remained in storage. It fell into desuetude, she likes to say, though really it fell into disrepute. She didn't so much as want to look at it. It pains her to play—she's such a pale version of what she once was—but she's driven to do it nonetheless. Music calms her in a way nothing else does, in a way it never used to when she was playing seriously.

They've been hoping to beat the holiday traffic, but now, as they drive through downtown Brooklyn, it seems the traffic has beaten them. On Flatbush Avenue, they're stalled across the street from an Italian restaurant. "We could stop for a whole meal," Nathaniel says, "in the time it would take us to get down this block."

The Brooklyn Bridge is backed up, too. A couple of police officers flank the entrance ramp, one of them checking the trunk of a van.

"It's only July second," Clarissa says. "Imagine what it will be like tomorrow and the Fourth." Green threats, yellow threats, orange threats, red threats: it's hard for her to remember what means what. Hard, too, to stay on high alert. Watching the police officers search the van, she thinks of Leo, of course, though Leo was in Baghdad when he was killed, not on the Brooklyn Bridge. And heightened security was the last thing on his mind. For as long as she can remember, he preferred heightened insecurity.

"When does Noelle get in?"

"Two?" she says. "Maybe two-thirty?" She rifles through her bag to find her date book.

"I haven't seen her in . . ."

"A year." Noelle flew in for Leo's funeral, but when it was over she returned to Jerusalem, and she hasn't been back since. Money is tight for her and Amram. Still, Clarissa thinks, how can she have absented herself for so long? When they spoke in February, Clarissa told Noelle she'd pay for a flight, but Noelle refused; she said she'd fly in for the memorial.

"And Amram," Nathaniel says.

"Mister Asparagus Pee." It's what Clarissa and Lily still call Amram. Amram and Noelle went to high school together, though back then he was known as Arthur. Arthur was the class prankster, overweight and disheveled, well liked in the way that overweight boys can be well liked, whereas a girl as heavy as Arthur would have been ostracized. Arthur was always turning scatology into philosophy. He wove elaborate theories as to why people liked the smell of their own farts; he considered suitable for scientific inquiry the question of why some people's pee smelled after they ate asparagus while other people's didn't. Apparently, it was a matter of having a particular enzyme, but Arthur hypothesized that it wasn't the pee itself but the ability to smell it that distinguished the two groups. One day, when asparagus was being served at lunch, a bunch of ninth-grade boys could be seen shuttling in and out of the bathroom under Arthur's supervision to smell each other's pee.

Now, as they head up the West Side Highway, Nathaniel gives a desultory wave in the direction of his office. Above the branches, Clarissa can make out the tops of the buildings on Riverside Drive. It's the neighborhood where she spent much of her childhood. Evenings, from her family's balcony, she used to stare across the Hudson at the Palisades, the amusement park flickering, the Ferris wheel lit up like an enormous necklace.

"Are you ready for the next few days?"

She looks at him forlornly: how could she possibly be?

An airplane streaks across the horizon, drawing something in chalk, but the writing disappears as soon as it's been printed, lost in the cloud cover and the darkening sky, the hints of impending rain.

"Did you write out your speech?"

She shakes her head.

"You'll have time when you get there."

"It might be better just to speak it. Sometimes when you prepare it's even worse."

A car backfires. Or maybe it's fireworks already going off. Even as a girl she was indifferent to fireworks, the boom like a rifle's recoil, the smear of color across the sky; you've seen one firework, she thought then, you've seen them all. Now, though, it feels like taunting: all that enforced good cheer. She thinks, The nerve of Leo to die on the Fourth. As Nathaniel drives on, she falls asleep to the hum of the movement, the ticking of the grates beneath their tires. She dreams of Leo. He's not doing anything—he's just hovering on the edges—but she has an image of him as a baby, and of her changing him on the table beside his crib. Another image comes to her, a Saturday and it's raining out, and she's watching Leo, who's only ten months old, thinking he's going to talk someday, that he's going to have opinions. It seemed inconceivable at the time, and in that inability to conceive lay a sorrow too, that her brother would grow up and eventually leave her. Often now, when she reflects on her newfound maternal impulses, she thinks back to how she felt about Leo, and she realizes these impulses have always been there and they've simply been submerged.

She is woken by the sound of a cell phone ringing. She reaches into her bag, but it's Nathaniel's phone, not hers.

He pulls over to the side of the road. He's nodding, nodding, taking in some news.

"Who was that?" she asks when he hangs up.

"The chair of the department," he says. "It seems I've won some award."

"Nathaniel!" she says. "Congratulations!"

"I guess."

"What do you mean you *guess?*"

He's quiet.

"Well? Aren't you going to tell me what it's for?"

"Outstanding teacher of the year. I'm supposed to give a final lecture."

"A *final* lecture?"

"Exactly. I'm forty-four years old, and they're already packing me off. They'll hang me like antlers from the wall."

"Look at you. It's amazing news, and you turn it into a cause for mourning."

"I'm just dreading it, that's all."

Nathaniel is a professor at Columbia, a behavioral economist turned neuroscientist, possessor of not one but two PhDs. He doesn't like to talk about this—his PhDs, his success, his work in general. Now, though, the secret is out, because last year he appeared on the cover of the *New York Times Magazine* in an article called "The New Frontier: How Neuroscience Is Reshaping Human Consciousness." To Nathaniel, this has all been mortifying. The photograph, certainly—he still gets ribbed by his colleagues—but also the phrase "whispers of a future Nobel Prize," which appeared in the article next to his name. He's aware of these whispers; he'd just prefer it if the rest of the world weren't aware of them, too. Clarissa likes to say that his carefully honed reputation for sloth has been ruined. But that's not what bothers him. He's simply embarrassed by it all. "It's the life of an extremely small-time rock star." Only that, he says, overstates matters. He doubts there's a rock star small-time enough to rival him.

Now, on the Merritt Parkway, he's close to the car in front of him, too close, Clarissa thinks, so she tells him this, and he touches his foot to the brake. There's construction ahead. A car is pulled over at the side of the road, and people stop to rubberneck. From behind them comes the sound of a police siren. "I think I'm about to ovulate," Clarissa says. She has this idea that there's an exact moment they're supposed to have sex, though the window is a good deal larger than that, twenty-four to thirty-six hours, most people say. But within that window, certain times must be better than others.

"We don't have to do this," Nathaniel says.

"Do what?"

"Be so precise about things."

"Precision matters."

Still, he wonders aloud whether there might not be a better approach. No basal thermometers or home ovulation kits. Just have sex when they want to. It would relieve the pressure from them.

"It would decrease our chances."

"It's just that you're so anxious," he says.

Anxiety, she knows, can contribute to infertility. Not getting pregnant is making her anxious, which is making her not get pregnant. Maybe if she pretended she didn't want it so much it would come to her unbidden.

"Worse comes to worse, there's adoption."

She knows this, of course, but it stings her to hear it. There are subjects she simply can't contemplate, as if merely to entertain them will bring them on.

Ahead of them, the traffic moves so slowly it appears not to be moving at all. She thinks of drives to the Berkshires when she was a girl, those weekends when it seemed to her that everything was one long car ride, she and her sisters jostling in the backseat, Leo on their mother's lap in front, their father behind the wheel singing songs, making up word jumbles and dictionary games, doing whatever he could to distract them.

A mist settles on the car. Nathaniel sprays wiper fluid across the windshield, and for an instant it feels as if they're driving through a carwash before the view in front of them clears up.

She removes a Kit Kat from the glove compartment, then puts it back. She knows what Nathaniel would say. If you couldn't eat chocolate the entire French population would have died out by now. But you could say the same thing about wine, and she's staying away from that.

They cross the Massachusetts border and make a pit stop, and when she returns she says, "I'm ovulating."

"How do you know?"

"I just took a test."

"In the middle of 7-Eleven?"

She explains to Nathaniel what he should already know, that when the test turns positive you're set to ovulate in twenty-four to thirty-six hours. But at that point you should already be having sex; the best time to start is two days beforehand. "We need to have sex right now."

"Absolutely," he says. "We'll just pull over to the side of the road. We'll hump unobtrusively on the hood of the car."

"That's not what I'm saying."

"What *are* you saying?"

"Let's check into a motel."

"We can't," he says. "We're supposed to meet your sisters."

"We'll make it."

"Not if we stop, we won't. Anyway, you can't just check into a motel at one in the afternoon."

"Of course you can." She directs him to the nearest exit, where the signs promise food, gas, and lodging and where, when they get off the ramp, they see a Holiday Inn, a Red Roof Inn, a Hampton Inn, a Howard Johnson. "Which will it be?" she says, her voice a singsong, taking on a jocund air she doesn't feel.

But Nathaniel won't play along. He simply sits next to her, making clear through his silence that this is her project. When she pulls out her credit card at the Hampton Inn, he stands so far behind her it's as if he doesn't know who she is.

She walks down the hall to the elevator, but Nathaniel is still standing at the front desk, staring vacantly at the Coke machine.

"It's a nice room," she says when they get inside, realizing as she says this how inane she sounds. It's like any motel room off the side of the road anywhere in the country.

Nathaniel goes into the bathroom to get a drink, and when he comes back inside he flips on the TV. He removes his shoes and lies down on the bed. He's making a show of settling in.

"What are you doing?"

"Renting a movie."

"No, you're not."

"Actually, I am." He has purchased a German movie, a black-and-white affair, a documentary, it seems. Clarissa recognizes the sky-line of Berlin, a museum, plumes of smoke rising from refineries, the Bavarian countryside. "You could have chosen a language we actually speak."

"I speak a little German."

"Okay," she says. "You've made your point. The court registers your objection."

Nathaniel turns off the movie and goes into the bathroom. She can hear the shower being run.

"Nathaniel, come on, what are you trying to prove? You win. I cry uncle."

The bathroom is fogged up; in the mirror, she can make out only the barest outlines of herself. "You keep this up and we'll really be late."

But he doesn't answer her.

When he gets out, he towels himself off and puts on his clothes: his underwear, his socks, his shirt, his trousers, moving slowly, meticu-lously, smoothing out the wrinkles. He opens the front door and steps out into the hall.

"Where are you going?"

"To get us some food."

"Nathaniel!"

But the door has already shut behind him.

He returns a few minutes later with two cans of soda, a couple of bags of corn chips, and a few candy bars. He pops open a bag of chips and offers her one.

"So what are you saying? I need to take you out to dinner in order to get laid?"

He tears open a chocolate bar, and she thinks of the early days with Nathaniel, a sex act involving chocolate syrup, and hoping to hark back to those times, she drags her finger through the chocolate and touches it lightly to his cheek.

"I'm sorry," she says. "I know this isn't very romantic."

"No," he says. "It's not."

Sex stripped of all sentiment, she thinks, though she does her best to inject sentiment into the act. It has never been this way with Nathaniel, and it won't always be this way, but at the moment it's hard for her to remember what sex was like between them, hard for her to envision anything but what it is now.

She's on her back, legs up in the air, while Nathaniel, mute as a Buddha, plunges in and out of her. He ejaculates inside her, and when he's done she lies utterly still, following the experts' advice, a pillow beneath her rear end to assist with gravity, while his sperm swims through her, swims toward its unknown destination.

And then, because she and Nathaniel are exhausted, because they're at a Hampton Inn where they've paid for their room and no one cares what they do until checkout time tomorrow morning, they allow themselves to close their eyes before driving to the airport. Limbs entwined, clothes strewn across the floor, they fall into a heavy sleep.

2

They're over the Atlantic, having commandeered a whole row, Noelle with two boys on one side, Amram with the other two across the aisle, though Akiva, their eldest, always animated and voluble, especially when given the chance to speak English, has seated himself a row back next to a retired couple from Phoenix returning from their annual pilgrimage to Jerusalem. Noelle recognizes the type. UJA dinners and Israel Bond drives. Grandchildren's bar mitzvahs in hotel ballrooms bedecked with palm trees (more bar than mitzvah, Noelle calls these affairs), not so different from the bar mitzvahs she used to attend, but she had no say in that, and now, twenty-five years later, she can afford to be disdainful. She has earned it, she thinks, sitting with her four sons on the flight to Boston, models of decorum, when she knows what boys are like, Israeli boys especially, soldiers as soon as they emerge from the womb.

Akiva is eight, Yoni six, Dov five, and Ari three; it's not so different from Noelle and her sisters. Her mother likes to say the girls were in diapers at the same time, testament, it would seem, to how close they were spaced, or perhaps to the fact that Clarissa still wore diapers at night when she was five. There must be some lesson in this, some predictor of what Clarissa has become, but Noelle can't find any. She doesn't wish to make too fine a point of this, but when she sees her children now, Akiva a row back chatting amiably in his unaccented English, she and Amram surrounded by the other boys, knit yarmulkes on their heads, their prayer fringes sticking out from under their T-shirts, she feels that she has outdone her mother, four small children at once instead of three—Leo came along later—no difficulty with toilet training.

The flight attendant comes down the aisle dispensing snacks, and the boys negotiate over chips, pretzels, and cookies.

"Let them have what they want," Amram says.

"Who's stopping them?" says Noelle.

"Where are we now?" Yoni asks.

"Over the ocean," she says.

"But where?"

"He wants a country," says Dov.

"There are no countries in the ocean," Yoni says.

Akiva says, "Three-quarters of the earth is covered by water."

"What difference does that make?" Yoni says.

"The difference is, it's true." Akiva is only eight, but he thinks of himself as a surrogate parent. When the family sings *zemirot* during Shabbat dinner, the boys take turns sitting on Amram's lap. Amram thumps his legs up and down and folds over the edges of the boys' yarmulkes, trying to make them resemble cowboy hats. Friday night at the rodeo: you sing *zemirot*, you get to ride the bull. Once, when Amram was away, Akiva sat in his father's seat and drank from his kiddush cup, and when it came time to sing *zemirot* he said, "Okay, boys, who wants to sit on my lap?"

Yoni drops a pretzel into Dov's soda, and Dov punches him in the thigh.

"Boys!" Noelle says.

Yoni drops another pretzel into Dov's soda.

"Would you take over for me?" Noelle says to Amram.

"Doing what?"

"Refereeing."

"I'm right here."

"You're right here," she says, "but you're reading."

"They're boys, Noelle. Let them be." Amram closes his magazine. But a minute later, he's reading again.

"I just want you involved."

"I *am* involved."

"Listen to me, Amram. Step up to the plate."

Dov says, "Eema and Abba are fighting again."

Dov's right, Noelle thinks. The past few months, she and Amram have been arguing more and more. Amram complains that he has spent the last year listening to stories about Leo, hearing her describe a relationship he never knew existed. Because the relationship Noelle lays out on the phone to her friends, the stories she tells their boys, the memories she says assault her, they're a kind of fiction, Amram believes. How often did they see Leo in all their years in Israel? They didn't even go to his wedding, because Thisbe wasn't Jewish.

Originally, Amram was threatening not to come on this trip, but Noelle convinced him to join them. It's her brother's unveiling: how can he miss it? And Amram is a buffer when she's with her family; his simple presence reminds her that she lives six thousand miles away, because when she sees her parents and sisters, when they're up in Lenox as they will be soon, another July Fourth, it's easy to forget that her life is elsewhere. It's how she felt when she first left home, what everyone must feel that first Thanksgiving back from college, except she's thirty-seven now and she still feels it. Sometimes she thinks that's why she moved to Israel: to put enough distance between her and her family. She recalls Abraham and Lot. *Behold, all the land is before you. If you go left I will go right, and if you go right I will go left.*

She rests her head against the window, trying to fall asleep, but the vibrations of the plane are too disruptive. So she leans the other way and, arranged like this, her head covered in a kerchief as it always is, she manages to fall asleep.

She's woken by the sound of carts rolling down the aisle. "More food?" she says sleepily.

"It's a Jewish airline," Amram says. He used to work for a catering company, and the reigning wisdom was, a third more food for a Jewish event, a third less drink.

Reflexively, she checks the wrapping for kosher certification, though she doesn't need to: all the food on El Al is kosher. Years ago, El Al used to fly on Shabbat, but no longer. Which is how it should be, Noelle thinks; Israel is a Jewish state. She knows what the secular say, that it's the tyranny of the few over the many. But in a parliamentary system you have to negotiate, and it's the religious the government negotiates with. The fact is, the Orthodox are becoming stronger. They have more children—most of Noelle's and Amram's friends have four—and almost all the new *olim* are religious, too. And they have the truth on their side; she's not ashamed to say that.

Once, visiting the States, she took Akiva, who was four at the time, to see the Christmas windows at Bergdorf Goodman. She likes the tinsel and lights; Christmas doesn't threaten her any longer. Still, she's happy not to have Christmas forced upon her, and that day, when Santa Claus was sitting in front of Bergdorf and all the children were screaming out his name, there was a moment of silence, and a voice called out: "Who's Santa Claus?" It was Akiva. That, Noelle thinks, is why she lives in Israel. So her children won't have to know who Santa Claus is, so they'll live their lives as God intended, speaking Hebrew and observing the commandments, so their own children will be Jewish, while the secular Israelis, who knows where their children will be, off to India and Thailand once they've finished the army, devotees of Buddhism and Transcendental Meditation, searching for meaning—of course they are, Noelle thinks—because being a secular Jew in Israel, of all places, is a hollow existence.

My sister the Hasidic Jew, Lily likes to say. The rabbi's wife. Well, Lily can say what she wants to. Amram isn't a rabbi, and they aren't Hasidic. She and Amram both work, and their boys will serve in the army. They won't spend their lives in yeshiva as the ultra-Orthodox do, expecting the rest of the country to protect them. Yes, she covers her hair, and she wears skirts and dresses instead of pants, and she won't swim at the beach or pool when men are present. And, yes, her children go to Orthodox schools and they'll marry Orthodox girls and marry them young. But don't let anyone tell her she's cut herself off from the modern world, that she's placed herself inside a cloister.

"Abba?" Dov says.

"Be quiet," Akiva says. "Abba's working."

"Abba's not working," Noelle says. "He's reading a magazine."

That's the other thing they've been fighting about. Amram lost his job, which was bad enough, but worse, he didn't even tell her when it first happened. He kept going to the office for another couple of weeks; at least, that was where she thought he was going, until she phoned his office and discovered that he'd been fired. She's angry about that—she can't stand dishonesty—and also about the fact that he's been fired again; they have four children to support.

The boys are speaking Hebrew to each other, and though she would normally object—English-only is the house rule—she allows them to go on. It's vacation, she figures, and they'll be in the States soon, where everyone speaks English. Her own Hebrew is fluent, but it will never be as good as her English is. In many ways, her children's Hebrew is already better than hers. With Akiva, there are phrases in his homework she doesn't understand, and he has to explain them to her.

It wasn't like that for her growing up—feeling like she was better than her parents, especially at anything having to do with school. She would daydream all semester in math, then rely on her mother to help her before the exam, but they would always end up fighting, with Noelle in tears. Even now, Noelle remembers math, remembers all of high school, really, as a word problem with water pouring into the bathtub at one rate per minute and being drained simultaneously at another rate per minute and she had to figure out how long it took to fill the tub. These problems seemed designed to assail her: why couldn't someone just put in the plug and the bath would fill up as baths normally did? Angry at her mother, abandoning her math homework to smoke a cigarette, Noelle would say to her mother as she was leaving for the hospital, "Fine, you want me to fail my math test?" (Her mother, a physician, was a rabid anti-smoker; there was nothing Noelle could do that would infuriate her mother the way smoking did—nothing until Noelle became Orthodox and moved to Israel.)

"Believe me," her mother would say, "I'd rather be home than going in to the hospital at three in the morning."

"Rather be helping me?"

"Yes, sweetie, I would."

Always the *sweetie* to taunt her, when Noelle understood even then that it wasn't a taunt. She still listens for that word when she calls home from Jerusalem. It returns her to infancy; she's nothing but clay in her mother's hands. Take me back, she wants to say. Make me whole again. She wants to crawl inside her mother, to return to some vestigial tadpole state. Coming home from the hospital, her mother would find her asleep, curled into herself like dough, and she would wake her gently to study again because Noelle demanded that she wake her, although her mother insisted those extra few hours wouldn't make a difference and what she needed most was sleep. (No one, Noelle thinks—not Amram, not her children, not her sisters, not Leo when he was alive—no one has ever woken her as gently as her mother did, the act of waking her as if an apology.)

It's like the dream everyone has. You realize you've forgotten to go to class all semester and tomorrow's the final in introductory Chinese. But for Noelle it's not just a dream; it's her life. She is, in fact, enrolled in introductory Chinese. She is, in fact, naked in school, always about to be discovered, because there's something at the core transparent about her, the organs, the veins and arteries carrying the blood to and from her heart, just a body spread out for all to see, redheaded Noelle with the blue, blue eyes, fourteen years old and the prettiest girl in Mamaroneck High School. It's where her family moved, to West-chester, when Noelle was thirteen because she'd gotten expelled from two schools in Manhattan and her parents thought if they removed her from the city they might keep her out of trouble. (That, more than anything, Noelle thinks, is why Lily can't stand her. Lily never forgave her for banishing the family to the suburbs, for making her leave her friends and start over in a new school. Well, blame their parents, Noelle thinks; she didn't want to leave the city any more than Lily did.)

Look at her, they would say, the boys on the football team and the swim team, Noelle's own teammates, the boys who tried out for the swim team just to see her in a bathing suit. *Why don't you wear a bikini, Noelle?* Thinking about her at night in their beds, beneath the sheets they soiled, not washing them, not wanting their mothers to wash them, not wanting to wash Noelle out of them. *You're killing me, Noelle. Just thinking about you makes me come.* Noelle lived for their voices, feeling she was nothing when the boys didn't talk about her, that she didn't exist at all. *Noelle the nympho. The girl who couldn't say no.* When her mother was on call, Noelle, who promised her she'd be studying, was instead out with Campbell, the next-door neighbor's boy, or Bruce Weinstein from around the block. She knew who was awake and who wasn't, whose parents were out, could feel her way around the streets near her home, moving stealthily through the bushes, avoiding the occasional passing headlights, following her own internal compass. In basements and attics, behind locked bedroom doors, lovely Noelle, her hair sliding across her face, the almost soundless sound of it, like the almost soundless sound of Noelle's panties dropping to the floor. *Man, that girl's efficient*, Casey Hopkins would say—Casey, whose father was a doctor at the same hospital as Noelle's mother—and sometimes, hearing a parent come home late at night, the sound of others stirring in the house, Noelle would escape out the window.

"How 'bout we go rock climbing," Noelle says, this to Mark Hathaway, Noelle guiding Mark's hand beneath her shirt, Mark, only thirteen, a year younger than she is. Noelle's heart goes out to the boys like this, the timid ones, like birds, the peach fuzz on Mark's cheeks, the two of them in the audiovisual room where Mark spends most of his time, because he's vice chair of the AV squad, shining the strobe lights on the students during the productions of *Guys and Dolls* and *Our Town*. Noelle runs her hands across Mark's body, the smooth hairlessness of him, thinking of her mother back in medical school sticking her hands inside a cadaver. Mark is used to shining the lights on others, only now, with Noelle, the lights are on him and he wants them off; he doesn't believe in kissing a girl with the lights on. But Noelle wants to see him; she won't do anything with Mark unless she can watch what they're doing. "How 'bout we go spelunking," Noelle says, and she guides Mark's hand down the inside of her jeans under the waistband of her panties. And it's true what the boys say about her, *Noelle, just thinking about you makes me come*, because Noelle can see it on Mark's face, the mere anticipation has caused him to ejaculate, and it's as if Mark has forgotten his cue and everyone onstage is looking up at him, and Mark, humiliated, runs out, leaving Noelle alone, and now Mark has told the rest of the school what Noelle said, *How 'bout we go spelunking*.

Soon everyone is saying it, the boys chanting it in Mr. Hampton's English class and along West Boston Post Road, waiting for their parents to retrieve them from band practice. They say it on the way home from synagogue and church, seeing Noelle in a white bikini in front of her parents' house sunning herself on a lawn chair, placing a halo of tinfoil around her neck so the sun will reflect off it to give her a better tan, her red hair settling in the crevice between her breasts. *Hey, Noelle, how 'bout we go spelunking*. And Noelle just laughs.

She does it everywhere with these boys, even in her parents' house, in her bedroom when they're asleep, and once in her parents' bed when they were out, with a boy named Stanley, who said, "Doesn't it creep you out, doing it in your parents' bed?" but Noelle simply shrugged. *Noelle's enterprising*, the boys say. *She makes do with what she can*. She's had sex standing in the school elevator, having learned how to stop the elevator between floors, elevators having always been her thing. (One Halloween, when her family still lived in Manhattan, she told Rudolph, the elevator man, he could go home for the night, and she, at twelve, took over for him, offering the tenants candy and other trick-or-treats as she took them up to their apartments.) Her parents moved to Westchester to keep her out of trouble, but there's plenty of trouble to be found in Westchester, Noelle caught with the construction worker, Jimmy, twenty-three, blond and handsome, with that tool belt dangling from his slim waist, and, frankly, Noelle is tired of high school boys, Noelle who feels in that instant when a guy is about to come, in that moment of rapture that crosses his face, that everything's okay and somebody loves her. She stands in the glaring light, knock-kneed as a foal, saying through the simple stance, the fragile pose, *Here I am, do what you want with me.*

Noelle the slattern. Lubricious Noelle. Licentious. Lascivious. Wanton. Slut. Noelle knows these words, having taken Ms. Pickens's vocabulary-building class, the boys in the hallway staring up at her from their Barron's books as she walks insouciantly by. Noelle doing her best to study for the SAT, the way her sisters are doing, Clarissa and Lily off to Yale and Princeton while Noelle is going nowhere (*Nowhere Noelle* is how she thinks of herself, up in her bedroom, crying, alone). But then she reminds herself that no one is calling out her sisters' names at night and no one is staying up late to help them with their math homework the way her mother is doing with her. But her mother loses patience with her; it's hard for her to understand how school doesn't come easily to Noelle. Her mother graduated number one in her class from the University of Pennsylvania and then again from NYU Medical School; like Clarissa and Lily, she has never failed at anything in her life.

"In that case," Noelle says, "why don't you take my test for me?"

"I can't, sweetie."

But in that *I can't*, Noelle's hears *I would if I could*, and she hates her mother for having no faith in her. "Go ahead," she says. "Tell me you hate me."

"How could you even think that?"

"You wish I'd never been born." Then Noelle starts to cry, and she says, "Why do I fuck everything up?" because there's something about her, she thinks, that's at core unknowable, unlovable.

Even now, looking back, she wonders what her parents could have done differently. They tried counselors and therapists. They sent her to a summer camp for troubled youth. They punished her. They bribed her. But nothing worked.

She was twenty-five when she arrived in Israel. It was random that she landed there, another stop on a round-the-world plane ticket. She figured she'd work on a kibbutz, wake up at four in the morning to pick melons, then sleep away the afternoons with the other volunteers. She'd fall in love with an Israeli air force pilot, get up in the morning and put on his uniform and march like a soldier through the streets.

"Look at me." Ari has dumped his pretzel twists into his ginger ale and is admiring how they float.

"Ari!" she says, then thinks better of it. It's a twelve-hour flight; at a certain point you have to surrender.

"They look like fish," Ari says, peering into his cup of pretzels.

Dov says, "You put pretzels in soda and you get Goldfish."

"Not the food," Akiva says. "Actual fish." He looks up at his brothers. "Okay," he says, "who can tell me what's happening in Israel right now?"

"People are playing soccer," Dov says.

"They probably are, but what I meant is, who can tell me what time it is?"

No one answers him.

"I'll give you a hint. London is five hours later than Boston, and Jerusalem is two hours later than that."

"In Israel, people are asleep," Yoni says.

"The kids might be," Akiva says. "But the grownups are eating dinner, or sitting at a café."

On the screen above their seats, CNN is broadcasting NBA highlights, and Akiva snaps to attention. Like other Israeli basketball fans, he dreams that an Israeli will play in the NBA, though his real dream is to be that Israeli. He has memorized the names of the Israeli basketball players who almost made it to the NBA, and he has become a fan of the University of Connecticut, whose former star, Doron Sheffer, was drafted by the Los Angeles Clippers, only to accept a safer, better offer from Maccabi Tel Aviv. In a few years, the NBA will have its first Israeli player, but Akiva doesn't know this yet, so it's Sheffer who preoccupies him, Sheffer, who played for the University of Connecticut before Akiva was even born. But Akiva acts as if he'd been alive then, and at eight he, too, shares the burden of Sheffer's failure. Akiva sees America as all-basketball-all-the-time, so when he meets an American who displays no interest in the sport he can't help but feel that the person's pulling his leg. He's happy in Israel; it's his home. Yet he believes that his parents, in moving to Jerusalem, voluntarily left heaven for the false consolations of earth. It's as if in making aliyah they left the NBA itself, and so he inquires about their lives in the United States, thinking there must be something more than what his mother has told him, that they're Jews and they want to live in the Jewish homeland.

Occasionally, Akiva will spot a tall African American on the street, a former NBA player extending his career and given, as Israeli law requires, a quickie conversion, and he will ask the player for his autograph. But he's always being frustrated. Just last month, when Noelle told him about their trip, he said, "Why does it have to be during the summer?" Meaning why not during the NBA season when he could watch a game live? Another time, Noelle said. But when Akiva persisted, she explained to him about July Fourth, American Independence Day. "A long weekend," she said, though this year July Fourth falls in the middle of the week. Every weekend in America is long, she explained. It's one of the things she misses most about the States—sleeping in late on Sundays when she was a girl, bagels and whitefish, afternoons at her parents' house sunning herself in the yard next to her mother's bougainvillea—because in Israel Sunday is a workday like any other day of the week. Leo's yahrzeit was coming up, she explained, which made it a more complicated occasion. "Bittersweet," she said, realizing as she said this that Akiva didn't understand what the word meant.

But he pretended he did, or simply chose not to ask, which is what he always does when he doesn't wish to discuss something. Noelle would like to talk to the children about Leo, but what is there to say? So many senseless deaths. Why compound them with another one? It's Akiva she's most tempted to talk to, because he's older and might understand, and because he has memories of Leo, though it's hard to know what he remembers and what he has gleaned from the stories she has told him and from the photograph of Leo, which stands on the shelf in their living room, her brother's face looking down at them like some imperious god. But then she reminds herself that Akiva's only eight, which was why when he said, "Well, I wish he'd died during the NBA season," she let it pass.

"Is there a basketball hoop at Grandma and Grandpa's?" he asks now.

She shakes her head.

"Why not?"

"Probably because Grandma and Grandpa don't play basketball." There was once a hoop in the driveway, but Leo and his friends used to stand on each other's shoulders and grab onto the rim, and eventually they brought it down. The summer before he died, there was talk of putting up a new hoop, but it never happened, and now the court remains as it was, the downward slope of concrete going to the garage, the bare wooden backboard with the holes where the rim hung, the discoloration from the wind and rain, from the years of balls shot against it. "The next-door neighbors have a hoop."

"Will they let me use it?"

"Maybe," she says. "If you ask nicely."

Ari starts to cry. To distract him, Noelle devises a game that involves figuring out what portion of the trip has elapsed, but because Akiva is getting all the answers right, his brothers lose interest.

Then they're on to the next game, this one led by Amram, which involves guessing which of the passengers are undercover; there are rumored to be soldiers on every El Al flight. But the boys go about this too loudly ("That guy in the brown pants!" Yoni calls out), and Noelle is forced to make them stop.

The children order Sprites, their fourth of the trip, and Noelle says,

"That's enough, kids, you've had too much soda already," but the flight attendant has already poured the drinks, and Amram says, "It's an airplane flight, a special occasion," and the boys all cheer and gulp down their sodas before their father can change his mind.

A couple of people wearing yarmulkes walk down the aisle looking for men to help make a minyan, and Amram gets up and joins them. Noelle doesn't count for a minyan, but she decides to pray, too, doing so quietly from her seat.

Judaism, Lily likes to say: just another installment in the random life of Noelle Glucksman. (Lily was the one who wasn't surprised when they learned after months of not hearing from her that Noelle, at twenty-six, had become an Orthodox Jew, living in Jerusalem, engaged to Amram.) *Hey, Noelle, what are you, deaf?* This when Noelle was a mere six and Lily seven, and sometimes Lily would shout and Noelle seemed not to hear her. Noelle ten and Lily eleven, Lily singing The Who to her, changing the words to *teenage spaceman*. In the morning when the alarm went off, Noelle slept right through it. And there Lily was again, coming out of the shower, screaming, "Would you turn off the fucking alarm, Noelle!"

It turned out Noelle did have a hearing problem, discovered when she was a freshman in high school, and maybe that was why she was doing so badly in school: she couldn't hear what the teacher was saying. There had been hints of this earlier, Noelle at seven saying to her mother, "Why if people have two ears do they only hear out of one?"

"What are you talking about?" her mother said, but Noelle insisted she was only joking.

At fourteen, when she went to the audiologist and discovered she had moderate hearing loss in her right ear and a little in her left ear too, Noelle began to blame everything on her hearing loss. She had a slight lisp, which she'd always attributed to an overbite, but now, sitting in the ENT's office going over the results of her test, she became convinced that her lisp was because she couldn't hear well. She was listening to the doctor even as she wasn't listening to him, turning him off as she'd learned to do, and when he asked her if she'd be willing to wear a hearing aid, she said, "Sure," even as she was thinking, *No way I'm wearing a hearing aid, hearing aids are for old people.*

Later, at home, she overheard Clarissa and Lily talking about her.

"Now are you proud of yourself?" Clarissa said. "Saying, 'What are you, deaf?' She's hard of hearing."

"Oh, come on, Clarissa," Lily said. "She's faking it."

How, Noelle wondered, did Lily know? Although she wasn't faking it, her hearing loss wasn't as great as the doctor believed, because when the audiologist tested her she intentionally got some of the answers wrong. It was the same way with school. She wasn't an A student and would never be one. But if she tried harder she could have gotten B's. But who wanted B's? You got B's and no one noticed you. She would get C's and D's. She'd flunk out. She'd get left back.

Home from the audiologist, she asked her parents to enroll her in a sign-language course. At first they refused, saying she needed to focus on high school, but then they struck a deal with her that if she did better in her classes they'd let her take sign language. And for a time her grades improved.

Once she saw a group of deaf teenagers on her subway car, and though her signing had gotten better, she still had trouble following them. She watched them, glanced away, then watched them again until, finally, one of them shouted, "Stop staring at us!" her voice as high-pitched as a hyena's.

She went to a party sponsored by the New York Association for the Deaf, but not knowing anyone, she stood in the corner sipping a beer, feeling excluded and alone. She would use sex, she thought; she'd make a pass at someone. But she found herself, a hearing person among the deaf, unusually self-conscious in front of the guys, and when she tried to approach one she was convinced all the girls were staring at her, accusing her of trying to steal one of their own when all she wanted was to talk to somebody. Then the dance music came on—everyone danced by feeling the vibrations beneath their feet—but it was so loud she couldn't tolerate it, and she had to go out onto the balcony. Standing next to the chips and the keg of beer, watching everyone gesture to each other, the beautiful choreography of sign language, she resolved to go back inside and dance, thinking if she exposed her ears to the noise maybe she would really become deaf.

At home, she tried to facilitate the process. She practiced backflips on her bed, treating the mattress as a trampoline, and she began to do this with Q-tips in her ears, hoping to block out the world of sound, but also thinking what if she slipped and landed on her side, plunging the Q-tip into her ear.

She learned about someone who had gone deaf at age twelve and could read lips so well you couldn't tell she was deaf. She was a graduate student at Columbia and taught a section of introductory European history. She could even talk on the telephone; she would be on one receiver and her roommate would be on the other repeating what the person said, and when she spoke there was no lag time. Noelle tracked her down, pretending she was a student studying for her midterm, until, revealing she didn't know anything about European history, she heard the woman ask who she was, and she panicked and hung up.

For days after that she felt disgusted by herself. She was always impersonating people: her sisters, her mother, the girls at school. Only in a boy's arms: that was the one time she felt she belonged, huddled like a duck in the AV room, attending to him, the look on his face, the grimace, the *Oh, Noelle, oh, God*, the feeling that they'd melded. But then he would roll off her and she'd be alone again, a lump of shame, and his gaze was slack and distant, his eyes like sea glass, and she swore she would never do it again, never have sex with another boy, but then the next one came along and she convinced herself this one would be different.

Even as a baby she was self-punishing. She would tug on her hair and squeeze her stomach. As a teenager, she developed trichotillomania; she pulled out clumps of her own hair. Sometimes she thinks she was simply born this way. Other times she traces it back to Leo. She was four when her mother got pregnant again, and from the start of the pregnancy there were complications. Finally, labor was induced at thirty weeks. In the delivery room, Leo's heart rate plummeted, the umbilical cord was noosed around the baby's throat, an emergency C-section had to be performed. There was some question about loss of oxygen. Leo developed late; he didn't walk until twenty months and he spoke even later. The doctors said there might be brain damage, maybe simply learning disabilities, maybe nothing at all. Those first few weeks, no one except Noelle's parents was allowed to handle him. The quiet, the delicacy, her mother sick, the baby sick, the baby's sleeping, don't wake the baby, don't disturb the baby, don't hold the baby, don't drop the baby. Always the baby, as if it were hubris to give him a name. Don't touch the baby, as if telescoping to Noelle's most unspeakable thoughts: her wish to drop the baby, to kill the baby, to be the baby. It was what she'd been her whole life; she'd always assumed she'd continue to be that.

She was the last one to see Leo alive. He spent Shabbat with her and Amram in Jerusalem, and a few days later, in Iraq, he was abducted. Then came the week when the family was on TV, pleading with his captors for his release, handsome, buoyant Leo looking drugged. And when his body was flown home, President Bush called him a martyr in the war to rid the world of evil. He invited Noelle's family to the White House. Publicly, her mother refused to go. She wouldn't allow her son to be used that way, to become an instrument in the service of the war.

Immediately, the family was frozen out. Rumors were floated, the sources unnamed, that maybe Leo wasn't as innocent as people had said. He'd violated journalists' protocol; he'd wound up where he wasn't supposed to be. Why, Noelle wonders, did these rumors surprise people? You slap the president in the face and he slaps you back. And she speaks as someone who voted for Bush, who sent in her absentee ballot from six thousand miles away. Her brother is dead—she still grieves for him—but Bush is the best friend Israel has ever had. She's the one who has to live with the terrorist attacks, the sounds of katyusha rockets going off at night.

Brain damage? Learning disabilities? In no time, Leo had outstripped her, as successful in his own way as Clarissa and Lily were in theirs. It was a relief to move to Israel; finally she wasn't simply someone's sister. She views the girl she was in high school with disapproval, but it's a faint, abstract disapproval, as is the pity that accompanies it. She regards the sex the way she regards everything else. She wouldn't deny it was her, but it doesn't trouble her any longer.

Across the aisle, Amram is flipping through a computer magazine. He's in the software industry; at least he was until he lost his job. She still doesn't know what happened—Amram won't talk about it—but the specifics are almost beside the point. What happened is what always happens. Amram is smart, but he alienates people. Temperamentally, he's meant to be the boss and he hasn't accommodated to the fact that he isn't the boss, so the real boss fires him. Noelle knows what people say behind Amram's back. She feels embarrassed for him, and for herself as a result, but there's nothing she can do about it. Amram is good-hearted and he's misunderstood, but after this last firing she, too, has grown exasperated.

It's an unspoken lie in their marriage, perhaps *the* unspoken lie, that Amram's salary supports them. His paycheck certainly helps, and Noelle is hardly in a position to complain; she brings home barely any money herself, working two mornings a week as a teacher's aide, though she knows that if she were paid for raising their children, she would—or at least should—be well compensated. But their own situation is tinged with regret because her grandmother, Gretchen, gave each of the grandchildren a substantial sum of money when they turned twenty-five, and Noelle frittered hers away. Strangely, the regret comes principally from Amram, who didn't even know Noelle when she was twenty-five. He spends considerable time talking about what they would have done with the money if only they'd gotten it a few years later. Because they didn't, they've been forced to rely on Noelle's parents for help, which humiliates Amram; he feels his masculinity is being impugned. He has become frugal to the point of unreason, deploying tricks to save money, when the real trick he's playing is to convince himself he isn't accepting help from his in-laws. He buys the cheaper brands of yogurt and cottage cheese, gets the *lachmaniot* in bulk though the bread becomes stale quickly, and having salved his conscience and saved a few shekels, he places the money he's accumulated into a piggy bank that he hides beneath his and Noelle's bed. Noelle finds this endearing and a little sad; her husband, thirty-eight years old, veteran of the Israeli army, has a piggy bank into which he places his shekel coins, thinking of this money as a vacation fund, what will send the family on a *tiyul* to the Negev, when what's in there will likely cover gas money and little else.

Yet at the same time, Amram will invest a thousand dollars in a company on a tip from a friend; he'll shirk his responsibilities at work.

Penny-wise and pound-foolish, the saying goes, but it's more than that. Amram believes in reinventing himself. He has done this already by becoming religious, and he's done it in other ways too, by shedding seventy-five pounds in a year only to gain the weight right back again. He believes in spectacular acts—miracles, essentially—not just by God but by man, and given the choice between caution and glory, he'll choose glory any day. This is what has gotten him into trouble, and it's what he and Noelle have been fighting about. Though they've promised themselves to stage a truce, for the sake of Leo's memory, and for the sake of their vacation, which they're hoping to enjoy.

A flight attendant distributes wipes, and the boys shred the packets and wave the wipes in the air. Soon Yoni starts to shred the wipe itself before Noelle reaches over and stops him.

Another flight attendant hands out customs forms, asking the passengers are they U.S. citizens, are they Israeli, and Akiva, proudly, says they're both, to which the flight attendant says, "Well, someone's double trouble," and she hands Akiva the forms for the whole family.

A voice announces, first in Hebrew, then in English, that the captain is beginning his descent; they should be touching down at Logan in forty-five minutes.

"*G'virotai v'rabotai,*" Akiva mimics. "Ladies and gentlemen . . ."

Yoni and Dov get into an argument about whose English is better, and then they're on to the question of whether there are more Americans or Israelis on the plane, a subject about which they also disagree.

"Come on, kids," Amram says, "we're almost there."

Noelle, to lend support, points out how well behaved everyone has been on the trip.

"Ari didn't even throw up," Yoni says.

"You see?" says Noelle, who in the cab to the airport had to mediate between the brothers, none of whom wanted to sit next to Ari, thinking he would vomit on their laps.

At customs they get their visas stamped, and then they head over to the baggage carousel, which Yoni and Dov promptly mount. They ride around on it, pretending they're luggage, until Amram insists they get off. Then they're through the swinging doors and out into the terminal, where Noelle scans the crowd for her sisters.

3

"Jesus Christ!" Lily says. She's standing in Logan waiting for Clarissa, who's an hour late. She looks up at the arrivals screen above her head, but what's the point: Clarissa and Nathaniel are coming by car. She waits a few minutes longer, then heads over to international to meet Noelle alone. She skips the automated walkway; she'll get there faster on her own two feet. She cuts a striking figure, a pretty redhead in capri pants, threading her way between the travelers.

She checks her voicemail and finds a message from Clarissa. She's been waylaid, it seems. It's hard to hear her sister over the voice of the P.A. telling travelers to pass to the left, stand to the right, issuing an endless loop of gate changes, but the upshot is clear: Clarissa won't be making it to the airport; she'll meet up with them at the house. *I'm truly sorry*, Clarissa says. *You'll have to strap those kids to the roof of the car. I love you, Lil. I owe you one.*

Lily mouths the words back—*I love you*—then presses on. Clarissa: her older sister, her best friend. She does love her, but right now she's annoyed. Strap those kids to the roof of the car, indeed! Though even that won't be sufficient. With Noelle and Amram and their four boys, with all the luggage and car seats (Lily and Malcolm's friends are always transporting their car seats wherever they go—it's as if they're cabled to their arms), they'll have to rent a car as well.

Lily doesn't know Noelle's flight number—all Clarissa told her was the airline—and when she arrives at international, she looks up at the screen and sees multiple flights from Tel Aviv.

Terrific, she thinks. *Lovely.*

At information, she asks to place an announcement, but no sooner does she do so than she hears her name being called out—"Lily! Lily!"—like some clarion call from years ago. It's Noelle, followed by Amram and their four boys, two of whom are sliding shoeless through the terminal. Another of them (The second? Lily thinks. The third?

There are so many of them, and they're so closely spaced, it's hard to keep track) has gotten hold of Noelle's pocketbook and is sifting through the contents.

"Hello there," Lily says, and she kisses Noelle on the cheek. Then she kisses her on the other cheek, in a show of gallantry, of European-ism, she isn't sure what. Mostly, she realizes, it's a show of discomfort, because, Jesus, Noelle is her sister, but the fact is they can't stand each other, and when Lily feels uncomfortable she goes for high drama; histrionics is her point at rest.

"Hello, Lily," Amram says.

Lily takes a step toward her brother-in-law. Then, remembering that Orthodox Jewish men don't kiss women they're not married to, she reaches out and shakes Amram's hand. "How are you, Amram?"

"I'm all right." Amram looks warily at the crowd funneling past him.

"You're here," she tells them.

Amram nods. "Land of the free, home of the brave."

It looks to Lily as if Amram has put on weight, but she can't be sure; he has always been fleshy-faced and heavyset. He's standing next to Noelle with his hands behind his back, looking ahead expression-lessly, as if waiting to be instructed what to do and already resenting those instructions. He has blue eyes, and blond, thinning hair pasted to his head by a sheen of sweat, on top of which lies a black velvet yarmulke. His face is tinged with color as if he's been exerting himself. He's exhibiting what appears to be a willed calm.

Lily trains her gaze on her four nephews, whom she hasn't seen since Leo's funeral. One by one, she takes them in a hug, and now she steps back, looking at Ari, the baby. Except he's not a baby anymore. "My God."

"What?" says Noelle.

"He looks so much like Leo."

"You think?"

"It's like I've been transported back thirty years." Saying this, and looking at her nephew, Lily feels her throat constrict. It makes her soften for an instant, even toward Noelle. "Well, you made it." She touches her sister on the sleeve. "Welcome home."

"Thanks," Noelle says, and for an instant she seems less guarded, too.

"How was your flight?" Lily asks.

"It was long," Dov says.

"Twelve hours long," says Yoni.

"It felt more like twenty-four," Akiva says, looking at his brothers in exasperation. Lily remembers this about him, the way, in his siblings' presence, he assumes the pose of an adult.

"Come here," Lily says. "Let me have a look at you." And now she's crouching before her nephews in the middle of the terminal, two on one side, two on the other, her arms draped over them. "You probably don't even remember me."

"Of course we remember you," Akiva says. He elbows his brother in the ribs, who elbows another brother, and soon they're all nodding, one after the other, like dominoes that have been toppled.

They're all blue-eyed and pale-faced, with delicate features: little Aryan Israelis, Lily thinks. What would the Nazis have made of this? Akiva, especially, is curious-seeming, as if absorbing some signal the world is sending out. Yoni, the second oldest, is slightly darker-complected, though he, too, has eyes the blue of quartz. All four of them look like they spend time in the sun; they appear remarkably healthy next to the other travelers wheeling their luggage into Wendy's and Krispy Kreme and T.G.I. Friday's and Sbarro. "So this is what the army does to you. It makes you handsome."

"Hush, you," Noelle says. "The army, thank God, is years away."

"Seriously," Lily says. "You could put these kids in commercials."

"Okay," Noelle says. "That's enough." But she says it gently, and Lily can tell she's secretly pleased.

"What happened to Clarissa?" Amram asks. "Weren't you supposed to meet up with her?"

"She didn't show," Lily says.

"What do you mean she didn't show?"

Lily shrugs. "She left me a message saying she'll meet us at the house. Luckily, I brought the van." Most of the time the van sits in the parking lot at Malcolm's restaurant. He uses it to go on runs to the farmer's market and the liquor wholesaler. But he won't need it over the holiday, so Lily has commandeered it; she figures if she can't bring Malcolm himself, she might as well bring his van. Still, she says, they'll need to rent a car, too.

Dov, meanwhile, has spotted someone eating an Auntie Anne's Pretzel. He wants one, he announces. He wants a bagel as well and, while he's at it, a slice of pizza, all of which requests his younger brother reminds him can't be fulfilled because the food isn't kosher.

"Nothing in this country is kosher," Dov says forlornly.

"There are kosher restaurants in America," Akiva says.

"Not as many as in Israel," says Yoni.

"Let's get going," Noelle says. "It's two and a half hours to Grandma and Grandpa's house."

Amram has a suitcase in each hand and a duffel slung over his shoulder. The two older boys are wheeling suitcases themselves, which leaves the last suitcase and the car seats to Lily and Noelle, sister beside sister moving through the airport toward the rental car counter where they'll divide forces, as Lily has suggested. Lily will take Noelle, the two older boys, and most of the luggage, and the two younger boys and the rest of the bags will go with Amram.

Noelle puts down the car seats.

"Is something wrong?"

"I got lipstick on you," Noelle says. "It must have been when I kissed you." She licks her forefinger, and now she's putting the finger to Lily's cheek, and when that doesn't work she takes out a tissue and places it against her sister's skin. And there Lily is, standing in the airport, and she feels as if she's going to cry, the touch of Noelle's hand to her face. Where is this feeling coming from? Always she finds herself caught unawares. And now Noelle is licking her finger again, telling her to hold still, and Lily does as she's told, feeling her pulse flutter within her. She's back to years ago, their parents taking them to the beach, the Pavlovian sound of the ice-cream truck, the four of them beside each other in the sand with their rainbow ice pops and chocolate malteds, the handing out of Wet Ones. Lily's mother is wiping one of their mouths, and then it's Noelle wiping Lily's mouth, and Lily is wiping Clarissa, who's wiping Leo, the four of them in a row the way Lily's nephews are now, marching determinedly through the airport. Lily hears her mother's voice, *They're like monkeys, David, pulling nits out of each other's fur.* They had been that, Lily thinks, hadn't they—four little monkeys? And Noelle is saying, "There, I got it off," and she's telling Lily a story about synagogue, how you always know which prayer books have been in the women's section because they're the ones with the lipstick smudges across the page. But Lily hears only the outlines of this. She has her hand to her cheek, is saying "It's off, right, the lipstick?" and now she realizes Malcolm's van is still in domestic, and so she tells Noelle she'll go get it and drive over to the rental cars to retrieve her.

Now, in the van, a quiet settles on them; Lily can sense they're going to fight, or if not fight, then remain silent, which feels to her like its own sort of fighting. She and Malcolm don't argue much, but when they do, there's no place she'd like to be less than in the car, the endless hum of the tires, the rubber clicking over grate after grate. Noelle sits beside her in the passenger seat; the two older boys are in back. Noelle is wearing a yellow blouse and a denim skirt down to her ankles, and her hair is hidden beneath a kerchief.

They pass Cambridge and Newton and are headed toward Worcester; it's a straight shot west on the Massachusetts Pike. It's four-thirty, and they're supposed to be in Lenox for a seven o'clock dinner. They should get there on time if the traffic isn't bad, but now the cars in front of them have stalled and a pickup truck is pulled over at the side of the road, an orange pylon flattened beneath it.

It goes on like this for eight, ten miles, the cars proceeding at their own haphazard pace, the vehicles moving slowly around a bend, swaying like beads on a necklace. Lily turns on the radio to "Traffic on the 3's," and the holiday is coming so everything is logjammed, the turnpike worst of all.

She exits in Framingham, and now, off the main highway, they drive past Fayville. To the sides of the road, the grass is lined with realtor signs and little American flags pitched into the ground. In the distance is a Red Rooster drive-through, with a giant-sized soft-serve vanilla ice-cream cone perched on top. A billboard reads, WHEN WORDS FAIL,

MUSIC SPEAKS. The van in front of them says Kennedy Livestock. They pass telephone pole after telephone pole, all that wire running west. Lily glances over at Noelle, who wears a mystical, faraway look, as if wherever she's been since Lily last saw her, she has left a part of herself. "Aren't you going to say anything?"

"What do you want me to say?"

"You could say, 'How are you, Lily?'"

"How are you, Lily?"

"I'm fine."

Noelle is silent.

"And how are *you*, Noelle?"

"I'm fine, too."

Behind them, the boys have fallen asleep, each with his head pressed to the window, thumping against the glass as Lily accelerates, as she winds around the occasional bend. She turns on the radio and music comes through the speakers, bad music, she thinks, but at least there are other voices in the car.

A Saab brakes in front of them with a bumper sticker that reads JESUS LOVES YOU BUT I'M HIS FAVORITE. A deer stands at the side of the road, still as a signpost, looking at them so intently it's as if he's trying to make out their words.

Presently the news comes on, and it's bad news, of course. Lily lives in D.C., an entire city dedicated to making bad news and watching it spread like a disease. Right now, that disease is Iraq, where, the broadcaster announces, another car bomb has gone off. Two Americans were killed, and dozens of Iraqis. "Occupation, occupation," Lily says glumly.

"You better get used to it," Noelle says.

"I am used to it. That doesn't mean I have to like it."

The car in front of them seems not to like it either: on its bumper is a sticker that says NO BLOOD FOR OIL.

But when Noelle looks up at the sticker, she says, "That's a stupid slogan."

Lily doesn't respond.

"You disagree?"

"It's stupid in the sense that all slogans are stupid. As far as slogans go, it's less stupid than most."

On the radio, the newscaster goes on about the war casualties. Lily hears the words *Baghdad, Mosul, Basrah*, and dejected, disgusted, she turns the radio off.

"Taste of your own medicine?" Noelle says.

"What medicine?"

"All those years the U.S. criticized Israel, and now look at the world's greatest superpower. A couple thousand people die in Manhattan and the heavens have fallen in. Your country lectured everyone for decades, and now that it's happening here, no force is too excessive."

Lily certainly isn't going to disagree about that. Though she can't help adding, "*My* country, Noelle? Have you renounced your U.S. citizenship?"

"Not technically."

"I didn't think so. A lot of people would kill for your passport." She looks over at her sister. "Just don't fight with Mom, okay?"

The sides of the road are thick with brush, the rock formation jutting out above it. Clouds block the sun, it's getting harder to see, and soon it starts to rain, so Lily turns on the windshield wipers. "Does Mom send you her op-eds?"

"She doesn't need to," Noelle says. "The one that ran in the *Times* a couple of months back? It was reprinted in the *Jerusalem Post*."

But Lily doesn't want to talk any more about this, doesn't want to argue with Noelle about the war, about anything having to do with Leo. But it's all she can do to stop herself. Noelle voted for Bush—not just once, but twice! She voted for him even after Leo died! Lily holds all fifty million people who voted for him responsible for Leo's death. With Noelle, though, it's worse; she was Leo's sister. *You killed your own brother!* she wants to shout.

They're past Worcester, where an enormous pumpkin sits at the side of the road, as if waiting, derelict, for Halloween. In the distance is a sign for Wachusett Lumber. Election Day is months off, but already campaigning has begun; little flags are staked at the side of the road with candidates' names printed on them. County legislator. County court. Town supervisor. Someone named French is running for something. Lily turns the radio back on, but all she gets is static. "Surprise, surprise. They still don't have radio towers in the Berkshires."

"We're not even close to the Berkshires," Noelle says. "We're more than an hour away."

"Well, it's anticipating us." A gob of bird shit splats against their windshield; Lily turns the wipers on higher. "The last time I was in Lenox, no one could get cell phone coverage. It's like the fucking Stone Age up there."

"Lily!" Noelle thrusts her thumb over her shoulder to where Akiva and Yoni are sitting. "Watch your language."

Ah, yes, Lily thinks. The fucking Stone Age. Noelle who when she was eight had her mouth washed out with soap by her third-grade teacher. Noelle who as a teenager used to say about some guy or another, "That's the one I'm balling," and Lily would look at her in benign amusement and say, "You're balling him, Noelle? My under-standing is he's the one balling you." Now religious Noelle with her long skirts and head coverings has become the language police. "I'm sorry, Noelle. The dang Stone Age. The gosh-darn Stone Age. The dickens of a Stone Age."

"How about just the Stone Age?"

"All I'm saying is I'd like to get cell phone coverage up there."

"And all *I'm* saying is I'd appreciate it if you minded your language."

"Yes, Noelle. You've made your point."

Ahead of them, a deer stands next to the road, looking from side to side, as if checking out the traffic. "Don't you dare," Lily says.

"What?"

"I was talking to the deer." She drives around a bend, and when they emerge into the clearing, they are surrounded by huge stalks of corn and, beyond them, patches of butter lettuce. A sign at the side of the road reads MEATBALLS, NACHOS, WATER. They pass an ad for an animal clinic, with the words IAMS SOLD HERE.

"Why do you need cell phone service, anyway? Can't you stand to be unwired for a few days?"

"I have work to do, Noelle. This holiday hasn't exactly come at a good time."

"Well, it's not good for any of us. Do you think it's easy to fly in from Israel? Or cheap?"

"I assumed Mom and Dad helped you out."

"Well, they didn't."

"Or Grandma. You're always asking Grandma for money."

"That's not true."

Lily looks at her.

"Well, sometimes."

Lily nods, feeling as if she's proven a point, though she doesn't even know what that point is.

They drive past Brookfield, where the grass is lined with yellow flowers and where, beyond a wooden fence, horses are at a feed trough and a woman in a straw hat is navigating a tractor. Through the window, Lily takes in the smell of freshly mown grass.

"Grandma could help you out, too," Noelle says. "And if you weren't so pigheaded you'd let her."

"I don't need Grandma's money."

"But Malcolm does, doesn't he? Isn't he trying to open his own restaurant?"

"What does that have to do with Grandma?" Malcolm has found a building on Capitol Hill, where there's been a dining boom, and he's been getting good press—he had a full-page photo in the *Washingtonian* in an article about D.C.'s best young chefs—and now all he needs is financial backing. A lot of it. But if Noelle thinks Malcolm should ask Gretchen for help, she misunderstands their grandmother entirely. Gretchen could fund Malcolm's restaurant singlehandedly and she wouldn't even know the money was missing. Gretchen's first husband, Lily's paternal grandfather, died of a heart attack when Lily's father, their only child, was six, and she subsequently outlived two other husbands, both of whom were CEOs of Fortune 500 companies, neither of whom had children. So Gretchen inherited everything they owned. She speaks of this with pride. What others might call greed she sees as discernment: she knows whom to marry. Gretchen is ninety-four and lives alone in an enormous apartment on Fifth Avenue overlooking the Met, where, Lily suspects, she's busy honing those powers of discernment, determining whom best to bat her eyelashes at. At heart, she's an insecure woman who believes people value her only for her money; if that's true, Lily thinks, it's because she has brought it on herself. She's always promising people money, then breaking those promises; she rewrites her will every year. She demands strict devotion from her family, and she likes to pit the grandchildren against each other, writing a check to one that's slightly larger than her check to the next one, all based on her quixotic assessment of who reveres her most.

If Malcolm wants Gretchen to fund his restaurant, he'd do well to move to Fifth Avenue and show up every morning with a mimosa. Even that would do him no good, because he'd cross her in a way he hadn't divined and then all his hard work would be for naught. Lily's family is comfortable, but it's possible that when her grandmother dies—though Lily doesn't believe this will ever happen; Gretchen is too iron-willed to die—she and her sisters could become very wealthy. Just as likely, Gretchen could give all her money to the New York Horticultural Society; she'd do it simply because she could. For all these reasons, Lily has resolved not to win Gretchen's favor. She received the money all the siblings received at twenty-five and she doesn't want anything more. If her grandmother offered to fund Malcolm's restaurant, Malcolm would think the money came without strings, but there are always strings with Gretchen. In no time, she'd be taking the train down to D.C., where she would camp out in Malcolm's kitchen cooking her favorite breakfast, scrambled eggs with horseradish cheddar. She'd have the restaurant closed in a matter of months.

"Anyway," Noelle says, "it's not just money, it's time. Do you know how long it takes to fly here?"

"Probably about as long as it took me to drive up from D.C. You should have seen the traffic. I was stuck with all the soccer moms." Lily gives the dashboard a firm, affectionate rap, as if she's thumping the rear of a horse.

"Well, I'm sorry Leo's death has inconvenienced you."

"Tell me something, Noelle. Do you think Leo would have wanted us to have this memorial?"

"I have no idea."

"Well, I do. He'd have hated it. If he were here, he'd be off vomiting in the corner."

On the other side of the road, two scarecrows are pinned to a tree. An American flag hangs from a pole, folded over on itself like a napkin.

"Where's Malcolm?" Akiva asks, leaning over from the backseat.

"I left him behind," Lily says. "He's been grounded."

"He's not coming?" says Noelle.

"He's too busy at work. He had a hundred reservations for dinner tonight." What Lily doesn't tell Noelle is that, once he leaves work, Malcolm will be driving down to the Outer Banks. One of his roommates from culinary school is in from London, so the roommates have decided to make a North Carolina beach holiday out of it.

They pass a road sign with a picture of a cow on it, and a few hundred yards later a pasture with cattle opens before them. At the exit is a sign for miniature golf.

"How long have you guys been a couple, anyway?"

"Ten years," Lily says. "We celebrated our anniversary last month."

"Have you ever thought about getting married?"

"You mean, have we thought about getting married since the last time you asked me if we'd thought about getting married?"

"Well, have you?"

"No, Noelle, we haven't." Lily considers asking Noelle why she wants her to marry Malcolm. Malcolm isn't Jewish, so if she were to marry him Noelle and Amram would boycott their wedding just as they boycotted Leo and Thisbe's wedding. But there's no point in pursuing this path. Noelle will disapprove of her not marrying Malcolm the same way she'll disapprove of her marrying him.

"Because you don't believe in marriage," Noelle says.

"How can I possibly not believe in marriage?"

"You certainly don't seem to."

"For several years there, I was spending every weekend in a cocktail dress at some winery, allocating my disposable income to bridal gifts. Now my paycheck goes to baby showers. I should take it as a tax deduction. Hazard of the job."

"What job?"

"Exactly."

"So you're above it all," Noelle says.

"Believe me, Noelle, I'm not above anything."

"But you're not going to have kids."

"Noelle, you're having enough kids for both of us."

"That wasn't my intention."

"To have so many kids?"

"To have them for you. Doesn't it bother you that your line will run out?"

"My line?" Lily says. "What is this? Divine right of kings? Heir to my throne?"

"Why do you think we were put here on earth?"

"We weren't put here," Lily says. "We're just here."

Noelle sniffles, blows her nose, and for a second Lily thinks she's crying. But when she glances over, Noelle is just sitting there impassively, staring straight ahead.

Now Yoni has woken up, and Lily finds herself rattling to the percussive thump of her nephew's foot against the back of her seat.

"Yoni," Noelle says, "stop kicking Aunt Lily."

"I don't mind," Lily says.

"Well, I do."

From behind the wheel, Lily can hear the sound of elbows jamming into ribs; one of the boys has slugged the other.

"Kids!" Noelle says.

Yoni reaches into his mother's bag and removes a tube of apple sauce and a container of Jell-O.

"Be careful," Noelle says. "You don't want to dirty Lily's car."

"It's already dirty," Lily says. "They can litter it to their hearts' content."

Now one of the boys has switched on the interior light, the better to play finger baseball by.

"If we weren't running late," Lily says, "I'd take you kids to Fenway Park. I could show you the Green Monster."

"Are you a Red Sox fan?" Akiva asks.

"Only when they play the Yankees."

"Why?"

"Because I'm a Mets fan." In 1986, the year the Mets won the World Series, Lily accompanied Leo, who was fourteen at the time, on the subway to Flushing, to watch Dwight Gooden and Darryl Strawberry play at Shea Stadium. Everyone in the family was a Mets fan, and in the bleachers at Shea even Lily and Noelle got along. Lily has no patience for Yankees fans, especially the newly minted New Yorkers, the arrivistes. She knows suffering: she's witnessed the Mets endure hundred-loss seasons. So when Akiva announces he's a Yankees fan, she says, "Too bad for you. I guess we'll have to eat at separate tables."

Akiva is silent.

"I'm only kidding," she says.

Though Akiva, perhaps to make sure, says, "I like basketball better, anyway."

Now the boys have grown quiet, and Lily and Noelle turn quiet, too. Noelle's phone rings, and she answers it in a whisper.

"Who was that?" Lily asks when she hangs up.

"Amram," Noelle says. "He was checking on our progress."

"And?"

"We're progressing, aren't we?"

More bird shit hits the windshield. It's as if a flock of geese is following them, dappling them with waste.

The news is on again: there's the possibility of a hailstorm. In July! Another reason, Lily thinks, to be back in D.C., land of March cherry blossoms and sweltering summers. Or on the Maryland shore. Or on the North Carolina shore with Malcolm. The summer she met Malcolm, she could occasionally get Mets games on the radio in Des Moines, when the team was playing the Cubs. Now she and Malcolm have gone in with friends to purchase Washington Nationals season tickets, though as often as not they have to give them away; it's what they've done for tomorrow's game. Lily wouldn't mind being back home, sitting with Malcolm and their friends in their appointed seats, drinking beer and eating peanuts.

From the back of the van comes a sneeze, and another one.

"Does he have a cold?"

"Allergies," Noelle says.

"Hay fever?"

"Some." Noelle rolls down the window, but soon the rain starts to come in, so she rolls it up again. "It feels doggy in here. Has Svengali been in the van?"

"At some point," Lily says. "Malcolm likes to take him on errands."

"On errands?" Noelle says. "He's a dog."

"I know what he is."

"Does he still drink from the toilet?"

"Whenever possible. We try to leave the seat up for him. That way, he has more room to maneuver."

"I hope you at least flush beforehand."

"If we remember to."

"The things you let that dog do. I remember one time you went for a run, and afterward Svengali was licking your forehead."

"He likes salt," Lily says.

"Well, I wouldn't let a ninety-pound Rhodesian Ridgeback lick my forehead no matter how much I loved him."

"Yes, Noelle, you've made that clear." When, Lily wonders, did Noelle become so squeamish? She remembers years ago catching Noelle peeing in the shower. "We do have toilets in this house," she said. To which Noelle responded, "What's a WASP? Someone who gets out of the shower to pee." And afterward, Lily and Clarissa, the ostensible WASPs, would do little riffs on Noelle's words. "What's a WASP?" Lily said. "Someone who puts on clothes to go to school." "What's a WASP?" Clarissa said. "Someone who wipes her butt after she takes a dump."

The boys have fallen asleep again, and Lily can hear them breathing in quiet syncopation. Through the rearview mirror, she sees a line of drool descend Yoni's mouth and settle on his chin. "I have a tissue."

Noelle shakes her head. "Better to let him sleep."

"They're cute," she says.

"Who?"

"Your kids. The other ones, too. In the car with Amram." But the words come out hollow. It's always that way with Noelle. Even when Lily's doing her best, Noelle looks at her askance, as if whatever she says smacks of pretense.

The Berkshire mountains surround them now, the clouds perched low above the summits. Lily recalls the car rides when she was a girl, going past Brewster and Pawling and Harlem Valley Psychiatric Center, stuck behind a Winnebago with the words OVERSIZE LOAD printed across it, then on to the familiar Berkshires towns, to South Egremont and Great Barrington and Stockbridge, closer and closer to their summer home. "Soon, soon," she says, but Noelle doesn't answer her.

The boys wake up long enough to play tic-tac-toe on the window, but now they've fallen asleep again, moving in and out of wakefulness.

They go over a small bridge, the car reverberating along the wooden planks. Deer signs lie up ahead, one after the other like mile markings. "Those signs are ridiculous," Lily says.

"They're warnings," says Noelle. "They're for our own good."

"Those deer are always prancing—looking happy when they're about to get killed. And us along with them, if we're not careful."

"The problem in Israel is cats," Noelle says. "You can't open a dumpster without having one jump out at you."

"At least they don't have antlers."

"Israel used to have a mice problem," Noelle says. "So they brought in the cats. Next they'll have to bring in the dogs."

"And then the buffalo."

"What?"

"Forget it."

Lily glances up at the rearview mirror. Akiva's head, which was leaning against the window, is now lolling to the other side; he's bent over himself like a puppet. For an instant, she has an image of Leo as a baby, so rubbery, so pliable—he resembled Gumby—and of herself up late holding him against her chest, trying to quiet him as he cried, tiptoeing down the long hallway of her parents' apartment, around and around as if they were doing a waltz.

"I'm sorry," Lily says. "Let's try not to fight."

Noelle doesn't respond.

Soon it starts to rain harder, and there's nothing but the beat of water against the windshield and the sound of the boys sleeping quietly in back, nothing in Lily's head but her own voice reminding her what she told Malcolm before she left, what she said to Clarissa on the phone last night, what she's been resolving to herself for weeks now, that she won't fight with Noelle on this trip, for her own sake, for her parents' sake, for the sake of Leo's memory. So she stays quiet as she drives, taking occasional sips from her Coke, focused only on the goal of navigating them through the traffic, everyone pressed like boats stern to prow as she drives along the road to her parents' house.

4

Thisbe's breath catches as she walks up the path; her heart throbs in her forehead. It's just Marilyn and David, she reminds herself, but to no avail. Calder, blond, long-lashed, is asleep in her arms. It's six in the evening, an hour before his bedtime, but his clock has been thrown off by the day's travel. His head thumps against her shoulder to the beat of her walking, but he remains undisturbed.

The front door looks different. Have they painted it? she wonders. It's green now; she could have sworn it used to be white. Above the knocker is a note that says "Welcome Home!" with three stick figures beside it. Clarissa, Lily, and Noelle, their arms touching. Marilyn and David have always been this way, the welcome home signs greeting the adult children, the happy birthday notes appended to bedroom doors, but when Thisbe poked fun at this ("What are you guys, seven?" she used to say to Leo), he would turn defensive. Though now she wonders if it's envy she feels and, as always, that undercurrent of exclusion: was she, despite everything, hoping for a fourth stick figure?

She rings the bell, and when no one answers, she finds the door unlocked. "Hello? Is anybody home?" She's in the foyer, next to the coat rack and umbrella stand; beside them sits the shoe cubby with David's running sneakers spilling out of it. "We're here!" she shouts. "It's Thisbe and Calder! Marilyn! David! Your grandson has arrived!" She's going for animation, engaged, she realizes, in willed histrionics, hoping to lose herself in the hubbub of the reunion. Calder turned three in February. He hasn't seen Marilyn and David in months, and to compensate for this, Thisbe has placed their photograph beside his bed. Her own parents live in Santa Cruz, a mere hour and a half away, so they see Calder all the time. They're simply Grandma and Grandpa to him, but in anticipation of this trip, she has started to refer to them as Grandma Natalie and Grandpa Ivan, as if to prove she's not playing favorites.

In the car ride from the airport, she brought out her treasure trove of memories, recounting to Calder the times he'd spent with her in-laws, the elevator in Marilyn and David's building in Manhattan that catapulted them to the seventeenth floor. (Calder insisted on pushing all the buttons; Marilyn and David even allowed him to press the alarm.) Do you remember this? Thisbe asked. Do you remember that? It's possible Calder does, though it's hard to know: you get him on a roll and he'll confirm anything. ("Did you play with Jacob?" she asks when he returns from preschool. "Yes," Calder says. "Did you play with Sophia?" "Yes." "Did you play with Donald Rumsfeld?" "Yes.") Still, she's hoping that the promptings on the plane going east will carry the weight she wants them to—she brought an entire photo album to show Calder, filled with photos of Marilyn and David, and of Clarissa, Lily, and Noelle. "Those are Daddy's sisters," she said. "Don't they look like him?" She fears Calder won't recognize his grandparents or, if he does, that he'll hide his face—he can be shy when he first sees someone, even someone he knows—and that this will reflect badly on her, will confirm whatever suspicions her in-laws have been harboring.

"Marilyn and David? Clarissa? Lily? Noelle?" For an instant she wonders, does she have the wrong date? But no: of course it's the Fourth. She sets Calder on the couch and goes to remove some stray items from the car, and as she heads back inside she sees two figures coming up the road, carrying groceries. She can't make out their faces yet, but their carriage is unmistakable. "Hello!" she calls out.

Simultaneously they wave, each holding one hand overhead, like two traffic cops. As they approach, a shyness overtakes them; no one seems sure what to do next.

Marilyn takes her in a hug, and Thisbe feels the anxiety leak out of her, though her pulse still flutters in her forehead like a sail.

"Where's Calder?" David asks.

"Inside," she says. "Asleep."

"Did the girls get here?"

"Not yet."

Marilyn looks at her watch. "They promised they'd be here for dinner." Marilyn's hair is red, the family trademark, though hers is shot through with long stripes of gray. She wears it back in a ponytail;

not many sixty-nine-year-olds could keep their hair that long without looking like a hippie or a fading ingénue, but Marilyn is neither of those things, certainly. She's tall and thin, a wearer of shawls and long dresses, and with her sharp chin and rapidly descending nose, she has the look of an especially handsome bird. One of Thisbe's most distinct memories is of Marilyn shooing off some pharmaceutical representative (Marilyn believes there's a special place in hell for the drug reps, and she makes a point of not prescribing any medication that's been pressed too forcefully on her), chasing after him, her doctor's coat flying behind her. David is thicker-set and fleshier-faced; he has Clarissa's green eyes, though he's the only non-redhead in the family. His hair has turned silvery, and he has let it grow longer, though mostly it's grown out instead of down.

"How's retirement treating you?" Thisbe asks.

"He's keeping busy," Marilyn says. "David's the most unretiring person I know."

"Second to you," David says.

In the living room, Marilyn stands above the sleeping Calder. "He's darling," she says. "I can't believe how much he's grown." She leans so close to him their noses almost touch.

"I bought him new shoes in February," Thisbe says, "and already he's too big for them."

"It was the same way with Leo," Marilyn says. "You got him home from the shoe store, and you had to go right back."

Thisbe doesn't blame Marilyn: whom else should Calder remind her of if not Leo? But it makes her uncomfortable nonetheless. The last time she saw him, Marilyn slipped a few times and called Calder Leo, and Thisbe wondered whether it was really a slip or whether Marilyn was staking a claim. Thisbe and Leo gave Calder a hyphenated combination of their last names, a fact Marilyn seems to have forgotten, or has chosen simply to ignore. On Calder's birthday, on holidays, whenever Marilyn sends Calder a card, it's always to "Calder Frankel" that she addresses it.

It's that name, in fact, that stares up at Calder now, on a gift Marilyn and David have gotten him. It's a jigsaw puzzle. There must be a thousand pieces in it; Thisbe has no idea how she'll pack it for the trip home. Long ago she learned that the weight of your baggage is inversely proportionate to the weight of your traveling companion. "Marilyn," she says gently, "that's not his name."

"What?"

"It's Godsoe-Frankel."

"I'm sorry," Marilyn says. "I forgot."

Now, though, Thisbe feels bad, because what difference does it make what her mother-in-law calls him? This is how it always is with Marilyn, the swinging from resentment to self-blame. Although Thisbe misses Leo for countless reasons, one of them is that he was a buffer between her and Marilyn. He was her perspective, her ballast, and now that he's gone, she feels the recriminations bloom once more.

"How's grad school going?" Marilyn asks. "Was it a good year?"

"It was," Thisbe says. It was as good a year as it could be under the circumstances, certainly the grad school part.

"And now?"

"Now it's summer. Like they say, the three best reasons to go to grad school are June, July, and August."

"So what comes next?" Marilyn says. "More classes?"

"One year down, ten to go. Or twenty. Or forty." Thisbe knows the stories about humanities PhDs, those perpetual graduate students marooned in college towns, working in bars, bookstores, and cafés long past an age when it's seemly to do so. Marilyn knows those stories, too. Years ago, David himself was an English doctoral student before he dropped out to teach high school.

"Come, come," Marilyn says. "You're not like that."

And she isn't, Thisbe knows. She's likely to finish sooner rather than later. She's never been one to tarry, when it comes to school or anything else.

"Leo would have loved Berkeley," Marilyn says, and Thisbe understands that this is a peace offering. Because when Thisbe applied to anthropology programs, when she was deciding among good graduate schools on the east and west coasts, Marilyn implied without ever directly saying so that she thought Thisbe was taking Leo away from them, back to where she'd grown up. Marilyn was right—Thisbe *was* taking Leo away from them—but Leo had been the one who wanted to move to Berkeley. He had his own fantasies about shorts in November, had fantasies, too, about U.C. Berkeley itself. Born in the 1970s, raised just blocks from Columbia, he'd missed out on the student protests. "I wouldn't have minded occupying a building," he told Thisbe once, and Thisbe just laughed. "What you wouldn't have minded was free love."

"Sure," Leo said. "That would have been good, too."

When she decided to go to Berkeley, Leo gave notice at *Newsday*. He had landed a job at the *San Francisco Chronicle*, on the foreign desk. They would be moving in August. The day he was killed, they had already booked their flights.

"I look at you and it just kills me," Marilyn says. "You're thirty-three years old, and you've already been through so much."

"I'll be all right," Thisbe says.

"Will you be?"

"I hope so." Thisbe looks down at Calder, who remains asleep, flat as a flounder on the living room couch, his arms flung to the sides. "What about you, Marilyn. How are *you* doing?"

"Terrible," Marilyn says. "Just dreadful."

"I'm so sorry." It's been the hardest year of Thisbe's life, yet it's different for her. Marilyn and David were Leo's parents. Whereas she . . . she can barely say the words, even to herself. She has come east for many reasons. For Leo's sake, of course, and to pay respects to his family, but also because she needs to tell Marilyn and David about Wyeth. *I have a new boyfriend.* It makes her heart palpitate just to think this. Lily is the only one who knows about Wyeth, and even she doesn't know how serious it has become.

Thisbe goes into the kitchen, passing through the swinging door where Leo, when he was three, caught his finger and had to go to the emergency room to have it reattached. It was the first of a series of injuries he suffered (several years later he almost lost a toe, cutting it on a Pringles can during a water fight), victim of his own heedlessness and bad luck. Thisbe was twenty-one when she met him, waitressing at a bar in town, and it was the first thing she noticed about him, that misshapen forefinger, how he held his beer so it looked like he was pointing across the room.

Now, in the kitchen, she finds food warming on the stove. She has half a mind to try something. If Leo were here, he'd be breaking into the food, serving himself a pre-dinner (an *amuse-bouche*, he'd have called it, though the way he'd have heaped his plate, it would have been hard to describe it as mere amusement), all too happy to join in the second seating when everyone else arrived. Once, at a Japanese restaurant, he shambled over to another table and returned with a plate of abandoned fish. "It's all-you-can-eat sushi," he said. "Why let it go to waste?" He'd done this to shock her, though she was long past being shocked. He's been gone a year, and she still envies him his impropriety.

It's an old wood house with a mansard roof, two stories plus a base-ment that, when Leo was a teenager, held the family's air hockey table and pinball machine and was witness to epic games of Ping-Pong between Leo and his father (when the girls came home from college they got in on the fun, too), and late at night when his parents were asleep served as the pot-smoking venue for Leo and his friends. (It was the same way for Thisbe growing up; the American family basement, she has long believed, was invented with marijuana in mind.) Even after Leo moved out, there remained an upstairs-downstairs divide, with the basement serving as rec room, while the rest of the house was consecrated to more high-minded pleasures, to the piano—Marilyn and David still play—and to a slew of board games, which were packed into the cabinets beneath the bookshelves. When Thisbe met Leo, the summer after her junior year at Bowdoin, she would come over to find various Frankels spread across the rug playing Scrabble, Pictionary, Boggle, Taboo. Most of the time she refused to join in; the competi-tion was so explicit it unsettled her. Though she's competitive herself. Those times when she agreed to play, she was as resolved to win as anyone else.

In the dining room, a couple of booster seats are perched on the table, and next to them stands a high chair. Marilyn and David had it made after Noelle's first son was born. "We wanted it to be an actual piece of furniture," Marilyn said, and Thisbe, back when procreating seemed at best a theoretical enterprise, said to Leo, "What does she mean, she wants to it to be an actual piece of furniture? It's a high chair!" Later, she took to surveying the other baby accoutrements, purchased for a grandson who lived six thousand miles away. "I think the diaper disposal should be a real piece of furniture. And the training potty, too."

In the living room she finds a deck of playing cards, a set of keys, and a flyer from the local policemen's benevolent association advertising the upcoming auction. An antique reading lamp sits next to the couch, and beside it lie Marilyn's glasses on top of an open copy of the *Times*. (The image Thisbe retains is of Marilyn and David up late reading, the smell of wood in the fireplace and of Marilyn's mulled apple cider, Thisbe and Leo coming home from the bar to find Marilyn and David asleep with their books toppled on their laps, Leo saying, "Come on, kids, time for bed.") Magazines are strewn across the top of the grand piano—*The New Yorker*, *Harper's*, the *TLS*—along with some medical journals and, stuck between them, an errant copy of *Blueberries for Sal*. Thisbe sits down to read, but then, distracted, she wanders across the living room and around the bend, through this house filled with alcoves. One Christmas, she and Leo house-sat for her college professor, and half the fun was seeing what they could find snooping through the closets. She's suspicious of people who don't snoop; she thinks it suggests a lack of curiosity. Besides, she has a proprietary regard for this house. It's here, in Lenox, where she and Leo met, where they spent their first months together.

On the rafters are the siblings' names and the names of old boyfriends and girlfriends etched into the wood. After she and Leo started to go out, he climbed up a beam and, in a ritual of mock seriousness, crossed out the name of his old girlfriend, Nora, and carved in Thisbe's name instead. *Her gallant boyfriend.* It's been twelve years since then, but she can still make out her name on the rafters; it flusters her to see herself here, living on in this house after he's gone. A shudder runs through her, though it could be from the cold as much as from anything else. The house feels damp, as it always did, perhaps because it wasn't winterized when it was first built and because, once it was, the process was done haphazardly and on the cheap. You'd think going to Bowdoin would have acclimated her to the cold, but it hasn't; even San Francisco feels chilly to her. Berkeley is warmer, which is one reason she's staying there, though she's a city person and if Calder weren't so happy at preschool, she might move across the Bay.

In the closet are arrayed sandals, flip-flops, and tennis sneakers— shoes of languor, Thisbe thinks, meant for traipsing through town, and for hitting a shuttlecock behind the house. There's even a pair of snow boots amidst everything else, though the family is in Lenox mostly during the summer. In the off-season they rent out the house for weeks at a time, though no one can remember when it's being rented; more than once somebody drove up, only to find the house occupied. It was Leo one time, and he so startled the renter that she pointed a hunting rifle at him. After that, Leo told Thisbe always to ring the doorbell when she arrived unless she wanted his parents to shoot her. A laughable notion: Thisbe can think of no one less likely to shoot a gun than Marilyn or David. Apparently, when Marilyn was growing up she refused on moral grounds to touch a weapon—she even opted out of archery practice at summer camp—and when she became a parent, she didn't allow her children to play with toy guns. "Good liberals," Leo said of them, only half derisively; they'd turned him into a good liberal, too.

Upstairs in the hallway everything is as she remembers it—the Kathe Kollwitz etchings on the wall, the faded portraits of Leo's great-grandparents, the old charcoal street map of Paris. On a glass table sit the family photos, where Thisbe finds a younger version of herself standing next to Leo at his Wesleyan graduation, and another photo, from their wedding, at the New York Aquarium, she in her wedding gown holding a glass of champagne, and behind her, in his tank, the walrus pressed against the glass, making his walrus noises. That walrus alone, Leo used to say, was worth the cost of the wedding; he kept referring to the walrus as his best man. In another photo- graph, this one taken after Leo's death, she's holding Calder, just two years old. In all these photos she plays a supporting role—the girl- friend, the wife, the mother—though there's also one of her alone, in a yellow sundress, a look of perplexity across her face, taken when, she isn't sure. This photo, in particular, makes her feel obscurely vio- lated, which is strange because for years there were no photos of her in the house, and she took this as evidence that she wasn't welcomed by Leo's parents, at least not by Marilyn, who from the start was suspicious of her, why, she doesn't know. The only reason she can come up with is that she wasn't Nora, Leo's high school girlfriend, who lingered on haphazardly into college, showing up in Middletown when she and Leo weren't with someone else to perpetrate another act of high drama. *The girl with the extra toe*, Thisbe called Nora, which, she understood, was mean-spirited (though Nora did, in fact, have an extra toe, at the base of where her first two toes met), and was, besides, the least remarkable thing about her. More remarkable was her capacity for self-destruction, for putting things into her body that didn't belong and failing to put in things that did. Leo's mother helped Nora get treatment (for drugs, for anorexia), and because of this, and because Leo knew Nora as long as he did (they were in the same nursery-school class in Morningside Heights), Marilyn saw Nora as a surrogate daughter and was almost as protective of her as Leo was.

The happy girlfriend, Marilyn called Thisbe. Why? Because she was blond and pretty and from California? Because she didn't have an eating disorder? Thisbe was tempted to protest that she wasn't happy and to argue, at the same time, that happiness was nothing to be ashamed of, both of which led her down a path she didn't wish to take, of defending herself to her boyfriend's mother. What had Marilyn been hoping for? That Leo would marry Nora? It should be illegal, Thisbe thinks, to marry someone you dated in high school; marrying someone you dated in college is hard enough. The story goes that after Thisbe was born her parents made placenta soup. It was a ludicrous ritual, but this was Santa Cruz in the 1970s, when everyone was engaged in ludicrous rituals. And she was only a few days old at the time: it wasn't her idea to make placenta soup. But Marilyn saw this story as confirmation. Of what? Thisbe thinks. That she's a pagan? That she wasn't worthy of Marilyn's darling son? From the start, David was more generous—Thisbe *likes* David—but he was overshadowed by Marilyn, who has the larger, blunter personality. Over time, Thisbe grew fonder of Marilyn, but for years she felt as if she were competing with the ghost of Nora and with the photos of her that still remained in the house long after Leo and she had broken up. Standing in the hallway in front of the family photos, Thisbe feels vindicated, but she experiences it as false consolation, because now that she's been given such a prominent place on the mantel, she isn't sure she wants to be there.

David comes up the stairs, carrying her suitcases. She doesn't know where she'll be sleeping, but as he guides her through the long corridor, she realizes he's leading her to Leo's old bedroom. They're halfway down the hall before she can so much as expel a breath.

"Is there—"

"I just thought . . ."

"I'm sorry," he says.

"David, you don't need to apologize."

"*Mi casa es su casa*."

"I know . . ."

It's a big house, he reminds her. There's the basement and the attic and the other bedrooms. But the truth, he admits, is that with so many people coming he hasn't given much thought to who will sleep where. Then, as if to belie his claim about the size of the house, he bumps into her in the hallway. He's still holding her suitcases, one in each hand like a set of weights, and they do a clumsy dance to escape each other.

Now they retrace their steps through the hall and down the stairs, where, in the basement, a bed has been made and where David deposits her suitcases. "Is this all right?"

"It's perfect."

"Calder can sleep here as well."

Thisbe starts to unpack, but then the doorbell rings and she goes upstairs to find Lily, Noelle, Amram, and the boys standing in the foyer with their luggage.

David hugs Lily, Noelle, and the boys. He shakes Amram's hand.

Marilyn, behind him, lines up her grandsons. "You kids are huge. Positively mammoth. What have they been feeding you in Jerusalem?"

"Falafel," Akiva says.

"Beans make you grow," Noelle says, shrugging, and she reaches down to grab a suitcase.

It isn't until they're inside that Marilyn realizes they're not all there. "Where's Clarissa and Nathaniel?"

"Beats me," Lily says.

"What do you mean, beats you?"

"She left a message saying she'd meet us at the house. I guess she's running behind schedule."

"Why hasn't she called?" Marilyn goes over to the window, but there's nothing to see but their driveway, which winds down a hill amidst a thicket of trees. She tries Clarissa's cell phone but is sent straight to voicemail. She tries Nathaniel's cell phone and is sent to voicemail, too.

"Come on," Lily says. "Let's eat. Those slowpokes can catch up with us when they get here."

But Marilyn won't countenance it. She looks to David for support, but he gives her his signature shrug, his gaze tunneling beyond her. She wants to shake him, really she does, though no doubt he wants to shake her, too.

In the kitchen, she tries to make herself look busy, tasting the gazpacho, the corn, the pasta salad, but there's nothing to taste but what's already been tasted, and so she floats around the room in her black silk skirt, fearing that she's overdressed, that she looks at once too decked out and too funereal.

In the living room, she places books on top of one another, on coffee tables and lamp stands, whatever will sustain them. At the foot of the grand piano sit copies of the *Times*, which have piled up from summers past, the way they pile up in Manhattan. She should just tie them in twine and leave them out for recycling, but David is still going at them. He reads the paper in order, every day from front to back, and in this manner he has fallen years behind, the fact of which he likes to report with a mixture of self-mockery and mulish pride. But the sight of those papers assails her now, and so she makes a pile of them and ties them up, then leaves them out front beside the garbage bins.

A bulb is extinguished in the reading lamp, but when she goes to replace it all she can find is a halogen bulb, and this one takes fluorescent. She returns to the closet, and this time she comes back with the right bulb, but when she unscrews the extinguished one it slips from her hand and shatters on the floor.

"Shit!" she says. "Damn it!" There are shards of glass all over the floor and spilling onto the carpet.

She gets the broom and dustpan, the vacuum cleaner for good measure, but when she turns it on, the sound of the motor feels like a drill going off, and she thinks, What if Clarissa is trying to call, so she puts the vacuum away. The shards are embedded in the rug, and she tries to remove them with a pair of tweezers, then resorts to using her hands.

Now Amram comes inside carrying the last of the luggage. He's halfway to the second floor when Yoni runs past him down the stairs. "My tooth is loose!" he cries.

"I'm going to yank it out," Akiva says. He's running down the stairs himself, a few steps behind his brother.

"You will do no such thing," Noelle says.

"It will be quick and painless," says Akiva.

"Let me have a look at it," Marilyn says, happy to have something, anything, to distract her.

Yoni opens his mouth for his grandmother to see, and his teeth sparkle in the kitchen light.

Now Akiva is telling Yoni to make sure his tooth falls out in America; that way, the tooth fairy will pay him in dollars. "Never get shekels," Akiva says, "when you can get dollars."

A coil of lightning slashes the sky. Thunder rings out a second later. Marilyn presses her nose to the window, and her breath comes back along the glass. A car drives by on the road below them, but she can't see it through the brush. All she can make out is the diffuse yellow of the headlights and the sound of water spraying against trees.

Soon David joins her, and for a minute they're standing there, looking out the window for their daughter and son-in-law. Reflexively, Marilyn puts her hand to David's shoulder, but he flinches, and she pulls away.

It's nine o'clock when a light comes up the driveway. Lily says, "Is that Clarissa's car?"

Everyone cranes their necks. The car blinds them as it tacks up the path, mist dispersing from its headlights, which glare at them like a disco ball.

"They're here!" Marilyn says.

Clarissa and Nathaniel emerge, looking drawn.

Everyone hugs so that, bathed in the porch light beneath the wrung-out sky, they look like they're doing a dance. Clarissa's clothes cling to her, her hair flat and sopping as a retriever's coat.

"You look like you walked here," David says.

"We did," says Clarissa. "From the driveway to the front door. It's that bad out there." She bends forward in a yoga pose: downward Clarissa. Her long red hair flips over itself; she shakes it from side to side.

They're inside now, drying off, and through the window Marilyn can make out the dripping exteriors of her daughters' cars, arranged in the driveway nose to tail, a fleet of them beside her own car. "Where in the world were you?"

"Oh, Mom, you don't want to know."

"Actually, I do."

"We fell asleep," Clarissa says.

"While you were driving?"

"You know what, Mom? It's private."

"What?"

"They're here now, Marilyn," David says. "What difference does it make?"

She gives him a scathing look, because, once again, he has to paper things over. Because the world could be imploding—the world *is* imploding—and he'd find some good in it.

She hands Clarissa and Nathaniel each a towel, and now she's drying off her daughter's hair, and Clarissa, laughing, poised in the foyer beside the standing lamp, says, "Mom, I'm almost forty, I can dry off my own hair."

"Come on," David says. "The food's getting cold."

Marilyn guides them through the living room, crossing one Persian rug after another, flattened by years of feet, all those summer flip-flops.

In the kitchen, the food, on trivets, is arrayed along the counter. The stove is on, keeping the leeks warm, the flame the dull blue glow of an extinguished campfire. In the corner beneath the spice rack the rice cooker flickers from *cook* to *warm* to *cook* again, as if it can't make up its mind.

"Dad's spice rack," Lily says, grabbing a bottle of fenugreek and a bottle of cream of tartar.

"Sixty-four bottles," Clarissa says. "Enough spices to last a lifetime."

"Not *my* lifetime," David says.

Noelle grabs a couple of bottles herself. "Dad's a spice addict," she says. "He keeps getting more."

"They mask the deficiencies in my cooking," David says.

"Now, now," says Lily.

Marilyn puts one arm around Noelle and another around Thisbe, and with her elbow she's nudging Nathaniel, too, into the dining room.

At the center of the room is a long table of pale blond wood, which was passed down from Marilyn's parents, who are now dead, and which she's overlaid with a white tablecloth. The cutlery is sterling silver, David's mother's, which she gave to them when she remarried for the last time. Marilyn is looking at it all, cataloging it, the silverware, the tablecloth, the table itself, the wineglasses, which she and David were given as a wedding present by a friend, also now dead, as if trying to remember it all.

It's the nine of them standing behind their seats, eight adults plus Akiva, who was supposed to go to bed with his brothers and his cousin; he's on Israel time, and it's four-thirty in the morning there. But he claimed he wasn't tired, and Noelle and Amram were too tired themselves to argue with him ("He's already a teenager," Noelle told Marilyn. "What am I going to do when he's a real teenager?"), so they agreed to let him stay up for another half hour.

Marilyn is at one end of the table, and David is at the other. Everyone is still standing, waiting for Marilyn to tell them what to do. "Sit," she says, but she remains standing herself, and it's not until she pulls out her chair that everyone else does as well.

She smooths her skirt beneath her. She brushes some hair from in front of her face. "This is just . . ." Her voice cracks. She tries to gather her composure. "This is the first time we've been together since Leo died." It's not like she needs to tell them this. Yet she feels as if she does, as if she has to remind them why they're here.

Everyone casts their glances down, even Akiva, who is running his feet along the floor, the only sound Marilyn can hear besides the muted noise of her own gulping. She thinks of the food in the kitchen, of the meal they've prepared, and it's not lost on her that what she and David are serving is what Leo himself would have ordered if she'd asked him to choose the menu.

She raises her wineglass to make a toast, but nothing comes out. Her reflection undulates in the china, coming back to her murkily as if from under water. "This past year has been awful. Dad and I, it's like we're going through this cloud cover, and then there's more cloud cover and more cloud cover and it never stops."

But David has gone into the kitchen, and soon he emerges with the gazpacho on a cart. Now he's recalling for the family a memory from when he and Marilyn were first married, living in a one-bedroom apartment on West End Avenue, when they had a dumbwaiter that went down into the courtyard.

But Marilyn can barely hear him. She's sitting at the table, staring vacantly ahead, unable to pay attention to anything he's saying.

"Amram and I need to wash," Noelle says, and Marilyn remembers: the ritual hand-washing before they eat bread, which they do at the start of every meal. How quickly she forgets, when the easiest thing is to remember Noelle as she was years ago, when there was no washing or ritual blessings, when there were, it sometimes seemed, no meals at all, when dinner for Noelle, despite Marilyn and David's objections, was a couple of Hostess Twinkies washed down with a Tab. Is it possible she longs for that now?

Amram breaks a challah roll into three and gives a piece to Noelle and a piece to Akiva and leaves the last piece for himself. Akiva leads them in the *motzi* blessing, and it astonishes Marilyn to listen to this, the language her grandson speaks so effortlessly, the things he knows that she never will.

Noelle removes a plastic bag out of which she produces a couple of turkey sandwiches and a tub of sliced cucumber. She passes out plastic cutlery and disposable plates to Amram and Akiva.

"What's that?" Lily says.

"Our food," says Noelle.

"And paper dishes," says Amram.

"You brought your own?" Lily's wearing a bright red shirt, which matches her hair, and a silver chain from which dangles an amethyst. Her skin is pale, but she flushes easily in the heat, and beneath the bulbs of the chandelier color rises to her forehead.

"We always do," Noelle says. "Don't tell me you've forgotten."

Lily hasn't, exactly, though it startles her every time. She feels vaguely offended, on her own behalf and on her parents', as if everything they do, everything they touch, is contaminated.

"But the food is kosher," Marilyn says. "Don't you remember?" She escorts Noelle into the kitchen, where, laid out in a row, are the chicken thighs, the caramelized vegetables, the corn on the cob, the pasta salad, the slushies.

"That's nice of you, Mom. It's just . . ."

"What?"

"The dishes," Noelle says. "They would need to be kosher, too."

"They *are* kosher," David says. "Don't you remember? We bought new dishes."

Noelle is quiet.

"What?" Marilyn says. "I don't understand."

"You know how strict Amram and I are."

Marilyn opens the fridge and shows Noelle a package of Miller's Swiss Cheese, with the rabbinic seal of approval laminated across it.

"The kitchen itself would need to be kosher," Noelle says. "The oven, the dishwasher, the microwave, everything."

"Are you kidding me?" David says. He's ready to chronicle the hours he and Marilyn spent cooking, the trips to the kosher butcher, ready to lay out the receipts for the dishes and pots, all so Noelle and Amram and their four boys could eat in their house, so they wouldn't feel excluded over the holiday.

"I'm sorry," Noelle says. "I should have told you not to bother."

"Well, we did bother," Marilyn says.

"I'm sorry," Noelle says again. But what do her parents want her to do? Eat something that's not permitted?

Now Marilyn is back at the table, and she's looking at everyone and she starts to cry.

"Oh, Mom," Noelle says. "I'm so sorry. We know how hard you and Dad must have worked."

"I don't care about the food," Marilyn says. "You and Amram can eat what you want to."

"What's wrong, then?"

Marilyn glances up at David, but he's looking away. She thought she could wait until after the memorial, but she sees she can't. All her plans, her whole life, feel like folly. "Dad and I need to tell you something."

Everyone looks up.

"We have some news you need to know."

"Marilyn," David says sharply. "You said we were going to wait."

They *were* going to wait, but she can't do it. She can't do anything but sit here and stare at her family, even as she knows she must talk.

Outside, in the distance, a siren blares. From upstairs comes the sound of a grandson coughing. "Dad and I are separating," she blurts out.

"You're what?" says Lily.

"We're splitting up," she says. "I'm leaving Daddy."

For several seconds there's pure silence.

"Are you kidding me?" Clarissa says.

David says, "Do you think we'd joke about something like this?"

Meanwhile, Marilyn is trying to explain things, though she can't explain them, even to herself. She won't say those words, that she doesn't love him anymore, because they're not true. "We lost our son," she says. "It's ruined us."

Again there's silence, and Marilyn can't stand it, because the quiet is worse than anything else. But her daughters just sit there, punch-drunk and mute, and David does too.

"It will be better this way," she says. Certainly, she thinks, it can't be worse.

Noelle, rising from her chair and grabbing hold of Akiva, says, "This is a grown-up conversation," and ushers him upstairs to his room.

When she returns, Lily says, "When did this all start?"

Marilyn doesn't know how to answer her. It started with Leo's death, of course, but at the same time it has sideswiped her. You put a frog in cold water and turn on the flame, and the water heats up so slowly it doesn't know to jump out. That's what it's been like for her. Only she *is* jumping out: she's leaving David. "You had to know we were arguing. We've been fighting all the time. It's been horrible."

"But it's only been a year," Clarissa says. "That cloud cover you were talking about? I'm just beginning to emerge from it myself."

"But I'm not going to emerge from it," Marilyn says. "That's what you don't understand."

Again everyone is quiet.

"I wake up every morning and look at Dad and all I can think about is Leo. Jesus, girls, we were his parents."

"Shouldn't that be bringing you together?" Lily says. "I mean, it's been hard for me and Malcolm, too."

"But no one else is giving up," Noelle says.

Is that, Marilyn wonders, what they think she's doing? Because she tried. All year long, she's been trying.

"You could go to couples counseling," Lily says.

"We did," Marilyn says, "and it didn't work." She looks up at David pleadingly. He's flanked on either side by Thisbe and Nathaniel; Amram is a couple of seats away. Her daughter-in-law and sons-in-law, Marilyn thinks, none of whom have said a word, looking, the three of them, like trespassers on their property, though she knows this is a shock for them too.

"You need to explain," Clarissa says.

So Marilyn tries. A few months ago, she and David went to a cocktail party up at Columbia Presbyterian. They were talking to this man, sixtyish, pleasant enough, doing his best to keep up his end of the social compact, and somehow they got on the topic of children, and he asked how many they had. "I said, 'Four,'" Marilyn says, "and at the same instant Dad said, 'Three.'"

"And she was angry at me," David says.

"Livid," says Marilyn. "Finally, I say, 'Eight months after he dies, and you're already saying we have three children?'"

"And I'm thinking, well, we *do* have three children, and does Mom want me to tell this stranger who's probably as bored at that party as we are, 'We had four children, but one of them died tragically in Iraq, you've probably heard of us, we've been on TV'? Twenty years from now, if we're even still alive, someone asks how many children we have, am I still supposed to say four?"

"It wasn't twenty years," Marilyn says. "It was eight months."

Everyone is silent again, and Marilyn is thinking, Please don't do this to me. But she doesn't even know whom she's addressing or what she's begging them not to do.

A beeping comes from the other room; the oven timer has gone off. She can't look at any of them, so she stares through the open door into the kitchen, where a mesh bag of shallots dangles from a knob. A single onion skin pierces through the mesh, trapped like a sparrow's wing.

"You called one time," David tells Lily, "and I remember what you said to us as we got off the phone. 'Make sure you get out. Be good to each other.'"

"But we weren't," Marilyn says, and she thinks this has been her great failure, that it will be the great failure of her life—that she hasn't been able to be good to David, that now, when they should be cleaving together, they have instead been cleaved apart.

Rain whips against the house. The tree branches lift over and again, as if trying to fly off.

"Dad just wants to make things better," Marilyn says.

"What's wrong with that?" says Lily.

"Because it's so damn *teleological*," Marilyn says. "Therapy, couples counseling—it's all there to deny the truth."

"What's the truth?" David says.

"That our son died and things will never be the same for us."

A crack of lightning illuminates the porch; thunder rolls in obligatorily. Besides that, no light comes in from outside, no sound either. Marilyn tries, vainly, to catch David's glance, but he's looking down, at his half-filled plate and cutlery.

"Do you think Leo would have wanted this?" Noelle says.

"I have no idea what Leo would have wanted. That's the point. He's not here." Marilyn closes her eyes, and when she opens them again everyone is still staring at her exactly as they were. She had a feeling they would object, that they'd try to convince her she was being foolish, but she's saddened now, disappointed in them, disappointed in herself for wishing they'd responded differently.

Now dessert is before them, loosed from its box, sitting on a doily in the middle of the table, a key lime pie, with the words *kosher* and *pareve* on the discarded wrapping. A kosher key lime pie, Marilyn thinks, bought for their daughter who won't eat it, and now it seems her other daughters won't eat it, either: no one is hungry anymore.

They sit silently around the pie, which is beginning to bleed beneath the chandelier bulbs, and presently, Lily rises to clear the table. The rest of them remain seated, listening to Lily in the kitchen as she topples the chicken and the half-eaten corncobs into the garbage pail.

Then everyone disperses and it's just Marilyn alone in the kitchen, feeling disgusted with herself. She leans over the grill and eats a chicken thigh with her hands, the marinade dripping onto the floor, and now it's gotten onto her skirt and fallen onto her espadrilles.

The sisters do the dishes, standing beside each other in such stupefied silence it's as if they've been pummeled. The rest of the family is elsewhere, scattered to the living room and upstairs. Outside, the rain pelts the roof and comes at the windows sideways. Clarissa washes and Lily dries and Noelle puts the dishes back in the cabinets. They move with the mute efficiency of an assembly line.

"Can you fucking believe it?" Lily says. She waits for Noelle to rebuke her for her language, but even Noelle knows better.

"I saw them just last week," Clarissa says, "and they seemed fine. I mean, they were bickering, sure, but I didn't think anything of it."

"I always thought they had a good marriage," Noelle says.

"I did too," says Lily. Though no one, she thinks, pays attention to their parents' marriage until they're forced to do so.

Clarissa, letting the water decant onto a plate, is recalling a toast she gave at her wedding. Standing next to Nathaniel, she told the assembled guests that her parents were an inspiration for them, that the greatest gift they'd given her and Nathaniel was their relationship. "And, sure," she tells her sisters, "weddings are these big public events where people get sentimental, but I meant what I said about Mom and Dad. I wouldn't have said those words if I didn't think they were true." She looks down at the sink, filled with soap and dirt and mashed-up watermelon rind, everything a turbid gray.

"They used to do everything together," Lily says. "Remember in elementary school how all our friends got picked up by babysitters and we got picked up by Mom and Dad? I'd have soccer or music or swimming, and there they were, like conjoined twins. They were the most inefficient people in the world."

"Maybe Dad's retiring was a bad idea," Clarissa says. "Now he has his own activities. He goes running. He studies opera."

"He has his vegetable-chopping course," Lily says. "Mom's always making fun of him for that." The plate she has been drying slips out of her hands, and it hovers momentarily in the air before she reaches out and catches it. Bravo, she thinks darkly. Someone should hire her. They should send her off to the circus.

She takes over the washing because she can't just stand there waiting to dry, and now she's going through the dishes at an incredible clip, piling them in the drainer for her sisters.

"Nathaniel and I see them every Tuesday," Clarissa says. "We have a regular dinner date with them."

"And nothing seemed different?" Noelle says.

"I mean, everything's been different since Leo died. But in the last few weeks, the last month?" And she thinks: Was it obvious? Was there something she was missing, something right beneath her nose?

"What about you?" Noelle asks Lily.

"I saw them maybe six weeks ago. Mom was down for a meeting at NIH. Dad came along with her."

Noelle reaches into the cabinet to put a bowl away and she stops mid-motion. "Wait a minute. What was Dad doing coming down with her if they were about to split up?"

"I have no idea." Something has gotten stuck in the drain; without Lily's noticing it, the water has risen to overflowing. She turns on the garbage disposal, but it makes a terrible cracking noise, so she turns it off. She removes a corn husk from the drain, and soon the water starts to seep out. A residue of endive and chicken skin settles on the dishes. She feels as if she might retch. She takes off the dish gloves and places them on the counter, where they lie, rubbery and immobile, like two dead fish.

"That's all you're going to say?" says Noelle.

"What do you want me to say? Malcolm and I took them out to dinner. We went to a nice restaurant."

"But what did you talk about?"

Lily racks her brain for what they discussed, feels a panic overtake her at all the nothingness she retrieves. "It was six weeks ago," she says. "Maybe more."

"Come on, Noelle," Clarissa says. "Do you remember what you were doing six weeks ago?"

"Well, I haven't seen Mom and Dad since the funeral. I can't be expected to know what's going on."

"And if you'd seen them?" Lily says. "Do you think you'd have figured things out? What would you have done, anyway? Staged an intervention?"

"I'm just saying," Noelle says.

"What?" Lily says. "*What* are you just saying?"

The sink fills again, a few bay leaves bobbing to the surface, flipping over and over on themselves.

"You don't notice things that are right in front of you, Noelle. Remember that guy you used to date who was so obviously, flamingly gay?"

"I don't know what you're talking about."

And the words return to Lily, her own words, from years ago. *Hey, Noelle, what are you, deaf?*

Though it's Clarissa whom Noelle is attacking now. Because what, she wants to know, was Clarissa doing showing up at the house at nine at night when she was supposed to be here at seven? "You fell asleep in the car?"

"What difference does it make?" Lily says. "She lost track of things."

"Well, the timing could have been better. It's Leo's memorial. Mom and Dad spent days making dinner for everyone."

"Mom and Dad spent days making dinner for *you*, and you refused to eat it." Lily opens the refrigerator and rifles through the shelves. She finds a piece of watermelon wrapped in tinfoil and dispenses with it in a few bites.

"You know how they worry about us," Noelle says. "I call every Sunday night at seven, and if they're not home I leave a message. Since Leo died, I haven't missed it once."

"Well, that's very noble of you," Lily says.

"It's not noble," says Noelle. "It's just what I do."

Clarissa, meanwhile, remains silent. She's doing the dishes again, the tendons in her forearms ballooning as she applies pressure to the steel wool. The water is as hot as she can tolerate, her hands turning pink as jellyfish. She's thinking of their childhood, of the chorus that rang through their days. Go bring Noelle her knapsack, she forgot her homework. Go pick up Noelle from school, she lost her keys. Go take care of Noelle, she fucked the wrong guy. And now Noelle is lecturing her on responsibility. "You're right," she says. "Nathaniel and I should have gotten here sooner."

"Okay," Noelle says. "That's all I was saying."

"Jesus, Noelle. Would you leave her the fuck alone?"

"Forget it," Clarissa says.

"I have forgotten it," Noelle says. "It's over."

Clarissa looks at them squarely. "You want to know why Nathaniel and I were late? We stopped at a motel." She hasn't told anyone she's been trying to conceive, but she's tired of all this secrecy.

"You what?" Noelle says.

"I've been trying to get pregnant," she says. "I was in a 7-Eleven and I started to ovulate." She explains it all to them, how she and Nathaniel have been trying for a year now. "I mean, I'm thirty-nine. Why did I think it would be so easy?" She lets her hands drop against her thighs. "Anyway, we stopped to have sex at a motel and then, when it was over . . ."

"You fell asleep?" Noelle says.

Clarissa says, "I know you're Orthodox, Noelle, but don't tell me you've forgotten what can happen after sex."

"I'm so sorry," Lily says. "I honestly didn't know."

"How could you have?" Clarissa hasn't let Nathaniel breathe a word of it; she hasn't breathed a word of it herself. And now she feels despicable. Because with her parents splitting up, what difference does any of this make? "Noelle's right," she says. "She lives in Israel and you live in D.C., and I see Mom and Dad every week. How could I have been so oblivious?" She slaps a dish towel against the counter: once, twice, three times, four times. A few drops of water come spraying off and land on her jeans.

She hears footsteps now, and when she looks up her mother is in the entryway to the kitchen, her father behind her. Nathaniel is there, too. And Thisbe and Amram: all the adults in the family.

"Is something wrong?" Marilyn asks.

"We're just doing the dishes," Lily says.

"It's okay, Mom," says Clarissa. "Everything's fine."

Noelle, on tiptoe, hooks a skillet onto the pot rack hanging from the ceiling. Clarissa turns on the garbage disposal one last time. Standing over the sink, Lily wrings out the dish towels.

"Thank you for cleaning up," their father says.

"We should be thanking you," says Clarissa. "You're the one who cooked dinner." But she feels all formal and stiff making such ceremony out of this, the way her father has made such ceremony out of their having done the dishes.

"It's late," Lily says. "Time for bed."

But they remain where they are, standing in the kitchen and just outside it, as if they're soldered to the floor.

Marilyn says, "I guess Dad and I really rained on the parade."

"Some parade," Clarissa says. "Get out the floats for Leo's memorial."

"Bad news on top of bad news," Lily says.

The clock above the stove chimes midnight. A bird is chirping, a mechanical bird, the clock a gift from one of the girls, for someone's birthday, Marilyn thinks, though she can't remember whose. It's a different bird for every hour, care of the Audubon Society, and now it's chirping, chirping, issuing its relentless call. "We could certainly use some better news."

Her mother, Clarissa thinks, is staring at her, asking her to be the bearer of good tidings, and standing there surrounded by her family, she blurts out, "Nathaniel won a prize." Instantly, she regrets having said this, and Nathaniel, she can tell, regrets it, too.

"What prize?" her mother says.

"It's nothing," Nathaniel says. "It's utterly irrelevant."

"Prize at the bottom of the Cracker Jack box?" Lily says.

"Pretty much."

Clarissa hates herself for having brought this up, for having panicked in the silence. But she has no choice but to go on. She tells her family what little she knows, how Nathaniel won Columbia's teaching prize. She listens to her own words as she says them, endures the sound of her voice bragging about her husband (oh, how she hates herself!), and now she endures their response, the *congratulations*es and the *oh-that's-wonderful*s and the *where-did-you-get-such-a-talented husband*s, even Amram participating, Amram, who, as the other brother-in-law in the family, has a history of feeling shown up and who may, for all Clarissa knows, actually be fuming. But he's putting on a good show of it, offering his glum congratulations, and Nathaniel, in turn, is glumly receiving them, as is Clarissa, and now Thisbe, a graduate student herself, says, "I'm just happy when my students don't throw spitballs at me," and everyone is saying, "Now, now."

Soon they all disperse, and it's just Clarissa alone in the kitchen. A minute passes, and Lily comes in. They're standing at the corkboard beside the refrigerator, thumbtacked to which are their mother's publications. There's an op-ed from *USA Today* and another op-ed from the *Washington Post*. Beside them are letters from parents of other journalists who have been killed in the war. "Mom's support group," Clarissa says darkly.

"She'll have to start another one," Lily says. "Mothers of dead journalists who dump their husbands. It will be a support group of one."

"It will be a support group of many," Clarissa says. "There are a lot of idiots out there." Also on the corkboard in their mother's handwriting is the number of dead in the ongoing war, both U.S. and Iraqi. The same numbers are tacked up in their parents' kitchen in the city, on the tiny chalkboard beside the phone. Constantly updated, Clarissa thinks, like the national debt. The Iraqi casualties are a matter of conjecture, but her mother has certainly educated herself. Every week she spends hours on the Web, keeping up with the news the papers don't report. Pinned on the corkboard near one of her op-eds is a photo of the toppled statue of Saddam Hussein, the U.S. flag raised beside it. And, next to it, her mother's commentary. *So much for that.*

"We should use it for target practice," Clarissa says, and in frustration at everything—at Leo's dying, at her mother, at Saddam Hussein himself—she takes a spoon and tosses it at the corkboard.

She emerges into the foyer, where the rest of the family is silently standing, everyone still pinioned to their spots.

"I'm beyond exhausted," she says, and she goes upstairs and

Nathaniel follows her; Noelle, Amram, and Lily ascend the stairs, too. It's exactly, Lily thinks, how it used to be, the line for the bathroom, and somehow, as always, Noelle has gotten there first. Lily waits outside, needing to pee, her bladder pounding against her pelvis. Then the door opens, Noelle emerges, and it's Lily's turn to go in.

When she steps out of the bathroom, she sees Thisbe standing in the dark hallway, her head leaning against a picture frame.

"Careful, you. You don't want to topple the art."

"That would be some end to the evening."

"It would be the coup de grâce." Lily can barely make out Thisbe in the darkness. The only illumination is from the crack beneath the bathroom door and from the dwindling glow of the nightlight.

"I should have stayed in Berkeley," Thisbe says. "I'm an interloper here."

"Oh, Thisbe, how can you say that? You're part of our family."

"And now I'm watching your parents' marriage split up. I just want to close my eyes."

"I wish I hadn't opened them in the first place." Through the skylight, Lily can see a glistening shard of moon hanging like a comma in the darkness. She hears breathing down the hall. "Our snoring nephews."

Snoring nephews, Thisbe thinks. Kissing cousins. She closes her eyes, wishes she were far away, back in Berkeley with Wyeth. "Where's your father?"

"In their old bedroom," Lily says.

"And your mother?"

"Downstairs."

"On the couch?"

"Presumably."

"Oh, Lily," Thisbe says. "We can't let her do that. She's almost seventy years old. If only . . ."

"What?"

"If only I'd stayed in better touch. If only I'd been a more accommodating daughter-in-law."

"Then everything would be perfect?"

"Do you know how often I called last year? Once every few weeks, at most? They're Calder's grandparents. I could have brought him east more. I could have made them feel more welcome in Berkeley. If only Leo were here."

"Well, yes," Lily says. "That would be nice."

Leaning against the wall, Thisbe runs her hands through her hair. She presses her palms to her eyes so she can't see anything but her own skin. "I should go to bed."

"Stay up here," says Lily.

"Where would I sleep?"

"In my room. We can have a slumber party. Girls' night out."

"Calder will wonder what happened to me."

Lily's thinking how she misses Malcolm, how tonight, of all nights, she doesn't want to sleep alone.

Now Noelle emerges from her bedroom in a complicated caking of moisturizer and face cream. She's wearing a long pink nightgown, which makes swishing sounds across the floor. "Thisbe," she says, seeing her sister-in-law. "Lily."

Thisbe reaches out and takes her hand, and now Lily does, too. They're standing, the three of them, in the hallway, in a dark little huddle.

"I can't believe this," Noelle says. "Oh, God." From beneath the doorway, they see the light go off in Clarissa and Nathaniel's room.

Thisbe walks softly down the stairs, trying not to creak as she goes. But it's an old house, and with every step she sends a noise through the hall. She gets to the bottom of the stairs, and there Marilyn is, lying on the couch, a mohair throw blanket tossed haphazardly over her, her fuzzy slippers lined up on the floor. She's on her back, with a medical journal open across her face, as if she's at the beach, sunning herself. Thisbe tiptoes past her, but Marilyn whispers, "I'm awake." She's sitting up now, her pale yellow nightgown tucked under her, her back straight against the pillow.

Thisbe points at the journal. "That's quite an eye mask you've got on."

"Now all I need are ear plugs."

"Anything interesting in there?" Thisbe wouldn't mind flipping through the journal herself, a break from her own journals, all those hidden truths about dead civilizations when there's so much she doesn't know about the living ones.

"Just the usual array of malady and disease. I figure I'll drown my sorrows in death and disfigurement."

"Does it work?"

"It can prove distracting." Marilyn makes as though to get up, but then she hesitates, as if she doesn't want Thisbe to see her half dressed. "Can I get you anything?"

Thisbe shakes her head.

"There's food in the kitchen. No one touched dessert. You can have yourself an entire key lime pie."

"I don't think that would be good for my girlish figure."

"Oh, come on, Thisbe. You have the metabolism of—"

"Someone who can eat an entire key lime pie?"

"Exactly."

"I'll have some tomorrow." Thisbe hears the clock in the kitchen, those chirping birds going at it once more. "I feel terrible that you're sleeping here. It's like you're a college kid sacked out on the floor."

Marilyn laughs. "Do I look tawdry?"

"Not tawdry. Just uncomfortable."

"I can sleep anywhere," Marilyn says. "It's a gift I have." Growing up, she tells Thisbe, she used to sleep on a captain's bed, her mattress perched on top of her drawers. "My parents used to call it my bed of nails. It trained me well."

"Calder and I could switch with you. I'm a lot closer to college than you are. Calder is, too, from the other direction."

"Don't worry," Marilyn says. "I'll be okay."

Thisbe hesitates for a moment, then leans over the couch and kisses her mother-in-law goodnight.

Then she's down the stairs to the basement. She hears water dripping, thinks there may be a leak, but she realizes it's coming from the bathroom: someone left the faucet on. Calder is lying precariously on the edge of the bed. She considers rolling him back on, but she fears she'll wake him. Though falling off the bed will wake him, too. Back in Berkeley, she doesn't share a bed with him, but they're away now, far from home, and she doesn't want to sleep alone tonight, so she nudges him over, and he gives a small, resigned sigh. Then she pulls back the covers and gets into bed beside him.

5

Alone in her old bedroom as the clock approaches one, Lily feels wretched and heartsick and angry at everybody. She didn't want to come here in the first place, and now she really wishes she hadn't come. Years ago she loved Lenox, loved even the drive up, pressed against her siblings in her parents' old Volvo, the perennial fighting of the car ride. But now she finds the town suffocating, her parents' house especially. She's always opening doors, looking through closets, half believing she'll come upon some portal she hasn't discovered in her decades of vacationing here. She resolved long ago never to live in a city that has no subway system; that's her threshold for a habitable hometown. D.C. itself only barely qualifies; the Metro resembles a toy train set, a Madurodam-like version of a real subway, its five color-coded lines like proto-nerves stretching out from the spine of the capital, as if in some lower-level vertebrate. She mocks D.C. with the best of them. Its self-importance, its isolation, a city without so much as a congressional representative. But though she's ashamed to admit it, she's still awed by the buildings. The Lincoln Memorial lit up at night, the Washington Monument, the White House, the Supreme Court: she's more seduced by power than she lets on.

She picks up her cell phone and calls Malcolm.

"Lily?"

She's quiet.

"Are you in Lenox?"

"Of course I'm in Lenox." She feels impatient with him for so many things. For not knowing what's going on, for having allowed this to happen, most of all for being there while she's here, though she knows she can't blame him for that either. The clock says 1:29, the green glare of the digits reflecting back at her like Silly Putty. "Did you make it to the beach?" She thinks she can hear waves, as if her ear is pressed to a shell.

"About an hour ago," Malcolm says. "There's talk of spending the night in the sand. Forget the hotel. We'll sleep by the ocean until the police wake us up with their billy clubs."

"Sounds nice," Lily says. She wouldn't mind being there herself.

"I miss you," Malcolm says.

She misses him, too, but right now she can't say it. He's there and she's here; she needs to get through the next couple of days. She's determined to divest herself of feeling, to strip herself of all senti-ment, to hunker down. "Malcolm, you're not going to believe this. My parents are splitting up."

"They're what?"

She says it again.

"Jesus, Lily. I *don't* believe it."

"Well, you better start."

"Is it because of Leo?"

She thinks: what isn't because of Leo? Yet it feels like excuses to her, glib and insincere and downright insulting, as if her brother is being forced to take responsibility for this.

"I'm so, so sorry."

And all she can think to say is she's sorry, too.

"Where are they now?"

"In their respective quarters. My father's in their old bedroom and my mother's downstairs on the couch. Because I guess when you're getting separated it's bad form to sleep together."

Malcolm doesn't respond.

"It's crazy," she says. "They'll be seventy next year. Isn't it a little . . ."

"Unseemly?"

"Well, there's that. They've been married for forty-two years. I thought there was a no-returns policy."

But Malcolm stays silent, and Lily hears in that silence that there are always returns. "You must think this is normal."

"Not exactly, Lil."

But for Malcolm it *is* normal. His own family is fractured and far-flung. A mother in Georgia, a father in Indiana, a sister in Utah, a brother in New Jersey. He gets along with each of them, but things go best when he sees them one on one: a dinner when somebody's coming through town, a stop for a few hours at a roadside pool, he and his brother sipping cherry slurpies on beach chairs before one of them has to depart. Malcolm enjoys people, yet he's also wary of them. It's one reason he likes being a chef; he's in the company of others, but at the same time he's alone. He thinks of family reunions as Jewish traditions, probably because Lily's family reunions are the ones he's most familiar with. Malcolm's parents got divorced when he was so young he can't remember their ever having been together. And Lily now realizes she's always counted on that, on having that bedrock feeling that her family was okay, and that it was Malcolm, his family, that was the fucked-up one.

He appears to have guessed what she's thinking, because now he says, gently, "You can't lord it over me any longer."

"Come on, Malcolm. I never lorded it over you." But she understands what he's saying. She thought he was the one from the post-nuclear family. Now it seems there's room for them both. "Everything I thought about my family turns out not to be true."

"I imagine that's hard."

But that's the problem: Malcolm can only imagine it. And Lily wants someone who can more than imagine it. She wants someone who can live it, who can feel what she feels. There are her sisters, of course. But their situations seem different, she doesn't know why. She thinks of Leo—he would understand—and she misses him more than she's missed him all year.

She's sitting on the bed, her feet resting against the floor. Her mother once said it was good to be married because you'd take care of each other when you were old and infirm. "And now my parents *are* old," she tells Malcolm, "and eventually they'll be infirm, and they've decided they don't want to be together anymore, which makes me wonder why they got married in the first place." She closes her eyes, tries to launch herself far away. "And on top of everything else, Clarissa's trying to get pregnant."

"As we speak?"

"For all I know. I'm doing my best not to listen." She swings her legs back onto the bed, and as she does so, her head bangs against the headboard. "And Leo's memorial is tomorrow and I haven't even written my speech."

"Have you started it?"

"I've tried, but every sentence is riddled with platitudes. *My brother was so amazing! What zest for life!*"

"In his case, it's true."

"Someone dies tragically and young, and they're automatically thought of as amazing. Which makes them less amazing than they actually were." She drums her hands against the bed. Her shadow dances along the ceiling, a jittery figure in the darkness. "I'm probably just jealous."

"Of what?"

Until a year ago, she reminds Malcolm, she wasn't anyone's sister. Now everybody she meets asks her about Leo. She's at the doctor's office, he has that stick down her throat, and he's telling her what a hero her brother was, which makes her gag even more than she already would. "Malcolm, promise me if I die you won't stand in front of the assembled mourners and tell them how tremendous I was? Promise you'll tell them I was a jerk?"

"Okay," he says, laughing.

"Because I *feel* like a jerk. Maybe I didn't love him enough."

"Lily, of course you loved him."

"Then why can't I get with the program?"

"What program?"

"Even Noelle is carrying on, and she and Leo couldn't stand each other. Do you know what Noelle used to do when Leo was a baby? She would dangle him by his ankles so she could watch the blood rush to his head. She would blow her recorder in his ear. I tell myself I was five years older than Leo."

"You *were* five years older than him."

"When I left for college he was barely a teenager. In a way, I was more like an aunt to him."

"And you were a girl," Malcolm says, "and he was a boy. From the first time I met him, he was off on his own adventures."

"What about Clarissa?" Lily says. "She was *six* years older. Yet when he died, she was undone."

"It sounds like you're engaged in competitive grieving."

"If I am, I've lost."

"Come on, Lily. Have you forgotten what you did after Leo died? You and your mother campaigned for Kerry together. You did that in your brother's name."

Lily remembers, of course. She and her mother signed up as volunteers, first in Missouri, and then, when the state polls looked bad and the campaign had pulled out, they moved to Ohio, where they lived out of a hotel the last month of the campaign. Leo had been dead for nearly four months, but Lily's mother still hadn't gone back to work. Lily herself took a leave from her job so she could campaign with her mother. They left Ohio the night before the election and flew to Pennsylvania, where the next day, in the Philadelphia suburbs, they handed out campaign literature door to door. "And then I went back to work."

"What were you supposed to do?" Malcolm says. "Not go back to work? Everyone else went back to work, too."

"Clarissa, my parents—their lives haven't returned to normal. My parents' lives will never return to normal. They're making sure of it. They're splitting up."

"Lily . . ."

"Please, Malcolm. Don't *Lily* me."

"Okay," he says. "I'm sorry."

"People used to say these things about me. *That Lily, she picks herself up and dusts herself off. She gets back in the saddle.* I was six years old, I didn't even understand what they were saying, but they were right." She takes a quick breath, emits air like the click of a shutter. It's almost two in the morning and she's in the dark, and the only thing she can see is the light from her cell phone. She's thirty-eight years old, and she's lying naked in her childhood bed.

She tries to picture Malcolm in his swim trunks, kneeling over a grill, her boyfriend tan, low-slung, crouching in the sand in his rolled-up shirt and flip-flops, eyes burning from the charcoal smoke. "Malcolm," she says, "let's move far away. I want to start over someplace new."

"Where in the world would we move?"

"Auckland?" she says. "The moon?"

"What would I cook on the moon?"

"Moon pie?"

"Lily, we're settled in D.C."

And he's right, of course. They've each been in Washington for over a decade now. Their rent is reasonable, and they have an extra bedroom, which they use as an office. It's where they're staying put, though their friends are buying homes and moving to the suburbs. *The thirties affliction*, Lily calls it. She detests the suburbs and finds all of D.C. unvaried and dull. People bemoan it so frequently there's no point in complaining it's a one-industry town; it's like complaining about the traffic in L.A. But it's true, no matter how often people say it, and it's not her industry, even if she went to law school and has been interested in politics since she was small. If she and Malcolm could live anywhere, she'd rather it be in New York or San Francisco. But people know Malcolm in D.C.; it's where he'll have the best chance of opening his own restaurant. And her work is there, too. If you're going to be a lawyer for government whistle-blowers, it's probably best to be near government.

She met Malcolm in Iowa, in the summer of 1991, working on the Democratic presidential campaign. She had volunteered for Tom Harkin and Malcolm had signed on with Paul Tsongas. It was a bunch of kids in their twenties staying up late playing Trivial Pursuit and smoking pot. Afterward, when they came down with the munchies, Malcolm would try out new recipes on the group in the small makeshift kitchen in the back of campaign headquarters. A number of romances had begun that summer, but Lily wouldn't sleep with Malcolm because he worked for a different campaign.

"You mean if I worked for Harkin you'd sleep with me?"

"Could be," Lily said.

"It's not as though I like Tsongas. I'm barely even political."

"Then why are you working for him?"

"Because he offered me a job. I figured it would be fun to come to Iowa. I thought I'd get to meet you."

"Well, lucky you. You did."

"Look at James Carville and Mary Matalin. They're married to each other."

"Then go sleep with Mary Matalin."

Sometimes late at night it would be just the two of them, and Malcolm would make smoked paprika-cured hamachi with eggplant caviar (how, Lily wondered, did a person find these ingredients in Des Moines?) and lime grapefruit soup with lemon-vodka sorbet. This was before cooking shows were staples on TV, before chefs had become hunks and celebrities, but Malcolm seemed to anticipate the trend. He would make pickled beef tongue with fried mayonnaise and onion streusel and serve it to Lily. "So this is it?" he said. "You're not going to sleep with me?"

"Not as long as both our candidates are in the race."

The fact was, if the summer had lasted longer Lily probably would have slept with Malcolm; mostly she was having fun toying with him. In September, she moved to New Haven for law school and Malcolm returned to Baltimore; he was between jobs, getting ready to start culinary school. But on the night of Harkin's concession speech Malcolm drove up to New Haven to watch it with her. "I've come to collect my IOU."

They didn't meet again until several years later, when Lily was clerking on the Supreme Court and Malcolm was catering a dinner there. Bill Clinton was in the second term of his presidency, and Tom Harkin was the senior senator from Iowa; Paul Tsongas was dead. Even now, Malcolm will say to her, "Look at you, sleeping with the enemy." Lily remains the most obdurate, most bullheaded, most unyielding person he knows.

The bistro where Malcolm is chef doesn't serve foie gras. He'd like to, and his customers would like him to as well, but it's not his customers he shares a bed with. Lily's no bleeding heart—she finds the very term patronizing—but she believes foie gras is beyond the pale. Malcolm doesn't disagree about the facts. It's just that when it comes to food he thinks ethics are beside the point; what matters is satisfying his customers. The way he sees it, ducks would make foie gras out of him if they could. But he has capitulated because Lily is so insistent and because when Lily insists on something he relents.

She hears a crunching through the phone. "What's that?"

"It's me," Malcolm says. "I'm eating potato chips."

Lily laughs. When Malcolm's not at the restaurant he likes junk food. Cheez Doodles, onion rings, French fries, sloppy joes. It's as if he's been let loose from the prison of haute cuisine. Leo was a junk-food fanatic, too, and he and Malcolm used to go out for ribs together, then top them off with a couple orders of fries. One July Fourth, Leo covered the hot-dog-eating contest on Coney Island; Malcolm came along for the trip, and when the contest was over he and Leo got in on the fun, seeing how many hot dogs they could eat, dunking the buns in water and gulping them down. "I wish I were there," Lily says.

"And I wish I were there."

"Then I'm happy to switch places with you. I'll go south and you come north. We can swap prisoners."

"I'm serious, Lily. Jesus, it's your brother's memorial. I loved the guy. Even if I didn't love him, how can I be down here when you're up there? And now your parents are splitting up."

"You can't be here," Lily says. "You're too busy at work."

"If I'm too busy at work, why am I at the beach?"

"Because your roommates are in town. Because you deserve a vacation."

"Well, it's not much of a vacation if all I'm doing is thinking about you."

They've been through this already. Malcolm believes he should be in Lenox, he *wants* to be in Lenox, but Lily insists on going it alone. She'll get this over with, do what she needs to do, and then she can return to her life. Because her sisters, her parents, this house she used to spend her summers in: they're not her life. Her life is with Malcolm, and if he'd just let her be, she could get back to her life with him, to their life together.

But yes, she admits, it's hard that he's not here. "Promise me something, Malcolm?"

"What?"

"Promise you'll take care of me when I'm old and infirm?"

"What if I get old and infirm first?"

"Then·I'll take care of you." Her hands are slicked with sweat, silver with it in the glowing moonlight. For a second the phone slips out of her hand and lands softly on the bed. "Malcolm?"

"I'm here."

From outside the bedroom come the sounds of tapping. Someone is padding down the hall; Lily hears the staccato beat of footsteps. "Malcolm, I don't want to become old and infirm."

"I don't, either."

"I have to go," she says. "I love you, Malcolm."

But there's a hollow hissing sound coming back to her. Malcolm has hung up already. Or maybe she's disconnected him.

6

"Do you hear that?" Clarissa says, sitting up in bed. She's in that startled, semiconscious state when she's not sure where she is. The bedroom is dark; she can't see anything. Slowly her eyes acclimate. Shadows chase each other across the walls. The water stains on the ceiling swell and buckle. She turns on the bedside lamp.

Nathaniel has a pillow across his face, in protection and protest; it looks as though he's trying to asphyxiate himself. "I don't hear anything."

And now she can't, either. But she's already awake, sitting up in bed. On the nightstand, the alarm-clock numbers peel back from themselves. "Come on, you. It's morning."

"It's five o'clock," Nathaniel says. "That's not morning."

"Actually, it is." But she doesn't resist when he turns off the lamp.

Her hair settles in clumps on her shoulders; a few tangles plunge down her back. She curls into Nathaniel, feels his breath against her arms. Outside, beyond the bulrushes, a siren keens. "Are you up?"

"Do I have a choice?"

She's quiet.

"Okay," he says. "Yes, I'm up."

For now, the rain has stopped, replaced by humidity hanging thick over town. She should put the air-conditioning back on. "Aren't you hot?" she says, but Nathaniel shakes his head. It's the cold that bothers him. If only they could divide it up, like Jack and Mrs. Sprat. She removes her T-shirt and lies in only her underwear. Nathaniel rests his hand on her stomach.

And what, she says, are they supposed to do now? Go back to having sex whenever they can?

"We could still try," he says.

She shakes her head.

"Well, for the record, I'm willing."

She's wearing a white tank top and red satin boxers. Nathaniel is shirtless, in a pair of gym shorts, and it seems he's waiting for her to mount him, and she, in turn, is waiting for him. For a second she wishes Nathaniel's own parents had split up and they could commiserate. The next second she wishes they had a blissful marriage and she could take vicarious comfort in that. But they have neither of those things. They have a workmanlike marriage, something low-fire and dependable, something that appears to suit them. Nathaniel doesn't understand them, nor, it seems, does he really want to. It's as if he's bewildered at having grown up where he did, in Nebraska City, dweller in his parents' home, inheritor of their genes. He's the aberrant one—the freak—destined from the first to get out and never to return. Sometimes it feels as if he raised himself, as if he were born fully sprung as an adult, tenured professor at Columbia. There's a way in which Clarissa's own parents have adopted him ("The orphan from the Midwest," her mother once joked), and so it doesn't surprise her now when he seems almost as shell-shocked as she is.

She turns off the light and rolls onto her stomach. She has her nose pressed to the pillow, the edge of it tucked into her mouth. "Let's try to get some sleep."

But she can't follow her own advice. She stares up at the ceiling, pocked as a piece of cheese. She walks over to the closet; she'll choose her clothes for the day. But there are hardly any clothes in there, just items in storage from over the years: a lacrosse stick, a flock of rain boots, a ripped board game a couple of whose dice have come loose from the box and are lying desolate on the floor. Behind it all sits her cello case. Growing up, she kept one cello in the city and another in the Berkshires. A cello in every port, her sisters used to say.

A car passes on the road below them, floodlighting the room. Presently, there comes a knock on the door. "Are you awake?"

"Mom?" Clarissa puts on a pair of shorts and steps out into the hall.

"Here," Marilyn says, and she takes Clarissa's hand and they tiptoe through the dark to the boys' bedroom, where Noelle's children are arrayed in matching blue sleeping bags, head to foot. "They're darling, aren't they? No matter what else is happening, at least I have them."

Clarissa remembers how, when Akiva was born, her mother said,

"I'm too young to be a grandmother." Or maybe it was just that the baby was Noelle's, and a grandson in Israel, raised an Orthodox Jew, made everything seem doubly anomalous. When her mother turned sixty-five, she refused to apply for the senior citizens' discount on the city's buses and subways; she figured anyone with her cross-court backhand didn't need to be coddled by the MTA. But when it comes to being a grandmother, she has done an about-face. She's *doting*, Clarissa thinks, a word she never would have associated with her mother.

Marilyn is over at the window, looking down at the tennis court. "There it is," she says. "All those years of Dad's and my life." The court lights are on, and scores and scores of balls still dot the clay from when she was hitting serves last night. In the illumination cast down from above the trees, the balls look golden, like apples. And it occurs to Marilyn for the first time that they're going to have to sell the house.

They've been in Lenox for forty years now; she and David bought the house before the girls were even born. Later, they figured out that they'd signed the contract five years to the day from when they were first introduced. They met on a camping trip, David arriving with his then-girlfriend, Marilyn with her then-boyfriend, each of whom was an inveterate camper, having hiked the entire Appalachian Trail. It wasn't until a year later when they ran into each other at the information booth in Penn Station that they discovered that the friendship they'd struck up on that trip, the two of them lagging behind the rest of the campers, sticking their hands into the bag of trail mix, hadn't been an accident. They'd been loath to admit it at the time, but now, having ended their respective romances, they discovered that they didn't like to camp; in fact, they both despised it. "My boyfriend was testing me," Marilyn said. "Could I carry the big backpack? Could I start a fire with two sticks? Would I moon over every mountain and sunset?" Afterward, over coffee and cinnamon doughnuts at Chock Full o' Nuts and continuing on into the evening, and later, into the years when they were married, it became a joke between them: the couple that hated camping had met while camping. Marilyn's father had fought in World War I, and when Marilyn's mother suggested they take the children camping, he said, "I spent a year and a half of my life in a tent. That's not my idea of a vacation." When Marilyn and David married, they promised that they would love each other till death did them part and that they would never spend the night in sleeping bags beneath the stars, never navigate through thistle with Calamine lotion dripping off them, and no amount of s'mores, a snack they both loved, was going to dissuade them. So years later, when Clarissa and Lily erected a play tent in the living room, and when Noelle demanded that they buy her a play tent, too, when Marilyn and David awoke in the morning to find their daughters not in their beds but in their tents, they knew they were getting their comeuppance.

A house in Lenox? Where, Marilyn wanted to know, were the museums and subways? The smell of salsa from the corner taqueria, the truck horns peppering the cityscape? But David had this idea about a country house. They would have children before long; it would be a place to get away with the family. And the Berkshires wasn't the country, exactly. It was more like a Massachusetts outpost of the Upper West Side. A friend of David's swore he was going to open a branch of Zabar's in Lenox. And Marilyn, who remained skeptical, finally relented when David promised he'd build her a tennis court. No more waiting for the courts in Central Park, sitting on the benches, banging her racquet against the ground, hoping to scatter the other players with her temper.

Zabar's never made it to Lenox, but it was a good decision, Marilyn thinks, to have bought the house. She found the place peaceful, and she discovered, to her surprise, that peaceful wasn't so bad. Still, as the years passed, she and David spent less and less time here. The girls had grown up, and the drive, even without the fighting in back that had punctuated their trips for decades, felt duller and less compelling, less worthwhile, ultimately, now that the children had moved away. Even July Fourth and Labor Day, which had been family mainstays, began to be met with protests and no-shows, certainly from Noelle, who was in Israel now, but soon from Lily too, who never seemed able to make it up from D.C., and so the family had trouble reaching critical mass. Marilyn and David rarely came up alone, and when they did, it was with a sense of obligation, as if they were tending to a dying friend they no longer liked. Although they'd paid off the mortgage, they still had property taxes, not to mention other costs: leaky roofs, freezing pipes, squirrels trapped in the insulation, a snowstorm last winter in which an electric line was toppled and singed a hole in the roof. It got to the point that whenever the phone rang, Marilyn thought, *What's it going to be now?* A year ago Memorial Day, she and David came up alone and, faced with the heat and the mosquitoes, they returned to the city and spent the weekend there. They've been back only a few times since, mostly for maintenance and repairs, on a house they're most consumed by when things go wrong, and in April, during tax time.

Leo alone remained committed to Lenox. He once calculated that he'd spent over eighteen hundred nights there: five years of his life. It's because of Leo, Marilyn realizes, that they've kept the house, and it's because of him that she and David continue to come here. They were in Lenox when they got the news. A phone call in the middle of the night, exactly as she would have imagined it if she'd allowed herself to imagine such things; even in the week when he was being held captive, she didn't permit herself to think it would end as it did. Back in their apartment in Manhattan, where they moved when Leo was in eighth grade, his room has been cleared out. But here his possessions remain, his bedroom door always open as if the room itself is waiting for his return. The clothes lie folded in his drawers, the pressed shirts hanging in the closet, the medicine cabinet still filled with dental floss and nail clippers and shampoo and Ace bandages, shelf upon shelf of a young man's sundries.

You're so brave, everyone told her after Leo died. *You're so unbelievably courageous.* Why? she thought. Because she didn't just expire? No one gave her that choice. Though it will take courage, she realizes, to prepare the house for sale. They will need to divide up Leo's possessions. There was some of that already, in the weeks and months after his death, a parceling out of objects to family members and friends in what seemed at the time like a macabre auction. But that, she realizes, was simply an overture.

After Leo died, she spent the first week sleeping on his bedroom floor, but once she left, she didn't return. She looks in sometimes through the open doorway, but it's as if the room has been cordoned off. In the weeks after he died, friends trailed through the house bearing flowers, quiches, lasagnas, pies; others returned possessions of his dug up from basements and attics. When people arrived, Marilyn directed them upstairs to Leo's bedroom, where they deposited what they'd brought. And then, not knowing what to do, how to stay or how to leave, they stood uncertainly in the kitchen, shifting their weight from leg to leg, leaning against the refrigerator, the stove, poking idly at the pies, quiches, and gratins they had brought, the price of admission to this house that had been a second home to them and where they stood now, silently gawking.

Marilyn stares down at the tennis court. "I have a half a mind to take it with me. To remove it patch by patch." The Venetian blinds sway in the breeze, casting segmented shadows across the room.

Clarissa, beside her, stares down, too. "What are all those balls doing there? It looks like someone was conducting a clinic."

"Someone was."

"You?"

"I was hitting serves before you girls got here. Taking out my rage."

Clarissa tries to count the balls. "That's a lot of rage."

"Wait here," Marilyn says, and she steps out into the hall. When she returns, she's holding two tennis racquets.

"Oh, Mom, you want us to play?"

"Not play. Just clean up. We can use these to sweep."

Quietly, they descend the stairs, their feet tapping out their hushed rhythm. Marilyn slides open the porch door, and now, past the rosebushes, they light out for the tennis court behind the house, bushwhacking their way through the tall grass. Sunrise is a little after five, but it's overcast again, and the night's darkness has only just lifted. "Come on," Marilyn says. "Hup two."

She's at one baseline with a bucket at her feet, and Clarissa, at the other baseline, also has a bucket. They pick up the balls, working their way across the length of the court, moving toward each other. Clarissa is bending over to pick up the balls, but Marilyn, as promised, is using her tennis racquet to assist her. She has sandwiched the ball between the racquet and her shoe and, with a single jerk, she lifts her foot and the ball flies into the air and lands gently in the bucket. Now she's using her racquet like a giant spatula, scooping up several balls at a time. "I'm way ahead of you."

"You'll turn anything into a competition, won't you, Mom?"

"Whenever possible."

Clarissa's kneeling at the service line, scooping up balls in each hand. She deposits them into the bucket, and when she rises, clay is caked to her calves. Outside the fence lie more balls, and as she goes to retrieve them she recalls a childhood game of tennis with Leo, when he must have been no more than five, and she, the forbearing big sister, spending the afternoon among the dandelions, fishing out errant balls.

It starts to rain.

"Hurry up!" Marilyn says. "We're almost done!"

But there are still thirty, forty balls to be retrieved. Clarissa runs into the garage to seek cover, but Marilyn remains on the court, jogging from ball to ball, using that quick jerk of the foot to flip them into the bucket.

Finally, drenched herself, Marilyn runs across the court to the garage, the balls hopping as she goes. She subsides onto a folding chair next to Clarissa. She wrings out her hair at her feet.

"Mission accomplished?" Clarissa says.

"We rescued what we could."

It's raining harder now. Fog settles heavily on the court. Clarissa leans back in her chair so it's resting on only two legs. She's staring straight ahead of her.

"Talk to me, darling," Marilyn says. "With everything that's been happening between Dad and me, I haven't heard a word about you."

"What do you want to know?"

"Whatever you want to tell me."

But that's the problem, Clarissa thinks. She isn't sure what she wants to tell her mother, especially not now. "I've started to play the cello again."

"You have? Since when?"

"Since Leo died, I guess. Just a little here, a little there." She reaches down and picks up a tennis ball. She bounces it on the ground at her feet. "A few weeks ago, I ran into Mrs. Pritchett on the subway. I hadn't seen her in twenty years, and there she was, looking the same as she always did. It was as if she'd been keeping tabs on me."

"She was good at that."

"She was." And an image comes to Clarissa of Mrs. Pritchett's apartment on West End Avenue, their cellos poised in front of them, as if they were squaring off. And afterward, when her lesson was over, Clarissa would join Mrs. Pritchett in her car and they would circle the streets of the Upper West Side, talking about music, about the cello, while Mrs. Pritchett negotiated the hazards of alternate-side-of-the-street parking, moving back and forth between West End Avenue and Riverside Drive. "Do you know what she told me? 'Two decades later, and your shoulders have finally straightened out.'"

"I don't understand."

It was the family joke, Clarissa reminds her mother. One of her father's shoulders was lower than the other from having carried his briefcase all those years. And then the same thing happened to her, from all that time lugging her cello. For one of her birthdays, her parents got her a cello case on wheels. She would roll it on the subway to and from school. Her friends used to make fun of her; they would call her the stewardess. I'm Clarissa, they would say. Fly me.

It was Leo who used to call her the Andre Agassi of string instruments. She picked up the violin when she was three, which was how old Agassi had been when he'd first held a tennis racquet, and soon he was sent off to tennis boot camp, where he practiced eight, nine hours a day. But Clarissa's parents never pushed her. They played piano themselves, and later her mother took up the clarinet (Clarissa still remembers playing duets with her, home concerts for the entertainment of her siblings), and while they were reasonably skilled, they certainly weren't gifted, and neither were Clarissa's siblings or, as far as she knows, anyone else in her extended family, which was unusual, Mrs. Pritchett said; these things tended to run in the genes.

And Clarissa *was* gifted. She'd been gifted at the violin, and she was even more gifted at the cello. Eight years old, ten years old, fourteen years old: she was up early practicing, up late practicing, and in the meantime she was going to a good school, where homework was expected of her and where the students did their homework. Had any child in the history of New York City ever gotten so little sleep? Her parents weren't forcing her to practice. If anything, they were telling her to take it easy, to have fun. But Clarissa didn't want to have fun. She wanted to practice the cello.

Freshman year in music school, at Indiana University, she was start-ing to play less and less. She would spend her days wandering around Bloomington, her evenings drinking tea at the Runcible Spoon, in whose bathroom sat a tub filled with goldfish. She would sit in that bathroom, watching those goldfish do laps, and then she would return to her dormitory.

Late at night, her boyfriend, also a cellist, studying at Eastman, would berate her for her dwindling practice hours. She was marooned in the Midwest, he reminded her, and what was she doing in the Mid-west if she wasn't playing music? What was she doing on *earth* if she wasn't playing music? "Aren't you happy playing the cello?" Her boy-friend meant this rhetorically, but the question floored Clarissa. No one had ever asked her this before, not her parents, whose exhortations to cut back must have been motivated, she realized later, by fear that she might not be happy; certainly not Mrs. Pritchett, who believed she had a gift and owed it to the world to pursue it.

Now, though, having finally been asked, she realized that while she wasn't unhappy, exactly, she wasn't exactly happy either. And then, a week later, having allowed herself to take that step, she allowed herself to take another one. She *was* unhappy. Spring break of freshman year, she spent the whole week in bed. She didn't eat; she didn't answer the telephone; she didn't see any of her friends. She decided right then to drop out of music school. She didn't so much as return to Indiana to say goodbye to her classmates and professors. She couldn't stand the thought of being back in Bloomington, of seeing her friends, her roommates, all those musicians, and so she sent her father to retrieve her belongings. The following year she transferred to Yale, which had an orchestra, a chamber music society, a jazz ensemble, but she refused to play in any of them. She majored in political science; she had left her cello back home in New York.

For weeks, Mrs. Pritchett tried to convince her to change her mind, and when she saw that she couldn't, she stopped calling. They didn't speak again for twenty years, not until a few weeks ago, on the subway. Clarissa told Mrs. Pritchett what she was doing now, how she's dol-ing out money for international relief ("You know the Open Society Foundations? We're like that, only smaller—we don't have George

Soros to bankroll us"), saying it all self-dismissively, because she *is* self-dismissive, and because she knew Mrs. Pritchett would be dismissive, too. She didn't tell Mrs. Pritchett that she has started to play again. Because she didn't—she doesn't—want to be beholden to her, and because she didn't wish to pretend she's doing anything but dabbling. She hates being terrible at something she was once so good at. Not that she's terrible, really, not by most lights, but by her own lights, by the lights of what she once was, she *is* terrible, and it pains her.

An image comes to her of Leo as a toddler, bursting in on her lessons. He wanted to turn everything into a duet so that when she was practicing her scales, when she was having a go at Bach's Cello Suite No. 1, he was having a go at it, too, pounding the keys on their parents' grand piano. Even Mrs. Pritchett, focused as she was on the task at hand, didn't have the heart to tell him to stop, and so it was left to Clarissa's father to haul him off so she could continue her lesson uninterrupted. And another image comes to her, a Halloween when he was seven, Leo taping himself up with her sheet music, getting ready for trick-or-treating; he called himself the Music Mummy. Her irrepressible little brother. Every year he would come home with more candy than anyone else. He was forever negotiating with the neighbors for extra Mars Bars and Blow Pops.

"I might play something at the memorial," she tells her mother.

"What would you play?"

"Something basic," she says. "Something Leo would have enjoyed."

"I know he would have liked that."

She's quiet.

"I remember what exquisite care you took of Leo. Dad used to call you the wet nurse. You kept pressing him to your chest, hoping he would nurse from you."

She laughs. "So this is why we have parents. So they can remind you of the embarrassing things you did when you were young."

"You were always Leo's favorite," her mother says.

And he, in turn, had been her favorite, too. She'd been the first of the siblings to meet him. Born premature, he was in the NICU for weeks, where, when she visited, she would press her nose to the glass and make faces at him the way she did at the gorillas at the zoo. "Smile at me," she would say. "Come on, Leo, smile at me." Every day, her father retrieved her early from school and brought her to the hospital. Finally, when it was time to take Leo home, she was the one who unveiled him to her sisters. "Wash your hands before touching him. Leave him alone. He needs to rest!" She began her patrol outside his bedroom, one night actually collapsing on the floor. "Sleeping on the job?" her father said as he carried her down the hall to her bedroom. But the next day she was back at her station, even offering her mother advice on how to nurse. "If he's going to get bigger, he needs more milk."

"I've never seen anyone so proprietary," her mother says.

"Or such a taskmaster."

"For a while there, you were pretty insufferable, but you were also an amazing big sister."

"What about now?" Clarissa says. "Will I be a good mother?"

"I didn't realize you wanted to be one."

"Why? Because I'm thirty-nine and . . ."

"I guess that's part of it."

She's quiet.

"You were always so focused. It was cello, cello, and more cello. You were good at blocking everything else out."

Again Clarissa thinks of Andre Agassi, running around with his tennis racquet when he was only three; that racquet must have been bigger than he was. There's a photo of her when she was a girl, with her cello standing next to her like some gangly older cousin.

"You never said anything about children," her mother says, "so Dad and I assumed you weren't interested in them."

"For a long time, I wasn't."

"And we didn't want to put pressure on you. We didn't want to be the kind of parents who breathed down their daughter's neck."

"Well, Nathaniel and I have been trying for a year."

"Have you seen . . ."

"A doctor?"

"Besides the one you're sitting next to now?"

Clarissa gets up and walks onto the tennis court, picking up more balls as she goes. She's never been able to stand disorder, and it seems she can't stand it now. A few strands of hair are slicked fast to her cheeks. Rain drips down her forehead. "Listen, Mom, I really don't want to talk about this."

"What do you want to talk about?"

"I want to talk about you, Mom. Why in the world are you leaving Dad?"

"I told you already. If you didn't understand it the first time, I don't see how I can do any better now." A giant elm tree gives them cover, though now, when a breeze comes through, it washes water onto them.

"Think about the practical things," Clarissa says. "Is there going to be a big court case? Will you be hiring expensive lawyers?"

"Clarissa, Dad and I have decided to separate. Hiring lawyers is the farthest thing from our minds."

"But it could come to that."

"We're not that way."

"No one's that way until they become that way."

"What do we have to fight over? This house?"

"For one."

"We'll sell it and split the proceeds. I don't need Dad's money and he doesn't need mine. I make a good salary. Dad did fine, too, when he was teaching, and now he's collecting retirement."

"Grandma will cut you out of the will."

"If she does, so be it. I never planned to marry rich."

"But you got used to it."

"Inasmuch as anyone gets used to Gretchen. It's like getting used to gravity. She's just there."

"But it's a good kind of there. It gives you a cushion."

"Maybe so, but mostly I just try to ignore it. And when I'm not ignoring it, I'm paying attention to it in such a way that I might as well be ignoring it."

"How?"

"By not buying something I could buy anyway and probably *would* buy anyway were it not for the fact that I'm afraid I'd be buying it because I could come into a big inheritance someday."

"What wouldn't you buy?"

"A necklace, a nice coat, the strawberries for six dollars at Dean and Deluca when I could get the same strawberries elsewhere for half the price. Dad's even worse. He always thought Grandma was spoiling you kids. 'Why can't she visit without bringing gifts?' he would say, and I would say, 'Because she likes to bring gifts, it makes her happy, indulge her, David.' So he did for a while—at least he tried—but then her second husband died and she married again and she was living in New York, we were seeing her all the time, and she was still bringing gifts. I remember your childhood as one enduring battle between Dad and me over which of Grandma's gifts we could keep. Her last husband owned a fleet of Jaguars and one time Grandma brought Leo a toy Jaguar. Dad hated that car. If his son was going to ride around in a toy car, it wasn't going to be in a toy Jaguar."

"And look at Dad's wreck of a car now," Clarissa says. "When is he going to get rid of it?" She's staring at the car dripping rain in the driveway, bathed in the vestigial glow of the tennis court lights.

"I'll tell you when he's going to get rid of it. Never. Dad says he likes Volvos, so I say, 'Fine, buy yourself a new Volvo,' but he doesn't want a new Volvo, he wants an old Volvo, preferably one that's about to break down. It's the same thing with his clothes. Nothing gets thrown out until it's threadbare. So if you think we're going to take each other to court, you don't have a clue." She starts to cry.

"Mom . . ."

"Do you think this is easy for me?"

"I have no idea."

"Well, it's been dreadful."

"Then why are you doing it?"

"I told you," she says, rising from her seat, and her voice is full of impatience. "Dad and I can't talk to each other."

"Of course you can. I saw you two last night."

"Listen to me, Clarissa. Dad says he's tired, but he's not too tired to come home after midnight and refuse to tell me where he's been. He started running after Leo died, and do you know how many miles he runs a week? I'm busy, too—I'm the one who still works—but I come home at night, I'm available to him."

"Have you told him this?"

"Come on, Clarissa. Even when he's there, he's not there. He spends his time practicing his librettos. He sings more than he speaks. Most of the time when I hear his voice it's in Italian."

Clarissa's quiet now. She looks down at the racquets, which lie at her feet, like two giant fly swatters.

"If you want to blame me, I'm fine with that, but I have just one request. I want these next couple of days to be normal."

"Oh, Mom. How in the world can they possibly be normal?"

"I want us to have the memorial exactly as we've been planning to have it. I want us to be sad in exactly the way we were going to be sad. And then, when it's all over, if you want to hate me—"

"Mom, I don't hate you."

"As long as you don't hate me for the next couple of days, that's all I care about. The memorial—this whole holiday—is for Leo."

"Okay," Clarissa says, but then she's off, back to the house, her sneakers hitting the wet pavement. She passes her father's Volvo, the beige paint peeling, the chassis looking as if it's about to cave in on itself. She walks under the bird feeder and beyond the geraniums that line the front path, and just before she moves out of sight, she looks back at her mother still sitting in her chair beneath the garage over-hang, the bucket of tennis balls at her feet. She steps quietly into the house, and when she reaches the landing she removes her shoes so as not to track mud across the floor.

When she gets upstairs, she finds Lily and Noelle standing in the hallway.

"How's Mom?" Noelle asks.

"Bullheaded as ever. She wants us to act as if everything's normal."

"*Normal?*" Noelle says.

"What are you going to do?" says Lily.

"I guess I'll have to try," Clarissa says. "What about you?"

"I don't know."

Down the hall the door has opened; one of the boys is stumbling toward them, wrapped in a sheet.

"Dov, honey," Noelle says. "Go back to bed."

"Is it true?" he says. "Do Grandma and Grandpa not love each other anymore?"

"Who told you that?"

"Akiva," Dov says.

"Oh, honey."

"Well, is it?"

"I don't know."

Lily bends over to pick Dov up.

"What do you think?" Dov asks her. "Have Grandma and Grandpa stopped loving each other?"

"It's complicated," Lily says.

But Dov is only five, and that answer itself is too complicated for him.

Now Lily has handed him to Noelle, who carries him, wrapped like a burrito in his sheet, back to the bedroom where his brothers are sleeping.

"'It's complicated,'" Lily says to Clarissa. "Isn't that something from Facebook?"

"I wouldn't know," Clarissa says. "I'm not on Facebook."

"The last of her kind," Lily says darkly.

Now another of Noelle's boys appears in the hallway, and another, and another. They move in slow procession down the hall.

"My tooth fell out!" Yoni says. "I lost a tooth!" He's walking through the corridor toward Clarissa and Lily.

"Yoni lost a tooth!" Akiva says. He has emerged from the bedroom in his blue briefs, a quilt wrapped around him like an enormous mane.

"The tooth fairy is coming!" Yoni says.

"Thank God you're in America," Akiva says. "If you were in Israel, the tooth fairy would give you shekels, but you're in America, thank God, so you'll get dollars."

7

It's six-thirty now and the boys are back in bed; it's early afternoon Israel time. For the moment, Noelle feels as if she's in a bubble, lying awake next to Amram while the children are asleep. She presses her ear to the wall to see if her sisters are awake; it's been a fitful night for them too.

She rolls over onto her stomach and back again. She wonders what she looks like from up on the ceiling, lying sleepless in her childhood bed. This is where she spent summer after summer. And Christmas vacation and spring break. Amram, who has risen, is in a T-shirt and cutoff jeans, his thighs thick as ham hocks, his prayer fringes sticking out from under his shirt, twisted as always around his belt loops. His yarmulke, blown by the breeze coming through the open window, flips over itself so that it's barely hanging from a few tendrils of hair; it droops to the side like a single earmuff.

He's standing now with his ear to the wall. "Your brother-in-law's awake." He says these words with such derision Noelle is forced to remind him that Nathaniel is his brother-in-law, too.

"Ah, yes," Amram says. "The fucking genius. He's in lecture mode again."

"Come on, Amram. When has Nathaniel ever lectured you?"

"His very existence is one big lecture."

"He's one of the most unassuming people I know."

But it's his very unassuming nature that assails Amram. Amram has a history of hating the smart kids, starting in high school and continuing into college, at SUNY Oneonta, where only by studying hard did he pull B's. Even at yeshiva, he resented the students who picked up the Talmud's logic faster than he could, and he would compensate for his weaker analytic skills with more strenuous religious devotion. For Amram, there's nothing worse than an academic, even an academic like Nathaniel, who rarely talks about his work. If anything, that makes

Nathaniel more detestable. Amram sees Nathaniel's regular-guy manner as a form of pretension; it's his way of mocking him. "If everyone was telling you you'd win the Nobel Prize, would *you* be modest?"

"I hope I would." But the truth is, Noelle doesn't know. It's beyond her ability to imagine winning the Nobel Prize. Even contemplating it is ridiculous.

"Clarissa acts like his PR rep."

"She's proud of him, Amram. I'd be proud of you, too, if you won a prize. I'm already proud of you."

"For what?"

"Just for being who you are."

She rests her hand on Amram's shoulder, and for a second he allows her to leave it there, but then he brushes it off. "Whose side are you on, anyway?"

"Why do there have to be sides?" But then she adds, because it's true, that she's on his side, of course. She loves him: he's her husband.

He goes out onto the balcony, where, with his back to her, he smokes a cigarette. She wishes he wouldn't smoke, especially not at her parents' house. She herself has resolved not to smoke this holiday; she doesn't want her mother to judge her. Or to judge Amram either. She will criticize Amram, but if anyone else criticizes him, especially someone in her family, she'll rush to his defense.

Back in their bedroom, Amram gets down on the floor and does fifty pushups and fifty sit-ups, then follows those with one-handed push-ups, ten with his left hand, ten with his right, the way he was taught in the Israeli army. An *oleh* at twenty-eight, he could have served in the army for only a few months, but he wasn't interested in cutting short his duties; if anything, he'd have liked to do the full three-year stint required of Israeli eighteen-year-olds. But Noelle persuaded him to serve only a year and a half. He's a man of routine. He does the same number of pushups and sit-ups every morning, takes the same route to synagogue each Shabbat, and Noelle always packs him the same lunch: a turkey sandwich on rye, two pickles—one sour, one half-sour—a bag of corn chips, a piece of marble cake, an Orangina.

"Help me stretch." Amram lies on his back, his knees bent, his soles planted firmly on the floor. He ran twelve miles the other day, and he's still suffering the consequences. He's a weekend warrior, only those weekends have been coming less and less often. He won't exercise for weeks, and then, inspired one day to go for a jog, he figures that, since he's at it already, he might as well run ten, fifteen miles. Then he'll spend the next week recuperating. Now he's enlisted Noelle in his recovery: the lady he saws in half. Except she worries she'll saw *him* in half, or, at the very least, that she'll injure him doing what he tells her to do. Right now, she's pushing so hard against his thigh it's as if she's trying to budge a stalled car. "Amram, I'm no good at this."

"Actually, you're quite good. I can feel the muscles being stretched."

"Why don't you hire yourself a personal trainer?"

"Because it would be expensive to fly him here, don't you think? Other leg," he says, grabbing hold of his left knee and pushing it toward the right one. "Okay," he says, "that's enough."

He checks his stocks on the computer. His portfolio is small, but he follows it closely. He can talk at length about the companies he has invested in, and he keeps his holdings for the long term—he's resistant to admitting a mistake—with the kind of determination that some might find pigheaded but that Noelle sees as evidence of more general loyalty. He's always invoking Warren Buffett, whose newsletter he subscribes to. He's a very poor man's Warren Buffett, but this makes him no less dedicated to his principles.

Noelle flips through the *Berkshire Eagle*, which someone has left up in their room. She's checking out the TV listings. "Look what's playing tonight. Another one of those Entebbe movies."

"Surprise, surprise," Amram says. "They turn our heroism into entertainment while they rebuke us at the UN."

Noelle doesn't disagree. But she'd rather not agitate him now. Already, he seems riled up. "Do you want to watch it?"

Amram shrugs. It's been twenty-nine years since Entebbe. It's one of Noelle's early memories, America's bicentennial, up in Lenox for July Fourth, she and her sisters eating roast beef sandwiches while in the background the TV played. She recalls the footage of the boats tacking up the Hudson, then the news reports breaking in, her parents cheering at the announcement that Israeli commandos had stormed the airport and saved the hostages. A hopeless raid in a hostile country,

Idi Amin providing haven for the PLO. Noelle can't explain it, but she felt pride watching TV that day, as if she were Israeli and this was already her homeland, the instinctive sense of belonging in a country she didn't even know. In the years that followed, when those TV movies kept being played, she would stay up past her bedtime to watch, in defiance of her parents' orders. She can still see the flight taking off, the camera scanning the rows of seats, knowing there are hijackers in the cabin, but who they are she can only guess. Then the hijackers commandeer the plane and hold guns to everyone's heads and they're screaming things in a language she doesn't understand. Even now, when she wants to irk her mother, she'll say, "I'm in Israel because of you, Mom. I saw you cheering that day in front of the TV, and I got inspired."

In her closet, she finds her old wedding dress hanging in plastic. It's the one from her first engagement, before she met Amram. Amram knows she was engaged, but he doesn't like to talk about it, and the truth is, neither does she. He's across the room from her now, and a feeling of revulsion sideswipes her. "I like you better in Israel," she says.

"Well, I like you better in Israel, too."

Israel is where they met, a Friday night at the Wailing Wall, a group of American backpackers congregating in the shadows behind the men lining up to pray. A few of the Americans were playing hacky sack, and Amram, trying to get into the mood of things, removed a harmonica and piped out a tune.

Noelle, smoking a cigarette, watched him from the steps where she was sitting. "I know you," she said. "You're Arthur Glucksman. Mamaroneck High School, class of eighty-five? You were in my sister Lily's class. I'm Noelle Frankel." Between them, like a wreath of smoke itself, a group of yeshiva students danced up the steps of the Old City.

It seemed for an instant as if her name had set off something, and Noelle wondered, Does he remember me? The girl who slept with half the class? Would she never be able to escape that? But if that was what he was thinking, he didn't let on. He just continued to play his harmonica, and soon he was accosted by a guard, who told him there was no harmonica playing at the Wailing Wall, that playing music was forbidden on the Sabbath.

Meanwhile, another guard approached Noelle and told her to extinguish her cigarette. Smoking wasn't allowed on the Sabbath, either.

"That's another thing we have in common," Arthur said. "We both broke the rules."

"And to think," Noelle said, "that I flew all the way to Jerusalem just to be a bad Jew."

"When you could have been a bad Jew in Mamaroneck."

"Or a thousand other places."

The Old City, Noelle had heard, specialized in bad Jews. She knew the stories about Friday night at the Wailing Wall, rabbis inviting you for a Sabbath meal, and one rabbi in particular, a charismatic American who was legendary among the local backpackers for retrieving lost souls. "Is that what we look like?" Noelle said to Arthur. "Lost souls?"

Arthur shrugged. He said he was happy to look like anything if there was a home-cooked meal in the bargain. He hadn't had one in months.

So they ended up at the rabbi's house, a large building made of Jerusalem stone from whose living room window you could see the Wailing Wall itself. Noelle and Arthur and ten other lost souls, all being fed by the rabbi's wife, the rebbetzin, who brought out chicken soup and gefilte fish and roast chicken and noodle kugel (so people really did eat these things, Noelle thought; it wasn't just something you saw in the movies), and presently the rabbi was singing Hebrew songs and the rebbetzin was serving poppy-seed cake. The rabbi spoke about the weekly Torah portion, how Jacob wrestled with the angel and injured his sciatic nerve and after that he was called Israel, not Jacob.

When dinner was over, Noelle and Arthur said goodbye, and they walked through the hushed, redolent streets of the Old City. "Lookie here," Arthur said, and he opened up his coat flap to reveal the bottle of Manischewitz wine. He'd filched it right off the rabbi's table.

Noelle laughed. "If you ask me, a certain someone isn't getting invited back to the rabbi's house."

"At least we got a souvenir."

They passed the Wailing Wall once more, and Arthur, feeling glad-hearted and transgressive, took out his harmonica and began to play again.

"Arthur, you'll get yourself arrested. I'll have to bail you out."

"So be it." He played a few more notes. "I bet I'm the first person to play the harmonica at the Wailing Wall."

"Are you kidding me? It's probably been done hundreds of times. Maybe even thousands."

"Come on," he said. "Humor me."

"Okay," she said, "you're the first person to play the harmonica at the Wailing Wall."

"Not the harmonica. Lynyrd Skynyrd. On the Sabbath. In defiance of Jewish law. And badly."

Noelle laughed. "You're right. No one's played it this badly." She held her black pumps in one fist, Arthur's hand in the other, and they walked through the Old City, back to Arthur's sublet apartment.

And there it was. A single Bunsen burner in what passed for a kitchen. And, in the main room, a futon and an armchair with one of the arms missing. "I figure it's the Middle East," Arthur said. "I'm lucky the building has a roof."

That night, standing in the dim light of Arthur's bathroom, using a toothbrush he'd given her, Noelle said, "Look at my teeth."

"They're beautiful," Arthur said.

That's what everyone told her. The stuff of mouthwash commercials: lovely Noelle with the smile like meringue. Her teeth, her hair, her breasts, her buttocks: every piece of her like the cut of a cow. She could hear the boys' voices, the sound of them so loud they drowned out everything else. "For a time I was studying to be a dental hygienist, but I made people's gums bleed."

"Isn't that what you're *supposed* to do?"

"I did it more," she said. "I did it worse."

"So what happened?"

"I quit. In high school, I used to cut my sisters' hair, and everyone complimented them on it, so I enrolled in beauty school. But I quit that too. I've spent my whole life quitting things. What about you?"

"What have I quit?"

"Sure."

"First law school, then accounting. Do you think the rabbi sensed something about us?"

"What do you mean?"

"I don't consider myself a lost soul, but my parents moved to Arizona to play golf and gin rummy, and my sister is in Seattle, married to a banker, and if I don't ever see them again—if the entire U.S. were to fall into the Pacific—I wouldn't be the worse for it."

Noelle slept with Arthur that night, because there had never been a first night when she didn't sleep with the guy (lately she'd been trying to find a reason, but there was never a good reason, and she didn't want to seem like a tease), but the next morning Arthur said he wanted to take her on a proper date. No one in Israel wears a tie (Amram himself doesn't even own one any longer), but the following night Arthur showed up at the youth hostel where Noelle was staying wearing a starched white shirt and a navy print necktie, holding a pint of cherry tomatoes. "For you," he said. "I was planning to get flowers, but the florist was closed."

Noelle laughed. "You're sweet, Arthur."

"My last girlfriend told me I was sweet and anxious."

"That's my favorite combination."

They planned to see a movie that night, but when they got to the theater it was sold out. "What bad luck," Arthur said. "No flowers, no movies."

So they settled for eating fish and chips at a restaurant on Ben Yehuda Street, where they sat outside under a blue and white umbrella, the colors of the Israeli flag. Afterward, they got lost wandering along Jaffa Street, through the back alleys lined with cats, and soon they came upon a fortune-teller who, for twenty shekels, promised to read their palms.

"Let's do it," Noelle said. She dropped a twenty-shekel bill in front of the woman, who scooped it up like a hunk of bread. Then she took Noelle's hand, gazed at it for a minute, and said in a language Noelle had only just started to learn, *Kol chaya'yich tihiyi smeicha.*

All your life you will be joyous.

She'd been taken for a ride, Noelle understood, but she didn't care. She was with Arthur, getting lost in a city thousands of years old, and it made her feel older herself, less likely to be carried off by the things that had always carried her.

The following Friday night, she and Arthur returned to the rabbi's house, where another bottle of Manischewitz sat on the table, and this time they didn't steal it. The Sabbath after that they went back again, and the one after that, too, and soon they were seeing the rabbi not just on Friday nights but on an occasional weeknight, staying up late to study the weekly Torah portion. Before long, Noelle had enrolled in a yeshiva for women and Arthur had enrolled in a yeshiva for men; slowly, they were taking on the strictures of religious observance. Noelle stopped eating bacon and shrimp; Arthur, in a ritual of mock ceremony, announced to Noelle one day that she was witnessing him eat his final cheeseburger, and when he got to the last bite she stood up and cheered.

She felt as if they were on a venture together (even now, she can't imagine having taken this journey without Amram at her side), and also that she was peeling back layers of herself, molting an identity she had wanted to molt for years and hadn't realized she was capable of molting. Six hours after they'd met she and Arthur were having sex, but now, eight months later, they stopped sleeping together because they weren't married. They shared a bed but they didn't have inter-course, and soon they stopped sleeping in the same bed, and then they stopped touching altogether. Noelle knew what others would say, that her newfound chastity was just another side of the same coin, but she didn't care. She had finally found something she could claim as her own. It was as if she'd unhusked herself, and this was what lay beneath it. She *was* joyous: the fortune-teller had been right.

One day Arthur said, "I'm changing my name. From now on, I'm calling myself Amram."

"Okay, Amram," Noelle said, trying it on for size. Arthur was like Jacob changing his name, and he hadn't even had to wrestle an angel, hadn't wound up with an injured sciatic nerve.

Early on, Noelle and Arthur had gone to the beach, where he dragged her out into the waves. His Hebrew was still better than hers, and he spit water out of his mouth and shouted Hebrew words to her, and she was supposed to shout them back: they were conju-gating Hebrew verbs. And there was Arthur's voice as he emerged from the water—*pagashti, pagashta, pagasht, pagash, pagsha, pagashnu, pagashtem, pagashten, pagshu, pagshu*—and Noelle, emerging from the water herself, was repeating after him. Then Arthur was hit by a wave, and suddenly Noelle said, "Wait a minute, Arthur. You don't know how to swim! You could drown!"

"At least I'll die knowing you learned Hebrew."

Noelle, dragging him back to shore, felt a warmth rise in her. Arthur had risked his life for her; she knew right then that she loved him.

She still loves him. But it's different now, and sometimes when she sees Amram in the pool with their boys, her husband who doesn't know how to swim but who nonetheless insists on teaching them swimming, she remembers differently what happened at the beach—remembers less the fact that Amram risked his life for her than that he was teaching her how to conjugate Hebrew verbs, that he always has to have the answers.

It's worse when he's in the States, an entire country where he doesn't know how to swim. In Israel, they have their life, they have their friends, they have their routine, they have their customs, but here in the States, and especially in Lenox with her sisters and parents, she finds herself growing embarrassed by him. Where, she wonders, was the young man she met, Arthur, at twenty-seven, sweet and anxious, giving her that box of cherry tomatoes? He's immersed beneath layers, covered in the sediment of what he has become, the sweetness eclipsed by something else, the anxiety redirected into bullying.

Now, in her old bedroom, she reminds herself of the ways she still loves him. How he reads to her in bed at night, only the little pen light illuminating the page, how he continues to read to her after she's gone to sleep because she likes to hear his voice in her dreams. How every anniversary he buys her a stuffed animal, and now there are ten of them at the foot of their bed, one for each year of their marriage. Last week, when she came down with a fever, he went out at three in the morning in the rain, driving vainly through the desolate streets, searching for an open pharmacy. In those early months, he would take her dancing, though he didn't like to dance, his feet on the dance floor moving this way and that, his arms jerking up and down like a robot's. How he can pop open a bottle of champagne and catch the cork in his mouth. On her thirty-fifth birthday someone in a gorilla suit walked into her classroom and strung a wreath of bananas around her neck;

the gorilla, it turned out, was Amram. How he can't wink, though he tries to—he holds his hand over one eye and winks with the other one—and she loves that about him, loves the fact that he can't wink, because she's never trusted winkers. How one time when she needed to pee and the women's room was locked, he stood guard outside the men's room while she went, shouting, "Sick lady, sick lady, out of the way, sick lady!" How they were in a restaurant when there was a bomb scare and he rushed her and the boys out to make sure they were safe, then returned to the restaurant to help out. How in another restaurant, just weeks ago, they were out on a date, eating Chinese food, and when their fortune cookies arrived she asked him to switch fortunes with her, sight unseen. "Your fortune is my fortune," Amram said, handing her his cookie—her handsome husband like the biblical Ruth, *Your people are my people, your God is my God*. How he can change a diaper with a hand behind his back. How one time he tried to do it with his feet—poor Akiva!—and she was behind him in their son's bedroom, cheering him on. How he got her that box of cherry tomatoes.

But doing this feels self-defeating. She's making a list of the things she loves about him, but the very act of making lists ruins things for her. Because if she really loved him, loved him the way she loves him when she's not making lists, she wouldn't need to make them. In Jerusalem, she thinks, she doesn't need to make lists.

Amram is standing outside on the balcony, smoking another cigarette. She calls out to him, but he doesn't hear her. "I wish you wouldn't smoke," she says, but her voice is too soft to carry through the glass door and she doesn't want to wake the rest of her family. "I'm sorry," she says, but this, too, he doesn't hear. She's a smoker herself; she knows how hard it is to quit, and in a way she doesn't want to. Neither does Amram. They like to smoke. They just don't like that they like to smoke, like even less that their children know they smoke, so they do it out of sight, the way they did growing up. All those years you hide things from your parents until you start to hide things from your children. They're romantics, besides, when it comes to smoking. They've given up so much; it's one thing they wish to hold on to. That and Amram's motorcycle, which he drives around Jerusalem. Noelle comes along, too; in her dresses and head scarves, her long-sleeved blouses, she rides with her arms wrapped around Amram, who's decked out himself in religious garb, a baseball cap on his head so his *yarmulke* won't fall off, his prayer fringes dancing to the sides of him. It makes them complicated, she thinks. Or maybe it just makes them a mess.

"Hey, you," she calls out. If they could just connect a tube from his brain to hers, if she could know his thoughts, share them, if they could be like conjoined twins, one brain for a single organism. She doesn't mind feeling alone when she's alone; it's when she's not alone and feels alone that she grows desperate. "Come to bed with me."

"It's seven-thirty in the morning," Amram says. "The kids will be up soon."

"I just want to hold you." He's her husband, she thinks, but it's been months since they've held each other. She wants that, certainly, but she also wants sex, because sex has always been a kind of forgetting. When it happens, Amram is touching her there and he's touching her there and he's touching her there, and she's retreating into nothing but skin and nerves, everything obliterated into sweet thoughtlessness.

Amram sits on the bed in his T-shirt and dungaree cutoffs, his prayer fringes draped across him. Now he strings the fringes over the nightstand. He's lying beside her with his hand on her stomach.

She sits up.

"What are you doing?"

"Taking my clothes off."

He hesitates.

"What?"

"It's just so sudden, that's all."

"What's wrong with sex at seven-thirty in the morning?" Most men prefer sex in the morning. At least that's been her experience.

He's staring at her as she undresses, and she feels an awkwardness overtake her and she wants to cover herself. It kills her to feel this way, in front of her own husband.

"The boys are down the hall," he says.

"In Jerusalem they're down the hall, too." In Jerusalem, in fact, they're even closer to them.

"They're on Israel time," Amram says. "It's afternoon for them now."

"I checked on them earlier. They're out cold."

He looks out the window, to where he was standing before. "I'm not in the right mood. It's not the right moment."

"That's what you always say."

"I can't help it. It's true."

She sits on the bed, half undressed.

"We could try tonight," he says. "We could go to bed early."

"And then tonight will come and you'll suggest tomorrow night instead. It's never the right mood."

He doesn't respond.

"Something has happened to your sex drive, Amram."

"That's not true."

But it is true. Or, if it's not true, then something else has happened. Already the laws of family purity are designed to help the mood. For the five days of her menstrual period and seven days afterward, she and Amram are forbidden to have sex. Then she goes to the *mikvah* and comes back clean; they're supposed to be rejuvenated.

"There's nothing wrong with my sex drive," Amram says. He's sitting up now, looking as if he might walk away.

"Okay," she says, because she doesn't want to fight about this. Besides, it's not the route she wants to take. It might make him have sex with her, but it would be for the wrong reason. He'd be proving something to himself, and so in a way it would be as if he were having sex with himself, which would be worse than not having sex at all.

But it's too late—her insinuation has worked—because Amram is unbuttoning his dungarees, saying, "We can try."

She hesitates.

"Isn't that what you wanted?"

It was what she wanted. And she's thinking about what her rabbi said, *Me'toch she'lo l'shma ba l'shma.* If you start to do something not for its own sake, you will eventually do it for its own sake. The rabbi was talking about Torah study, but can't it be true, Noelle thinks, for sex as well?

She's naked now beneath the covers, and Amram is naked, too, but there's a noise downstairs, a clanking of pipes. She hears the bathroom door open and the sink go on. The sound of the television comes up from the living room.

Amram is on top of her now, the weight of him square on her, and

Noelle, gasping for breath as he pushes down on her solar plexus, says, "Good God, Amram, what did you eat last night?"

"What?"

"Go easy on me. I'm a featherweight here."

He's utterly still, poised above her, his arms taut against the mattress, bearing his bulk. He rolls off her.

"Amram."

"I've been trying to lose weight."

"I was kidding."

"No you weren't."

"Amram, please. I'm sorry."

He rolls over onto his back and stares up at the ceiling. His hands are clasped behind his neck.

"I apologize," she says. "That wasn't fair."

He allows her to mount him, but he's cold beneath her, his gaze slack, his heart beating dully against her chest.

"You don't think I'm attractive," he says.

"That's not true."

"Remember when you said you didn't like the hair on my shoulders?"

"I was joking."

"You weren't."

"I don't even remember having said that."

He's inside her now, though he's still half dressed, his T-shirt on one shoulder and off the other, his boxers coiling around themselves, down at his ankles. He thrusts—once, twice, three times, four times—but there's an obligatory cast to the movement. She takes his face in her hands. "Look at me, Amram. Please look at me."

His elbow knocks into her rib cage.

"Ouch!"

"Are you all right?"

"No," she says, "I'm not."

"Well, okay. I'm sorry."

She rolls back on top of him, but he's just lying beneath her, unmoving, his palms placed against her ribs, as if he's preparing to push her away.

A moment passes, and he does just that.

"What's wrong?"

"I need to go to the bathroom."

She waits for him, lying as still as she can, as if by not moving she will make him come back to her.

But when he returns he says, "Great, I'm not hard." He guides her hand to his penis, which, sure enough, is shriveled as a fig. She flinches at the touch of it.

"You could use your mouth."

She hesitates: oral sex is prohibited by Jewish law. The spilling of seed, like Onan.

But Amram assures her he won't come. "It's just to get me going."

She tries to go down on him, but she feels self-conscious. She hasn't done this in years, not on him, not on anyone. She doesn't want Amram's semen in her mouth—the very thought of it repulses her—and now her jaw is bumping against his pubic bone and she feels his hair, rough as steel wool against her chin. She takes him in her mouth, and her head is going up and down, up and down, but she feels leagues away. She has taken him in too deep, and she's coughing now, lying beside him on her back, gagging quietly. "Maybe *you're* the one not attracted to *me*."

"Of course I'm attracted to you." He's lying next to her, his organ at half-mast, flopping to the side like a fish.

"It doesn't seem like it."

"I could masturbate," he says.

She gives him a look: this, too, is prohibited.

"Just to get us going," he says again.

She catches sight of herself in the mirror still wearing her baseball cap. She was already dressed, had her hair covered to start the day, and she neglected to remove the cap when she took her clothes off. And there she was, hammering at Amram's crotch as she went down on him, and she laughs now, recalling this, thinking, What a turn-off, of course he couldn't get hard.

"We could do it from behind," he says.

That's how dogs do it, she wants to say. But even the thought of it sounds absurd. When did she become so squeamish? She's on her hands and knees, and Amram is behind her, pounding against her like a rump roast, and as she looks over her shoulder she can't see him, only feels him ramming against her flesh. She closes her eyes, presses her face against the pillow, and when she looks back from between her legs she can see nothing but her breasts hanging pendulously from her. "Amram, are you hard?" But he doesn't answer her, and she's thinking, *Enter me already, for God's sake!*

He's inside her now, but then she's not sure. She feels a smothering pressure; she's being rammed in the rear as if with a cattle prod.

There's a wetness against her buttocks, and before she can say "What was that?" she realizes.

"Oh, man."

"You came." Semen drips down her rear end, viscous as egg yolk.

"Fuck," Amram says.

She reaches around with the pillow to wipe herself off.

"Oh, God, Noelle."

She covers her breasts with the bedspread, shielding them from his gaze. "You weren't inside me."

"No."

She burrows deeper beneath the covers. "You said you weren't hard."

"I wasn't."

"But you came," she says. "I thought that wasn't possible."

"Me, too." He's mopping at his pelvis with a wadded-up tissue, and then he's mopping her up as well.

Already the backs of her thighs are caking up. Regret sloshes through her, rising in her stomach.

"The sheets," he says. "They're soiled." He grabs at the edge of the fitted sheet, and now it has come off and he's lying on the mattress pad, trying to extricate himself, and she's trying to extricate herself, too.

"I'll put it in the wash," she says.

"I'll do it."

She goes to object, but she doesn't have the strength to stop him. "You were right. The kids. What was I thinking?"

He's standing far away from her now, across the room.

"We'll try again later. It will be different tonight."

"There won't be a tonight."

"It's my fault," she says.

"*Your* fault? I'm the one who came in two seconds."

"Amram—"

"I did," he says, "and don't try to sugarcoat it."

The fitted sheet is still half on, half off. She does her best to right it, but it won't stay on. There's a stain on the middle of it, and another one on the peak of her baseball cap; she'll have to wash that as well. "You should get dressed," she says. "The kids will be up soon."

"They're already up. I can hear them."

There's a knock on the door, and she goes to answer it, but there's no point. The boys have burst in, decked out in their prayer fringes and knitted yarmulkes, so she herds them downstairs, the four of them in a row attached like sausages, where the rest of the family is waiting for them.

At breakfast, Noelle sits with her bagel and peanut butter, the food she and Amram brought, while the rest of the family surrounds her, eating their eggs and French toast. She spreads cream cheese on Yoni's bagel, but because the knife is plastic and the bagel a day old, because she's feeling an aggression well up inside her, the knife breaks in half, one piece flying across the room and landing on the floor. She goes to retrieve it, and as she bends over she feels Amram's semen cake against her thighs (oh, for the chance to shower!), and the humiliation revisits her once more.

Back at the table, she sees Lily whispering to Clarissa. It's as if they know what happened. She tries to look away, but she can't. The mere sight of them gets her worked up. She swore on the plane ride to the States that they would have no impact on her. And now they're here—her sisters!—and she has lost her resolve. In bed last night, she found herself listening for them—listening in on Clarissa and Lily the way she did as a girl, and she forgot for an instant that they weren't sharing a room, that Lily was in her bed, alone, and Clarissa was next door, in bed with Nathaniel.

In the kitchen, pouring one of her boys a glass of juice, she turns on Lily, who is tending to the waffle iron. "I saw you guys whispering."

"What?"

"If you have something to say, why don't you say it aloud?"

Lily simply stares back at her.

"I'm part of this family, too, you know." She hurries out of the kitchen, past the table where everyone is seated, and up the stairs to her and Amram's room.

"What was that?" Clarissa says. She has come into the kitchen to make a waffle herself.

"That," Lily says, "was our little sister throwing a hissy fit. Apparently, we were telling secrets about her."

"Were we?"

"I have no idea. Big things are happening in this family—huge things—and Noelle focuses on trivialities."

The kitchen door swings open and their mother comes in. "Something's burning in here."

"It's the waffles," Lily says.

"Well, don't just stand there, girls."

But that's what they do, and so it's left to Marilyn to pull the plug from the socket and toss the waffle iron into the sink. Smoke rises through the kitchen, and Marilyn has to stand on the step stool and remove the smoke alarm to make sure it doesn't go off.

When breakfast is over, the dishes cleared, Marilyn opens the porch door, and presently, a butterfly enters the house. Calder and Ari snap to attention. They're both three, though Calder is quick to point out that he's two months older than Ari. He has his sights set on Dov, who, at five, is playing tag with his older brothers, but Dov isn't interested in Calder. So on the principle that a mutual enemy makes you a friend, the boys settle on stalking the poor butterfly. It's up on a beam, out of reach, but they swat at it, and when that fails, they try to spear it with a broom. "My father carries a gun," Ari says, in response to which Thisbe explains that Ari means back in Israel, when Amram is on army reserve duty, that Amram isn't carrying a gun at this very moment, information she intends as reassurance but that instead seems to disappoint Calder.

The older boys have gotten permission to use the neighbors' basketball hoop, and intermittently from across the yard come the sounds of exultation and distress, fouls called and disputed, a more free-ranging discussion about ethical play as the boys hurl themselves at the ball and at each other. Akiva, Yoni, and Dov play a series of round robin one-on-ones before settling on one-on-two, Akiva against Yoni and Dov. Now Ari and Calder have gotten in on the act, each of them grabbing hold of one of Akiva's legs until, collectively, they bring him down.

"Hey," Akiva says, "that's against the rules." But his cousin and brothers are on top of him now, pounding their fists against his chest.

"Is that rugby you're playing?" Marilyn says, but all she gets in response is a succession of grunts. She's wearing a white sundress and sandals, and she's moving around the perimeter of the house, replenishing the bird feeder, pulling weeds from between stones, stringing out towels on the laundry line. Clarissa and Nathaniel are in the garden, swatting a shuttlecock back and forth.

"Here," Marilyn says, "make yourself useful." She tosses a few towels Clarissa's way, one of which lands draped over the badminton net.

Thisbe has come outside in a tank top and shorts, back from her morning run. She's holding a grasshopper, which she caught in the driveway and which she shows now to Calder. He's holding something himself—a four-leaf clover—that he presents to the group.

"What's that?" David says. He has emerged from the kitchen, barefoot, in cutoff jeans, the brim of a Brooklyn Dodgers baseball cap pulled down over his eyes. He has a frying pan in one hand, a dish towel in the other, and he's trying to figure out what everyone's been saying. "You can make a wish on that," Thisbe tells Calder.

But Calder's already off, back to playing with his cousins, leaving the clover at his mother's feet.

"*Seventeen-year-old, legally,*" Lily calls out. She's on the porch, doing the *Times* crossword.

"*Jail bait,*" Amram says.

Lily shakes her head.

"*Underage,*" says Marilyn.

"Five letters." Lily knows the answer: she's just quizzing them. It's

Tuesday, which means an easy crossword, and since no one has gone into town to buy the paper yet, she's doing the Monday crossword, which is even easier.

"*Minor*," Clarissa says. She's good at crosswords herself, though she doesn't bring to them Lily's competitive ebullience.

"Who wants to take me on?" Lily means who wants to do the crossword next to her and try to finish first? It's why she bought another copy of the paper: an extra dollar-fifty so she can kick someone's butt. But Clarissa's already getting her butt kicked at badminton, and Marilyn is too busy folding laundry, and no one else seems interested either. Lily considers coming off the porch, but she's feeling sensitive to the heat. Last week, she fell asleep on the grass outside her apartment and got herself a sunburn. Now, with her red hair pinned to the top of her head, her nose peeling, a little lipstick smudged across her mouth, she has the hue of an overripe nectarine. "*Surprisingly lively for one's age.*"

"*Sprightly,*" says Marilyn.

"Four letters."

"*Spry,*" Thisbe says.

"*Ninth-inning pitcher.*"

"*Closer,*" says Amram. When it comes to sports, nobody can touch him. Back in Jerusalem, a group of American *olim* have started a fantasy baseball league, and late at night when he's not checking his stocks he's charting the progress of his players. Last year, he won his league's version of the World Series, which netted him the $1,500 first prize.

"*Old woman's home in a nursery rhyme.*"

"*Shoe,*" Thisbe says.

"*What the love of money is, they say.*"

"*The root of all evil,*" says Marilyn.

"*One who mounts and dismounts a horse.*"

"*Jockey,*" says Nathaniel.

"Seven letters," Lily says. "Begins with a *g,* ends with a *t.*"

"*Gymnast.*"

"*Iranian money.*"

"*Rial,*" Thisbe says.

"*Summit.* Four letters. Begins with an *a.*"

"*Acme,*" Clarissa says.

"Man, this family's fast," Amram says. He's going for joviality, Noelle can see, but it makes him breathless. The game reminds Noelle of speed chess, which Amram played once in Washington Square Park and lost in a dozen moves. He was terrible at speed chess, probably because he wasn't much good at regular chess either. Apparently, he was the same way with skiing, insisting at nine, when he first skied, on going down the expert slopes, refusing so much as to consider the bunny hill, the very name of which repelled him. His skis fell off on the first try, skidding down the slope on their own, and he wasn't far behind, on his rear end, spraying ice in all directions like a Zamboni.

"*Nitroglycerine or dynamite,*" Lily says. "Nine letters. Starts with an *e.*"

"*Explosive,*" says Marilyn.

"I'm tired of this game," Amram says.

"Try this one, Amram," Lily says. "*It may hang out in a sports stadium.*"

Amram hesitates. Another sports question: he can't help himself. "*Fan,*" he says.

Lily shakes her head.

"*Vendor!*"

"Four letters," she says.

"*Player! Umpire! Mascot!*"

"I said four letters."

"*Scalper! Ball! Outfielder! Referee!*" Amram jumps up as he guesses, sending his laptop spinning across the table. He tugs on his prayer fringes, which have come untied from their belt loops. He's trying to convey enthusiasm, but there's a belligerent, abrasive quality to his voice, a combativeness that makes Noelle anxious. "Easy does it," she says, reaching out to him, but he slaps her hand away.

Lily holds up the newspaper in front of her face. Amram is staring so hard at the pages it's as if he's trying to see through them.

"Do you want a hint?"

"Not a chance."

Twenty seconds pass, half a minute, a minute. Dov comes back from the basketball game with a point of dispute, but Amram shoos him off. "Okay," he says. "I give up."

"It's a four-letter word that begins with a *t*. The penultimate letter is *e*."

"The *penultimate* letter?"

Lily looks at him wryly. "As in second-to-last?"

"*It may hang out in a sports stadium?*" Amram says. "What kind of sport?"

"Sorry, Amram, no can do." Lily fans the newspaper in front of her face. A smudge of lipstick has come off on the paper. She emits an exaggerated yawn. "Time's up," she says. "The correct answer is '*tier*.'"

"*Tear?*" says Amram.

She spells out the word for him. "*Hang out*," she says, "as in *jut out*."

Amram slams shut his computer. "That's ridiculous!"

"Why?" she says. "Because you couldn't get the answer right?" She folds the newspaper in half, and in half again, and places it beneath her chair. Soon, though, she reconsiders. She has her nose in the page once more and is scanning the crossword. "Okay, Amram, here's an easy one for you: *assassinated Israeli prime minister*."

"*Rabin*," Noelle says.

But Amram just sits there stonily.

"Try this one," Amram says, rising from his chair. "A plane crashes and the debris lands on the border of Arizona, New Mexico, Colorado, and Utah. Where do you bury the survivors?"

But Lily couldn't be less interested. She has moved from the crossword to the rest of the arts section and is flipping through the book review, the movies. "I give up."

"Sorry, Lily, there's no giving up."

"Is that so?"

"Amram," Noelle says, "leave her alone." Noelle isn't used to defending Lily, and that's not her intention now; it's Amram whom she wants to save from what she's sure will be humiliation.

"Survivors don't get buried," Amram says.

"Ah, so they don't," Lily says, not even bothering to look up.

"That's it for me." Amram grabs his bottle of mineral water and heads inside. He's going to take a nap, he tells everyone.

But not five minutes have passed before he reappears, holding a sand timer. "Who wants to play Celebrity?"

Everyone is arrayed haphazardly across the garden, like croquet rings. Marilyn is back to weeding, crouched on her knees in the dirt. Thisbe is lying on a beach chair, reading a novel, and Lily is sprawled across a towel in her T-shirt and shorts, trying to get some sleep. The boys, indefatigable, have moved from one-on-two to HORSE and back again. Now Marilyn has come inside holding some weeds. Her knees are brown, she's gotten her sundress muddy, but she looks like she's achieved what she set out to do.

"I'm tired of games," Noelle says. She's especially tired of Celebrity, where she's always paired with Amram and where, invariably, things go wrong. Any game with a timer rattles Amram, the sand descending, the depletion of which occurs implacably and makes him quietly frenetic. It's like standardized tests, all of which he aced when he was preparing for them—at least that's what he told Noelle—but when it came time to take the actual test, sitting in the classroom, everyone silent, the sound of pencils filling in those bubbles and the tick-ticking of the clock on the wall, he panicked that time was going by too fast, and then it *was* going by too fast: the test was over and he hadn't managed to answer even half the questions. In Celebrity, with the other players looming and that relentless minute glass, Amram jumps in too soon, his voice reverberating as if from a bullhorn, and Noelle, sitting mute beside him, becomes exquisitely embarrassed.

The game is already familiar to the others, but Amram explains the rules to them anyway. Each player writes down the names of ten celebrities and places them in a bowl. They don't have to be real celebrities, Amram says. They can be fictional characters, or simply people everyone knows. Noelle, for instance, would be a celebrity for these purposes. "We can play couples against couples," Amram says. "You guys"—he points to Lily and Thisbe—"can be a couple, too."

Everyone starts to write down their clues, but David gets up and walks out onto the porch.

Marilyn runs after him. "Aren't you going to play?"

"No, Marilyn, I'm not." He's in the garage now, and he grabs a hoe and heads over to the marigolds. He starts to dig some dirt.

"What are you doing?"

"Gardening." He gets down on his knees and yanks a few weeds out, then tosses them over his shoulder in the direction of the compost. He's wearing shorts, and when he stands up two pale patches of dirt are caked to his thighs, like blush. "Please don't tell me to be a sport."

"I was simply going to ask you to play with us."

"You already asked me that."

"Well, I'm asking you again."

"I'm not going to play couples against couples."

"Fine," she says. "Play with whoever you want to."

The hoe is beside him in the flower bed, and he leans against it like a staff. "You want me to act like things are normal, but things aren't normal, Marilyn. I didn't bag out of this holiday, though I might have liked to. I came up to the country with you, and at dinner last night I sat there civilly while you said your piece, and then I retired to my quarters. I've been more than a sport if you ask me."

"I know you have."

"But I'm not going to play parlor games with you. I don't care if it's couples against couples or boys against girls or lefties against righties or tall people against short people."

"Okay," she says. "You've made your point."

He jams the hoe into the ground and walks around the side of the house, to where their car is parked.

"Where are you going?"

"To the hardware store."

"For what?"

"Hardware." He has his keys out, and he stops for a moment before he opens the trunk. "We need to sell this house."

"I know we do."

"Unless you're planning to turn it into a timeshare—a week for you, a week for me?"

"I'm not."

"Then we should fix the place up, don't you think? It would be nice if it looked good for potential buyers."

"I don't care how it looks."

"Well, I do."

"Fine," she says. "Go make your purchases."

She comes back inside, where the rest of her family is seated on the floor, waiting for her to resume playing.

"Where's Dad?" Clarissa asks.

"He's run off." And then, because this is not how she wants to leave things, she says he needed to run some errands, which, she supposes, is true.

Across from her, Amram has finished writing down his clues. He's looking at Lily, his arms folded across his chest, seeming uncommonly, uncharacteristically cheerful.

"Amram," Noelle says. "I think we should be on different teams."

But Amram, running his hand through a day's growth of stubble, will have none of it. "Those who play together, stay together. You live with me, you play with me." He blinks and grins. He's a collection of tics, all nervous energy.

Marilyn joins Lily and Thisbe, and they all move clockwise, from team to team. Winston Churchill. Elvis Costello. Wilt Chamberlain. Robert Downey Jr. Maury Povich. Billy Baldwin. Babe Ruth. George Eliot. Slobodan Milošević. Someone has in fact written down Noelle. After the first round, Amram and Noelle are losing, but Amram gives off an air of confidence that borders on haughtiness; he'd have everyone believe he's simply biding his time.

Lily opens up a clue. "I've never heard of this person."

"That's part of the game," Amram says. "Sometimes you know things and sometimes you don't."

"Try to guess," says Thisbe.

"*You* try to guess," Lily says. "I can't even sound out the words."

"Time's up," Amram says.

The same thing happens with Clarissa and Nathaniel. They get a couple of clues right, but then they're stumped. "These are supposed to be celebrities," Clarissa says.

"This is ridiculous." Marilyn shows everyone the name she's holding. "It's in Hebrew."

"It's not in Hebrew," Amram says. "It's the Roman alphabet." He spells out the words.

"*Yisrael Salanter?*" Marilyn says.

"That's right," says Amram, though not before correcting his mother-in-law's pronunciation.

When it's his and Noelle's turn, it's as if Amram knows which pieces of paper to choose. He gives the hints with assurance, and Noelle guesses them correctly. *Rav Kook, Yossi Beilin, Yerovam ben Nevat, Abaye, Arik Einstein, Naomi Shemer.* They get six answers right in the course of a minute.

"*Eldad?*" Lily says when it's her turn again.

"Sorry," Amram says. "You said the name. You lose a point."

"*Eldad?*" Lily repeats.

"El*dod*," Amram corrects her. "The word rhymes with *rod*, not *dad*."

"And who, may I ask, is this famous person you've concocted?"

"I haven't concocted him," Amram says. He quotes to Lily. "*Eldad u'Meidad mitnabim ba'machaneh . . .*"

"In English, please."

"Eldad and Meidad were false prophets," Amram says. "They're in the Torah. Or the Bible, if you prefer. The Old Testament? The Pentateuch? I take it you've heard of those books?"

Lily doesn't so much as move an eyebrow.

"But have you read them? Did Leviticus make it into the syllabus at Princeton? Or did you only read the Bhagavad Gita?"

Lily holds up the clue in front of Amram and tears it in half. "That's very clever of you, Amram, quoting some obscure biblical figure. Do you think that makes you smart?"

"He's not obscure," Amram says. "My eight-year-old knows him. Hell, my three-year-old knows him."

"I don't care what your eight-year-old knows or what your three-year-old knows. My dog knows as much as they do, and he'd have been happy to demonstrate were it not for the fact that your three-year-old is allergic to dogs. Or is it your four-year-old?"

"We don't have a four-year-old," Noelle says.

"You say the name of this false prophet is Eldad?"

This time it's Noelle who corrects Lily's pronunciation.

"Well, there's no end to your false prophets, starting with Moses and Joshua and continuing on down to Sharon and Netanyahu. You and Amram, too, living in your warmongering country, practicing your delusional religion."

"It's your religion, too," Noelle says.

"It most certainly isn't."

"Amram's and my country," Noelle says, "we'll welcome you whether or not you deserve it. Have you heard of the Law of Return? Every Jew gets automatic citizenship, no questions asked? If the Holocaust comes to America, what will you do then?"

"The Holocaust!" Lily says. "Always the Holocaust! The world's greatest conversation stopper!"

"You don't think it's possible?" Noelle says.

"Anything's possible. Right now, the world has more pressing concerns, and so do I."

"Like what?" Amram says. "Your little bleeding-heart job? Your boyfriend's new restaurant—that pipe dream of his?"

"It's not a pipe dream. And let me remind you, in case you forgot, that when Malcolm first had the idea to open his own restaurant it was you, Amram, who wanted in."

"Holocaust or no Holocaust," Amram says, "Israel will welcome you, because you're a Jew and it's your homeland."

"Oh, spare me the Moonie-in-the-airport talk."

"Why?" Noelle says. "So you can continue to live your soulless life?"

"What makes my life soulless? Because I don't believe in God?"

"Because you're a single woman in your thirties," Noelle says. "Because you're essentially alone."

"I'm not alone. And before you tell me I'm living in sin, let me say this as clearly as I can. I would take my relationship with Malcolm over your relationship with Amram any day of the week."

"Lily!" their mother says.

"Listen to the two of them, Mom, with their self-righteousness and false prophets. All these Orthodox Jewish couples with their marriage certificates framed on the wall. Have you read about spousal abuse in the Hasidic community?"

"We're not Hasids," Noelle says, "and you know nothing about Amram's and my relationship."

"And you know nothing about my relationship. But I'll say it again, in case you didn't hear me the first time. If I were a betting woman, I'd bet on Malcolm and me over the two of you."

"In that case," Noelle says, "why isn't he here?"

"Come again?"

"Leo died a year ago, it's his memorial, for God's sake, and your boyfriend can't make it because he's too busy? Amram's busy, too, but he flew six thousand miles so he could be here."

"Malcolm wanted to be here," Lily says. "He practically insisted on coming."

"Then why isn't he here?"

"Because I wouldn't let him come."

"Why in the world?"

"Because that's just what I'm like, Noelle. So would you get off your fucking high horse for once and stop blaming Malcolm?"

Now Thisbe starts to cry. Still in her running shorts, a couple of clues gripped in her hand, she's hunched over on the floor, sobbing. Marilyn touches her arm, her hair, says, "What's wrong, sweetie?" Lily's hand is resting on her, too, and Thisbe just wants everyone to stop touching her. Soon the boys come inside, Calder among them, in front of whom Thisbe has resolved not to cry on this trip, and now she's breaking her promise. "What's wrong?" Calder asks, but she can't get the words out, doesn't even know what she would say if she could. She just wants to be left alone, but all she can do is sit there, the bowl of clues at her feet, being attended to by everyone, her former family, as she cries and cries, unable to stop.

"You were brilliant," Amram says.

"*Brilliant?*" says Noelle.

"We won," he reminds her. It was twenty-two to nineteen to sixteen, in favor of him and Noelle. "And what you said to Lily? You were absolutely amazing."

But if she was amazing, why does she feel remorse running through her? She told her sister off, said the things she has wanted to say to her for years, but now she's upstairs with Amram, the walls pressing in on her again, their soiled sheet still affixed to the bed, the stain staring back at her.

"Come on," Amram says, poking her in the ribs. "How about a little smile?"

She tries to give him one.

"Perhaps a measly congratulations?"

"Congratulations to us," she says gloomily. She's happy they won, too, but whatever pride she felt has been erased by how Amram is carrying on. His semen is still spackled to her thighs; she feels a mute humiliation.

Amram is whistling a song, but she doesn't want to hear music coming from him; she doesn't want to hear anything at all. He's lying on the bed in only his T-shirt and boxers; a red spot stains his sleeve. "I proved something," he says.

"The only thing you proved is you could make Thisbe cry."

"Are you kidding me? If anyone made her cry, it was you."

She retrieves her pocketbook slung over the bedpost. She rifles through it, she has no idea for what.

"Look—"

"Could you please stop talking to me that way?" *Look. Listen.* Amram always starts his sentences like that. She hates how he hectors her, how he holds forth.

"Why can't you just be happy we won?"

"It was only a game."

But if it was only a game, why can't she let him enjoy his victory? She's always attacking him, diminishing his small pleasures; she detests herself. She drums her fists so hard against her thighs welts start to bloom beneath her skirt.

"You think I'm not as smart as Nathaniel, is that it?"

"Oh, Amram."

"Well, do you?"

"Honestly?"

He nods.

"No," she says, "I don't think you're as smart as Nathaniel. Not many people are. Certainly no one I know."

"Then why didn't you marry him?"

"Because I didn't want to marry him. I wanted to marry you. There's only one thing Nathaniel has that I want for you."

"What's that?"

"A job."

"A job?" he says. "Is that all you can ever think about? A fucking job!?"

"I'm worried," she says. "Don't you understand? You have a family to support."

"Do you know how long it took Nathaniel to get his PhDs?"

"If you say his name again, I'll scream!"

"Thirteen years total. And do you think Clarissa was hounding him during that time? Do you think she was telling him to make a living?"

"Clarissa didn't even know Nathaniel when he was getting his PhD. He already had it by the time she met him."

"Not the second one. And do you think she told him not to get it?"

"I have no idea."

"Well, I do. She allowed him to pursue his dreams."

"Is that what I'm doing? Preventing you from pursuing your dreams?"

"In a way, you are."

"We have four children," she reminds him. "That was our dream. To raise our boys and settle in Israel. We're *living* our dream, don't you remember?"

"Maybe I want to change careers."

"To what?" Ever since she's known him, Amram has worked in computers. It's hard for her to imagine him doing anything else.

"What if I want to go back to school?"

"You hated school. You cursed the very town of Oneonta."

"I was twenty then, and I'm almost forty now. Maybe I'd like to experiment."

"Doing what?" All her life has been one big experiment. Amram's life too. Finally, she has stopped experimenting. It scares her to hear him say this.

"I used to be good at art," he says. "Or emergency medical training. That's something else I've been thinking about."

She'd like to be more patient with him, she would, but something stops her. "You need to send out your résumé. That's the first step. The next step is to get an interview."

"I've already gotten one." Amram is standing over her now. It's as if he's inflating before her, like one of those balloon animals released to the sky. "I got an e-mail last night. This company wants me to come in and talk."

"Amram! That's wonderful!"

"Not when you consider what the job is."

"What is it?"

"It's entry level, the kind of thing I did when I was just starting out."

"Entry level's better than nothing."

"Not for me, it isn't. Anyway, it's too late. I told them I wasn't interested."

"You what?"

"Oh, don't act so surprised, Noelle. You'd have done the same thing in my position."

"I most certainly wouldn't have."

"If they offered me a job that was worthy of my talents, I'd consider it."

Worthy of your talents? she wants to say. What talents? But she's not being fair. And if he's not talented, what does that say about her? She married him. What talents does she have? Part-time teacher's aide. Mother. It took her five years to graduate from high school, another five years to finish college; she got expelled from institutions up and down the East Coast. And here she is, vacillating between self-pity and self-reproach, issuing her scattershot accusations.

"Look," she says, pointing at the bed. The stain has gone through to the mattress. "What am I going to tell my parents?"

"You don't have to tell them anything. You're thirty-seven years old."

"And just leave it like that?" She glances up at him, but the sight repulses her and she turns away. "It happened once before."

"I don't know what you're talking about."

"A few months ago. Don't you remember?"

He gets up from the bed and walks across the room. He's standing far away from her. "You humiliate me, Noelle. Every day you wake up and humiliate me."

"That's not true."

"It's the truest thing I've ever said."

She's quiet.

"I'm tired of everything."

"Tired of me?"

He rushes out of the bedroom, and she follows him. Down the stairs they go and out into the garden, where it has started to rain again. They're getting wet beside her mother's rosebushes. "Amram, what's happening to us?"

He walks around the perimeter of the house and heads straight for their car.

"Where are you going?"

"For a drive."

"You can't just take off like that."

"Watch me." He has the key in the ignition; he's talking to her now through the open window.

"Amram, please, it's my brother's memorial!"

"Believe me, I won't be missed."

Would you please stop feeling sorry for yourself? she wants to say, but the car has jerked forward, Amram is peeling out of the driveway. He's just a taillight now at the foot of the road, and then not even that. Standing in front of her parents' house, she screams, "I'm sorry, Amram, we'll work this out! I promise we'll do better!"

But he's already gone.

When she steps back inside, her mother and sisters are seated in the living room, having witnessed what took place.

"Well," she says, and she lets her hands drop against her thighs; they make a little thud of resignation.

"What was that?" her mother says.

That, she wants to say, was my idiot husband stalking off. But she understands that to cast Amram in such light is to do the same to herself. "He just went for a spin," she says, and since everyone knows this isn't true, they simply sit there, not saying anything, until Dov comes in and starts to bang on the piano keys. Ari follows, saying, "Eema, if I fall from somewhere high will you catch me?" and Noelle feels briefly rescued. But then the boys are gone and she's alone again, and her mother says, "Come here, Noelle, sit down next to me." Her mother places her arm around Noelle's shoulder. "Dad left, too. All the men in the family have run off."

"Great," Lily says. "We should stage a bra-burning."

"Amram will be back soon," Marilyn says. "How far could he have gone?"

But that's the problem, Noelle thinks. He could have gone any-where; he could be on his way back to Israel, for all she knows.

An hour later, Amram still hasn't returned. Noelle looks out the liv-ing room window, but she sees no sign of his car, no sign of anything besides her boys playing tetherball in the yard. David, meanwhile, has come back from the hardware store with a bucket of paint and a paint roller and two large bags of supplies. He's in his and Marilyn's old bedroom when Noelle knocks on the door. "Am I bothering you?"

"You're never bothering me, darling."

She steps softly inside. Her father's on the bed with his clothes on: a pair of cargo shorts and a khaki T-shirt, his tube socks pulled up to his knees, his running shoes tightly laced. He's holding open a book whose title she can't make out. "Were you taking a rest?"

"That's okay. I can rest later. I always like company, especially yours." His hair is disheveled, zigzagging across his scalp, as if it can't make up its mind which way to go. His nose is red, and there's a crumpled-up tissue on the bedside table.

She has brought him a bowl of ice cream, which she lays now at her feet. "Are you okay, Dad?"

"I guess."

Across the room sits a photo of her, and another of Clarissa on all fours, Leo perched on top of her, taken when they were just children. Her mother's dresser is unlatched; a pink camisole peeks out of the drawer. "I'm glad you came back."

"Did you doubt I would?"

She shrugs.

"One missing husband down, another missing husband to go?"

"So Mom told you."

He nods.

A nail file sits on her mother's nightstand. Beside it is a bottle of No-Poo. It's shampooless shampoo, from what Noelle understands, the idea being that regular shampoo leaches out your hair's essen-tial nutrients, though the one time she tried No-Poo, she found that in addition to leaching out essential nutrients, regular shampoo also leached out dirt.

"Are you worried?" her father asks.

"I'm always worried about Amram." But now, she admits, she's worried even more. She can hear the piano being played downstairs. "What are you reading, Dad?"

He holds the book up to her. "Civil War biography."

She didn't know he was interested in the Civil War. Or in biographies, either, for that matter. She's standing across the room from him, as if waiting to be invited further inside.

"Mom's always saying that women read fiction and men read biographies of Civil War heroes."

"Yet all those years you taught your students to read great literature."

"You're right." *Great Expectations. The Great Gatsby.* Great books with the word *great* in them. He should have named the course that. And not a Civil War general in the bunch. Or a president, either. Again he holds up the book for her to see. It's about Ulysses S. Grant. "Mom got it for me for Father's Day."

"Since when does Mom get you gifts for Father's Day?"

Since forever, he admits. When the children were small, she used to get him Father's Day presents on their behalf and he pretended the gifts had come from them. Over time, it became a habit.

She looks up at him, hesitates.

"What?"

"I didn't get you a Father's Day gift, Daddy. Not even a card."

"It's okay," he says. "Clarissa and Lily didn't get me anything, either. Everyone has other things on their mind."

And it occurs to Noelle that Father's Day was only three weeks ago. "Wait a second, Dad. Mom got you a gift just last month?"

"You're saying that's strange?"

"Don't you think?" She's looking out the window, where, below her, the bird feeder sways in the porch light.

"Whatever's happening between Mom and me, it's not the book's fault."

She looks up at him. For an instant, she thinks she sees tears in his eyes.

"And I'm learning something. There's value in that."

"You always liked to learn things, didn't you, Dad?"

"I still do."

The closet door is open across from him, the mirrors lined up so she can see her reflection, a row of them, one after the other like a chain of dolls.

"How about you?" he says. "Do you like to learn things?"

"Sure," she says. When she first came to Israel, she didn't even know the Hebrew alphabet; twelve years later, she's fluent. And the prayer liturgy, the kosher dietary laws, the dos and don'ts of Sabbath observance: they were all foreign to her once and now she's mastered them. Still, the details can elude her—she often relies on Amram to remind her what's what—and though she can sit for longer than she could as a girl, she prefers to watch a movie or talk to a friend than read. The Jews, she thinks, are the People of the Book, but in this regard, at least, she's not one of them. "Do you miss teaching?"

"Sometimes," he says. "Mostly I miss my students. The smart ones, at least, and the majority of them were smart. Occasionally I'd get a student who wasn't really interested in literature, and by the end of the semester something clicked."

"And you ended up changing their lives?"

"I wouldn't go so far as that. But, sure, you do your best to make a small impact." The truth is, there are only two things he doesn't miss about teaching. Grading is one. If he could have taught without having to grade exams, he'd have been happy to do it for half the salary. The second thing is the parents. Though that's really the first thing. The phone calls, the angling for good grades, all that anxiety about college. It was private school and it was Manhattan, so it came with the territory. Still, if it hadn't been for the parents, he suspects he'd still be teaching now.

"I wouldn't work if I didn't have to," Noelle says. "I don't know a lot of people who would."

"What would you do instead?"

"I'd raise my boys."

"And once they were raised?"

"I'd find something."

"Wouldn't you be bored?"

"Even if I was, it wouldn't be such a bad thing. Given the choice, I'd rather be bored than busy." She looks up at the photo across the room, the one of Leo on top of Clarissa. "It's funny, Amram's not a teacher, but sometimes I think he was born to be one. He certainly knows how to hold forth."

"And that bothers you?"

"Sometimes." Though it can be reassuring in a way. It's nice to be with someone who seems to know the answers, even if you resent being told what they are. "How did you end up becoming a teacher in the first place?" And she realizes, asking this, how little children know about their parents, how few questions they ask.

"Originally I was getting my PhD, but I never quite finished." He'd gone to Columbia for graduate school, only a few blocks from where the children were born. He's never been able to escape that neighborhood. He completed his coursework and took his comprehensives, but when it came time to write his dissertation he got stuck. It wasn't writer's block, exactly; it was more like inspiration block. He had a crisis of the spirit. He saw an advertisement for a high school teaching job. It was a replacement position for the year; an English teacher had gone on maternity leave. She gave birth, presumably, but she never came back, and one year became five years became forty. He fell into what he ended up doing, which, he suspects, is what happens to most people. At this point, he can't believe he was ever going to be a professor. He's always saying that his high school students were better, smarter, and more interesting than the students he would have taught at college. They were better, smarter, and more interesting, he often thinks, than he is himself.

Noelle steps tentatively toward him, as if she's waiting for him to offer her a seat, but there are no seats in the room, just the bed, with a clearing below where his feet extend. But it makes her uncomfortable, a grown woman sitting next to her father on his bed, so she simply stands across from him.

She hears a car move past the house, the sound of it reverberating, then drifting off. "I'm sorry about last night."

"What about it?"

"The food you and Mom made."

With a toss of his hand, he waves her off.

"I should have been more flexible."

"At least we were all there. It's what Mom wanted. To have the whole family together again."

"And you didn't?"

"Under the circumstances, I don't know." He's flipping through the book, and she recalls her parents, years ago, rebuking her for breaking the spines of her textbooks, for leaving them facedown on the desk and floor.

"I brought you some ice cream," she says. "Butter pecan. Your favorite."

"Darling."

"But it's all melted now. You'll have to drink it." She looks past him, at the photo of her on her mother's dresser. "Amram was fired," she says. "He lost his job."

"I'm sorry."

She is, too. She hears water running down the hall. Someone is getting ready to take a bath.

"Mom and I can help if you need money."

She always needs money. That's the given. But no, she tells him, she doesn't want his help. It's not that she's above asking for assistance. She has received money from her grandmother, certainly. But Gretchen is at a further remove, whereas to ask money from her parents would be to admit failure, and Amram, certainly, wouldn't countenance it. Still, she's grateful for the offer, happy to know that if it comes down to it she won't end up on the street.

Her father closes his eyes. His book is lying open on the bed, and she removes a tissue from the tissue box and places it as a bookmark between the pages. Staring up at her is a picture of Ulysses S. Grant, and for an instant she's back in high school, asked to recite the names of the presidents, but she can't do it, her mind's a sieve. Another humiliation revisits her, her math teacher, Ms. Rinehart, returning the exams in reverse order of the scores, and there Noelle was, sitting in the back of the classroom, her head lowered, her red hair tenting her face, as exam after exam was returned, each name lowering her score even further. How easy it is for her to remember such things. How quickly she turns on herself. "Do you want to rest?" she says. "I can turn out the lights."

He shakes his head. "I got all these supplies from the hardware store. Come," he says. "Let's start with the bathroom."

She follows him inside, where the mirror above the sink is halfway off its hinge. He takes a screwdriver and removes it completely and examines the back for missing screws. She thinks she hears a car coming up the driveway, but when she goes to the window she sees it's nothing, just some engine across the hedge, probably the neighbor's lawn mower.

Back in the bathroom, she finds her father leaning over the tub.

"False alarm?" he says.

She nods.

For several seconds there's silence.

"Thank you, Daddy."

"For what?"

"Thank you for not saying that Amram will be back soon."

He gives her a sorrowful look. "Count on me to be the voice of pessimism?"

She shakes her head. "Just the voice that understands there are things you can't know."

The mirror is leaning against the base of the sink, and she moves it to the wall to steady it. Then she approaches her father, who's bent over the tub, and gets down on her knees to help him.

8

It's noon in California when Thisbe reaches Wyeth, but he sounds as if he's still asleep. Calder is napping in the basement. Thisbe sits quietly beside him in the dark listening to his breath draw out.

"Did I wake you?"

Wyeth doesn't answer.

"It's noon, Wyeth. Time for lunch."

"I was up earlier, but I fell back asleep. It's good you called. I'm supposed to be studying for both of us."

Yet he's in bed at noon: a laggard on the job.

"Let me guess. You ordered in pizza." Wyeth is the cook in their relationship, but he finds it depressing to cook for himself, so when no one else is around he reverts to a college-kid existence: the half-emptied Styrofoam boxes, the takeout menus fanned across the floor.

"Chicago-style pizza," Wyeth says. "Deep dish." As if to reassure her he hasn't completely gone to pot.

"In my honor?" Coming east, Thisbe and Calder had a stopover at O'Hare and they spent a few hours wandering around Chicago. Now Wyeth is eating food that tracks where they've been. Proof that he's been thinking about her. Though she worries she hasn't been thinking about him.

It's hot in the basement; there's no cross-breeze. She removes her running shorts and leaves them in a heap on the floor. Sweat trickles along her arms and down the backs of her knees. Her pulse jangles in her forehead. "Wyeth," she says, "I haven't been able to tell them about you."

"That's okay."

"No, it isn't."

She met Wyeth last fall, her first semester of graduate school, though she likes to say she's known him for years. Wyeth is an old friend of Lily and Malcolm's. In an earlier life he was a political organizer; he spent several years registering voters down south. Thirty years late to the ball, is how he puts it: a nineties version of Goodman, Schwerner, and Chaney. But after a few years, the job wore on him. He found the weather in the South oppressive, and he didn't like making conversation with strangers, much less knocking on their front doors. He was, he discovered, one of those antisocial social people: he liked the idea of a party more than the party itself. And the idea of people more than actual people. "Except, of course, for you." That was why he became an anthropologist. Ultimately, he preferred Cro-Magnon man.

As a break from his job, Wyeth spent a summer in D.C., where, to supplement his income, he waited tables at Malcolm's restaurant. Late at night after the restaurant had closed he and Malcolm would hang out in the kitchen while the dishes were being cleaned, drinking beers and watching the World Cup on TV. Lily would join them when she got off from work and the three of them would ascend the stairs to the patio. Often they were still there at three in the morning; one time they fell asleep outside and were woken up the next day by Malcolm holding plates of eggs Benedict.

"Do I get paid overtime for sleeping here?" Wyeth asked.

"Absolutely," said Malcolm.

"Waiters have to report for duty in a few hours," Lily said.

"I'll be here for my noontime siesta."

And there he was, back at the restaurant in the afternoon, still there late at night after everyone else had left and it was just him, Malcolm, and Lily drinking beers on the patio. "What do you know?" Lily said to Malcolm. "We've made a new best friend."

One weekend, Leo and Thisbe came through town. Thisbe recalls the bar they went to, thinks she remembers Wyeth himself, though it's hard to know what she remembers and what she's been told so many times she simply believes she remembers it. But she takes solace in the fact that she met Wyeth, and in the fact that Leo was there, too. She has come to believe that Leo liked Wyeth, as if Leo's presence, and his liking Wyeth, were a kind of telescoped approval of what has happened now.

At the end of the summer, Wyeth returned to Alabama, and he stayed in only sporadic touch with Lily and Malcolm. But when they learned he was moving to Berkeley to study anthropology, Lily said to Thisbe, "You have to meet this old friend of mine." And to Wyeth she said, "You have to meet my sister-in-law."

Thisbe and Wyeth were on the lookout for each other, but they didn't need to be. It's a small department; their first semester, they were paired in seminar for oral reports and they took potshots at Clifford Geertz (reactionary) and Margaret Mead (even more reactionary). After class, they would drink lattes at a café near campus until it was time for Thisbe to pick up Calder from day care.

One time, she invited Wyeth along. She was testing him, she figured, though Calder was two at the time, willing to be held by whoever wished to hold him, and she wasn't even sure what the test was, what constituted passing and failure.

They went out for coffee after class one day, and later, strolling down Telegraph Avenue near her apartment, she invited Wyeth up.

"Look at you," he said. "You're raising your son smack dab across from People's Park. How's that for political indoctrination?"

"I'm raising him across from a fraternity," Thisbe said. "He gets woken up by hooting in the middle of the night. I tell him there are owls outside his window, but he's starting to know better."

There were photographs of Leo all over the apartment; you couldn't so much as walk a few paces without bumping into one.

"Shrine to the late husband?"

"I know," she said. "It's macabre."

"How long has it been?"

"Four months."

"Jesus," he said. "I'm so sorry."

"You didn't know?"

"I knew it was recent. I just . . ."

"It's okay."

For a second he just stood there staring at the photos.

"I'm sorry," she said. "I probably shouldn't have invited you up."

"No," he said. "I'm glad you did." He was wearing a gray T-shirt in the back of which was a small hole; she could see the movement of his shoulder blades as he walked through her apartment. His hair was the color of cork, and he had the beginnings of a beard, which was darker than that. His shoulders were expansive. All of him was; he filled up every room he entered. He was six foot three, so much larger than Leo. In bed with him for the first time, Thisbe was startled by how much of the mattress he took up; whichever way she rolled, she was pressed to him. She hadn't imagined she'd end up with someone who looked like Leo, though in the months after his death everyone reminded her of him. Yet that first time with Wyeth, she hadn't thought about Leo, and realizing this, she panicked.

That day in her apartment, seeing all those photos, Wyeth said, "What better way to dissuade potential suitors."

Yet he hadn't been dissuaded.

The next day, Thisbe called Lily. Lily was the worst person she could have called: she was Leo's sister. Yet Thisbe felt at the same time that Lily was the only person she could talk to; besides Malcolm, she was the one person in the world who knew both Leo and Wyeth.

"I went on a date," she said. She didn't even mention who the person was, but when Lily said, "Good for you!" she told her it was Wyeth.

"Does that make it better?" Thisbe said.

"Better, how?"

"That you and Malcolm know him? I figure I'm not cheating as much. I'm keeping it in the family."

"Cheating?" Lily said. "I *want* you to date."

"But it's only been four months."

"It's not as if you're getting remarried."

No, Thisbe thought, it certainly wasn't. But then one date became another became another, and because they were in graduate school and didn't need to date—their life *was* a date: they saw each other all the time—their relationship progressed without their even noticing it. That, at least, is what Thisbe tells herself. Lily knows she and Wyeth have been seeing each other, but Thisbe hasn't told her how serious it has become—hasn't mentioned, for instance, that Wyeth has asked her to move in with him in the fall. She's considering doing it, but she has asked Wyeth to wait until she gets back from this trip. With Leo's memorial coming up, Wyeth—her whole life—has been put on hold.

She's still sitting in the basement in her T-shirt and underwear while Calder remains asleep. She hangs up the phone, and now she sees Lily at the top of the stairs.

"Are you all right?"

"Why wouldn't I be?"

"A couple hours ago you were in tears. Not everyone starts to cry in the middle of a parlor game."

"What can I say? I'm extremely competitive."

"Somehow, I don't think that's what it was."

And it wasn't, of course, though Thisbe herself doesn't know what it was. A year later, it still happens; she'll be minding her affairs and she'll start to cry. There are wells of sadness within her that even she can't excavate.

"Let's take a drive," Lily says. "My parents will watch Calder."

Then they're in Lily's van, and they're driving the route Thisbe and Leo used to take, past Belvoir Terrace, the summer arts camp for girls. It's late afternoon, but Thisbe can still recall those nighttime drives, the serpentine twist of the pavement, the smell of the woods as the rain came through the open window, the leaves flapping like bats' wings.

They enter the Historic Village of Lenox, established in 1767, as they're reminded on every sign, though the history Thisbe recalls is a history of bad art, which continues, she discovers, unabated. The sidewalks are lined with metal sculpture—of donkeys, of elephants, of human figures playing the tuba and the trombone. They park on Church Street, across from Twigs, where there hangs in the window a child's T-shirt that reads I'M ONLY DOING THIS UNTIL MY BAND GETS SIGNED.

Up on Housatonic, they go into the bar where Thisbe used to work. Walking past the patrons watching the Red Sox on TV, she half expects to see the waitresses she knew. But they're all gone now, another generation of twenty-two-year-olds pouring beer and serving curly fries.

"Can you believe it?" Lily says. "It's four in the afternoon and everyone's already drunk."

A girl in a pink halter top has draped herself over the jukebox. She's fishing through her pockets for change. "This is where Leo and I met," Thisbe says.

"It's where everyone meets everyone," Lily says. "There's nowhere else to go in this godforsaken town."

They're sitting at the bar, where the drink specials are written on a chalkboard. Keno cards are lined up behind a set of salt shakers. Thisbe stares down at her forearms laid out on the table, the veins running through them, milky blue.

"How are you doing?" Lily asks.

"Okay, I guess."

"Will you make it through these next couple of days?"

"Do I have a choice?"

A woman threads her way through the crowd, holding a pitcher of beer above her head, her T-shirt riding up her stomach. A waitress delivers a platter of nachos, and a man shouts, "Waitress, taste my soup!" but there's no soup for the waitress to taste and she just stares at the man dumbly.

"We could play pool," Thisbe says. But now that she's suggested it she doesn't want to, and she stays seated at the bar, and Lily does, too.

From across the room, it appears as if someone is waving at Thisbe, but then a girl in tight jeans and a pink cutoff T-shirt emerges from behind her and waves back. A Doors song is playing on the jukebox, and Thisbe has a vague, unsettling feeling from long ago, the taste of beer and a first rock concert, everyone pawing each other. She has never been comfortable in bars. Beneath the surface lie the seeds of repressed violence; she's always waiting for a fight to break out.

She flips through the menu. She used to take her customers' orders and, without a pad or pencil, commit them to memory. Nine or ten customers, food and drink: she never made a mistake. It was her waitress's legerdemain, the equivalent of balancing a ball on her nose, and she did in fact feel like a trained sea lion. But it earned her better tips and she needed the money. She was storing up cash for the winter, when she would drive to Middletown to visit Leo.

Above the bar, the chalkboard reads EVERYTHING'S BETTER WITH GUINNESS. Thisbe's holding a Guinness herself, and her fingers make stripes on the frosted beer mug. She taps her hand against the glass, the beat relentless, like Morse code. A peanut machine stands in the corner, and next to it a Chiclets machine. A hard-to-pinpoint sadness sideswipes her. She looks away, blinking, feeling as if she's about to cry. On TV, a Red Sox player does something acrobatic in the field, and the crowd emits a collective roar.

"You should eat something," Lily says. "Have a hamburger."

Thisbe shakes her head.

"Potato skins?"

"I'm not hungry." And she's not, though she didn't eat lunch and earlier she was famished.

Finally, she orders a turkey wrap, which she picks at like a rodent before leaving it uneaten at the side of her plate.

"I see you've kept your fast metabolism."

"It's more like I stopped eating."

"When?"

She shrugs. She's always been slender, but this past year she's hardly eaten at all.

Pool is being played behind them, the balls clanking against each other like nunchucks. A kid in a backwards baseball cap drums his pool cue against his sneaker and a plume of chalk floats through the air. A waitress passes them holding a tray of discarded chicken wings, a gob of blue cheese dripping off it.

Thisbe goes into the bathroom, where she stands at the sink letting the water wash over her. A sign reads EMPLOYEES MUST WASH THEIR HANDS BEFORE RETURNING TO WORK, but someone has crossed out the *h* in *hands* and changed the *d* to a *u*.

"Come on," she tells Lily. "Let's get out of here."

Outside, it has started to rain again. She has an umbrella in the car and she thinks to go get it, but Lily is headed in the other direction.

On Main Street, they pass the public library and the wine store. Wine and art galleries and hideous puns, Thisbe thinks: that's what Lenox is.

And now, sure enough, they walk past Tanglewool, where dresses hang in the window. A dismembered mannequin lies in the gutter. "Talk about throwing out the baby with the bathwater," Lily says.

In front of Town Hall, they're flanked on either side by the police station and the fire station. "Should we take a drive?"

"Where to?" Thisbe says.

"We can go to Stockbridge and see the Norman Rockwell Museum. We can continue on to Great Barrington." Across the street, they can make out Loeb's market and the health-food store.

"Actually, a museum doesn't sound so bad. It's better than going to Laos to sleep under mosquito nets."

"Why?" Lily says. "Is that what you're planning to do?"

"I'm an anthropologist, so I have to do fieldwork. Knowing me, I'll end up with a case of dengue fever."

"I'd make a terrible anthropologist," Lily says. "I'm the world's worst hypochondriac."

"You can't think about those things." Though Thisbe does, in fact, think about them. She's putting on a tough-guy act. It's as if now that Leo has gone it has devolved upon her to be the reckless one. Merely getting a PhD could be considered reckless, the academic job market being what it is. She suspects Marilyn and David would have preferred she go to law school. Her own parents probably would have preferred law school, too. Everyone, she thinks, prefers law school, except for the people who actually go to law school; anyway, that was never in the cards. She'd been preparing to go to graduate school when Leo died, so she feels as if she's following their plan, carrying out their joint venture.

"Would Wyeth go too?" Lily asks.

"Where?"

"To Laos. To get dengue fever."

"Are you kidding me? He'd be leading the brigade."

"Really? I don't remember him being a daredevil."

"No more so than any other guy." So often it's that way, Thisbe thinks, the man with his fantasies, his pleasing delusions, the woman left to draw the reins. She can see it even now with Wyeth, so different from Leo but who, like Leo, relies on her as ballast. *No, we can't go to Belize for the weekend. It's expensive and we need injections and I have a three-year-old to take care of.* Is that, she wonders, why women were created? To allow men to say "I would have done it if only she'd let me"?

They head to Lilac Park, where they walk down the hill past the benches and the gazebo. The rain has stopped, and a girl of about thirteen is sitting on the grass playing the flute. At the bottom of the hill is a thicket of trees, and as they wander past the brush Thisbe feels as if she's on a camping trip, taken blindfolded on a Girl Scout treasure hunt. There are no sounds, just the rhythmic thumping of their shoes making their soft imprint in the dirt; no sights either, save for the occasional fugitive headlight illuminating them, then casting them back into shadows.

Lily makes a growling noise.

"Very funny."

"I guess I'm not much of a mimic."

That had been Leo's specialty. He could make the sound of a squeegee running up and down a window so that if you closed your eyes you thought he *was* a squeegee. And a vacuum cleaner and a garbage disposal and a popcorn maker and a blender. He did the world's best cow; you let him loose in a pasture, and he would set off a chorus of lowing. "Me and my useless talents," he said.

But they hadn't been useless. Senior year at Bowdoin, she'd had an alarm clock that woke you to the sound of your choice—waves, wind, brook, hummingbird—and when the alarm clock broke, catapulted across the bedroom one night, victim of overexuberant sex, Leo himself took on the role of alarm clock, waking up early to make hummingbird sounds for her. He would even do them over the phone, calling her from his offices at the *Wesleyan Argus*, where he'd been up all night putting the newspaper to bed. On weekends he would come in person, taking the roads through New Hampshire and Maine; sometimes he'd show up on weeknights too, having prevailed upon a fellow editor to fill in for him. Thisbe saw his body when it came home from Iraq; she pulled back the sheet and looked at him. He had been flown to D.C., and afterward, walking on the Mall, the Washington Monument suspended in the distance, she felt so dizzy she had to sit down. Why, she wondered, had she insisted on seeing the body? She didn't have to be the one to identify him. But if she hadn't done it, she'd have always wondered whether it had been a mistake, a different journalist killed, and perhaps this was another trick of his, a final act of ventriloquism by the grand ventriloquist, and maybe he would still come back to her.

Nights in bed with Wyeth, falling into the fleshy slab of him, she can forget any of this ever happened. The whole Frankel family: they're nothing but a mirage. But yesterday, when she stopped in town so Calder could pee, when she picked up orange juice at a convenience store, she thought she recognized someone, and there they were again, the stares, the whispers. *It's the Frankel boy's wife. Over on Reservoir Road? The journalist?* All it takes is putting her on a plane and depositing her in Massachusetts to make her feel that this country is an enormous slide propelling her along its slippery belly. She's here once more—will she ever get away?—and of course it's Leo she thinks about, and his parents, his sisters, everyone he knew.

Now, treading with Lily on their makeshift path behind the park, doing the kinds of things she and Leo used to do, she's thrown back to the life she left. Leo was a walking, talking bushwhacker. "They had to harness him," Lily says. "My parents will deny it, but they led him around on a leash one summer."

She thinks of the noises Leo used to make—his squeegee, his showerhead, his toilet flush, his popcorn maker—recalls his soothing, whirring sounds as she fell asleep, her own private white-noise machine, so that in the weeks after his death she didn't know how she would ever fall asleep again without his musical accompaniment.

Here in the Berkshires, land of bears, instructions were tacked to the front of the house reminding the renters how to secure the tops of garbage bins. Yet there had been a black bear not thirty feet away late one night outside the house. It was an April weekend and the tourists hadn't arrived yet, so Thisbe and Leo had the town to themselves. They were lying in the hammock strung like a pulley from the porch, half naked in the growing cold, a blanket tossed over them. Thisbe was in Leo's Wesleyan sweatshirt; the marijuana smoke was warming them. An open jug of apple cider stood on the porch, and next to it sat a box of glazed doughnuts. Thisbe and Leo were swaying in the hammock, and the bear was looking at them directly, so still it was as if he'd already been mounted and stuffed.

Thisbe laughed. Marijuana did that to you. It made you giddy: a laughter slut. She remembered what she'd been told. If you left a bear alone he'd leave you alone, but if you scared him he'd come after you.

"Hey, Smokey!" Leo called out. "Want a toke?"

"Leo!"

"We'll give that bear the munchies!"

You didn't need to give a bear the munchies. They were born that way; they came preprogrammed. Thisbe got out of the hammock and trundled inside, and Leo reluctantly followed her.

But they forgot the doughnuts and the jug of apple cider, and the next morning everything was gone, the cider container pulverized, pieces of it drifting in juice. All that was left was the flap of the doughnut box, which skittered across the porch like a giant bug.

"I guess bears like doughnuts," Leo said. "Big surprise. He's probably keeled over in the woods, victim of a doughnut-induced heart attack."

"We better be careful," Thisbe said. "If we eat out here again, we're liable to become food ourselves."

"You think that's why that bear showed up?"

Oh, Leo. She was menstruating, and Leo had this idea that bears could smell when a girl had her period. You would have thought he was twelve. They were twenty-one at the time, which, looking back, doesn't seem much older. She's thirty-three now, and she wonders whether in another twelve years she'll regard the person she is today with the same resigned disbelief, whether she'll always be disowning earlier versions of herself. It's surprising that Leo didn't die sooner, mauled by a bear with a bong in his paw, made to pay for his jubilance and high spirits. Not for the first time, she thinks it would have been easier if he'd died long ago, before she'd ever met him.

It's raining harder now. Lily holds her jacket like a tarp above their heads, but they continue to get wet, plunged over and again into the water as they emerge from beneath the trees into exposed air.

They head down Sunset and reach the nursing home, where, Thisbe recalls, she walked one time with Leo and Gretchen. "That's where you're going to put me," Gretchen said. "The old-age home."

"Are you kidding me, Grandma?" Leo said. "That's where *you're* going to put *me*."

They retrace their steps up the hill and back to town, past Bistro Zinc and Firefly, until they reach Lily's van, on the corner of Franklin, sitting alone in the rain, looking like a figure in a diorama.

Now, as promised, Lily is driving them toward Stockbridge and

Great Barrington. They pass Monument Mountain Regional High School, where a huge American flag has been emblazoned onto the grass. Across from it is Monument Mountain itself.

"How's Wyeth?" Lily asks.

"He's good," says Thisbe.

Lily gives her a look. "Is that all you're going to say?"

"What more should I say? Wyeth is just like me. He was born to be a grad student. We sit in the library all day reading these obscure journals. I never realized we were such dorks."

"I meant how are you and Wyeth together?"

"Oh," Thisbe says. "We're fine."

"That's a short answer."

"Would you like a longer one?"

"I wouldn't mind."

They're stopped at a red light near the bowling lanes and miniature golf. Berkshire Bike and Board is up ahead. "Wyeth wants me to move in with him."

Lily's quiet for a moment. "I didn't realize that was in the cards."

"How could you have? I didn't tell you."

"I mean, I knew you two were together, of course. I just thought . . ."

"What?"

"That it was a rebound relationship."

That, Thisbe thinks, is what everyone assumes, and though she understands why, it offends her in a way. It's as if people think she's acting out, the grieving widow throwing herself at whoever comes her way, when she didn't do that, not with Wyeth or anyone else. She's surprised how quickly things have progressed with Wyeth, but then everything in her life has been a surprise (she certainly didn't expect to marry her college boyfriend), so why should this be any different? It *is* a rebound relationship, she wants to say, but only in the sense that her life is a rebound life.

"So it's serious?"

Thisbe hates that phrase. It makes it seem like a disease. But yes, she tells Lily, it's serious.

"Are you going to move in with him?"

"I don't know," she says. "I can't even think about it till I get through this trip."

From behind the wheel Lily nods.

"Wyeth's not putting any pressure on me."

"That doesn't surprise me," Lily says. "Malcolm and I used to call him Waveless Wyeth. He was as calm as the sea."

"He just doesn't get jealous."

"That's a good quality," Lily says. "Though who is there for him to be jealous of, anyway? Leo's dead."

"There's his memory," Thisbe says. "And there are you, Clarissa, and Noelle. Not to mention your parents. I don't know what it is about being in California, but when I'm there and you're here it's easy to forget Leo and I'm just living my life. But I'm not just living my life, and as soon as I fly out here I'm back to where I was." She hesitates.

"What?"

"Do you really want to hear this?"

"I do," Lily says. "I don't like secrets. At least not ones that are kept from me. I'm tough, besides." She raps her fist against her chin. She's steering them now across a small bridge and onto Main Street in Great Barrington.

"Calder was only two when Leo died, and those last few months, when Leo was in Iraq, he didn't see him much."

"You're saying he doesn't remember him?"

"He does," Thisbe says, "but only because I've been such a pain about it." Sometimes she wonders what the point of it all is. She has spent so much time showing Calder photos of Leo, telling him stories about his father, she's half forgotten he was two when Leo died. She was careful to prepare Calder for Wyeth, introducing them slowly to each other and reassuring him that Wyeth would never replace his father. As if that was what concerned him. The fact is, Calder *wants* to replace his father. He's embarrassed by Leo's absence: all his friends have fathers, and he wants one, too. Though he can also, in the blunt way of three-year-olds, embarrass people with his forthrightness. More than once, he's been asked by some unknowing soul where his father is, to which he has responded, cheerfully, "He's dead!"

"On Father's Day," Thisbe tells Lily, "I went out with Calder and Wyeth for brunch. We weren't there to celebrate anything. We just didn't have any food at home. But everyone in the restaurant was celebrating Father's Day, and Calder starts saying Wyeth is his father, and when I try to explain the truth to him he won't listen to me. He keeps on saying Wyeth is his father, shouting it through mouthfuls of French toast, and finally I can't listen to it any longer and I run out. Waveless Wyeth, you call him? Well, you're right. Because Wyeth just sat there patiently and cleaned Calder up and he didn't care that everyone in the restaurant was staring at him. I don't blame Calder. Leo was his father, but he'll never know him."

They turn onto Railroad Street, and now, suddenly, Lily stops the car. She opens the door and steps out onto the sidewalk.

"Where are you going?"

"I just need to take a few figurative steps back. A few literal ones, actually."

"I know," Thisbe says. "It's a lot to digest."

Lily stands on the sidewalk for several seconds staring at a clothing shop across the street. Then she gets back into the car and refastens her seat belt. "Thisbe, I'm your sister-in-law. And Wyeth is my friend. If it's going to be someone, I'm thrilled that it's him. You're right, it's a lot to digest."

"But you're digesting?"

Lily gulps, as if to show that she is.

"And to think this is the easy part."

"You're worried about telling the rest of the family?"

"Wouldn't you be?"

"I guess I would."

They've parked the car, and now they're walking down Railroad Street, past 20 Railroad and Club Helsinki. "You haven't told anyone," Thisbe says, "have you?"

Lily shakes her head. "Nobody knows except for me and Malcolm."

"I was planning to tell your parents on this trip."

"And now you're not?"

"I keep thinking maybe I can hold off a little longer. If I told them in a year . . ."

"Then it would be more respectable?"

"It might be."

"There's nothing unrespectable about it now."

"Anyway, I can't tell them in a year because Wyeth and I might move in together. He'll be on the phone machine. Even if he isn't, they'll find out anyway. I'm surprised they haven't already found out."

"From Calder?"

Thisbe nods. "He's three years old, Lily. It's not fair to ask a child to keep adult secrets."

"It will be good practice for when he's older."

"I'd rather keep him out of practice."

Some of the stores look familiar to Thisbe, but others are gone now. The Deli has closed, which had, she still believes, the best sandwiches in the world. Leo would always get the Zonker Harris, and she would always get the Arlo. The summer she met Leo she saw Arlo Guthrie play at Club Helsinki. The show was okay, but she's never been much of an Arlo Guthrie fan. She liked the sandwich better. In the end, she preferred to eat Arlo than to listen to him.

Now, in the van, Lily drives in silence, and when they reach Stockbridge they come to a stop in front of the Norman Rockwell Museum. "Should we go in?"

Thisbe laughs. "It's after five, Lily. It's probably not even open now."

"There's only one way to find out."

But they just sit there staring at the museum, which looms above them in the mist. Thisbe reaches into a bag of Veggie Booty; Lily takes a handful, too. It tastes like Styrofoam, but Thisbe keeps eating it; she realizes now how hungry she's been. It's what she and Calder subsisted on during their drive from the airport. Veggie Booty and grapes. Though she sneaked a cookie when Calder wasn't watching. *Do as I say* is her motto, *not as I do.*

"Years ago," Lily says, "Leo and his friends used to steal into that museum."

"Why doesn't that surprise me?"

"They weren't very discriminating," Lily says. "From ages ten to seventeen, it was one big experiment in breaking and entering."

And it hadn't ended at seventeen, Thisbe thinks. One night, she and Leo hid in the Bowdoin library because you weren't supposed to graduate from college without having had sex in the stacks. Could it possibly have been her idea? She's afraid it was, though Leo, always happy to commit some infraction, didn't require much coaxing. She's been in libraries where the stacks are movable; if you're not careful, you'll wind up crushed. Which would have been their just deserts, flattened like sheet metal for their transgression, for their juvenile idea of what passed for fun. Once they were settled in the stacks, they realized they were stuck for the night, and so they spent their time reading, rising every few minutes to jump up and down between the light sensors so they wouldn't be left in the dark. Leo was on a Studs Terkel kick; Thisbe was in the middle of Sara Sulieri's *Meatless Days*, most of which she read lying on the floor, her head thrown back on Leo's lap. Finally, she fell asleep with the book splayed across her stomach. Leo must have fallen asleep, too, because they were woken the next morning by the sound of the janitor, his key chain clanking against his belt. They raced downstairs and outside, where the sun was beginning to ascend above Brunswick. When Thisbe got back to her dorm, she realized that her book was still in her coat pocket, realized, too, that she and Leo had stayed up all night and forgotten to have sex. It almost redeemed them.

Now, back in Lenox, they stop on Main Street to get gas. Thisbe hands Lily her credit card, but Lily refuses it. "I'm treating," she says. "It's my car, and I'm the driver."

"But you're driving *me*."

"Please, Thisbe. You're a graduate student."

"And what are you? A public-interest lawyer?"

"Believe me, I make more money than you."

"Not by much."

"Anyway, you flew out here. I didn't have to pay for a ticket."

Reluctantly, Thisbe agrees. She waits in the passenger seat while the gas is being pumped, and now Lily has returned and is saying, "There, we're replenished."

"You didn't have to do that," Thisbe says. "I could have paid. I'm doing fine."

"Are you? My parents tell me they try to send you checks, but you refuse to cash them. I hope your parents are helping you out."

"Not when I can avoid it."

"Why?"

"Because I don't want them to help me."

"You might want to rethink your position on that. From what I understand, it's hard enough to live on a graduate-student stipend even when you're not supporting a child. I don't imagine Wyeth has much money, either."

"Even if he did, I wouldn't let him help."

"Why not?"

"Lily, come on."

"You could ask Gretchen for money."

"I'd never do that."

"She'd probably help you unsolicited. In fact, she prefers unsolicited. She finds solicitation distasteful."

"Gretchen, she's . . ."

"What?"

"It's a long story."

"I have time."

Thisbe hesitates. The Sugar Granny, Leo called Gretchen. Like the other siblings, he received a gift from her when he turned twenty-five. "Six figures," he told Thisbe at the time. She didn't think she could ask him to be more specific, but even at the low end, six figures seemed like a staggering sum. Yet she learned that the money could be spent quickly, especially in New York, where she and Leo had moved. Leo was freelancing, stringing for newspapers, not making enough money to pay the rent. She was making even less; she was waitressing at a French restaurant in Tribeca, but her hours were erratic, the tips just good enough to allow her to pretend she was supporting herself. New York, she discovered, was filled with young people like her, engaged in financial dissembling. Her parents sent her an occasional check. She racked up credit card debt. A few years removed from college, she seemed to believe she was still there. She waitressed nights, so her days were free. She took courses in poetry and conversational Italian; she went back to the piano, which she hadn't played since she was a girl; she signed up for an Indian cooking class. She and Leo were living on the seamy outskirts of the Lower East Side in a fifth-floor walkup that was rent-stabilized, but on her nights off they ate out at expensive restaurants, invited by friends whose idea of expensive was different from theirs. Her friends would ask her what she was doing in New York, and she would answer with self-mockery and exaggerated drama that she was finding herself. Other times she gave up all pretense and simply said, "I'm consuming." As if by making fun of how she lived she would earn a pass for doing so.

She took on extra hours at the restaurant, and when that wasn't enough, she began to let Leo pay for her. She didn't like doing this—it went against her sensibilities—but he insisted he could afford it. He reminded her of Gretchen's gift; there was, he implied, the promise of more. Nothing explicit, certainly, but he was always saying how wealthy Gretchen was. Obscenely wealthy, was how he put it. He seemed to think Gretchen herself was obscene, but that didn't stop him from cashing her checks. He believed all would work out well, which struck Thisbe as the bearing of the rich. It certainly wasn't how she saw things, having grown up with a social worker mother and an economics professor father—and a Marxist economics professor at that, who, perhaps because of his Marxism, or because he was impolitic, never managed to get tenure.

Yet Thisbe ignored all this. She was drawn to the fantasy of an alternate life in New York. She would waitress twenty hours a week and spend the rest of her time conjugating Italian verbs and practicing her piano scales, perfecting her tikka masala and Rogan Josh.

Gretchen's gift must have been in the low six figures, because soon the money had run out. At a restaurant one day, Thisbe realized she didn't have enough money to pay for lunch. The manager made her hand over her driver's license and coat while she went out to find an ATM. It was twenty degrees outside, and she'd been forced to leave her parka as collateral! When she told Leo what happened, he said, "It's lucky they didn't make you leave your shoes!" He appeared to think the story was funny, but she found it a humiliation.

After that, she began to carry forty dollars in a separate fold of her wallet, reserved for just such an emergency. When Leo was a boy, back when New York was more perilous, land of graffiti and crack deals and extinguished streetlights, his parents had made him do the same thing. *Mugger money*, he called it. Though it wasn't being mugged Thisbe was afraid of. She was alone in the world, alone financially. She and

Leo were married now, but they were still poor. The only reason they had health insurance was that their parents paid for it, and counting on her new grandmother-in-law—was there even such a term?—was folly.

So she quit waitressing, abandoned piano lessons, Italian, the things she loved, and took a job with a political nonprofit. The pay was poor, but at least she had a salary. And when that salary didn't seem like enough, she started to work for an advertising firm. Daughter of the Marxist economics professor, resident of Santa Cruz, she found herself at twenty-nine working on Madison Avenue; it was perhaps the single job she was least suited for. But in some ways that was the point. Working in advertising proved she was unsentimental; it meant she had grown up.

Yet she hated advertising even more than she'd expected to. She was paid to convince people they needed things they didn't; her job was to make them feel bad about themselves. Placed on a beer campaign—she thanked God she didn't have to shill for the cigarette companies—she did her work dutifully, but she went home feeling sullied and, in what she later realized was subconscious penance, she stopped drinking beer, first from the company whose campaign she worked on and then from all beer companies. She longed for the courses she'd taken when she first got to New York, and, even more, for college, when all she did was take courses. She'd studied anthropology at Bowdoin, and on the subway to work she carried in her tote bag the recent catalogs from the university presses, which she would spread across her desk during lunch. Fifty-five dollars for the latest volume of anthropological theory! But she could afford it now; she had a real job. So she ordered the book, thinking of it as a reward to herself. Holed up in her office while her coworkers went out to lunch, she would lift her sandwich to her mouth, elbows pressed against the pages of her book, mayonnaise dripping on Hélène Cixous.

In the previous year, Leo had published articles in *GQ* and *Esquire*; he'd traveled to Somalia and written about it for the *Times* magazine. He'd recently been hired as a reporter for *Newsday*. He had a salary now; their parents were no longer paying for their health insurance. Maybe, Thisbe thought, she could consider graduate school. She could go to Columbia or NYU, perhaps even to Yale; New Haven was only an hour and a half away.

A month before the war started, a man came to their apartment building selling life insurance. When Thisbe saw him from the window, she thought, *Oh, please.* The only thing people sold door to door any longer was drugs, certainly on their block off Grand Street, where jittery teenagers slunk from alley to alley and dark cars stopped to disgorge their passengers, only to scoop them back up a few minutes later. When Thisbe and Leo moved in, the realtor had described their block as in transition, but now that seemed at best like wishful thinking, at worst like an outright lie. So when the life insurance salesman rang their bell, she refused to let him in.

But he left some literature under their door, and afterward she leafed through it. The war would start soon; it had been ordained, she believed, from the moment the Supreme Court gave the presidency to Bush. He would find a way to get there, and Leo would find a way to get there with him. If it hadn't been Iraq, it would have been Afghanistan, or the West Bank, or Sudan, or Zimbabwe. Thisbe would array these locations across her mental atlas, imagining Leo flying there, because he *would* fly there, because there would always be people like Leo, drawn to danger like a moth to light.

One evening, she dropped the life insurance brochure onto his lap. Instantly, he understood what she was thinking. "I won't do anything stupid."

She didn't respond.

"Are you saying you doubt me?"

"Of course not."

"If you don't want me to go, I won't go."

But she couldn't ask him to do that.

She continues to believe that, if she'd insisted, he wouldn't have gone. But it would have leached the spirit from him. Growing up, he couldn't simply smoke pot like any reasonable American teenager. He had to study it, grow it, turn it into art. He took up badminton in high school, and before long he was captain of his school team. At college he majored in philosophy, and for a time all he could talk about was Wittgenstein and Heidegger. And when he tired of philosophy,

when he tired in general of going to class and started to spend his
nights at the *Wesleyan Argus*, where he'd been named editor-in-chief,
he brought the same monomaniacal discipline to bear on the writing
and editing of what he was determined to make the best college newspaper in the United States. Later, when he flew off to some battle-
field, Thisbe said, "How about you do something a little easier on the
nerves?"

"You mean *your* nerves?"

She laughed, but he was right. If he needed mayhem, she would
have preferred it if he wrote for the police blotter. But he wasn't interested in the police blotter. And, truth be told, neither was she. They
talked about retiring early and traveling around the world; they would
die without a home, two octogenarian backpackers falling from a cliff
in the Himalayas.

After Leo was killed, when Thisbe recalled his words, *If you don't
want me to go, I won't go*, it wasn't her failure to say *Don't go* that assailed
her; it was, rather, that she'd doubted him. She feared Leo would die,
and so he'd gone ahead and done it.

Other people—Marilyn comes to mind—wanted revenge. If there
was a chance of success, she'd have quit her job and spent the rest of
her life prosecuting Bush for war crimes. But Thisbe didn't want a
penny out of what had happened to Leo; it would have compromised
her grieving. If she had taken out a life insurance policy, she'd have
refused to cash it in.

A few weeks after Leo died, living alone in their old apartment,
she agreed to go to lunch with Gretchen at an expensive restaurant
on the Upper East Side. She didn't know Gretchen well and, frankly,
Gretchen scared her. There was her money, of course. And there
was her temper, which was a thing of lore among the Frankels, how
Gretchen, caneless, alert, could simply raise her voice and everyone
would fall into line. Over prime rib and a whiskey sour, Gretchen laid
out her coterie of powerful admirers, the slights and indignities she'd
been forced to endure. The previous week, she'd shared an elevator
ride with Caroline Kennedy, and though Gretchen had met her more
than once, Kennedy ignored her. "She was talking on her cell phone,"
Gretchen said, "and she didn't even acknowledge I was there." Cell

phones led to rudeness, Gretchen believed. On this Thisbe didn't disagree.

"How are you doing?" Gretchen asked.

"I'm okay, I guess."

"It must be hard."

Thisbe nodded.

Gretchen was silent, and in that silence Thisbe realized it must be hard for Gretchen too, that when Thisbe lost a husband Gretchen lost a grandson. Gretchen had been at Leo's funeral, but Thisbe couldn't remember having seen her there, could recall nothing from that day besides the dark casket draped on the podium, the thrum of processioners, their heads lowered, as she sat beside Leo's sisters, unable to quiet the relentless beating of her heart. "How are *you* doing, Gretchen?"

Gretchen stared down at her whiskey sour. She'd grown up before people spoke about their feelings, and she didn't feel comfortable doing so. She glanced at Thisbe, then looked away.

Although none of the other diners were as old as Gretchen, everyone was of a certain age and means, lingering over their snapper and Dover sole, gesturing to the busboy with the same clipped impatience Gretchen displayed when her water glass had been drained, bearing an air of entitlement that Thisbe knew she could never possess even if she wanted to. It was a seafood restaurant, and on the wall across from her a swordfish was mounted. She had eaten at expensive restaurants before, certainly during her first couple of years in New York, but those had been noisy downtown establishments, and Gretchen preferred restaurants like this one, where stockinged women wore pins clipped to their breasts and the men had on jackets and neckties.

"How was your food?" Gretchen asked.

"It was delicious," Thisbe said. "Thank you for inviting me." She felt awkward saying this, as if she were being forced to engage in politesse. But it was true. She was happy to be here, happy to be with Gretchen because she was Leo's grandmother, the way that being with anyone who knew Leo helped dull the pain even as it made it sharper.

"You're a widow now," Gretchen said.

Later, it occurred to Thisbe that this was something she and Gretchen shared: Gretchen was a widow three times over. But at the time she was startled by the savage, icy precision of the word. She'd never heard herself described this way before, and sitting across from Gretchen, whose hair, white as coconut, was up in a beehive, looking as always as if she'd just come from the beautician, her dark silk pants suit without a wrinkle, the scarf around her neck knotted just so, Thisbe stared into her tiramisu and started to cry. She was thirty-two years old; most of her friends weren't even married yet, and she was already a widow. She was on the Upper East Side, a neighborhood that felt alien to her, in a restaurant that felt even more alien, where everyone was dressed up for lunch, and she'd made the mistake of wearing blue jeans; she'd half expected to be turned back at the door, if not by the maître d', then by Gretchen herself. She felt ugly, her blond hair pasted to her forehead; snot was coming out of her nose, she was crying and crying, blubbering into her dessert.

"I want to give you some money," Gretchen said.

"Oh, Gretchen, I can't let you do that."

From her pocketbook, Gretchen produced an envelope with her name embossed on it. "You're alone," she said. "You have a baby to take care of."

"Gretchen, please."

Gretchen reached across the table and handed her the envelope.

"What about the girls?"

"What girls?"

"Clarissa, Lily, and Noelle. Are you giving them money, too?" How, Thisbe wondered, could she accept money from Gretchen when they weren't related by blood, when, blood aside, their connection felt flimsy. She had been married to Leo for only five years, and during that time they'd rarely seen Gretchen.

"The girls will be fine," Gretchen said. "You're the one who needs my help."

"So the money would be for Calder?"

"It's not for me to decide."

She would lose this battle, Thisbe understood, the way everyone lost to Gretchen. No matter what Gretchen said, the money was intended for Calder. If Thisbe hadn't been the mother of Leo's son, Gretchen probably wouldn't have even taken her out to lunch.

She has no memory of what she did next, of anything, really, from the moment she left the restaurant until she got home. She convinced herself she had refused the money, but when she awoke the next morning the envelope was still in her coat pocket, in the envelope with Gretchen's name embossed on it.

Two hundred thousand dollars! Standing in the kitchen, holding the check with both hands as if the very number made it too heavy to lift, she began to cry. All her life, she had remained ignorant of money. It was a combination of laziness and futility at math, along with the idea, passed on tacitly by her parents, that excessive focus on money was deserving of contempt, that if you knew too much about money you knew too little about everything else. Leo had been in charge of their finances, and when he died she panicked. She bought a book about money management and enrolled in a one-day seminar on financial planning, which taught her just enough to make her realize how little she knew.

Was it even possible to cash a $200,000 check? If she deposited it, she'd be regarded as a fraud. She'd felt fraudulent enough eating at that restaurant with Gretchen, where the bill had come to $150.

A month later, when she got to Berkeley, the check was still in her wallet. If she waited long enough, it would be void. How long? Ninety days? A hundred and eighty days? The only thing that made her deposit it was that Gretchen would realize she hadn't done so and she couldn't bear to face her.

There are college savings plans now, and educational IRAs, but she hasn't invested in those. She could put the money in U.S. Treasury Bonds or C.D.s, tying it up to get a better interest rate, but she hasn't done that either. She simply deposited the money into the same checking account into which her monthly graduate stipend gets deposited, and then, not wanting to mix the two up, she opened a second account, just for the money Gretchen gave her. "I haven't told anyone about this," she says to Lily.

"Not even Wyeth?"

She shakes her head. She certainly hasn't told Marilyn and David, convinced that they will feel as she does, that the money isn't rightfully hers. She hasn't even told her own parents. She has two hundred thousand dollars plus interest collecting at the headquarters of Wells Fargo and her parents are helping pay for Calder's preschool! They're sending her additional checks whenever they can find an excuse—her birthday, Calder's birthday, Christmas, Mother's Day—trying to make it seem as if it's not outright charity. She feels terrible about this, and she keeps a careful tally of the money, promising herself she'll pay them back. "I haven't benefited from it," she tells Lily. "Not even a penny."

"Then you're crazier than I thought."

"Why?"

"You're a starving graduate student, Thisbe. I should have bought you more than a tank of gas. I should have paid for your therapist."

"Who are you to talk? You don't take money from Gretchen either."

"But if I were a graduate student—"

"Oh, stop it with the graduate student, already! It's insulting!"

"And if I were a widow with a three-year-old to take care of, I wouldn't have so much pride."

"Is that what you think this is? Pride?"

"You don't?"

"You're her granddaughter, Lily."

"And you're—"

"I lived in the same city as her for years and I hardly ever saw her. I'm just some girl who married into the family."

"You're the mother of her great-grandson, is what you are."

"Who, a year later, is shacked up with another guy."

"Ah," Lily says. "So that's the issue. Wyeth."

"It's one of them. I don't want the privilege of receiving Gretchen's gift. Or the burden of it, either. I'm alone now, and I want to do things on my own. You of all people should understand that."

"And so you'll deprive Calder in order to make your point?"

"Calder will manage."

"How?"

"The same way everyone else manages who doesn't have two hundred thousand dollars in his name. Which is to say the rest of the world."

"So what are you going to do with the money? Just let it sit there?"

"It's what I've been doing until now."

"Fine," Lily says. "I can see your mind is made up."

They stop in to O'Brien's to pick up some beers, and now, as they move silently around the bend, the Community Center comes into view, where Leo's memorial will be held tomorrow. It's six in the evening, and two women in their forties emerge from the center holding yoga mats. Above the entrance to the center is an American flag. "God bless America," Lily says glumly. "Don't forget to salute."

In back, beyond the long porch that spans the width of the building, sits a playground. Everything is made of plastic, the jungle gym and the slide curling back on themselves like those roller-coaster straws Thisbe used to drink from as a girl. The ground is lined with wood chips, and she spreads out her jacket and sits down. Lily subsides next to her. Across from them sits a basketball court and five tennis courts. Down the hill is an expanse of green with a volleyball net erected in the middle. An elderly couple has been playing tennis on the damp courts, but now they've put their racquets away, and it's just Thisbe and Lily alone.

They walk across the lawn to the Lenox Children's Center, where, when they sit down on the concrete steps, they can see the Community Center looming above them, the ballroom on the second floor where the memorial will be held. Behind the Children's Center Thisbe installs herself on a swing. Now Lily does, too, and soon they're swinging, climbing high above town, then descending in an arc toward each other.

"Look at me," Thisbe says, pointing at her open beer bottle. "I'm back in Lenox and I'm going to get myself arrested."

"You'll spend Leo's memorial in jail." Lily moves past her in the shadows, her legs and torso flashing by. The cables sway from side to side; their legs almost touch. Lily takes her hand, and now they're swinging together, as if they're on a trapeze.

Back on the steps, they stare up the hill at the Community Center. "That's where it's going to be," Thisbe says. "My late husband's memorial."

"Your late husband," Lily says, and she forces out a laugh.

"I figure if I talk that way it might be easier."

They sit quietly for several seconds, dragging their feet through the grass.

"Everyone who knew us says Leo and I were great together. Our tragic love story. There's no love like the love that's been erased."

"What about you?" Lily says.

"Me?"

"Do *you* say you were great together?"

"Sometimes we were great and sometimes we weren't." Toward the end, she admits, they were less and less great. In the months leading up to his departure for Iraq, she and Leo were fighting more and more. It was even worse when he got there. She would stay up like a schoolgirl waiting for his call, and when he finally did call, they would fight about the fact that he hadn't been calling. Calder's second birthday was coming up, and she wanted to know whether he would be home for the party. But he couldn't be sure, which was his answer to everything. They'd agreed, he reminded her, that he would go to Iraq. Agreed! As if he'd signed a contract! I agree to work for *Newsday* for a paltry salary! I agree to cover a war I'm opposed to, waged by a president I don't support, a president who stole the election! And she—she'd agreed to none of it!

Leo didn't make it home for Calder's birthday, and a week later, at four in the morning, she had to take Calder in to the emergency room. He was having an asthma attack; he couldn't breathe.

"Come home now," she told Leo.

"What do you mean come home now? What would I tell my editor? That my kid is sick?"

"I don't care what you tell your editor. Just come home."

Where, she wondered, was the boy she'd met, affable, winsome Leo who had once convinced his mother to grow pot for him; that way, she could be sure it wasn't tainted. Years ago, in that vast swath of his life before she came along, he used to argue with his friends about which was the better trick, putting the porn movie inside the Disney movie box or the Disney movie inside the porn movie box, both of which pranks they used to perform on torpid summer nights as they trolled the local video store. It was sophomoric, it was ridiculous, Thisbe didn't even know him then, but she'd have chosen that teenager over the man he had become.

Yet even early on she'd seen glints of his resolve. When he was editor of the *Argus*, he'd once stayed up for sixty straight hours.

"So the defense rests," Lily says.

"What defense?"

"Even if your marriage to Leo was perfect, you wouldn't have to justify what's happening now."

Maybe she doesn't, Thisbe thinks. But what she doesn't tell Lily, what she can't bring herself to say, is that late at night in one of their awful phone calls she told Leo she was through; she wanted a separation. Afterward, she had a premonition he was going to die. Silly, silly Thisbe, she thought. What did it mean to have a premonition your husband was going to die in Iraq? Someone aimed a gun at you, and you were long past the point of premonition.

"It's no fun being alone," she says. "I'm thirty-three and I have a toddler, and when people say 'How are you?' to me I wonder if it's a greeting or a question. Because if it's a question, the answer is long, and it's different from moment to moment." Everyone, she thinks, wants to know about the milestones—Leo's birthday, their anniversary—and those are hard, of course, but it's the everyday things that are the toughest. When she used to shop for groceries, she would get this cereal Leo liked, Great Grains Raisins, Dates and Pecans, and she mustn't have been thinking because a couple of months ago she ended up with a box of it in her shopping cart. There it was when she got home, sitting in her bag from the Strand, which was where she and Leo used to buy their books. She was clear across the country, holding that box of cereal, and she couldn't even eat it—she's allergic to nuts—and she was standing in the kitchen and she started to cry.

"Before Leo died," she tells Lily, "we talked about getting a dog. He had his heart set on a Siberian husky. He'd even picked out a name for her. He was going to call her Demeter. But I wasn't going to take care of a dog while he was in Iraq. You come back, I told him, you settle into a life in Berkeley, and we'll get a dog." But then he died and she was alone, and she thought, stupidly, she'd be less lonely if she had a dog, and Calder wanted a dog, too. But there was no way they could handle a Siberian husky. She had just started graduate school and she was taking care of Calder, who was as much work as a whole pack of Siberian huskies. "So we settled on a turtle," she tells Lily, "and sometimes when I'm home and Calder is at day care I'll go over to the tank and pick that turtle up. I'll take my highlighter and poke it in the back because I'm just the kind of compulsive grad student who always carries her highlighter with her, and the turtle will just lie there—dead, for all I know. There I am, in my T-shirt and underwear at eleven in the morning, thinking, This is the solution to my loneliness? A fucking reptile? A turtle I've named Demeter, which is a retarded name for a turtle, especially since it turns out he's male? And all I can think is, I'm never, ever going to get over Leo."

"You *are* getting over him," Lily says.

"Which is even worse."

Lily stares straight ahead of her. "If it's as serious with Wyeth as you say it is, you're going to have to tell my parents."

Thisbe nods. She also needs to talk to Noelle. Because Noelle was the last person to see Leo alive. Maybe Noelle can answer her questions. Thisbe doesn't even know what those questions are, but she knows she needs to talk to her.

They drive back to the house with the windows open, the breeze blowing Thisbe's hair against her face. Lily presses on the gas, and now they're hurtling up Cliffwood Street into the shadows.

When they reach the house, a single lantern is on next to the bird feeder, casting a ribbon of light across the porch. A lamp flashes on upstairs. Thisbe shuts the car door behind her and, using her jacket as an umbrella, she makes her way up the path.

When they step inside, David is in the foyer removing his rain boots. Amram, though, hasn't returned. Noelle, as if to make a point, has set the dinner table without a place setting for him.

"Don't worry," Marilyn says. "He'll be back soon."

"That's what you told me six hours ago."

Marilyn stands at the entrance to the kitchen, holding a ladle in one hand and an oven mitt in the other. "You were gone for quite a while."

"We had a lot to talk about," Lily says.

"Well, come help make dinner." Marilyn ushers them through the swinging door and into the pantry, where she hands them each an apron. She removes a bunch of carrots from the fridge, and a bag of arugula. "You can wash and chop these," she tells Thisbe. "The salad bowl is above the sink. And you," she says to Lily, "can help me make the fruit soup."

"Keep busy," Lily says. "That's your solution to everything."

"It's my solution to nothing," Marilyn says. "But people need to eat."

9

It's eight o'clock, but dinner hasn't started yet; everyone is stalling except Noelle. "Come on," she says. "Let's eat." If they wait until Amram comes back they may never eat again. Yet even as she's thinking this, she cranes her neck and looks out the window, hoping to see his car.

"Pavlov's bell is ringing," Marilyn says. She bangs a fork against the kettle, but all it makes is a dull thud.

"I hope Pavlov could hear well," Lily says.

"Certainly better than me," says Noelle. She set the table earlier, but she put the knife on the left and the fork on the right and the spoon on the inside of the fork, knowing as she did so that she was making a mistake but not sure how to correct it. It doesn't matter, she tells herself. As long as everyone has silverware. But it feels symbolic of something larger. If there's a right way and a wrong way to do things, she can be counted on to choose the wrong way.

"Where's Abba?" Yoni asks.

"He'll be back soon," Noelle says, doing her best to sound convincing.

"Where did he go?"

"Out," she says. "To run some errands."

"What errands?" Dov says. "Why has he been gone so long?"

"Boys, boys," Noelle says, drawing the four of them into a hug. "So many questions."

They eat at the same table where they ate last night, only now, with the children present, they're flank to flank as if at a trough. Marilyn has placed a long silk runner down the length of the table, all blues and reds and purples, in the hope that something colorful might brighten her mood. One of the chandelier bulbs has gone out, and she gets on tiptoe and taps at it until it comes on again. She spins the chandelier like a roulette wheel. It's what she used to do when the children were babies—the rotating lights mesmerized them—and when she does it now Ari snaps to attention, watching the bulbs spin and spin.

"In another life you'd have been Vanna White," Lily says.

"Whoever that is," says Marilyn.

"Oh, Mom, come on."

Marilyn has seated the children strategically, adult next to child next to adult next to child, but there's only so much strategic seating can do. At her table sit an eight-year-old, a six-year-old, a five-year-old, and two three-year-olds. A representative of every age group, like some child's version of the UN. Though they feel at the same time like one age group: the rabble. She didn't have enough dining room chairs to seat them all, so Clarissa removed two folding chairs from the closet, but now the boys are fighting over who gets the regular chairs and who gets the folding ones, and soon they're negotiating over the size of the cutlery—some of them got larger forks than others—and Ari is saying he wants the teddy bear spoon, but the teddy bear spoon, Noelle informs him, is back in Israel.

"It's not fair!" Ari says.

"It never is," says Noelle, blowing out air in mock exasperation, though the feeling is less counterfeit than she lets on.

"That's Calder's favorite phrase," Thisbe says.

Noelle says, "Sometimes I think it's Ari's *only* phrase. It's the first thing he says when he wakes up in the morning. I should put it on a T-shirt."

Marilyn wishes her grandsons would settle down, especially now, the night before Leo's memorial. He was your father, she wants to say. And your uncle. Show some respect. But they would just stare at her blankly, the way grandchildren have been staring at their grandparents for years, the way, she suspects, she stared at her own grandparents. So she decides to be Zen about it, a phrase and a concept she doesn't like, but if being Zen about it means surrendering, then that's what she wants to do.

"Will you be joining us?" she asks David. He's wandering about the living room, toolbox in hand, as if he's less a member of the family than the neighborhood contractor: foreman of the crew. He has finished with the hinge on the bathroom mirror, and now he's on to the other bathroom, where the paint has started to flake. Okay, she wants to say, you've made your point. They will have to sell the house, but they don't have to sell it this minute, or this week. David's just staging his mute protest, but at this point she's inclined to let him. Leo's memorial is tomorrow, and as the time has drawn closer, she has found herself buried among his possessions, absenting herself for the last few hours while she ransacked his room, she doesn't know for what.

"I'm not hungry," David says, and she's almost glad for it. She'd rather he not be in the way.

"Well, if you want anything, it's on the stove."

"Okay," he says tonelessly.

"I'll put the leftovers in a baggie."

"That's fine."

"I'll leave dessert out, too."

But David has already departed, back to the bathroom and then who knows where, to wherever his revolving workstation deposits him.

Even without him and Amram, everyone is crowded around the table like at a mess hall; the boys are all elbows as they reach over each other, fighting for the orange juice and the sweetened iced tea.

Marilyn serves the fruit soup while Noelle forks the kosher food onto her boys' plates, the corned beef on bagels, which she splatters ketchup and mustard on, dousing everything in condiments because that's how her boys like it. Through her eating restrictions she's separated herself from the others, but she feels as if they've separated themselves from her. She thinks of Joseph down in Egypt, of the ancient Egyptian custom of eating separately from the Israelites. That's how she feels now, not sure if she's the Israelite or the Egyptian here, only that she's been banished. The corned beef abrades her throat as it goes down; the pastrami feels no better. She doesn't like cold cuts, but that's all she has. She's overcome by the urge to dispense with everything: all these senseless rules. Amram's not here to watch over her, and it's only the shame of thinking this (Has that been his role? To keep her in line?) that makes her continue to eat what she's eating. She glances at her watch, then at her cell phone. He's been gone for seven hours.

"You've gotten a suntan," Marilyn says. She's looking up at Thisbe across the table.

"My life's one big suntan," Thisbe says. "That's the problem when you go to school out west. It's hard to study indoors." She thinks Marilyn might rebuke her; she can be a fanatic when it comes to sunscreen. A doctor *and* a mother, Leo used to say; it was a lethal combination.

Marilyn is wearing a row of bracelets, which clink against each other like wind chimes. She's looking up at Thisbe again. It's Leo she's thinking about, though she's thinking about Thisbe too, which is another way of thinking about Leo.

It's her own fault, she believes. She still doesn't know why she didn't warm to Thisbe. Was it because everyone else warmed to her, because everyone found her so congenial, so winning, everyone, that is, except for Marilyn herself, who felt compelled to stand up for some principle she couldn't even name? Everybody thinks Marilyn didn't like Thisbe because she wasn't Nora; it's what Thisbe herself believes. But that's not true. Marilyn knew Nora when she was four, when Nora used to run along the beach in her purple flip-flops and yellow one-piece, Leo, in his own flip-flops, dutifully trailing her. "Those two are going to get married," Nora's mother used to say, and Marilyn saw no harm in agreeing. She liked Nora. But there was always a species of compassion in the way she liked her. Nora was lovely, but she was troubled, and this was apparent to Marilyn even when Nora was in preschool, the way obstacles impeded her that other children could surmount; not infrequently, she reminded Marilyn of Noelle. As head-strong as he was, there was never a chance Leo would marry Nora; for all her drama, she was safe. She was the exact sort of girlfriend for a teenage son of hers to have: adventurous, explosive, ultimately anodyne.

But Thisbe, it was clear, was different. She was pleasant to Marilyn, but she didn't need her, and Marilyn doesn't like not to feel needed. Mere weeks into their relationship, Marilyn thought: Leo could end up marrying her. He was twenty-one, too young to be with the girl he would marry. But really, she knows, it was something else. Her baby, her only son, was being taken from her. It shocked her to feel that primal possessiveness, that oedipal urge but in reverse, and though she tried to hide it, she wasn't able to.

Did she think that, given a choice between his girlfriend and his mother, a young man would choose his mother? Did she believe that if she wasn't welcoming Thisbe would simply leave? Her error had been in thinking she could act out and that she and Thisbe would have time to reconcile. Years would pass and there would be a thawing between them. What had once been begrudging would become openhearted, warm. She and Thisbe would learn to like each other; perhaps the feeling would even blossom into love. Thisbe would be spending her life with Leo; she would be the mother of Marilyn's grandchildren. Marilyn even allowed herself to imagine her old age, David dead already, Thisbe coming to visit her in the nursing home, where the waiting rooms were filled with daughters and daughters-in-law. Mothers and daughters-in-law: such volatile, loaded relationships. Yet mother-daughter relationships could be loaded, too, and Marilyn had managed to have good relationships with her daughters. She saw no reason why she couldn't do the same with Thisbe. Only now, she realizes, she made a mistake.

She's looking at Thisbe from across the table, and for a moment it's as if no one else is in the room and it's just her and Thisbe, separated by all that burnished blond wood. A bee buzzes against the porch window, as if trying to ram its way in.

"Darling," Marilyn says. She can hear her heart beat like a thrush in her forehead.

"Please, Mom," Lily says. "Leave Thisbe alone."

"What did I do?"

Lily's thinking of Wyeth, of her conversation with Thisbe just hours ago, hoping to shield her as best she can, to protect her from her mother.

"It's okay," Thisbe says. "I'm all right."

Clarissa, trying to redirect the conversation, says, "Are we set for the memorial? It's at noon, right?"

"But we should get there early," Marilyn says.

"Did you finish your speech?" Lily asks Clarissa.

"No," Clarissa says. "Did you?"

Lily shakes her head. She has begun it and begun it and begun it again. She should stand at the podium and read twelve different opening paragraphs, each one more atrocious than the next.

"Will you be speaking, Marilyn?" Nathaniel asks.

Marilyn shakes her head. She spoke at Leo's funeral, and she's been speaking throughout the year in the nation's op-ed pages. She'll leave it to her daughters to speak.

"And Dad?" Noelle says.

"Last we spoke, he didn't know."

Clarissa, grasping for some subject, says, "Nathaniel will be wearing a tie. I can't remember the last time he wore one."

Noelle, too, trying to keep the conversation aloft, says, "I bought four ties for the boys duty-free at the airport." She got five ties, in fact, one for Amram, but it looks like that one won't be necessary. At least it will spare them another fight. Amram thinks ties are a woman's idea of how a man should look.

"I wore a tuxedo once," Dov says.

"Well, you won't be wearing one tomorrow," says Yoni.

Akiva spears his sandwich with a fork.

"Akiva," Noelle says, "stop playing with your food."

But Akiva goes on playing with it, stabbing the bread until it's bullet-pocked, and Noelle doesn't have the will to object anymore.

Ari, playing with his sandwich himself, says, "I never got to wear a tuxedo."

"You will someday," Noelle says. "If you want to."

"Count yourself lucky," Nathaniel says. "Some of us spend our lives trying to avoid wearing a tuxedo."

Ari says, "I want to wear a tuxedo to Uncle Leo's memorial."

"Well you can't, honey," Noelle says.

There's silence; again Marilyn is staring at Thisbe. She still doesn't know why Lily rebuked her, why anyone is rebuking anyone now.

Thisbe, as if sensing this, says, "It's okay." She's extending her hand to Marilyn, but she's across the table, out of reach.

"I don't know," Marilyn says.

"Me, either," says Thisbe, though she doesn't even know what she doesn't know. She's eating the chicken thighs and the leeks, the pasta salad, Noelle's food, the kosher food—the one gentile at the table and look what she's ended up with. She's thinking, stupidly, that the food doesn't *taste* kosher, feeling as always when it comes to Judaism like an ignoramus, a fool.

"I wasn't always the easiest mother-in-law," Marilyn says.

"Oh, Marilyn. Please don't say that."

"Well, it's true."

"You were a good mother-in-law," Thisbe says, feeling the words catch in her mouth, convinced she sounds insincere, ashamed she's forced to say this. With her right hand she's forking the food into her mouth while across her body her left hand moves of its own accord, trundling along her lap like a rodent. Where is everyone to rescue her? Where's Clarissa? Where's Lily? Where's Noelle? Where of all times is Amram, whom she can usually count on to distract the others? He has vanished, and everyone else is quietly chewing their food, a bunch of ruminants, unmoving and silent, as if they've been ossified by Marilyn's words.

"You must think I'm ridiculous."

"Why would I think that?" Thisbe says.

"Spending my life writing tendentious op-eds."

"They're not tendentious. I like them." Though what Thisbe feels is mostly a mixture of discomfort and relief. Discomfort that a year after Leo died he remains in the news, that her life is still fit for consumption. Relief that Marilyn has taken up the mantle, that she's become the public face of it all and, in so doing, has spared her.

"I could waterboard Alberto Gonzales himself and it wouldn't bring Leo back. I'd like to spit on Bush. The nerve of the man to claim my son as his ally. Leo hated that war."

He did, Thisbe thinks, though he hated it the way most people she knows hated it, idly at first, and then less idly, as things started to go bad. The war was over, in any case, by the time Leo was killed; he was covering the occupation, and though there wouldn't have been an occupation without a war, there would have been other occupations, and other wars too, and Leo would have found his way to them. Thisbe dislikes Bush as much as her mother-in-law does, but when Leo was abducted, accused by his captors of being a U.S. agent, when he was placed before the cameras, looking woozy, lobotomized, was it any wonder Bush enlisted him for his cause? Bush lied about WMDs; mischaracterizing Leo was small stuff by comparison. And the left, in embracing Leo, mischaracterizes him, too. Because Leo wasn't interested in being a hero, certainly not a political one. What Marilyn fails to understand is that Leo wasn't political; he was a journalist. He refused to tell Thisbe how he voted, and though she had no doubt, his political views were beside the point. What he wanted was adventure; in another era, he'd have traveled to Africa to hunt elephant tusk. But Thisbe can't tell her mother-in-law this, can't say what she believes, which is that if Leo were alive he wouldn't recognize the person she's writing about.

Now Marilyn is talking about an anniversary party she and David threw for themselves. "It was our thirtieth," she tells Thisbe. "I don't know if you remember it."

Of course Thisbe remembers. She'd been with Leo only a few months at the time, and Marilyn hadn't invited her to the party. She was twenty-one years old, and did she really want to drive down from Maine to eat canapés with her new boyfriend's parents? That had been Marilyn's defense. Christmas break was coming soon, and Thisbe would probably prefer to be off skiing. But when Leo found out she hadn't been invited, he was furious. And Thisbe herself was insulted, hurt. Yet it's been years since that party, so that now, when Marilyn apologizes for the snub, it takes Thisbe a moment to realize what she's talking about. "I haven't thought about that party in years."

"Well, I have," Marilyn says.

"I came to other parties," Thisbe says. "I was included in everything after that." And there's this, she thinks: she's here now, for the memorial.

"I was so sorry when you two broke up," Marilyn says.

For a second, Thisbe doesn't know what Marilyn is talking about. Then she realizes: Marilyn is referring to when they graduated from college and she and Leo split up. They were twenty-two at the time, not yet ready to marry, not yet ready to live together, even, and Thisbe was intent on taking the Foreign Service exam—she was hoping to go to Ghana—and Leo was off to his own far-flung places. They didn't meet again until a few years later, when they ran into each other on the Upper West Side beneath the marquee of the Beacon Theater. Neil Diamond was playing that night, and Thisbe said to Leo, "You're not going to that concert, are you? Please don't tell me you've started to like Neil Diamond."

He laughed. "Don't worry. I'm not at such loose ends."

"But you're a little at loose ends?"

"I *have* missed you."

"We were young," she says now. "It took us a while to figure things out."

"But you did," Marilyn says. "That's what's most important."

Thisbe tries to look away, but it's like those 3-D baseball cards from the cereal box: whichever way you hold Marilyn, she's staring back at you.

"I remember when you two met," Marilyn says. "Leo fell in love with you instantly."

And Thisbe, reddening, says, "I fell in love with him, too."

Only now, looking at Calder, who's been witness to all this, and at his cousins, staring down at their cold cuts in perplexity and embarrassment, Thisbe says to Marilyn, "Maybe this could wait." She worries what Calder will say if the conversation continues; she fears he'll mention Wyeth.

"Why shouldn't they hear this?" Marilyn says. "They should know about Leo."

"They do know about him," Thisbe says. "I talk to Calder about him all the time."

"Well, I want them to hear about him from me too. Anyway, I don't believe in protecting children, certainly not from something like this."

I'm not protecting him, Thisbe wants to say, even as she's thinking, *It's up to me to decide whether I protect him.*

But Marilyn has quietly left the table. When she returns, she's holding a large cardboard box with Leo's possessions inside it. She removes a photo album, which she passes around from person to person, the adults holding the album for the children to see, making sure nothing gets smudged.

Soon it's Thisbe's turn to look at the album, and she's thinking there's something unfair about photos; she'd like to have them banned. She flips to a photo of Leo from when he was six, playing the lion in a children's theater version of *The Wizard of Oz*. And another photo, from the cast party, when he's eating ice cream through his lion's mouth, fed to him in spoonfuls by his sisters.

"He was a bottomless pit," Marilyn says.

Noelle says, "He used to eat all of Mom's leftover apple strudel, then try to pawn it off on someone else."

"On his friends," says Marilyn.

"One time," Clarissa says, "he blamed a band of strudel-eating intruders."

"Strudel bandits!" Noelle says.

"Remember when he was a teenager," Marilyn says, "and he made Dad and me buy him a mini-fridge?"

"He kept it next to his bed," Clarissa says, "stocked with provisions for a middle-of-the-night meal."

"Thank God for his fast metabolism," Marilyn says.

In other photos, Leo is holding a lacrosse stick, a badminton racquet; he's wearing an old headband; he's drawing at an easel. "Who knows where all that stuff came from," Noelle says.

"He and his friends shared everything," Marilyn says.

"They were such girls," says Lily. "They even shared clothes."

Marilyn has risen from her chair and is standing now behind Thisbe, who holds the album next to her plate.

"Who's that?" Thisbe asks. She's pointing at a photo of Leo, who's spinning a basketball on his middle finger, showing off for some girl.

"Leo's first girlfriend," Marilyn says.

"Nora?"

Marilyn shakes her head. "The first girl Leo kissed, the summer after sixth grade. Kimball, I think her name was. He never told you about her?"

"If he did, I've forgotten about it. I knew about Nora, of course, but other than that, our past was the past and I was fine with that."

"Mom," Noelle says, "are you trying to make Thisbe jealous?"

"She has nothing to be jealous of," Marilyn says. "Not of Nora or anyone else. When Leo fell for her, it was like, *Wow.*"

Thisbe's thinking of Nora now, the wishbone image of her. They met only once, at the hardware store, and when Leo introduced them everyone was uncomfortable. She didn't see her again until Leo's funeral, where Nora inserted herself front and center, impresario of an event that wasn't hers. Nora's nothing to her now; she never was, really. So she's surprised to discover she still has animus for her, and it startles her, the quiet venom she feels, as she says, "Nora and her eating disorders."

"That was the least of it," Marilyn says. "You'd think Leo, the youngest child, allowed to do whatever he pleased, wouldn't have been attracted to someone like Nora. But beneath it all he had a savior complex. And then you came along and we all were relieved. Finally, Leo was with someone who didn't need taking care of."

"We all need taking care of," Thisbe says.

Akiva asks to be excused, and a palpable relief settles on everyone, as one after the other, as if forming a conga line, the children leave the room.

Now David comes through in his paint-spattered pants, moving quickly past them as if to say, Don't mind me.

Marilyn removes a set of weights from the box. "These were Leo's," she says. "You know what he called them? Dumbbells for a dumbbell. If only the whole world were as dumb as Leo." She reminds everyone how Leo, born premature, took to the weight room when he was eleven, and how, a year later, the family adopted a stray Labrador retriever he had found cowering beneath a bench in Riverside Park and named her Kingman, after Dave Kingman, the New York Mets home run king. The dog took a liking to Leo and didn't seem to mind, or was too feeble to object, when every morning as part of his weightlifting routine Leo would bench-press Kingman herself, three sets of twelve repetitions, Kingman prostrate, helpless but good-natured, as she was lifted and lowered and lifted again. And when Leo grew tired of bench-pressing Kingman, when the dog became less pliable, he took to bench-pressing Noelle, who was willing in this way to help him stay in shape: Leo on his back, thrusting lithe Noelle up and down, up and down. Leo, who beat up the school bully, then beat up the kid who made fun of the school bully for Leo's having beaten him up. Leo, Marilyn's little weightlifting philosopher of a son, bench-pressing Kingman, testing the premise that if you lifted a cow when it was born and kept lifting it every day there would never come a day when you couldn't lift the cow. "You know what I keep forgetting about Kingman?" Marilyn says. "That dog was a girl."

"Yet he named her Kingman," Noelle says. "He tried to get her to lift her leg to pee."

"He always felt outnumbered," Clarissa says. "That's why he liked to spend time with Dad. A break from all that estrogen."

Though the truth, Marilyn thinks, was that Leo was happy to be the only son in the family: he liked being the alpha male.

She lays the weights at Thisbe's feet. "I want you to have these."

"Oh, Marilyn, I can't."

"Why not?"

"I don't lift weights," Thisbe says, because it's the only thing she can think to say, though she does lift weights, and fearing that Marilyn knows this, she corrects herself and says she dislikes free weights, she prefers the machines, then adds that her luggage was already over the weight limit on her trip east and she was forced to pay a fee. She could buy weights, she says, for the price it would cost to carry them back. She *will* buy weights, she's tempted to tell her mother-in-law, knowing only that she can't return home, to Wyeth, with her dead husband's dumbbells in tow.

"Here," Marilyn says. "Take this instead." And she hands Thisbe a San Diego Chargers football pennant.

"Leo was the world's most avid Chargers fan," Clarissa says. "We never knew why he liked them."

Neither did Thisbe. The more the Chargers lost the more devoted he became; he was, in his own way, a lonely man of faith.

And now she's sitting with the pennant in her lap, wondering what she'll do with it when she gets home, and presently some gravy drips off her plate, staining the pennant brown.

She will do it now, she decides: she will tell Marilyn about Wyeth. But when she goes to speak, she falls mute. She grabs her wineglass, and she's holding the stem so tight she fears it might break. "Things are different now," she says. "A year has passed. A lot has happened since Leo."

"It's been endless," Marilyn agrees. "It's been terrible for the whole family."

"But it's changed—"

"I know."

"I—"

"Darling."

There it is, she thinks, that noxious word again, and why, she wonders, does she let it bother her when it's meant as an endearment? But it doesn't feel like an endearment; it feels like an assault. Marilyn doesn't have the right to call her that. If they'd had another kind of relationship she might have the right, but they didn't have that kind of relationship, and now, with Leo gone, they're not going to have it. "I need to be excused." She exits the dining room, and finding Calder with his cousins in front of the TV, she picks him up and carries him down the stairs.

In the basement, she gives Calder a bath, and when he's done, he comes back upstairs to watch TV with his cousins.

Soon, though, he runs into the kitchen. "Ari wet his pants! He got pee on Grandma and Grandpa's carpet!"

"That's impossible," Noelle says. Ari must hold the world record for earliest toilet training; he stopped wearing diapers before he turned two.

Calder directs her into the living room, where his cousins are crouched as if examining a dead bug. Marilyn is already wiping up the pee. "Should I get him a diaper?" she asks Noelle.

"He doesn't need a diaper." It's an absurd response, Noelle understands, coming from someone whose child just peed on the floor, yet she refuses to believe it. Ari never has accidents. She gets down on the rug and, in what feels like a humiliation, puts her nose to the fabric. Maybe Calder is mistaken and someone spilled a glass of water. Or maybe it *is* pee and Calder is the guilty party.

But of course Ari peed. He's standing right in front of her with his pants wet.

Noelle takes him upstairs and cleans him off, and in violation of everything the books advise about parenting and everything she herself believes, she says, "Why did you do that?"

"It was a *ta'ut*," Ari says. An accident.

Except it wasn't an accident. There are no accidents with Ari. "Is it because Abba drove off?"

"It was a *ta'ut*," Ari insists, and he starts to cry.

Back in the living room, she finds herself apologizing again and again, and every time she does so she feels worse for it.

"Really, Noelle," her mother says. "It's not a big deal."

But it feels like a big deal, and everyone's insisting that it isn't one only flusters her further. "I'll pay to have the carpet cleaned."

"Don't be ridiculous."

She's still down on the carpet, examining the stain. "I don't know how it happened. He was toilet trained at twenty-one months."

"Noelle. Please. Forget about it."

Amram drove off, so Ari peed in his pants. She's making too big a deal of it, but she can't help it. It's Amram's fault, yet it's her fault, too; she might as well not be able to keep her own bladder in check. Sleeping with whatever boy came her way. What good is her newfound modesty when she can't control things any more than she ever could? She can't control her husband and she can't control her children, and what good is she if she can't do that?

She puts the boys to bed, but when she comes downstairs everyone is silent and she's convinced they've been talking about her. Thisbe is trying to get Calder to sleep, but he's running around the living room holding his pajamas aloft, which gives her brief comfort—*she* got her children to bed—but soon Thisbe corrals him and brings him downstairs, and that feeling disappears, too.

She goes over the last couple of hours like a dog pawing over a clump of dirt. She measures her mother's affection for her grandchildren and it seems that her boys have gotten the short end of the stick. She thinks of the way her mother is with Calder, the *sweetie*s and *darling*s she doles out, words with which she herself once measured her mother's affection and found herself deficient. Her mother seems more enthusiastic, more open-armed, more *something* with Calder. Noelle can't blame her. Her mother sees Calder more often than she sees her boys; Calder may live across the country, but he doesn't live across the world. That was her choice. She's Orthodox now; that was her choice, too. Her mother has more in common with Calder; of course she favors him. Maybe she's imagining it, maybe she's being paranoid, but it doesn't matter, it's what she feels.

She goes into the kitchen, where food is strewn everywhere: on top of the microwave and spilling into the sink and perched precariously on the butcher-block table. A few leek tops have fallen from the counter, the thin white filaments spread like hair across the floor. Someone left the water running, and now, when Noelle tries to turn it off, she can't get the dripping to stop. She erred from the start by refusing to eat her parents' food, when by any reasonable standard it was kosher, by any standard other than her own. Even the dishes were new. So it was cooked in a nonkosher oven, on a nonkosher stove. What difference does that make? It makes all the difference in the world; at least it usually does. But now, with Amram gone, all the rules she abides by seem to have no purpose, and she thrusts a serving spoon into the bowl and shoves several spoonfuls of potato salad into her mouth.

A fence around the Torah. That is what the rabbis say. You must hold yourself to the strictest standard possible if you hope to avoid transgression. But she doesn't need a fence around the Torah. She needs a moat. She needs an entire city. She swallows the potato salad and washes the dishes, scrubs them as if to erase all evidence of what she's done, as if to erase her very self. Then she puts away the food and sweeps and mops the floor. When she's finished, everything is so clean she imagines the kitchen the way it was forty years ago, when her parents first bought the house.

Up in her bedroom, she can't find her nightgown. She rifles through her suitcase, but it isn't there. When she comes downstairs, she finds her sisters and mother in the living room, her father with his toolbox moving quietly about the house. "I need something to sleep in," she says. She's hoping Clarissa or Lily will lend her something. She recalls that song she used to listen to, "Big Sister's Clothes," and how, growing up, she loved to borrow clothing from Clarissa and Lily, loved how, over time, the three of them forgot whose clothes were whose, and their mother simply left the clean laundry on top of the washer and they took whatever they wanted, as if out of an enormous grab bag. But her sisters seem not to have a spare nightgown, or, if they do, they don't offer her one. Now it's her mother who goes upstairs and returns with a nightgown, and Noelle retires to put it on in the bathroom, which, smelling as it does of fresh paint, makes her retch.

Back in the living room, she deposits herself into an armchair, and since everyone else is reading, she tries to read, too. But she can't concentrate.

"That becomes you," her mother says.

"What?"

"My nightgown. You can keep it if you'd like."

"I have plenty of nightgowns."

"You can have one more."

She doesn't want to be here with her family, doesn't want to be waiting for Amram, pretending not to wait for him, knowing they know she's pretending not to wait for him. "I'm going to bed," she says softly, and her sisters nod and her mother comes over and kisses her on the forehead, and she feels as if she's going to cry and she can't let herself do that.

Upstairs, she checks her cell phone, but there aren't any messages. She refuses to call Amram; he can call her. She'll wait for him, she thinks, though it's as futile, she knows, as waiting for the Messiah. Part of her hopes he never comes back, because if he does come back what will she do then? Yet she rebukes herself for even thinking this way: he's her husband no matter what he's done. She thinks of the Hebrew words *ezer k'negdo*. Husband and wife, that's what they are, and remembering they have an agreement not to go to sleep angry, she tries to do the same when he's not here. She fluffs up his pillow and leaves him a wide berth to get into bed. Then she searches through her suitcase for her packet of mints, and when she finds one she places it on his pillow where it will wait for him like at a hotel, and then she turns out the light.

"Were you at the same dinner as me?" Thisbe says.

"I was there," says Lily.

"So I'm not crazy."

"I heard what you heard."

"I tried to tell her," Thisbe says.

"I know."

It's after midnight, and Thisbe has come upstairs, where Lily is readying herself for sleep. Thisbe, in her cotton pajamas, is preparing for bed, too; she's dabbing moisturizer on her face. A shadow passes over them, and Thisbe turns around, expecting to see someone, but it's just her and Lily illuminated in the hallway by the tiny nightlight. She thinks she hears the kettle whistling downstairs, but the sound is coming from the street.

"Think of it this way," Lily says. "In two days you'll be back home. You'll be thousands of miles away from here."

"And you?" Thisbe says.

"I'll be home, too."

"It was stupid," she says, "trying to bring up Wyeth at dinner."

"Wait until after the memorial," Lily says. "Then she'll be able to hear you."

Thisbe rubs her eyes and sees pinwheels, flashes of light coming to her in the darkness. Her pajama pants drag along the floor; she leans over and cuffs them. "These were Leo's."

"I thought I recognized them," Lily says.

"We were the same height, but they're still too big on me."

"He had long legs."

"Long legs, compact torso." And he was brawny, she thinks, while she's lithe. She leans against the plaster, and the passageway is so narrow she can stick out her feet and touch the opposite wall. "It's funny," she says, "I never wear pajamas."

"So why are you wearing them now?"

"They're my most modest nightclothes. Anyway, I like the feel of cotton." She looks up at her sister-in-law. "Remember what you said to me last night? How I could sleep up here if I wanted to?"

Lily nods.

"Can I tonight?"

"Oh, Thisbe. Of course."

It's a big bed, with room for them both, and Thisbe gets under the covers beside Lily, and soon they've fallen asleep.

She wakes at three in the morning with a jolt, thinking she hears Calder calling out to her. She rises from the bed without disturbing Lily and tiptoes silently out of the room.

But when she reaches the basement, Calder is asleep. She nudges him over and gets into bed, and she closes her eyes and takes his hand and soon she's asleep herself.

10

A bottle of grapefruit juice in one hand, a tube of lipstick in the other, Clarissa stands rooted in the aisle at the Village Pharmacy, where the fluorescent lights shine down on her beside the aspirin and cold cream and cleaning products and get-well cards. She has opened the grapefruit juice and started to drink it, though she hasn't paid for it yet.

It's nine in the morning, her brother's memorial is in a few hours, but what she really needs is space to breathe. She called home an hour ago to retrieve her messages, and her fertility doctor had called. He needed to talk to her as soon as possible. It was July Fourth and the office was closed, but he knew how anxious she'd been, so he gave her his cell phone number. Clutching that number in her hand, she stepped outside into her mother's garden; it was the closest she could get to privacy.

When the doctor picked up, all she could do was thank him for talking to her on the holiday.

"I'm happy to," he said, but his voice was somber, his tone severe. It seemed they'd discovered what the problem was. He said something about her LH levels and FSH levels, and she got lost in the thicket of gynecological terminology, but the bottom line, he made clear, was that without intervention she would have trouble getting pregnant; even with intervention it could be tough. She needed to start thinking about IVF. Then he told her to make an appointment for the following week.

It was eight in the morning and Nathaniel was still asleep. She thought of going back inside to wake him, but what difference would it make? She'd be just as infertile in an hour. So she drove into town and wound up where she is now, in the drugstore aisle, pulled there as if by some subliminal force. It's where she invariably circles back to, the pharmacy, though this time she has studiously avoided her usual port of landing, having steered clear of feminine hygiene, the pregnancy tests and home ovulation kits nestled right among the maxi pads and down the row from incontinence.

At the register, she bats away a mosquito with her grapefruit juice. In her other hand, she's clutching the lipstick so tight the cap has come loose and left a smudge on her thumb. "America the Beautiful" pipes through the speakers; "Born in the U.S.A." follows it. The man behind the register—a boy, really; he can't be more than sixteen—is dressed like Uncle Sam.

"You're in no mood to celebrate, I'm betting." It's the woman in line behind Clarissa, who looks familiar to her. An acquaintance of her parents, presumably; there's no one they don't know in this town.

"I hate the Fourth," she tells this stranger.

"I'm sorry about today."

She nods.

"Will you be speaking?"

"I'm going to try." She looks down at her hand, still smudged with lipstick. "You caught me."

"What?"

"Possessing lipstick."

"I didn't realize it was contraband."

"I just always thought makeup was cheating. What can I say? I'm trying to look pretty for my brother's memorial."

When she gets home, she finds Nathaniel in their bedroom, already dressed. His dark hair is slicked back, and he's standing in front of the mirror in a navy suit and tie. He has polished his shoes, and now he's bending over to tie them. At his feet lies a crumpled rag streaked with shoe polish. "Where were you?"

"In town," she says. "I was buying grapefruit juice." She raises the empty bottle to show him. She tries to imagine what she would do on a normal day, what she would have done before she knew everything she knows now, about her parents, about her LH levels and FSH levels.

She logs onto the computer and types "LH levels" and "FSH levels" into the search engine and gets seven hundred thousand results for FSH and thirty-five million results for LH. She'll be sitting at this computer when she hits menopause.

According to her parents, she didn't say a word until she turned three, at which point she began to speak in full sentences. She suspects the story is exaggerated, but it gets at an essential truth about her. After college, when she and Lily traveled through South America, it was Lily who did all the Spanish speaking, though Lily's Spanish is no better than hers; in fact, it's probably worse. Lily throws herself into things, whereas she's a watcher, she's cautious, she's a student first, and she doesn't like to make mistakes. It was why when she was growing up she refused to play baseball until she learned all the rules; like a general, she wanted to master the field of battle before she took up arms. It is, she supposes, what she's doing now, trying to figure out what's wrong with her in advance of a doctor's appointment she hasn't even scheduled yet, hoping to make up for how she was on the phone: incoherent, a child.

She starts to cry.

"Clarissa, what's wrong?" Nathaniel is standing above her in his handsome suit, while she sits on the bed, her head in her hands.

"I spoke to my fertility doctor," she says. "I can't have a baby."

"Is that what he told you?"

She tries to explain it to him, but she can't. "He said we need to start intervention."

"Soon?"

"Now."

"The test results were bad?"

"He wants me to come in next week."

Before Nathaniel can say anything more, she grabs her toiletry case and runs into the bathroom. She divests herself of her jeans and T-shirt, and now, standing in her bra and underpants, she flosses her teeth. But she jabs the floss so hard against her gums blood drips into the sink.

She removes a pregnancy test from her toiletry case, and an ovulation test for good measure, and she pees on them successively, though she knows she's not pregnant and her ovulation test was positive two days ago. Ha! she thinks. She'll turn out to be pregnant. She'll show the fertility doctor what he knows. But the results are exactly as she expected. She breaks the sticks in half and tosses them violently into the garbage.

Nathaniel is waiting when she returns to the room. "Get undressed," she says. She wants to have sex with him. Her parents may be getting separated, but she had her own life before they got separated and she will have her own life after they get separated, and she's ovulating, for God's sake, and maybe intervention is necessary but they need to be doing whatever they can, too.

"Come on, Clarissa," Nathaniel says. "Your brother's memorial is in an hour and a half."

"I know when it is."

"Well?"

"Pretend you're fifteen. It can be over in a minute."

"Sounds like fun," he says cheerlessly.

"Are you going to make me undress you?"

He's across the room from her, moving his head from side to side as if hoping someone will rescue him. His hair is dark and straight, and as he cants his head it falls across his eyes, physical manifestation of his reticence. He's narrow and lanky, with a jutting-out quality to his limbs, which, though he's six foot two, makes him seem even taller than that. He prefers to be the observer—on most occasions, he'd like to be a fly on the wall—and it was his misfortune to have his growth spurt take place when he was young, so that when he would have rather been out of sight, hiding under the staircase, simply watching the goings-on, he was always sticking out. It's what he's trying to do now: hoping to disappear. But it won't work. Because Clarissa has approached him and is removing his tie and shirt, and now she has him fully naked.

"Okay," she says, and they do the deed. That's what it feels like—a perpetration—and once it's over she lies silently on top of the covers.

She walks over to the mirror and examines herself. "Great," she says. "I'm starting to break out." She'll have a big zit on her nose for her brother's memorial. She rifles through the closet. She tries on a white shirt, but it looks bad on her, and so she's back to where she was, undressed.

She removes a scale from the closet and steps gingerly onto it. "Good God," she says. "I weigh forty-three pounds!"

"That's very light," Nathaniel says mildly.

"Now I know why I'm infertile." She has read that 12 percent of infertility is caused by weighing too much or too little, though if she were really forty-three pounds, she wouldn't be infertile, she'd be dead. She has the same scale at home, a battery-operated contraption that, if you don't step on it just right, will register something outlandish. Last week, she weighed 219 pounds. She weighs too much *and* too little. She wonders what percent of infertility is caused by that.

She threads her legs through the holes in her underpants and strings her bra over her shoulders. "My uterus is retroverted." She acts as if this is something she just learned, when, in fact, she discovered it when she was twelve, at her first gynecological check-up. The doctor left her with her feet in the stirrups and called in the medical students to have a look. This was unprofessional conduct, she knows now, but at the time she had no idea, and being a specimen like that, and at such a young age, felt like a humiliation. Later she would learn that it's not unusual to have a retroverted uterus, so her doctor's excitement baffles her now. Still, there's something about that word, *retroverted*, that continues to haunt her, and she recalls that doctor's appointment with a clarity and horror that surprise her this many years later. She feels a residual shame at having been treated this way, and even now, when a gynecologist is examining her for the first time, she's quick to announce that her uterus is retroverted, as if hoping to preempt a response.

Nathaniel gets out of bed and dresses again.

"Take two?"

He doesn't respond. He's buffing his shoes once more, though they're as dark and shiny as the outside of a limousine. "I'm sorry, Clarissa. I can't do this anymore."

"Can't do what? Have sex with me?"

"No," he says. "I'm always happy to have sex with you. What I can't do is have a baby."

"That's the thing, Nathaniel. You don't have to have the baby. All you have to do is stand there and shout, 'Push!'"

"I'm serious."

She can see on the wall behind Nathaniel a framed copy of Shakespeare's sonnet number 30. "When to the Sessions of Sweet Silent Thought." She had to memorize that sonnet in junior high school, and she still knows it by heart. Everything she committed to memory is still committed to it, the things she wants to remember and the things she doesn't want to remember: nothing ever leaves. She takes a step toward him. "What in the world do you mean?"

"I can't keep going on like this."

"Why?" she says. "Because I made you have sex in a cheap motel? Because I told you a minute ago to get undressed? A lot of guys would be happy if a half-decent-looking woman wanted to have sex with them."

"I'm one of those guys."

"Then what's the problem?"

"The problem is I can't continue like this."

"Like what?"

"With the pregnancy tests and the ovulation kits and the basal thermometers. Most of all, I can't continue with the disappointment—with my disappointment, with yours. Your brother died, Clarissa. Your parents are splitting up. How can we add more stress to that? It could break us."

"I don't care."

"You don't care about breaking us?"

He was the one, she reminds him, who wanted to have a baby; she, on the other hand, wasn't sure at first. They were at a standstill, doesn't he remember? For a time they considered breaking up. And now, more than ten years later, he's changing his mind? What is this, a seesaw? She says yes, and he says no? It's us against the world, they used to say. And the words come back to her: *star fucker*. She heard them once from her own sister, from Noelle. And it's not just Noelle. It's practically in the air she breathes. Married to the future Nobel laureate. It's always been that way. Her high school boyfriend became a Rhodes scholar. A young man she dated in college is now a star at the State Department. People think she can sniff out success. But she doesn't care about success; she hates it, in fact. Ambition: it ruins you. Accomplish this, accomplish that, and for what? She used to be a star herself and she was treated that way, but now she's not a star and she'll never be one. Is that why she wants this so badly—because she was once a star, because Mrs. Pritchett said to her, "You could make it all the way to the Philharmonic, Clarissa, if only you want it badly enough"? But she hadn't wanted it badly enough. She hadn't wanted it at all. So this is what she has left: becoming a mother. Sometimes it seems all she's doing with her life is trying to get pregnant. And the crazy thing is, she doesn't even know if she wants to get pregnant. She's not a kids person. They're cute, she supposes, at least some of them are, but she's not drawn to them, she really isn't, and here she is spending the holiday with her five nephews, and she likes them, sure, at least for five minutes, but then she's thinking, *You run along now.* "What do *you* want, Nathaniel? Do *you* want a baby?"

"I don't know."

And she thinks he can't not know, that in his quiet way Nathaniel has always known what he wanted, and it protected her, this knowing, when so often she didn't know what she wanted herself. "I just want to go to the doctor," she says. "I want to find out what's wrong with me and then I want us to decide."

"Okay," he says. "We'll go to the doctor and decide."

"Jesus," she says. "My brother's memorial is in less than an hour. Why aren't we getting ready?"

"I *am* ready." Nathaniel is sitting before her in his suit and tie. She, on the other hand, is in only her underwear.

"Okay," she says, "*I'll* get ready." And, choking back a sob, she runs into the bathroom and closes the door.

Now, fully dressed, she descends the stairs to the first floor, to where Noelle and her boys are waiting. Lily and David are already at the Community Center, setting up for the memorial. Marilyn emerges from the bathroom, and now she leans against the banister, bending down to adjust her shoes. Thisbe comes in from the garden holding her own shoes; she opens a compact and applies eyeliner, then dabs her eyelids and applies some more.

"Is everybody set?" Marilyn asks.

Noelle lines up her boys in the foyer. They all have on neckties except for Ari, who's wearing a clip-on bow tie, which Noelle found in Leo's old bedroom. "Do you kids have tissues?" she asks. They have been known to wipe their noses on their shirts and pants, on whatever piece of cloth presents itself to them.

They nod.

"Has there been any word from Amram?" Thisbe asks.

Noelle gives her a cross look. She's been telling the boys he'll be back soon, but she hasn't heard from him. "He's coming," she says. "He wouldn't miss this."

"Check that the lights are out," Marilyn says, and Nathaniel walks through the house extinguishing the lights while Marilyn goes to wash the last few dishes.

Thisbe is brushing Calder's hair, and now she's wetting down his cowlick.

"Do I look handsome?"

"You're the handsomest young man in the world."

Nathaniel adjusts his tie in the hallway mirror, and now Clarissa is behind him, examining herself, too.

"Okay," Marilyn says, grabbing her pocketbook. She opens the door, and one by one they emerge into the sunlight. Everyone gets into their cars.

11

"Could you give me a hand with this?" Lily says.

David hefts a case of beer, and now he's hefted another one, and he seems about to heft a third before he changes his mind and deposits what he's lifted onto the table in back. They're on the second floor of the Community Center, setting up for the memorial. It's ten o'clock, and the service won't start until noon, but Lily has insisted they get here early.

At the back of the room, Lily makes sure the white wine is chilled and the corkscrews laid out as they should be.

"Everything looks good," her father says.

She's on her knees now, placing beers in the cooler.

"As do you," he says gallantly.

"What?"

"You're looking pretty, Lily."

"Thanks, Dad." She had an early-morning hair appointment with Priscilla, the mother of an old friend from town. Priscilla, as always, has done a lovely job, but now Lily in her red dress and heels, anticipating everyone's arrival, finds herself sweating, tendrils of hair plastered to her forehead like papier-mâché. She's so intent on not disturbing a strand that she's been walking around with her head straight and now her neck is starting to hurt. It's hot out—it's supposed to hit ninety-five today—and she contemplates placing herself beneath the ceiling fan, but that will make her hair blow in all directions.

She was already dressed when her father woke up this morning. She told him she had a request to make; she wanted to preside over the memorial. "I'll just stand up front and call the speakers to the microphone. And I want to pay for everything."

"Lily," he said, "come on."

When they got into town, she left him in the car with the motor running and returned with the bottles of red and white wine and the cases of beer, with seltzer, Coke, 7-Up, and cranberry juice cocktail. And the snacks, which she lays out now on porcelain plates the color of bone. Nuts and dried fruit, raw carrots, celery, stuffed grape leaves.

She distributes the chairs about the hall, thinking they would look best in semicircles, expanding outward like the rings around a planet. But there's something too kindergartenish about sitting in a semicircle; the mood should be more understated, she thinks, and more severe. So she rearranges the chairs in rows of ten, each directly behind the other. The chairs are wooden, hardback, the fold-up kind, which her parents rented from a caterer in town. She counts them now, a hundred and thirty total. There are more chairs downstairs, in the old billiards room; she can take them out if she needs them.

It was Thisbe who insisted that this not be a huge event. She reminded Lily that Marilyn and David have summered in Lenox for forty years now. Marilyn, officially off duty, has been called on more than once to assist in medical emergencies; she even helped deliver a baby—on July Fourth, in fact—when the local doctors had evacuated town. And everyone knew Leo. And they know the girls. It doesn't have to be family only, Thisbe said, but neither does she want people draped from the rafters, gaping down from the nosebleed seats.

Lily doesn't want it to be a spectacle, either. And it couldn't be one even if she wanted it to be; the room holds only 150 people. Yet even as she thinks this, she finds herself worrying not enough people will show up and this will reflect badly on her brother's memory, on all of them. She has set up thirteen rows of chairs, but even in this small room they look paltry. She could put out the extra chairs and fill the hall, but what if they remain unoccupied? There's nothing worse than empty seats.

They have hired a security guard, who's already patrolling out on Walker Street. The family has agreed to allow a single member of the local press to attend the memorial, but aside from that, the event is closed off to all cameras and reporters. There were dozens of journalists at the funeral last year, and it won't happen again this time; the security guard will make sure of it.

Lily adjusts the doily on the podium, checks again that the seats are arranged right. She has written out her speech, and she checks that too, to make sure the pages are in order. She's rewritten and rewritten it and she still can't stand it. She might discard it entirely and extemporize.

Again she readjusts the doily on the podium.

"Caught you," her father says.

"What?"

"Being compulsive. And here I was thinking you were a slob."

"I am a slob. Remember my college roommate preference form?" She had to rank herself from one to five, one being "neat," five being "constructive disorder," and she gave herself a resounding five. Yet she ended up with a compulsive for a roommate. She could have had her own reality show, *Cluttered Eye for the Neat Guy*. Sophomore year, her suite was broken into, and when the police showed up, they took one look at her room and said, "Poor girl, her possessions were ransacked." But they hadn't been ransacked; they hadn't even been touched.

"You always said a cluttered room was evidence of an organized mind."

"It is," she says.

"So what happened?"

What happened was, she met Malcolm, and a chef needs order in his restaurant. The problem is, the order has started to spread to their apartment. Malcolm gave her the home office because he believed if there was a single room in which she could commit clutter, it wouldn't bleed into the rest of the house. He needn't have worried. Last week, she found herself balling up his socks; next thing she knows, she'll be color-coding them. And look at her now: she's practically lining up the carrot sticks and grape leaves.

"You look good, Dad," she says. He has only a couple of suits, one of which he's wearing for the occasion, a gray affair that makes him appear handsome in an effortless, rumpled way. He has even gotten a haircut, which he consents to do only when prodded—a task that has devolved upon her mother, who puts the word *haircut* on the calendar on the fridge, spaced out every couple of months. And now she's leaving him, Lily thinks, and his hair will be left to grow like a clump of weeds; what if he won't be able to take care of himself? "How are you doing?"

"Pretty much as expected." He's at the front of the hall, beside the stage, and he hoists himself up onto it.

"Meaning not good?"

"I'll be okay."

"Will you be?"

"I always have."

Her mother used to say that her father dealt gracefully with whatever was handed him, and though on balance, Lily thinks, what was handed him was good, he has had his share of misfortune, starting with his father's death when he was only a boy. And then his stepfather died as he was leaving for college and his mother got married again.

"What about you?" he says. "How are *you* doing?" He removes a grape leaf from the tray and takes a small bite, then sets it on a cocktail napkin, where the oil starts to bleed through.

"Mostly I feel numb, but then that's no surprise."

"What do you mean?"

"The girl who goes outside without her winter coat on? Too cool to feel the cold?" It's why she asked him if she could preside over the memorial. It's her way of doing penance.

He seats himself in the front row of seats. Then, reconsidering, he moves a few rows back, only to change his mind again, and now he's over at the liquor table, dipping his hand into the cooler of beer. He brings a bottle up, looking at it with surprise, as if he's caught a fish.

"No alcohol before noontime?"

He laughs. It's the rule they used to have when the children were growing up. No sweets before noontime. So Lily and her siblings would make a ceremony of standing by the cupboard where the cakes and cookies were housed, counting down until midday.

"Speaking of which, I got you this." He hands her a package of gummy bears, which he picked up this morning at the candy store in town. "You still like gummy bears, don't you?"

She nods.

"There was a sign in the store that said 'Unattended children will be given espresso and a free kitten.' I thought it was funny. I had half a mind to take it home with me. Back to my days of petty crime."

"What days of petty crime?"

"Just your typical adolescent things. Stealing road signs and filling my pockets with sweets. The occasional dustup with some neighborhood kid."

"*Dustup?*" she says.

"You see all the things you don't know about me?"

She steps out onto the balcony. The playground and tennis courts are arrayed below her; down the hill is the Children's Center, where she and Thisbe sat yesterday drinking beers. She wouldn't mind another beer now. Beer and gummy bears. It would be enough to make her sick. But it would be a good kind of sick, the kind of sick that would distract her from a deeper sickness, from everything that's about to happen.

The memorial is being held in the center's ballroom, though it's not anywhere Lily would want to hold a ball. It's more like an elementary-school auditorium. Sixty years ago, she wouldn't have even been permitted inside the building. Before the town took it over, the center was home to the Lenox Brotherhood Club, and the Saturday night dance was the only time women were allowed in. Lily has an image of herself in the 1940s being escorted to a dance by some club member. She'd almost rather go to her brother's memorial.

Leaning over the railing, she's startled by the touch of a hand on her shoulder. It's her father's hand; he has come outside to join her. He's drinking a ginger ale, which he offers her a sip of, but she's still working on her gummy bears.

"You're looking contemplative," he says. "What are you thinking about?"

"Nothing," she says. "Everything. I don't know." She glances up at him. "What are *you* thinking about?"

"I was just remembering that after Leo died Mom and I talked about moving to California."

"Oh, come on. Mom never would have moved to California."

"Actually, she was the force behind it. She had it in her head that she would close her practice and we'd settle in Berkeley."

"What in the world would you have done there?"

"Beats me. Become full-time grandparents? Though Thisbe's parents would have already been there. We'd have felt like hangers-on." He does a couple of knee bends, and now, with his legs locked, he touches his hands to his toes.

"You're all movement, Dad, aren't you?"

"I suppose."

She recalls Leo's words, "channeled hyperactivity." It was how he used to describe their parents. And now he's gone, unable to see just how hyperactive they've become. Her father has taken up running and become devoted to opera; her mother is on the tennis courts even more than she used to be. As a teenager, she'd been ranked in the junior division, and she went on to play women's varsity at Penn before dropping the team in favor of chemistry lab and, after that, medical school. Now she's up again at six in the morning, hitting ground strokes in Central Park. It isn't sport for her, it's exorcism and absolution, and she takes pleasure in dispensing in straight sets whatever hapless male colleague has the temerity to take her on. And, throughout, she has been keeping up a full schedule of patients. It wouldn't surprise Lily if in the last year her parents have gotten only a few hours of sleep a night. Though she's not one to talk. She knows about channeled hyperactivity; she hasn't been sleeping much herself. "You'd have hated California."

"You're right," he says. "We'd have been back in New York in no time."

She knows what he's thinking, because she's thinking it, too. What if they'd moved to California and her mother had left him? He'd have been alone then, even more alone than he is now, in a state, a part of the country, where he knew hardly anyone. Though maybe if they'd moved to California, had relocated themselves far from where everything had gone wrong, if they'd started over, the way people for generations have started over in California, they might have been able to work things out.

She follows him inside, where he filches another stuffed grape leaf. But this one, too, he takes a bite of before leaving it to bleed across a cocktail napkin.

"You're breaking into the storehouses," she says. "Laying waste to the vineyards."

"I eat when I get nervous."

"Looks more like you gnaw."

"In my old age, I've started to worry."

"Your old age, Dad? You've been worried as long as I've known you. Compared to you, Mom was a stoic." Nervous Nellie, they used to call him. Dithering David. He was always delaying them on their way to school. *Don't forget to look both ways. Make sure to cross at the light.* He made them wear bicycle helmets, and this was practically before bicycle helmets were invented. Their mother, on the other hand, was on the front lines with her AIDS patients. She was accidentally pricking herself with needles, saying it was all part of the job.

"Yet it's on Mom's behalf that I'm worrying now. She's terrified things won't go okay."

"What does she think will go wrong?"

He shrugs.

"And who is she, anyway, to saddle you with her worries? Don't you think she's forfeited that right?"

He doesn't respond.

"What happened to the man who was boycotting dinner last night—that guy walking around with his ladder and paintbrush?"

"You preferred him?"

"I did."

What can he tell her? That that man is still there, as surely as is the man who is standing before her asking her to be good to her mother? The truth is, it's not in him to fight. Perhaps he's just hardwired that way. Or maybe it's how he was raised, a boyhood spent alone in the company of his mother, a woman with her own whims and tempers. He mourns for Leo no less than Marilyn does even if he isn't bellowing it into bullhorns. It's not in him to write op-eds, just as it's not in him to rage about Bush, though he hates Bush, too. In a way, he thinks his response is more dignified. Whether or not it is, it's the only response he knows.

He gets up now and heads across the hall, and Lily, following him, says, "Where are you going, Dad?" but he doesn't answer her. They pass under the huge ceiling fan, and for a second she feels as if she's being transported by some gale, her dress billowing as though it's trying to fly off. But then she's outside again, on the balcony, and the heat assaults her. Sweat drips down her forearms. A big patch of it blooms across her father's white shirt; he buttons his jacket to cover it up. "Mom's afraid of upsetting you."

"Why? Am I such a loose cannon?" And she wonders: is she? Is she someone people need to steer clear of?

"She's a little scared of you."

What's so scary about her? Much of the time she's scared herself. Her mother is afraid of her? The woman who chases after drug reps, who brings the pharmaceutical industry to its knees?

"She thinks you don't suffer fools gladly."

What fools? she thinks. And whom does she need to suffer? No one besides Noelle. Is that what her mother is worried about? Noelle?

"Go easy on her, okay?"

"Don't worry," she says. "I won't pick a fight."

They descend the stairs to what looks like an old smoking room, everything upholstered in dark leather. In the corner stands an upright piano, and the walls are lined with black-and-white photographs of old Lenox Brotherhood sports teams. The 1920 Brotherhood Basketball Team. The 1931 Brotherhood Baseball Team. There's a display of dollhouses behind glass.

"Mom thinks you're the quickest to defend Thisbe."

"What's there to defend?" Lily says. "Thisbe's done nothing wrong."

"You've always been tougher on Mom than on me. Long before any of this ever happened."

He's right, she thinks. Maybe it's because she and her mother are alike. The lanky ones, the two of them, the reddest of the redheads, fueled by their impatience, which darts like a beam of light into every corner of the room. Compared to them, her father was always softer. He used to carpool Lily and her sisters, off to music lessons and tumbling class, on outings to the Cloisters and Wave Hill. When Leo was old enough, he came along, too. Her father liked being the car-pool dad, even in Manhattan, where owning a car wasn't worth the trouble. He was a frustrated driver, a man who loved to drive in a city with no real roadway; it was the one thing he disliked about New York. In his twenties, he bought a Peugeot convertible in which he drove the women he dated; it was, he said, a test of their will. He did it with Marilyn too; he wasn't about to marry someone who wouldn't ride in his convertible. With the children in back, he would make a game out of driving, taking them up Amsterdam Avenue where the traffic lights were staggered, seeing how long he could go without hitting a red light. But he was always safe. When Lily and her sisters were in junior high school and the carpooling stopped, when the only driving he did was late at night, moving the car from one side of the street to the other in deference to the city's parking restrictions, he would ask if they wanted to come along. "Come on," he said. "A little alternate-side-of-the-street-parking fun?" When they were small, he took a leave from teaching so he could care for them while their mother did her second residency, in infectious disease. In their picture books with the animal figures, they would mistake the mother for the father, the one with the apron standing over the stack of dishes. When they fell and hurt themselves, they instinctively called out, "Daddy!"

Lily takes his hand and they go out front, where the holiday traffic is approaching them. A car drives past with a bumper sticker that reads BUSH IS LISTENING. USE BIG WORDS. And another bumper sticker: PRACTICE GENTLE ACTS OF IMPEACHMENT. They're in friendly territory, David thinks. He points to Lily's van parked out front, with its KERRY-EDWARDS sticker on the window. Back at the house, his and Marilyn's car is parked, too, with its own KERRY-EDWARDS bumper sticker.

"I know how to attach myself to losers, don't I?" Lily says. She's thinking of the Mets—and now the Nationals—but also of John Kerry. It's been almost a year since the election, but she can't get herself to throw that sticker out. The fact is, she's happy to defend John Kerry. Everyone she knows voted for him, though they did so with the feeling that at least he was better than Bush. She alone was enthusiastic. The long, dour face, the patrician moroseness, the French speaking, the flip-flopping, the polysyllabism: all the things people disliked about Kerry are precisely what drew her to him. There's a way in which she was a little in love with John Kerry and she remains so to this day.

"You always were a contrarian."

"I suppose I was." Oppositional Lily, her friends used to call her. She was captain of her high school parliamentary debate team, which meant one day she argued one side and the next day she argued the other, and if she'd been a student at Princeton in 1979 she would have stood with Sally Frank, suing the all-male eating clubs, taking the case to the New Jersey Supreme Court. But she was twelve in 1979. When she got to Princeton, Cottage Club was about to settle; it held its first

coed Bicker when she was a sophomore. She had no interest in bickering Cottage—Cottage was still the old Princeton, even if it had capitulated and gone coed—but she bickered anyway just to prove she could
get in, and as soon as she was admitted, she resigned. She clerked
on the Supreme Court after graduating from law school, for Justice
Scalia. She was the only liberal clerk out of four (most years Scalia
didn't have even one liberal), for a justice she found clever and winning but whom she consistently disagreed with. (She likes to say that
if she could have only added the word *not* to all of Scalia's sentences
he would have written an opinion she liked.) She spent the whole year
shouting at the other clerks. The combat in the justice's chambers
("What's going on in there?" people would ask) and continuing over
lunch on the steps of the Court, the beers late at night when the arguing resumed, everyone going home for a few hours of sleep ("No hard
feelings," the clerks would say as they departed), only to begin afresh
the following morning—Lily still recalls that as one of the happiest
years of her life.

A man comes up the road in sunglasses and a seersucker suit, walking
his Newfoundland. From a couple hundred feet away, Lily can already
see the spit spraying out of the dog's mouth, testament to the breed's
affinity for drool, or to her own eyesight, which is still twenty-ten in
both eyes. In seventh grade, when Clarissa needed glasses but didn't
want them, she had Lily accompany her to the eye doctor and Lily fed
her the answers to the chart while the doctor was looking away.

Owner and dog seem headed toward the Community Center. A dog
at a memorial service, Lily thinks. That would have been Leo's idea
of fun. But now the Newfoundland has turned up the block, past the
center and into town, his owner pulled after him.

Out in front, her father, seated on a bench, is staring into the
distance.

"What are you looking at?"

He shrugs. "I'm gazing into the great beyond."

"All you need is your telescope."

"Now, that's an idea."

Lily hasn't seen his telescope on this trip, though she expected it to
be out, and for him to be behind it, peering into the heavens. He has

joined the local Berkshires astronomy club, and he's always dragging Lily's mother to some remote meeting place beneath the stars. "It's how I spend my summer weekends," Marilyn says, "standing in the dark in an abandoned field." When she tries to talk to him during these outings, David's always shushing her, as if he thinks she'll wake up the constellations. In the wilting heat, with the mosquitoes swarming around him, he can be found on the deck pointing his telescope at the sky, gazing into the stratosphere.

Lily leans against the bench, ruminating over a celery stick. She crunches on it like a hare.

"Come on," her father says. "Let's take a walk." But he seems to mean only around the building, because he has guided her out back to the porch, where they sit now, looking at the tennis courts. "No matter what's happening between Mom and me, I don't think she'd say she regrets this."

"Regrets what?"

"Our forty-two years together."

"Oh, Dad. How could you even think that?"

A representative from the Community Center steps out onto the porch, with paperwork for them to sign. Lily removes her credit card, but it's too late: her father has already paid the bill. "Come on, Dad, I asked you."

"Indulge me," he says. "Leo was my son."

"And he was my brother."

"Parents like to pay for their children. It's written in the genes."

Maybe so, she thinks, but they're her genes, too, and she'd have liked to do this for Leo, if only this once.

Now they're back inside the center, in the game room, which is housed in an alcove on the first floor. "Look at this," her father says. "If the grandkids get restless, we can send them down here."

On the shelves are piles of books and board games. *Angelina at the Fair, Clifford the Big Red Dog, Bears, Bears Everywhere!*, Junior Monopoly, Let's Go Fishing, Scattergories, Apple to Apple. Down the steps is a foosball table, and Ping-Pong, air hockey, a soda machine, a VCR. A sign is tacked to the wall that reads FOUL LANGUAGE AND ROUGH PLAY ARE NOT ALLOWED. They'll have to remind the grandkids of that, too.

Out front again, they settle onto the bench facing Walker Street. A blond boy in a tank top sticks a pinwheel out of a car, and it lights up momentarily in the heat. In the rear of a station wagon a poodle paces, around its neck an American flag.

"I'm sorry Malcolm can't be here," her father says.

"I am, too."

"Mom and I have always liked Malcolm. I don't know if we've ever told you that."

"You haven't."

"It's not because we haven't felt it."

Lily's quiet.

"It's just that to tell your daughter you like her boyfriend is to imply you could just as easily not like him. I've always thought praise was a double-edged thing."

"I suppose it is."

"And you're such a private person."

"Why?" she says. "Have I ever refused to answer your questions?"

"Not refused, exactly . . ."

"But?"

"You make it known when things are off limits."

"Such as?"

"If you're going out at night and I ask about your plans, you're likely to say, 'I'm getting together with a friend.' As if to ask you anything more specific would be an intrusion."

"You can ask me what my plans are."

"Okay," he says, "what are your plans?"

"My plans at the moment should be obvious. I'm sitting in the heat in this horrible dress."

"Oh, Lily, it's not horrible."

She doesn't respond.

"Come on," he says. "Help me along here. You've caught me at a sentimental moment. Or a weak moment, at least. I'm feeling bold. I'm asking you about Malcolm."

"You want to know if I'm happy?"

"You probably think I'm not entitled. Not with what's happening between me and Mom."

"You're no less entitled than you ever were."

"Well, *are* you happy?"

"Yes, Dad, I am."

He stares out at the traffic. At the edge of the lawn, a boy is playing "The Star-Spangled Banner" on the French horn, and now a car moves slowly along the street, the driver pressing on his horn, as if trying to play a duet.

"And now is when you ask me why we haven't gotten married. Why we've decided not to have children."

"But I can't ask you that when I haven't been much of an advertisement for it myself."

"For children you've been an advertisement. At least, I hope you have."

"But not for marriage."

"Dad," she says, "you and Mom were married for forty-two years, most of them happy from my perspective."

"From my perspective, too."

"And if Leo hadn't died . . ." She can't even finish the sentence.

His gaze bores past her, out into the distance where the sun is beating down. "Mom's right, you know. It's easy for me to cast her as the bad guy, but I haven't been able to talk to her. I've become a workaholic, and I'm not even working anymore. A few months ago when we switched to daylight savings time, I forgot to adjust my watch and I didn't discover it until Thursday. Thursday!" he says. "What kind of life am I living that I can block out the rest of the world for days at a time and not even realize it's going on without me?"

"Dad . . ." She touches her hand to his jacket sleeve.

"There's a shame in all this."

"A shame in what?"

"There's the shame at having failed at something big—at the biggest thing I know of. And there's the shame at having let down my family."

"Oh, Dad. You haven't let us down."

A hawk flies over them, holding something in its mouth. A fire truck rumbles past them. "Look at you," he says. "You've gotten me to talk about myself when I was trying to talk about you."

"You wanted me to explain why Malcolm and I aren't married?"

"Not explain," he says. "That makes it sound like I require a justification. I'm asking for a reason, which is something different. There are reasons for everything, presumably."

"It's actually quite simple," she says. "I don't want the state involved in my love life." He's right, she tells him—she's a private person—and whatever else, weddings are so public. If she and Malcolm were to get married, they'd do it alone, with a justice of the peace, but even that she doesn't want to do. It just seems—she doesn't know—*silly*. Not for everyone, but for her.

"And Malcolm agrees?"

She nods. She feels more strongly than he does, but then on most things she feels more strongly than he does. It's one of the things that make them well suited: there's room for only so much strong feeling in one relationship. "And just so you know I'm not that stubborn, if Malcolm and I were to have children, we probably would get married, just because it would be easier on them if we did. It may not always be that way, but it still is, I think, and I wouldn't want them to have to bear the burden of my principles."

"But you're not going to have children?"

She shakes her head. On this Malcolm feels as strongly as she does. She thinks of that saying, Why do they make two-year-olds so cute? Because if they didn't, there would never be any three-year-olds. But for her and Malcolm, two-year-olds aren't nearly cute enough to make them want to have a three-year-old. Or an eight-year-old or a fifteen-year-old, for that matter. She's happy to be an aunt, and Malcolm's happy to be an uncle, or whatever he is to Noelle's and Thisbe's boys.

"Married or not," her father says, "do you think you're in it for the long haul?"

"I do," she says. She and Malcolm have been together for ten years, which puts them ahead of a lot of people. Not that she can ever be sure. What's happening with her parents—well, it's enough to give anyone pause. She once read that when your friends get divorced it makes you twice as likely to get divorced yourself. Breaking up really is contagious. "I've been having this idea," she says. "I want you to move down to D.C."

"Oh, Lily. Why in the world would I move down to D.C.? I hate it there."

"I hate it there, too, and look at me. I've been living there for over a decade."

"And that should be incentive for me to move there? Because you hate it there, too?"

"You almost moved to California," she reminds him. "It's harder to picture you in California than in D.C."

"I didn't almost move to California. I simply humored Mom until she came to her senses."

"And if she hadn't?"

"I probably would have gone."

"And look where you'd be now."

"I'd be alone in California, and you're telling me instead I should be alone in D.C.?"

"You wouldn't be alone. I'd be there."

"Lily."

"Seriously, Dad. What do you have left in New York?"

"I have everything there. I have my friends, my life, I still have the apartment. Clarissa and Nathaniel are right across the East River."

"You could use a new start."

"I'm almost seventy, darling. There are no new starts for me."

"Come down to D.C., Dad. I'll set you up with a senator's widow."

"I don't want to be set up with a senator's widow."

"Or a congressman's, then."

"I don't want to be set up at all."

"Single or attached, I'll be happy to have you. You can help out at Malcolm's restaurant. He'll put you to work."

"As what? The world's oldest busboy?"

"No one would know you were. I've heard about your jaunts around the Central Park loop. You probably run the mile faster than I do."

"I don't know about that."

"You can run along the Potomac, Dad. There's opera in D.C., too. We can get you a subscription to the Kennedy Center."

"Lily," he says, laughing, "that's nice of you. I'll be all right, darling. Don't worry about me."

"I'm just saying I'd like to see you more."

"I'd like to see you more, too."

"Then can we rent you a place for a couple of months? You don't even have to move down there. Think of it as a test drive."

He hesitates.

"Will you at least consider it?"

"Okay," he says. "I will."

He's staring now beyond the lawn, out to the road girdled with traffic, where the rest of the family will arrive soon. For an instant he thinks he sees Clarissa's car. "I've faced tough times before and I've gotten through them."

"I know you have."

"Really tough times."

"You're thinking about your father?"

He is. He was six when his father died. He has memories from earlier than that, recollections that go back to when he was three, but even in those his father is curiously absent. There are a few glints. His father, tall and broad-backed, striding through the living room as dinner is being announced. A Saturday morning and his father is shaving, and he stands on the toilet, eye level with the man, and afterward, alone, he draws swirls in the mirror with the discarded whiskers. Breakfast, the feel of his father behind him, a whiff of mint, his father's hands in front of him as if they're his own hands, cutting his waffle into tiny squares so that his meal looks like a chessboard. But when he visits these memories they disintegrate, and were it not for the photographs he has kept in a drawer he doubts he could recall what his father looked like. A year after his father died, he had a stepfather, and when *he* died, ten years later, another one lay in wait, and though both of them were good men who treated him kindly, he hardly remembers them any better than he remembers his own father; they were but dim music in the background of his days. He recalls his childhood as having taken place alone and in the company of a few solitary friends. He knows it's not true, exactly, but he thinks of himself as a latchkey kid; it's as if he raised himself.

For a long time he looked to father figures—his seventh-grade social studies teacher, a high school soccer coach, his dissertation adviser whom he so wanted to please he didn't drop out of graduate school until long after he first wanted to, settling, finally, on becoming ABD only when it became clear that he'd sooner kill himself than do another semester of research. He's not that way anymore (his own father, dead more than sixty years now, would be over a hundred if he were still alive), but he still has a thing about fathers and sons, about fathers and children in general. Marilyn was the one who insisted they stop at four (if it had been up to him, they'd have kept going), and back when he was still teaching, he would gravitate to the students who had lost a parent, knowing instinctively who they were without ever having been told. He was, in practice, the English-teacher-slash-guidance-counselor, though he'd been trained for only half the job. Late afternoons when classes let out, he could be seen in his office consulting with these students, who would sit there casting him their fugitive glances. His own father, who ran a big shoe conglomerate, always said that in a different life he'd have been a schoolteacher. It was math his father wanted to teach, but it was the teaching itself that interested him, and it wasn't until David had his first teaching job, installed in the high school where he would remain for thirty-nine years, that he even made the connection. "It's funny," he says. "I always wanted a son, but then Mom gave birth to you girls and I figured I was destined to have daughters and it was probably for the best. I thought having a boy would be more complicated."

"Was it?"

He shakes his head. "Or no more complicated than having any child." When Marilyn was pregnant with Leo, it was the early days of amniocentesis and the doctor told her she was having a boy. David thought Marilyn was pulling his leg, so he called the doctor and made her tell him herself. It was as if she were telling him he was having a gerbil.

"Fathers and sons," he says. He's thinking about Calder, who certainly won't remember Leo; he barely remembers him already. It's probably better that way. It's the same thing with divorce. Best to get it over with before the kids are born, and if there are kids, do it when they're toddlers so they don't remember what they're missing. Still, he thinks, there's a loss.

And now, suddenly, he's crying. "I miss Leo," he says, and all Lily can think is *Don't cry, Dad. Please.* Because, if he does, she won't be able to make it. But he goes on crying, and she feels like a doll made of porcelain, her face about to crack.

She goes upstairs and walks across the ballroom, passing again beneath that monstrous ceiling fan. "Here they come," she says. Through the window she can see her family getting out of their cars, her sisters and Nathaniel walking slowly beside each other, the children in dark jackets trailing them, her mother and Thisbe bringing up the rear.

12

It's twelve-thirty, and the memorial was supposed to start half an hour ago. The crowd is upstairs lingering quietly outside the ballroom, some of them next to the wine and the beer cooler, the raw vegetables still laid out but covered in cellophane to remind everyone they're for after the service.

Out on the balcony overlooking the playground, Clarissa, Lily, Marilyn, and David are conferring; soon Thisbe and Nathaniel join them. "What do you think?" Marilyn says. She's talking about Amram, who still hasn't shown up. Outside on Walker Street, Noelle is patrolling the block, looking in every direction for his car.

"We should wait," Thisbe says.

Above them, a helicopter comes into view. "Who's that?" says David.

"Is it the fucking press?" Marilyn says. The one reporter who's been allowed in is already here, loitering in back in his dark jacket and sunglasses, his press pass hanging like a pendant from him, looking vigilant and dour. He was carrying a camera when he arrived, but Marilyn told him to put it away. No cameras, no recording equipment, all the speeches at the memorial are off the record: those were the ground rules she set. The reporter can talk to the immediate family, but no one else is to be interviewed.

"Where's Amram when we need him?" Clarissa says.

"What do you mean?" says David.

"Wasn't he in the Israeli army? He probably knows how to shoot down helicopters."

Lily stares up at the aircraft. "The only thing Amram learned in the Israeli army was how to strip-search Palestinians."

"Enough," Marilyn says crossly. "Not today. Not now."

A group of Leo's friends have returned and are chatting amiably beside the wine and the beer cooler. There's an older assemblage, too, most of them Marilyn and David's friends, having driven up from New York and over from Boston, though there are also a few acquaintances from Lenox who have known the family over the years. An old babysitter of the girls is back in town, and she introduces herself to Clarissa and Lily. "I remember when Leo was in diapers," she says.

"We all do," says Clarissa.

"I remember when *Clarissa* was in diapers," Lily says, "and I'm younger than she is."

In the front row, Thisbe is whispering to Calder. Beside him sit his cousins. Next to Akiva is an empty seat, which he's holding for Amram. Noelle has told the boys their father called and he's coming back soon. She didn't want to scare them. She has convinced herself she's helping Amram save face, though it's really her own face she's saving.

Outside now, she asks the security guard for a match, then lights up a cigarette. She looks into the sun, her hand at ninety degrees to her forehead, though what is there to see? Amram can be coming in one of three directions, and he isn't coming from any of them. Unless he's planning to parachute in, like the military commando he's always wanted to be; at this point, she'd put nothing past him.

Finally, this morning, she began to panic. He'd been gone for nearly twenty-four hours, and it was time, she realized, to give up on pride and stop waiting for his call. She phoned him but was sent straight to voicemail. She phoned him again and was sent there once more. She started to rifle through his belongings—his coat, his pants pockets, his datebook, his memo pad, even the velvet sacks in which he keeps his prayer shawl and phylacteries—looking for any clue to where he was. She turned his pockets inside out, but all she could unearth was a cough-drop wrapper. The only other thing she found was the number *41* written randomly in pencil in his hand, and feeling desperate, she got on the computer to see if there was a flight with that number to Tel Aviv.

She couldn't find one, but she called El Al, anyway, and when the representative came on, she asked if an Amram Glucksman had checked in from Boston. "He's my husband," she said.

"What flight is he on?"

"The one this morning."

But there was more than one flight this morning from Boston to Tel Aviv, and when the representative asked to put her on hold, she panicked and hung up. She didn't want Amram to get detained, didn't want to get detained herself if she and the boys had to return home without him.

Next she tried rental car agencies. She plundered her purse to find the information, but Amram was the one who had rented the car, and she hadn't paid attention to the company. She called Thrifty and Budget, thinking those were names Amram would like, but they had no more information than the airline did. Finally, she turned off her cell phone and gave up.

Amram, she reminds herself, loves a grand entrance. He was half an hour late to his own son's bris, and when he finally arrived he said, "I thought I'd keep the young man waiting. I figured I'd stave off his pain." Though it's her own pain she's staving off now by trying to convince herself he wouldn't miss this.

Her mother comes outside to join her. "He knows when the memorial is, doesn't he?"

"Of course he does."

"I just—"

"Do you think he's an idiot?"

"And he knows where?"

"He knows everything he needs to."

"Do you want *me* to call him?"

"Believe me, he won't pick up."

It's one o'clock now, and Noelle examines her watch as if for errors, but it's just her way of avoiding her mother's gaze, of avoiding the gaze of her sisters, who are leaning out the window looking down at her.

She lights another cigarette. "Don't tell me not to smoke."

"I didn't say anything."

She takes a lap around the Community Center, and another lap, and another, yanking out a dandelion as she tramples through the tall grass, tearing its head off and tossing it behind her in violence and disgust, in her other hand her cigarette diminishing to a nub so that she practically singes her cuticles.

When she returns, her mother is still waiting for her out front. "You know we want him here, Noelle. He's part of our family."

For a second Noelle softens, but then her mother says, "Aren't you scared?" and Noelle says, "Of course I'm scared, I'm fucking terrified."

The only thing blunting the edge of her fear is the anger trying to displace it. *He's part of our family.* She feels gratitude to her mother for saying this, but along with this gratitude comes shame, because maybe *she* doesn't want him as part of the family. He has spent the last day embarrassing her, and now he's embarrassing her even more; no doubt if he shows up he'll embarrass her further. Maybe she embarrasses easily. Or maybe this is just how he is. She's furious at him for not having shown up, even as she hopes he won't show up, which will allow her to be even more furious at him.

She walks out onto the street, into the July Fourth traffic, looking, she realizes, like some deranged police officer, as if by standing there amongst the cars she'll get Amram to show up.

Upstairs, heads swivel as she enters the hall. Her mother beckons her out onto the balcony. "Noelle, we have to—"

"I know."

"What?"

"You have to start without him."

"It's almost one-thirty. We only have the room for another couple of hours."

"That's fine," she says, but she starts to cry.

"I'm sorry, Noelle. I really am." She reaches out to hug her, but Noelle pushes her away.

She stays out on the balcony, watching everyone through the glass. Her father motions to her to come inside, but she pretends not to see him. If they want to go ahead without Amram, they'll have to go ahead without her too. Now her mother is gesturing at her emphatically, but she turns from her as well.

Through the window, she can see Clarissa seated onstage, playing the processional on the cello, and listening to her sister, to the mournful sounds of the cello, she's brought back to a time when the world felt open and young, when it was just her and her siblings and their days were marked by the sounds of Clarissa practicing music in the other room. Now those days are gone and Leo's gone with them, and now Amram is gone, too, and she feels as if she's gone as well; she doesn't know who she is any longer. She has a fantasy in which the

Community Center gets blown up and everyone is killed except for her. All the people she's ever known are dead, and she's alone now. What will she do? Who will befriend her?

When she steps inside, she sees the room has been partitioned in back, which makes it appear smaller than it is, and this has the effect of making the crowd seem larger. She's not good with numbers; when she attends an event, Amram's always asking her how many people were there, and invariably she doesn't know. He's constantly quizzing her, putting her on the spot. At dinner, presiding over his clan, he checks in with their boys, who sit around him like a constellation of moons, and then he checks in with her; he wants her to report on her day. She tries to do her best, but his questions fluster her. She's back in school, asked to remember the signing of the Constitution, the words Lincoln uttered at Gettysburg, who said, "Give me liberty or give me death." The glare of the lights is on her, her teacher's rebuking gaze; she'd rather die than to have to sit there and report. The sad thing is, she feels this way even now, with her own family, the people she's supposed to be comfortable with. That word *report* freezes her, and she can't remember anything. If Amram wants to know how many people were at the memorial, he should have shown up. Still, she reflexively scans the rows of seats so she can give him an answer when he asks. She counts seventy-five people, eighty-five, over a hundred now, her family's friends and acquaintances fanning out, a few faces she doesn't recognize.

Lily steps to the podium to introduce the speakers, but Noelle can't hear her. She tells herself it's her hearing loss. That's part of it, certainly; she has trouble making out voices in large rooms, has trouble placing voices, too. At home, one of the boys will call to her from downstairs and she'll think he's calling her from upstairs; she'll be in the supermarket and a friend will scream out, and she'll turn the wrong way. She has a hearing aid, but it's back at the house, in her suitcase. As a teenager, she would trumpet her hearing loss; now she doesn't tell anyone. She carries her hearing aid wherever she goes, the way she used to carry her diaphragm, but when it came time to use it, she would forget to, or wouldn't bother—it's a miracle she didn't get pregnant all those years—and it would stay nestled like an egg in her purse, the way her hearing aid does now. And though it's true the acoustics in the hall aren't good, that's only part of the problem. She can't concentrate on what Lily's saying. And now it's Clarissa's turn to speak and she can't concentrate on what she's saying, either.

Clarissa looks out at the audience. "How to start?" she says, arranging her papers on the podium. She could begin, she tells the crowd, by listing her brother's attributes, but she hates to reduce people to attributes. "And Leo was less reducible than most." So she describes a trip she and Nathaniel took to Wesleyan when Leo was a student there. Nathaniel came down with a cold, so she and Leo left him in the dorm with a bowl of instant chicken soup and went into town to pick up sandwiches. "It was December, and cold out, and a homeless man came over to Leo and said, 'Hey, Tom, how have you been?' and Leo said, 'I'm fine, Frank, how are you?' And I whisper to Leo, 'Do you know him?' and Leo says, 'I've never seen him in my life.' 'Then why did you call him Frank?' I ask, and Leo says, 'Why did he call me Tom?' So Leo and this guy he's calling Frank get to talking, and Frank says, 'You know what I could use, Tom? Ten dollars.' And Leo says, 'Why do you want ten dollars?' 'I want to see a movie,' Frank says. 'I haven't seen a movie in years.' 'Look at you, Frank,' Leo says. 'You're emaciated. You don't want to see a movie. You want to eat.' And Frank admits this is true. So Leo hands him his sandwich.

"A few other homeless men approach us now. They want to know what's going on. 'Tom's feeding the pigeons,' Frank says. But Leo takes offense on Frank's behalf. 'You're not a pigeon,' he tells him. 'You're not a damn pigeon.'

"Soon the other guys want in on the deal. Leo's standing on the steps of the sub shop, saying, 'Okay, who'd like a sandwich?' and they all raise their hands. One wants turkey, one wants roast beef, one wants meatballs. Leo takes down their orders and comes back with three subs, and when he's done passing them out he hands Frank a ten-dollar bill. 'For dessert,' he says. 'Go catch yourself the last screening of *Rocky Horror.*'

"It wouldn't have surprised me," Clarissa says, "if Leo had returned to his dorm and brought back Nathaniel's chicken soup too. He wasn't a do-gooder. He hated that phrase. He was just someone who got an idea into his head. He did everything in excess, but it was a good kind of excess."

A few people are nodding in back. A man removes his jacket and slings it over his chair. Leo's boyhood friends are clustered in a couple of rows, the men in blue blazers and khakis, the women in sundresses, as if they all got together to decide what to wear.

Clarissa says, "When I told a friend about today's memorial, she asked me why we'd decided to do it. I think she meant 'Why go through it again?' What could I tell her? That I'm always going through it, that my whole family will be going through it for the rest of our lives? But then my friend said, 'I understand, you want closure,' and I thought I could kill her. To me, *closure* is the most detestable word in the English language. It's what other people say to you when they think it's time to move on.

"My brother's funeral was so public we decided we wanted to do something different this time. To *own* the event, is the only way I can think to put it. But I'm realizing now that I was hoping it would be easier. A year has passed, so in a way it *is* easier, but in the ways that count it feels the same to me.

"I thought of myself as Leo's second mother. In a lot of ways, I thought of myself as his *first* mother. I remember being a teenager and wanting you to die, Mom, for all the reasons any teenager wants her mother to die, but also because I thought I'd do a better job with Leo. I mean, you did a great job, of course . . ."

Marilyn, smiling, raises her hand in front of her as if to say she understands.

But now Clarissa doesn't know how to go on. In the front row, Ari tugs on the edge of his bow tie, and now Dov is tugging on it, too. "Stop it, boys," Noelle whispers. A car horn honks out on Walker Street.

Clarissa looks up at her father. He didn't speak at Leo's funeral, but he left open the possibility that he might speak today. Now, though, he shakes his head. A year has passed, but he still can't do it. Clarissa steps down from the podium and returns to her seat.

The heat is smothering, so Marilyn gets up to turn on the ceiling fan. But it's a rickety contraption that emits more noise than air, and now, as the hall starts to vibrate with the sound of it, she switches the fan off. She opens all three doors to the balcony. Leaning out, she can still see that helicopter suspended above the building. She wants to scream. Someone's cell phone goes off and people turn around. It's an elderly man's and he's having trouble finding it; his wife searches through his bag.

Now it's Noelle's turn to speak. She considered writing something out, but she doesn't do well with prepared texts. She suffers from performance anxiety, but that's because she thinks of things as a performance, and so she has resolved not to regard her speech this way. If she stands at the podium and says nothing, that will be all right, too; it will be its own sort of testament. And she *will* say something. Even if it's simply, "I'm Noelle, the youngest of Leo's three sisters. My brother died, and I miss him." The words aren't eloquent, but they're true, and the truth, she thinks, has its own eloquence.

She rests her arms on the podium. Her hands flutter like birds. "My name is Noelle Glucksman. I'm the youngest of Leo's three sisters, and I was the last person in my family to see Leo alive. As many of you know, I'm an Orthodox Jew, and Leo spent Shabbat in Jerusalem with Amram and me and our four sons before he was captured. He stayed up late talking to us. He asked a lot of questions. About God and theology, about our lives. 'Such structure,' he said. 'That's amazing.'

"I have this image of my brother from when he was four. He's up here in Lenox, running around naked in our front yard. My parents told him to put on his clothes, but he wouldn't listen to them. He never would. He always did what he wanted. But there was another side to Leo—a thoughtful, contemplative side. It's not a coincidence that he studied philosophy in college. He was always interested in the truth. I saw that side of him when he visited Jerusalem. I told him he was welcome to sleep in on Saturday, but he wanted to come with us to synagogue. He couldn't read Hebrew, but he insisted on following along in the transliterated English. The service was close to three hours, but he stayed there the whole time.

"After he died, people said to me, 'How can you believe when something like that happened?' But I know Leo wouldn't have said that. If he were alive to reflect on his own death, he wouldn't have said you shouldn't believe. And he wasn't a believer himself. That Shabbat in

Jerusalem, I thought I could see my brother as an Orthodox Jew. I'm not saying he would have become one, only that he was interested in everything and he was up for anything. That's one of the reasons he ended up in Iraq. Leo was the most open, most curious person I've ever known.

"When the sun went down that day, Amram recited the havdalah service, which is the prayer Jews say to mark the end of the Sabbath. It separates the holy from the profane. There's a tradition that when a girl holds the havdalah candle she should hold it at the height she wants her future husband to be. Leo was the one holding the havdalah candle that night, and I must have told him about that tradition, because I noticed he was measuring the height of the candle, holding it just so. 'That's how tall Thisbe is,' he said.

"'But you're already married to her,' I told him.

"'I know,' he said. 'But I'd marry her again. I'm thinking about her. The next time you talk to her, please tell her that.'

"An hour later, he packed and left. It was the last time I ever saw him." Noelle wants to go on, but she doesn't have anything else to say. She steps down from the podium and walks back to her seat.

A hush descends on the room. For a second Thisbe thinks everyone is staring at her. She looks down at her lap, and when she glances up she sees Jules, Leo's best friend from childhood, and she smiles at him. She catches the eye of her college roommate sitting in back.

Then Ari calls out, "I miss Uncle Leo!" though he's only three and doesn't remember him. But he remembers his father, and when he says, "I want Abba to come back," his voice is loud and plaintive. He starts to cry, and now Calder has started to cry, too.

A blond woman in a crinoline skirt offers to take Calder and Ari downstairs to the game room. But the other boys wish to remain in the hall, and now, as Lily steps to the podium to deliver her speech, Akiva starts to cry as well.

"It's contagious, isn't it?" Lily steps down from the podium and gives Akiva a tissue.

A cough rings out; soon another one echoes it. Lily looks up at the crowd. She has, in fact, discarded her prepared speech and chosen to speak off the cuff. "Leo would have been uneasy watching us here today. He'd have told us to lighten up. I was five years older than Leo. I used to sit on him to get him to be quiet. But in a lot of ways he seemed older than me. Or if not older, then more sage.

"Dad, you and I took up running this past year, and for months we didn't even know the other was doing it. It was like we were in silent communion. Sweating out our grief, is how I think of it.

"When Leo was a boy, he used to cry when he watched the evening news. Terrible things were happening around the world, and it tormented him. He was touched by strangers. It made sense that he chose journalism, and it made sense that he wound up overseas. Yes, he liked danger, but there was something bighearted about him. Nothing for him was abstract or far away.

"Okay," Lily says. "This is what I really want to say. Noelle, there's this Hebrew phrase you sometimes quote whose meaning is 'Those who understand will understand.'"

"*Ha'mevin yavin*," Noelle whispers from the front row.

"The idea being," Lily says, "that those who understand will understand, and those who don't understand, it's probably better that way. When Leo was twelve we adopted a stray dog he'd found in the park. Mom, you used to say the dog had a special affinity for Leo, and I suppose that's true, if by 'special affinity' you meant Kingman ignored Leo slightly less than she ignored the rest of us. Kingman was wonderful and we all loved her, but if she could have found a way to pour her own food, she wouldn't have missed any of us. There was only one way you could get Kingman to pay attention to you. If, for example, Clarissa and I were walking her and Clarissa had to leave, Kingman would strain after Clarissa. But then if I was the one who had to leave, Kingman would strain after me. She didn't want us to separate. Leo called her the Togetherness Dog. And he was like that, too. He was the Togetherness Person. He was also—and I don't think a lot of you know this—the family mediator. Noelle, you're right when you say Leo did what he wanted, but he was always keeping an eye on us, and there were certain things he couldn't abide. One of those was conflict. Dad, I remember you saying they should have made Leo the Middle East envoy. Dennis Ross couldn't hold a candle to my brother. Put Leo in a room with the Palestinians and the Israelis, and he wouldn't have let them leave until they'd reached an accord. And maybe, I like to think, that's what he set out to do in going to the Middle East, and he simply got derailed.

"There are things happening in our family that I'm not free to discuss, so I'll just invoke Noelle and say that those of you who understand will understand, and those of you who don't understand, it's probably better that way. I'm not sure of a lot when it comes to Leo, but I'm sure that if he were alive, he wouldn't allow this to be happening. He would sit the parties down and refuse to let them leave. He'd have pulled on you both just like Kingman did, because that was the kind of person he was." As she speaks, Lily's not even looking at her parents. She's staring out at the audience, where a hush has settled again, and now someone in back has blown her nose and deposited the tissue into her pocketbook. "That's all," Lily says. "I have nothing else to say."

As Lily steps down from the podium, Clarissa and Noelle glance up at their parents, but Marilyn and David are simply staring straight ahead. They don't look at Lily either when she tries to catch their glance.

The security guard has come upstairs and is standing now outside the doorway. Clarissa's cello, which is leaning against the wall, wobbles briefly, and a man in suspenders and a paisley tie goes over to right it. Thisbe stares down at the folder in her lap. "Well," she whispers to Lily, "I guess it's my turn."

She approaches the podium and removes the papers from her folder. "Hello, everyone," she says tentatively.

People murmur back.

At the center of the room, Leo's friends straighten in their chairs. A couple of the men button their blazers. For an instant, Thisbe smells a whiff of perfume. They're all staring at her, just as she'd be staring if she were sitting where they were. She wants to do well by them, to do well by herself, but she doesn't know if she can, doesn't even know what doing well by them would mean.

Glance up, she thinks. *Pause. Enunciate.* She has written these words in the margins of her speech, and now she's trying her best to listen to them. "I met Leo here in Lenox," she says. "It was the summer before our senior year of college, and on our first date Leo and I and Leo's best friend Jules played paintball together." She looks up at Jules, and he nods. "I don't know how many of you are familiar with paintball, but it's a messier, more violent version of Capture the Flag. You're standing in the middle of some abandoned field, shooting at each other with pellets. Jules, you and I ganged up on Leo, but the two of you also had this game of your own, trying to see who could hit the other more."

Jules laughs, and Thisbe feels her nerves loosen. Briefly, she laughs, too. "I know there's supposed to be a lesson here. Live by the sword, die by the sword. You meet your husband when people are shooting at him, and . . ." She takes a quick breath. "But that's not the lesson I draw. What I think is that Jules was there on Leo's and my first date. You have a crush on a girl, and you invite your best friend along! I've never known anyone who had as many friends as Leo, and the friends he cared about most were here in Lenox. This was his second home, but it was really his first home."

Several of Leo's friends nod; one of the women dabs a handkerchief to her eyes.

"The day he left for Iraq, Leo said to me, 'I'm going back to the state of nature.' He was talking about Thomas Hobbes, whom he studied in college. Leo liked to say that Hobbes's description of life was really a description of him: nasty, brutish, and short. But he was none of those things, certainly not as I saw him.

"Marilyn and David, Clarissa, Lily, and Noelle—I'm an only child, and growing up, I always felt that my family was insubstantial compared to yours. That's one of the things that appealed to me about Leo—the tumult of you Frankels, as if in your presence I was being swallowed by a many-tentacled beast and made into a tentacle myself. Clarissa, Lily, and Noelle—you all were older by the time I came along, but I still felt that in marrying Leo I was getting you as sisters, and when he died I lost you, too. I know that losing a husband is different from losing a sibling, and it's especially different from losing a son. A lot has changed since Leo died, but I will always be part of your family." Thisbe's thinking of a phrase Noelle used to recite: "We shall do and we shall listen." It's what the Israelites declared at the foot of Mount Sinai. And why, Noelle asked, did the Torah say "We shall do and we shall listen" instead of "We shall listen and we shall do"? Don't you listen to God's commandments before you follow them? But that was the point, Noelle said. You did God's bidding whether or not you understood it, and the very act of doing that bidding caused it to make sense.

That's what Thisbe thinks as she stands at the podium. Saying the words will make her feel them. And she does feel them, even if she's not sure she wants to. She looks up at Leo's parents, at her sisters-in-law. *I will always be part of your family.* Shoulders shaking, breaths coming out in sobs, she steps down from the podium and hugs Marilyn and David, hugs Clarissa, Lily, and Noelle, and now, back in her seat, she wraps her arms so hard around herself she fears she might unspool.

Someone has extinguished the lights, and now slides are being shown on a screen above the stage. Photos of Leo and the rest of the Frankels, photos of Thisbe and Calder too. From her spot presiding, Lily watches herself move in and out of the light, as if a train is flashing past her in the darkness. She sees Malcolm reflected on the screen. He's in photograph after photograph, only now she realizes it's not him but his shadow, cast hundreds of miles up the East Coast. It's not until she has stepped down from the podium and made her way to the back that she sees him pressed against the wall, standing beside the cooler of beer, looming quietly in the darkness. "Malcolm?"

"I drove up here," he says. "I hope that's all right."

"All right?" She steps back from him as if to get a better look, to make sure he is who he is and not some impostor boyfriend.

"You told me not to come, Lily. You said you wanted to do this on your own."

"Oh, Malcolm." She takes him in a hug.

Now that the service is over, she leads him down the stairs and out behind the Community Center, past the playground and the tennis courts and across the open field, where, looking back at the balcony, she sees the memorial guests shrinking in the distance, appearing now like marbles in slots. She subsides onto the grass; Malcolm sits down next to her. "Malcolm, you're here!"

"I'm here," he says.

"Tell me all about you."

He laughs.

"Come on, catch me up."

He's wearing a seersucker suit, the pants of which he's gotten grass stains on, but he doesn't seem to care, and she certainly doesn't care about her own grass stains. She takes off her shoes and runs her toes across the ground.

"I went to the beach," he says.

She pokes him in the side. "I know you went to the beach."

"What else can I tell you?"

"Whatever you want."

"That guy I met with the other day? The financier, as you call him?"

"What financier?"

"Come on, Lily. Have you forgotten? I've been meeting with backers? Trying to open up my own restaurant?"

She remembers, of course. She just forgot Malcolm met with a backer the other day. Although now that he mentions it, she recalls a toe against her calf as she lay half asleep, the strong, animal tug of him and, some minutes later, a hand gentle on her neck when he emerged wet from the shower, the smell of coffee as he leaned over in the smear of dawn to kiss her goodbye, his words, *Wish me good luck.*

"Well, he called me this morning and said there's a good chance he'll fund my restaurant."

"Malcolm! That's amazing!"

"A good chance," he repeats. "The details still need to be worked out."

"Malcolm!"

"Lily, nothing's definite."

Nothing's ever definite, she wants to tell him. Look where she's been these past few hours. Look where she's been the last year of her life. "Master of your domain," she says. "Emperor of your empire."

"Lily, come on."

"Malcolm, you're going to have your own restaurant!" She takes his hand and they return across the field, back to the crowd sipping drinks and eating canapés, back to where her parents are waiting for her.

Now that the service is over, Thisbe greets people she hasn't seen since Leo's funeral, some she hasn't seen since their wedding, only now she's gotten the two mixed up and she can't remember whom she saw when.

She finds Calder down in the game room, where he's playing foosball against himself, twisting the handles around and around so that the players keep doing somersaults. He stands beside the woman who brought him downstairs.

"Thank you for rescuing him," Thisbe says. "And me, too, while you were at it."

"It was nothing. I got him away from the madding crowd. It was the least I could do."

"Well, thank you."

"Hello there." Jules has sneaked up from behind Thisbe and is standing next to her now.

"Jules!" she says, hugging him. "I hadn't even realized you were coming, and then I saw you in the crowd!"

"Oh, come on," he says. "I never would have missed this."

Thisbe tries to introduce Calder to Jules ("Jules was Daddy's best friend"), but Calder doesn't even look up from his foosball game, whose players he continues to spin and spin without regard for their kicking the ball.

Thisbe steps back to have a look at Jules. His hair is blond as it always was, but he has cut it short, and it's starting to grow gray at the temples. "How are you, Jules?"

"I'm okay, I guess. It's been a tough year."

"For all of us."

"I mean, I knew that guy when we were in first grade."

"He lived for you," she says. "He lived for all his friends in Lenox." She points at his feet. "Look at you, Jules. Your shoelaces are untied." And she remembers how Jules could never be bothered to tie his shoelaces, and how Leo made a point of stepping on them. She imagines Jules as a boy, imagines Leo as well, giving each other noogies and dead arms, kneeing each other in the thigh, shouting "Charlie Horse!" as they did so, as if by naming the act they were absolved of blame. All that sanctioned violence decked out as camaraderie so that it was hard to tell where one ended and the other began. And an image comes to her, of Leo and Jules in the mall on some bank of escalators, running up the down escalators and down the up ones, nearly colliding with the other shoppers. It's as if the memory comes from earlier, and she's been boomeranged back to when she wasn't around, trespassing on their former lives.

The summer she met Leo, Jules was still trying to get into movies for half price. At the local diner, where he and Leo would convene for a noontime breakfast, Jules would flirt with the waitress by insisting on ordering the kids' meal. "More fish sticks," he said. "And chocolate milk. And could you possibly get me a box of crayons?" They acted like children when they were together, probably because they'd met when they were six, a group of boys who spent the summer with each other, all of them parting ways when the school year started and reuniting like sparrows every July, claiming that school, their friends back home, meant nothing to them and they lived only for the summer and for each other, when they would return to Lenox. In Leo's case, it was true. He spoke of his friends from Lenox with near-reverence, no one more so than Jules, who lived the rest of the year in the suburbs of Boston and who would remain Leo's best friend until he died. It was all guys—five, six, seven of them—and even once they were older and had left for college, it seemed there was no room for girls. Early on, Thisbe discovered that by dating Leo she was also dating his group of friends and she was supposed to win their favor. But she didn't want to appeal to her boyfriend's buddies, some of whom she liked and some of whom she didn't. As it happened, they all liked her. She's always been good at being one of the boys, and she was especially fond of Jules.

Now Calder has lain down on the floor beside them; it seems that he's actually fallen asleep.

"He has your eyes," Jules says.

"Jules, he's sleeping."

"Your eyelids."

"You sound just like Leo." That night at the bar, the first time they met, Leo sidled over to her by the nachos and beer and said, "I like your eyes."

Thisbe laughed. He would need to think of a better come-on than that. "How about my nose?"

"That's good, too."

"And my ears?"

"I like those also."

"Seriously," Jules says. "He's your spitting image."

"It's funny," she says, "because I've always thought he looked like Leo." Though in a way she and Leo looked alike.

"Tell me about him."

"He's your typical three-year-old," she says. "He's the king of scatology. Everything's a poop joke with him."

"Tell me something else."

"He's just like Leo. He has absolutely no sense of direction. One time, I took him to a party with my anthropologist friends and he kept bumping into the mirrors. Everyone thought he was drunk."

Now Marilyn tells the crowd it's time for the unveiling, and Thisbe thinks this is a reprise. Because it was only a year ago when she was here, sitting up front at Leo's funeral, then on to the graveyard, the limousines flashing their garish lights. And everything she's been feeling these last minutes, that sense of solace, of things opening up, back with Jules again, even laughing a little: it's all gone now, and a gloom settles over her once more.

She drives with Marilyn in her rental car, and she feels that she can't look at her and can't avoid her either. They're two chickens in a coop, and she stares straight ahead, navigating along the twisting roads, and the word comes to her, *serpentine, serpentine*, as if someone is shooting at her.

A car horn goes off in the distance. A cow looks up from the side of the road, blank-faced, cow-faced, chewing its cud.

Now all that's left is the laying of the headstone, which the graveyard workers do without ceremony, and it seems no one in the family wants ceremony, either. There it is, removed from its wrapping, unveiled to them, Thisbe thinks, and of course it is; that's why they call it an unveiling.

LEO FRANKEL, HUSBAND, FATHER, BROTHER, SON
APRIL 10, 1972–JULY 4, 2004

"We forgot to say kaddish," someone says. Amram was supposed to say kaddish at the memorial, but he wasn't there. There are thirty, forty people standing around Leo's grave, more than half of them Jewish, but no one besides Noelle knows how to say kaddish. Lily says, "Will you say kaddish, Noelle?"

Noelle has never said kaddish before; even during Leo's shivah, Amram recited it for her. There has been a movement among the Orthodox to allow women to say kaddish, but Noelle isn't part of that movement. Even before she became religious, she wasn't a feminist, yet she feels like a crypto-feminist as she realizes that were she to say kaddish she'd probably stumble over the words. She speaks and reads Hebrew as well as Amram does, but she has never been called on to lead the prayer service. As she stands before the crowd, she's surprised to feel she's been kept under wraps.

She does, in fact, falter as she begins, especially since she's reciting from memory. And the kaddish is in Aramaic, the language of the Talmud, which she never studied. But she presses on, reminding herself that it doesn't matter if she makes a mistake because no one will know besides her. For a second she feels loosed from something, and when she thinks that Amram may not be coming back, it's with less panic than she felt earlier. If she has to, she'll take the boys back to Israel on her own. She'll find a way to manage.

When she finishes chanting, everyone stands quietly in the graveyard, waiting for what comes next. But there's nothing more to do. So they form a single line moving away from the grave, and one by one they get into their cars.

13

Thisbe drives home with Marilyn and Calder, none of them speaking; a heaviness corrodes the air. They move along Main Street, slowed by the holiday traffic, and when Thisbe turns on the radio no sound comes in.

They get to the house, and Marilyn goes upstairs and Thisbe and Calder go downstairs, and soon the other cars have arrived as well and everyone disperses to their quarters. The house feels empty, yet it's overcome at the same time by a low-grade clamor. Thisbe thinks she hears noise upstairs, but when she goes to search she can't find anyone.

In the garden, the sprinklers have gone off of their accord, and now, on the second floor, a bath is being run. The whole house is leaking water. In the living room, she finds the TV on, but no one is watching it. The news is playing: a pastiche of the holiday. Fireworks are being readied by the National Parks Service. A man is stoking a barbecue pit. President Bush is presiding over a service at Arlington National Cemetery.

Outside on the porch her nephews are spraying each other with Calamine lotion. Now it's sunscreen they're spraying. Soon Calder has joined the fray.

When he comes back inside, he looks like a ghost. A pink ghost, actually. Thisbe didn't realize they'd invented pink sunscreen. Or maybe it's pink Calamine lotion. Whatever it is, he's covered with it.

She takes him into the bathroom and cleans him up, and now, back in the basement they've been sharing, wearing a new set of clothes, he sits down to the computer. She has told him he can compose an e-mail, but since he's only three, he simply pounds on the keys. Seated on the bed with the screen open before him, he regards her computer with a glum familiarity that suggests he's been composing e-mails for years. When he was two, he insisted on having his own cell phone, so she gave him a phone that no longer worked. But he wanted an actual phone, something that lit up and made real cell phone noises. Now he wants his own laptop. Like most children, he loves buttons—what, Thisbe wonders, did the cavemen do?—but he seems especially preoccupied with them. This disappoints her—she wanted to raise a humanist!—though she takes solace in the thought that it will be good to have a handyman around the house.

She connects him to the Internet and goes upstairs, and when she reaches the landing she sees Noelle in the foyer putting on a pair of rollerblades. "Are you going rollerblading?"

Noelle gives her half a smile.

"Right," she says. "You're putting on rollerblades, but you're going for a swim."

"Do you want to come along?"

"Really?"

"You look like you could stand to get out of the house. I know I can."

"Calder's on the Internet," she says. "By the time we get back, he'll have hacked into the Pentagon."

"My mother will watch over him. Come on." Noelle is bent over in the hall closet, fishing around among the rain boots and beach towels and shuttlecocks and running shoes. She turns back to Thisbe. "What size are you?"

"An eight."

"Here," she says. "These might fit you." She tosses a pair of rollerblades at Thisbe's feet.

Noelle is at the foot of the stairs now, skating forward and back. "You should be a good partner, a California girl like you." She bends over and touches her toes, then skates around the foyer in circles.

They skate down Cliffwood into town. Thisbe may be a California girl, but the first time she skated was when she was four and her mother took her to the ice rink at Rockefeller Center in the shadow of that year's Christmas tree. Bowdoin had a women's club ice hockey team, which required less skill than enthusiasm, but she had enough of both to play for a couple of years. She could skate backwards and could whack at the puck with sufficient accuracy to send it skidding toward the goal. But what she liked best about ice hockey, about skating in general, was when she put her shoes back on. Those first few steps: it was as if she were being transported on helium. She feels the same way when she emerges from a sauna. Air! It's like the world is saying, "Come take me!"

When they reach town, the sidewalks have been taken over by window-shoppers, so they step out onto the street and skate between the cars. If the cyclists can do it, why can't they?

"Where are we going?" Thisbe asks.

Noelle doesn't know. She's skating forward now, with Thisbe behind her; they're weaving between the stalled cars.

It requires getting used to, Thisbe thinks, the sight of Noelle on rollerblades. As she moves along Main Street with a breeze at her back, Noelle's denim skirt bulges as if inflated with water, and her kerchief, knotted behind her head, flutters like a pennant. Cars pass them, belching out smoke, and the sounds of traffic make it hard for them to hear each other. Now Thisbe moves forward so they're skating abreast. Noelle crouches and comes up and crouches again, so that it looks as if she's doing knee bends.

It's six in the evening now. The fireworks will start in a couple of hours. And at seven o'clock, James Taylor will perform on the Tanglewood stage. On the corner of Main and Walker two teenage boys in Lenox T-shirts are holding up signs selling tickets to the concert.

"They should sell those tickets to their own grandparents," Noelle says. "How old is James Taylor, anyway? Sixty? For all I know, he's a grandparent himself."

"From heroin addict to grandparent," Thisbe says. "So there's hope for us all."

"If there's hope for me," Noelle says, "there's hope for anyone."

It's an hour before the concert, but already the traffic is thick with exhaust, with the smell of salami and pâté, of macaroni and cheese, pickles, mashed potatoes, and scones. The stuff of summer picnics, Thisbe thinks, recalling weekends with Leo, wandering past Kripalu to Tanglewood, where they would camp out on the lawn while the string musicians held practice. They used to fall asleep in the grass with their turkey sandwiches and watermelon spread across their stomachs: their own human picnic bench. Then Leo, waking up to the sound of the cellists practicing, would say wistfully, "Clarissa used to promise she was going to play here and she'd get us free tickets."

In Lilac Park, more James Taylor tickets are being scalped. "Beer here!" Noelle calls out, and now she and Thisbe are skating down Sunset to where the residential streets have been emptied out. Here they can move unimpeded in either direction, going past house after house, all those lawns flagged out front with their green *Berkshire Eagle* boxes.

"Do you rollerblade a lot?" Thisbe asks.

"Whenever I can," Noelle says. "It's the only exercise I get besides carrying my kids. What about you?"

"Not in ages."

"Rollerblading is my Prozac," Noelle says. "If I didn't have it, I'd have to take the real thing."

"Would you consider it?"

"Maybe," she says. "If it were permitted."

"It's against Jewish law?" It feels like a stupid question, the way most of her questions about Judaism feel stupid, but then it's hard for Thisbe to guess what's prohibited and what isn't. Just as often, she's thrown by what's allowed. She recalls learning that, if slaughtered properly, venison is kosher. Deer!

"The problem isn't Jewish law," Noelle says. "It's Amram. He doesn't believe in taking drugs."

"But he wouldn't be the one taking them."

Noelle thinks to say Amram sets the rules, but she's never thought of it so starkly, and it discomfits her to think of it that way now, so she doesn't say anything. "Anyway, he's not here to tell me what to do."

"Not at the moment."

"And he may never be. For all I know, he's never coming back."

"Do you really believe that?"

"Honestly, Thisbe, I have no idea. But when my mother promises me he'll come back soon, it sounds condescending, not to mention stupid. So don't go giving me false assurances either unless you know something I don't." Noelle skates into a driveway and Thisbe follows, and soon they emerge onto Yokun Avenue.

"So you haven't heard from him at all?" Thisbe says.

Noelle shakes her head. "He's been gone over a day now. You can't tell me Leo ever did anything like that."

"Not unless you count flying off to Iraq."

"I don't."

They've circled back to Lilac Park, where they stand unmoving on their rollerblades while beside them, on a bench, a couple is giving their rottweiler puppy scraps of a roast beef sandwich.

"I don't know how much longer I can take Amram."

Thisbe's quiet.

"I know what everyone's saying about him. And about me too as a result."

"Well, you're in good company," Thisbe says. "I can only imagine what they're saying about me."

It's true, Noelle thinks. She feels an alliance with Thisbe: the pariahs among her family, the ones cast overboard. "Honestly, Thisbe, could you ever imagine yourself with someone like Amram?"

No, Thisbe thinks, but then there aren't a lot of people she could imagine herself with. And she understands Amram's appeal. He has a kind of bullying charisma that would be more compelling if he didn't always act so aggrieved. "*De gustibus*," she says.

"What?"

"It's Latin for taste."

"Meaning?"

"Meaning love is particular. I wouldn't expect anyone to understand why I love the people I love."

"You're talking about Leo?"

"For one."

"Everyone loved Leo."

"Not everyone. But I loved him, and that's all that mattered."

As the time for the concert has drawn near, the streets have, in fact, started to fill with grandparent types. Or grandparent types trying not to be grandparent types. Women James Taylor's age in muumuus and peasant dresses, men in ponytails, too old, Thisbe thinks, to be men in ponytails—and she lives in Berkeley, the world's capital of men too old to be in ponytails.

"Come on," Noelle says. "Let's head down to the show."

"But we don't have tickets."

"We can lurk around the edges and watch the crowd. I hated James Taylor when I was growing up. We can see if I still hate him."

They thread their way past the row of stopped cars, and soon Noelle veers off into the Tanglewood Institute, where the grounds are lined with trees and where a couple of musicians walk past them now, carrying trombones. Noelle skates on her own, back and forth along the concrete, before coming to a stop next to Thisbe, who has settled herself onto the grass across from a sign that says BOSTON UNIVERSITY.

"How about you?" Noelle says. "Do you work out a lot?"

"When I can," Thisbe says. "Grad school comes with a gym, so I might as well use it. The problem is, I hate those machines. Leo used to say any exercise you can do while reading isn't really exercise, and I agree. I run a couple of times a week up in the Berkeley hills. It's my version of sightseeing."

"It's funny," Noelle says, "but I used to be the athlete in my family."

"Not anymore?"

She shrugs.

"You seem pretty good with wheels on your feet. I can't imagine you're worse without them."

"I was on the swim team in high school," Noelle says, "and I used to play in the father-daughter two-on-two basketball tournament. I fought with my father growing up, but not as much as with my mother. I liked playing basketball with him. Sports were this thing we had together."

"And now?"

"Now he's here and I'm there. And I doubt he plays basketball anymore. There's an over-fifty league, but once you get to sixty everyone but the crazies has been weeded out. At a certain point, people start to tear their ACLs."

"How about in Jerusalem?" Thisbe says. "Do you play basketball there?"

Noelle shakes her head. "It's hard to find women who want to play, and I can't play with men." She shrugs, half apologetically. "No physical contact with anyone but your husband. Basketball isn't football, but it's still a contact sport." She subsides onto the grass at the edge of the Institute. More musicians walk by; the brass section seems to have been released en masse. A cluster of young men move past holding tubas.

"Does it feel like a concession, not playing basketball anymore?"

"At first everything felt like a concession," Noelle says. "But after a while I began to see things differently." She removes a granola bar from her pocket. "Want some?"

Thisbe shakes her head.

"Though, sure, I wonder sometimes. I miss things, especially when I'm here." She dispenses with the granola bar in a few bites. Patches of sweat bleed through her kerchief.

Thisbe's sweating, too. Her blond hair is noosed behind her, and as she tilts her head forward her ponytail swings over her and slides across the ground.

"It was weird seeing everybody at the memorial. It felt like I'd left and everyone else was still here. I don't know why that should surprise me. Where did I think they would go?" Noelle grabs a clump of dirt and disperses it like grain.

"It was nice of you to say kaddish," Thisbe says. "It would have meant something to Leo."

"You think? I was afraid you'd disapprove."

"Why?"

"Imposing my religion on you? You may recall I skipped your wedding."

Thisbe does recall it, and it didn't please her at the time. How, she wondered, could Noelle not come when her own brother was the one getting married? And she, through no fault of her own, was to blame. Marilyn and David were frantic about it; they did what they could to get Noelle to change her mind. Leo, for his part, seemed not to care. "More cake for me," he said to Thisbe, which bewildered her. There had been years of this, she understood, years of having to endure Noelle, but she had grown up alone, always wanting a sibling, and then to be granted one and not have her come to your wedding seemed almost too much to bear.

Noelle is still sitting on the ground, her legs moving back and forth, digging little trenches with her rollerblades. "It's weird," she says, "twelve years ago I didn't even know the Hebrew alphabet, and now I'm fluent. If you'd told me Israel was where I'd end up, I'd have thought you were crazy. And the thing is, I could as easily have landed in Sweden."

"But you're happy in Israel, aren't you?"

Noelle shrugs.

"You tough Israelis."

"We just pretend we're tough."

"I can't imagine living in a place where my kids would have to go to the army."

"I can't, either."

"Yet you're there."

It's true, Noelle thinks. She's reminded of how, when she first moved to Israel, it was one of the country's attractions—how she could walk cavalierly through the streets while back home her parents were reading about the latest bombing. She saw her parents the way New Yorkers saw tourists—cautious, jittery, terrified of subway crime—when all they had to do was come visit. They did come visit, and at the end of the day when she dropped them off at their hotel she said, "Well, that's a relief. You made it back alive."

"Okay," her mother said, "so it's not so dangerous."

But when they returned to New York, they were afraid for her again. The first few years of their marriage, she and Amram lived on the West Bank, in a town that's been in Israel's possession since 1948; even under Oslo no one was talking about giving it back. "It's got everything we need," she told her parents. "The bank and the supermarket are just a stone's throw away."

"Very funny," her mother said.

"I keep reminding myself," Noelle tells Thisbe, "that after Christopher Reeve was paralyzed, his daughter joined the college polo team. It's how I buck myself up." She's sitting against a tree, and she tucks her rollerblades beneath her. A line of ants ascends the trunk, moving in procession. "Anyway, the army is years off. I have more immediate problems to worry about."

"You mean Amram?"

"Even if he comes back, what good does it do me? I joke that I have five boys to take care of, but it's not really a joke. He doesn't help out much with the children."

"Welcome to my world."

"Why?" she says. "Was Leo the same way?"

"Well, he drove off, too, didn't he? Or flew off, rather. It's hard to change a diaper when you're in Iraq and your son's in some walk-up in lower Manhattan. Before long, technology will solve that problem, but it will be too late for me."

"And when he was home?"

"When he was around, he was around. When he was available, he was available."

Beside them, the cars inch their way down to Tanglewood. The sun is unspooling across the sky. On someone's rear window is a HILLARY FOR PRESIDENT bumper sticker, though the election is still more than three years away.

"I probably shouldn't tell you this," Noelle says, "but after Leo died Amram tried to market his story."

"Market it?" Thisbe says. "How?"

"He knows some TV guys in Tel Aviv, and he had this idea for a script. A true-life story about Leo Frankel. It was around the same time he was talking with Malcolm about going in on his restaurant. He casts his net wide."

"Everyone needs to make a living."

"There are livings and there are livings."

This is true, Thisbe thinks, but she doesn't care. Another bad script about Leo: she's seen more than her share of them. In the weeks and months after Leo died, she received e-mails and phone calls from literary agents and Hollywood scouts. Her story had to be told, she was informed. A publisher intimated that she wouldn't even need to write the book herself; she could hire a ghostwriter. Everyone descended upon her like maggots on carrion. The rights to Leo's story, the rights to her story: she shooed them all away.

"It's funny," Noelle says, "but I've always taken comfort in the idea that Amram and I have known each other since high school. And the crazy thing is, we didn't really know each other in high school. I mean, I would have recognized him in the halls, sure, but I doubt we exchanged more than ten words our whole time there. Amram and I have the same birthday—May eleventh, a year apart. I was born at one in the morning and he was born at one in the afternoon. It's ridiculous to think that makes a marriage."

"Come on, Noelle. You can't convince me you married him because of that."

"Or the fact that we're both lefties? I'm the only lefty in my family, and I wore it like a badge. I insisted on being seated at the dinner table so I wouldn't bump elbows with the person next to me. I demanded special scissors for lefties, and a chair at school with the desk growing out of the left side instead of the right. I used to memorize the names of famous lefties. Julius Caesar, Joan of Arc, Leonardo da Vinci, Ty Cobb."

"Oh, Noelle. You didn't marry Amram because of that either."

"For a time, I was obsessed with horoscopes. If a guy was the right sign, then I'd think he was the one for me, and if he wasn't the right sign, I'd convince myself he was still the one for me." Noelle forces out a laugh, a single propulsion of breath like a pneumatic door being opened. "But you probably think I'm no different now, praying to some absurd God."

"I don't think religion is the same as astrology."

"When I told the rabbi at the Wailing Wall that Amram and I share a birthday, he said, 'You see? It's *bashert*.'"

"What does that mean?"

"According to Jewish tradition, God chooses your spouse for you. Your helpmeet, like Adam and Eve."

"Do you believe that?"

"I used to," Noelle says. "Now I'm not so sure." She plucks a dandelion and blows at the fuzz, which lands like little hairs on her rollerblades. She's been wearing a sweatshirt around her waist, but now, in the shade, with the sweat seeping into her clothes, she's starting to feel the evening's impending chill, so she puts the sweatshirt on. "I'm much more patient than Amram. He'll be in the bathroom washing up and the boys will be badgering him to go make them breakfast. But he won't be moved. He yells at the kids more than I'd like him to. But he's a good father. He's the fun parent—the one who swoops in and does the tickling and the card tricks, who gets the kids to levitate."

"To *levitate*?" Thisbe says.

"When the boys were babies, he would stand behind a wall and extend them out into the room so it looked like they were flying. That's what drew Amram to Judaism. The miracles. He'd like to perform a few miracles himself." Noelle rises, then sits down again, as if she's rubber-banded to the ground. She taps her rollerblade against the grass. "You probably think we're ridiculous, bringing our own kosher food."

Thisbe shakes her head. She's seen far stranger things than that. She lives in northern California, she reminds Noelle. They have all-liquid diets there, and entirely plant-based ones. She's at the epicenter of the raw-foods movement.

"And the crazy thing is, I passed a nonkosher hotdog stand this morning, and it was all I could do to stop myself from buying one."

"You don't mean that."

"I do. At the airport the other night when we were waiting for our luggage, I came across a *Playboy* at the newsstand. Back when I was in high school and Clarissa and Lily were in college, *Playboy* came to campuses to audition models. 'Girls of the Ivy League,' the issue was called. Clarissa and Lily were indignant, of course; they've made a life out of being indignant. But if I had been a student at Princeton or Yale, I'd have been the first to pose. Modeling for *Playboy*, having the whole world look at me—it was the only thing I cared about. You don't know me, Thisbe. I'm sitting here with my hair covered, but am I any different from who I was then?" With a single thrust, Noelle pulls her kerchief off, and for an instant Thisbe expects to see her bald. But beneath the kerchief is just her hair, red and matted to her forehead. Thisbe averts her gaze, and she keeps it averted as Noelle puts her kerchief back on and reties it behind her head. "I can feel myself slipping," she says. "What if I go back to how I was?"

"You're away from your surroundings," Thisbe says. "You just need to get home to Jerusalem."

"Maybe this is just who I am."

"It's not who you are." And then, because, despite having been her sister-in-law, Thisbe doesn't really know Noelle, and because she doesn't believe, in any case, that people are simply one thing to the exclusion of others, she says, "You're probably a lot of different things." Which comes off as patronizing.

"You're not listening to me," Noelle says.

"I *am* listening to you." But Thisbe realizes Noelle is right.

They're still sitting on the grounds of the Tanglewood Institute, where a couple of girls emerge from behind a copse of trees. They must be eight or nine, and they're chasing each other, clumps of mud flying from their sneakers, laughter swelling and dissipating as they orbit an enormous oak, appearing and disappearing and reappearing again like horses on a carousel, Soon they pick up paddle racquets in the shape of violins and start to hit a rubber ball back and forth. Tanglewood kitsch, Thisbe thinks.

But Noelle isn't paying attention to them. She's looking above her, where a helicopter has emerged from between the clouds. She wishes she were up there. She used to go on helicopter rides above Manhattan, hoping the pilot would fall sick and she'd be forced to take over the aircraft. When Leo was sixteen she took him hang-gliding, though she made him promise not to tell their parents; they'd have been apoplectic if they'd found out. She signed the consent forms, saying she was Leo's guardian, which she was, at least for the day. She and Leo were the risk takers in the family, the ones who jumped off high ledges on their skateboards, who went diving off the rocks at the quarry, coming within inches of their lives. "Come on," she says. "Let's follow those cars."

But the cars are all stuck bumper to bumper, and so Noelle and Thisbe pass them now, moving along the shoulder of 183 as the blacktop continues its steady downward incline toward Kripalu and Tanglewood.

When they reach the tent, teenage boys in matching Tanglewood T-shirts are guiding the concertgoers into the parking lot. A family of four walks through the gate, the parents holding beach chairs, two boys of about sixteen carrying a mammoth cooler, out of which sticks a plastic baggie, flapping in the air like a fish. At the edge of the road, an eagle pecks at a piece of hotdog. Someone is playing "Sweet Baby James" on a boom box.

There's a clearing ahead, and soon Thisbe sees it: the lake, Stockbridge Bowl, where she and Leo used to swim. Noelle is skating there now, so she follows her, to where Noelle sits down beside the water.

"It's getting late," Thisbe says. "Your parents will start to worry about us."

"Let them worry." Noelle removes her rollerblades, and now she removes her socks as well. She's sitting barefoot on the ground in just her blouse and long skirt.

"What are you doing?"

"I'm going for a swim."

"In what?"

"In my skin," she says. "Are you telling me I can't do that?"

"No," Thisbe says. She's not telling Noelle that. Though she does say, lamely, "Isn't that against your religion?"

Noelle laughs. "Since when have you become an authority on my religion?"

Since never, Thisbe thinks. And when Noelle points out that Stockbridge Bowl is desolate, that it's off the main road and no one's going to be here now—a Wednesday evening at seven o'clock with the July Fourth crowd roaring in the distance for James Taylor to emerge—that there's no lifeguard on duty, that it's just the two of them, Noelle and Thisbe, both of them women, relatives, in fact ("Unless you don't consider me your sister-in-law any longer"), that there's no injunction in the world forbidding Thisbe from seeing Noelle naked, Thisbe just nods. She continues to nod as Noelle removes her blouse and skirt so she's in just her bra and underwear, and then she removes those too. She's standing naked in front of Thisbe in only her kerchief, and Thisbe has a brief, absurd image of some photography exhibit, a photo of Noelle with the title *Devout Skinny Dipper*, but before the image is even complete, Noelle has removed her kerchief as well. She's bent over in the grass so that, from behind, Thisbe can see her genitals. Noelle folds her blouse, her skirt, her undergarments, her kerchief, and lays them in a pile at her feet. "Well?" she says. "Are you going to join me?"

Thisbe shakes her head.

"I trust it's not against your religion, either."

"No, Noelle, it isn't."

"Then what's stopping you?"

"I just don't want to swim." Though the real reason is that, though she has signed on for a lot by coming back east, one thing Thisbe hasn't signed on for is going skinny-dipping with her Orthodox former sister-in-law. As uneasy as she felt watching Noelle undress, she would feel that much more uneasy getting undressed herself. Just to make that clear, she doesn't so much as loosen her rollerblades as she settles herself onto the grass.

As she watches Noelle step into the lake, her red hair loosed from its kerchief, as she sees the water rise to her thighs, as she watches her sister-in-law throw herself into the water so she's fully submerged except for her head, Thisbe finds herself recalling Noelle, a hot August day shortly after she and Leo got married, wearing an evening dress that was long-sleeved and loose-fitting, as the rabbis dictated. *Dowdy.* That was the word Leo used to describe the women in Noelle's Jerusalem neighborhood. It was the word he'd once used to describe Noelle herself. But looking at her that night, Thisbe thought that, despite the kerchief and the dress, despite having given birth only three months earlier, Noelle was anything but dowdy. She'd been a lovely girl, and she was still lovely. The feeling returned—it returns to her again—of having been an only child, looking in solitary on the adult world. How she had wanted a sister! And now she had a sister-in-law. Three of them, in fact. This is what she's thinking as she watches Noelle do the crawl, remembering what a fine swimmer she is. Still, she cries out, "Be careful, Noelle! Don't go too far! There's no lifeguard here!"

But if Noelle has heard her, she doesn't let on.

Now the concert has begun. James Taylor has come onstage; Thisbe can hear the crowd cheering for him as she waits by the water for Noelle, who has switched from the crawl to the breaststroke and back again and who, having been in the lake for twenty minutes now, gives no sign that she's through. Thisbe's just sitting on the ground, feeling her shorts stick to the backs of her thighs, her feet growing sore in their rollerblades.

Finally, Noelle swims back to shore, and when she emerges she shakes her head from side to side, trying to drain the water from her ears. She sits down naked next to Thisbe and makes no move to put her clothes back on.

"I'd offer you a towel if I had one."

But Noelle seems not to care. She's sitting no more than two feet away from Thisbe, as if she's daring her to look, or not look, and so Thisbe settles on some compromise between looking and not looking, hoping that, whatever she's doing, she doesn't piss Noelle off.

The oak trees swirl above them, making low, guttural sounds. A few fireworks go off, and a few more. Noelle, still naked, is staring at Thisbe's hands. "I see you've stopped wearing your wedding ring."

Thisbe nods. "Why should I be wearing it?" Though the last time she saw Noelle she was wearing it. And even after that. Her first semester in Berkeley, sitting alone at a Chinese restaurant, her bag laid carefully on the seat across from her as if she were saving it for someone, she was approached by a busboy, who said, "Are you waiting for your husband?" and she started to cry over her spinach dumplings. Because she realized she *was* waiting for her husband, waiting for Leo to return from Iraq. When did a widow remove her wedding ring? The Jews must have had an answer for that, the Jews like Noelle. The Varsity Jew, Leo used to call her; he said Noelle lettered in Judaism. More than once after Leo's death she wished she were like Noelle, steadfast, consoled by religion's ministrations, not the doubter she was, without a ready-made community to take her in. Sometimes she thinks that's why she went to graduate school, to have a community, paltry as it is, her group of graduate students commiserating over their classes, her cohort of anthropologists. A month after she and Wyeth got together, she was washing up in the bathroom when her wedding ring fell off and rolled down the drain. She screamed as it disappeared, but she didn't call the plumber, and she suspects she was secretly relieved. The next day, Clarissa phoned. They hadn't spoken in months, and it was as if Clarissa knew what had happened and was watching out for Leo. Talking to her, Thisbe felt shaken, and when she got off the phone she went back to the bathroom and inserted her fingers down the drain, trying vainly to retrieve the ring. "It fell down the sink," she tells Noelle. "I took it as a sign that it was time to stop wearing it."

"You think that was a sign?" Noelle says. "That's idiocy."

"No more idiocy than marrying someone because you share a birthday. Or because your rabbi told you to marry him."

"That's not why I married Amram."

James Taylor is between songs—he's talking now—and someone in the crowd seems to have called out, but Thisbe can't decipher the words. A few piano chords ring in the distance. The audience starts to cheer. Noelle is still sitting naked on the grass, though now she reaches over and puts on her kerchief. "I miss Leo," she says. "I can't believe he's gone."

Thisbe nods.

"Don't you miss him?"

"Of course I do." A squirrel shoots down a tree, its tail moving spasmodically like a mop.

"How?"

"What do you mean, how?"

"How do you miss him?"

In every way, Thisbe thinks. Because how can she not miss Leo when all his mail still gets forwarded to her, when just last week she received a reminder for his six-month dental appointment, and she was tempted to call the dentist and yell into the phone that Leo didn't get a six-month dental appointment, he got a six-year dental appointment (his mother notwithstanding, he hated dentists and doctors both), and besides, he was dead, it was his very dental records with which they'd identified him, and didn't they know that, or did they not have such a box to check off? How can she not miss Leo when he was still on her phone machine when she moved to Berkeley, and he might still be on it were it not for the fact that it broke and she had to buy a new machine. How can she not miss Leo when on Calder's birthday she signed the card from both of them, though it didn't matter, of course—Calder can't read—but *she* can read, and for the week after his birthday she would read the card to him every night before he went to sleep, closing with the words *Love, Mommy and Daddy*. How can she not miss Leo when she still has his clothes, many of which have gotten mixed up with hers, and one time when Wyeth jumped out of the shower to answer the doorbell he threw on her shirt, which was lying on the chair, only it was Leo's shirt, and when she saw him in it, she screamed, "Would you take that fucking thing off!" How can she not miss Leo when she often thinks of her grandmother, dead for a decade, and of her grandfather, dead even longer than that, and how when her grandfather was dying, a slow, protracted, excruciating death, her grandmother didn't want him to go into the hospital; she wanted him to die at home. And how when he did die, early one morning, she got into bed with him one last time and held his body, already overcome with rigor mortis, and how Thisbe, when she heard that story, thought it was so beautiful she swore to herself that if she ever got married and outlived her husband, she would lie down with him one last time like that. Only the way she imagined it she was eighty or ninety, not thirty-two, and she didn't picture that he would be far away and there would be no body to speak of, nothing, certainly, she could lie down with even if he were there. Is that what Noelle means by how does she miss him? She thinks, Let me count the ways. But she's not going to tell Noelle any of this because it's private and, besides, she has nothing to prove to her. "I just miss him," she says.

"What if he's not really dead?" says Noelle.

"What do you mean, what if he's not really dead?"

"What if he's missing in action?"

"He's not missing in action, Noelle. He was a journalist, not a soldier. And his body was flown back. Don't you remember?"

"You're saying you never imagined it?"

Of course she did. Those last few weeks in New York, standing in the dark beside the East River, while behind her the cars cast their lights on her like stun guns, moving in procession down the FDR Drive. Queens was across the river, and beyond it, if she could only train her eyes, she could see all the way to Iraq.

And later, in Berkeley, already with Wyeth, she would say to herself, *What if Leo came back now?*

And a month later: *How about now?*

And now?

A memory comes to her, she and Leo going to the Price Chopper in Great Barrington, grocery list in hand, trying to decipher Marilyn's handwriting. One time, they had to turn around and go back to the house because they couldn't read what she'd written. Marilyn herself couldn't figure it out; it was only later that she remembered. *Bagged carrots!* And Leo's handwriting was even worse than hers. Last month, Thisbe found in her apartment a note Leo had written her. *Off for a run. Be back in an hour.* And for a moment it pierced her, and she needed to know when the note had been written and where Leo had run, before she allowed herself to ask the more obvious question: how had the note gotten there, across the country from where she and Leo had lived, moving with her from apartment to apartment, adhering to her like flypaper? She'd found it in her wallet, which surprised her: she wasn't someone who kept things. That had been Leo's task; he was a secret sentimentalist. Though sometimes she wondered whether it was sentimentality as much as an aversion to cleaning up. She thinks of his bachelor days at Wesleyan, if someone in college could even be called a bachelor, but he certainly lived like one. Having failed to sign up for the college meal plan, he lived for semesters at a time off pizza and ramen noodles. He ate from a set of rubber camping dishes that he kept in his dresser drawer, and whenever they got dirty he would dump them into the shower and rinse them off with shampoo. The problem was, he didn't own a dish drainer, so he would place the dishes, still wet, back into his dresser, and soon the wood would start to warp, the dishes to mold. His refrigerator was a specimen lab. A milk carton from every month, he liked to say. You could carbon-date things with it.

And suddenly she can't sit here anymore, letting naked Noelle drip-dry beside her in the fast-descending sun while in the distance James Taylor is crooning to whomever he's crooning to, and now the fireworks are starting to go off, issuing their staccato clamor. "Would you get dressed already?"

Noelle stands up. She's still in her paisley kerchief and nothing else, and this time, as she bends over her pile of clothes, Thisbe looks away: she's not going to be forced to stare at her genitals. Noelle puts on her underwear, her bra, her blouse, her skirt, moving methodically, unhurriedly, seeming to dare Thisbe to rush her. Now she's fully clothed except for her socks, which she puts on, methodically as well, and her rollerblades, which she begins to lace. Thisbe is still sitting beside her, staring out at the lake, which in the growing darkness looms before them like a dark blue dish, and for the first time the words *Stockbridge Bowl* make sense to her.

She recalls Noelle's speech at the memorial, the story she told about

Leo holding the havdalah candle, saying he'd marry her again. And his words to Noelle. *I'm thinking about her. The next time you talk to her, please tell her that.* "There's one thing I don't understand," she says. "When Leo said those words to you? Even when he was in Iraq, I talked to him every couple of days. Yet you could go months without speaking to him."

"So?"

"It's not like you two were close."

Noelle is silent.

"Then why did he ask you to tell me that?"

"Beats me."

"It was as if he knew we'd never speak again. Come on, Noelle. What are you hiding from me?"

But Noelle has taken off. She's gliding away, out past the clearing, skating along the blacktop up toward historic Lenox.

"Wait, Noelle! Come back! That weekend Leo visited you, did he seem reckless?"

"In Jerusalem?" Noelle says. Leo had Shabbat dinner at her and Amram's house. He dandled his nephews on his knee. How reckless could a person be doing that? *It's not like you two were close.* Thisbe probably meant no harm with those words, but they cut into her just the same. Well, maybe they weren't close, but Noelle would like to remind Thisbe that she preceded her by years. Leo was twenty-one when he met Thisbe; Noelle knew him his whole life. *K'heref ayin.* Like the blink of an eye. The whole world is like that for God. And, for a moment, Noelle feels like God herself. The last one to see her brother alive. Standing balanced on her rollerblades at the side of the road, her head covering in place, exuding the cool she always strives for but that consistently eludes her, she looks at her sister-in-law with a malevolent calm.

And Thisbe stares back at her just as malevolently. Foolish Noelle with her religious code, her sundry enjoinders and prohibitions, Thisbe's fatuous former sister-in-law standing kerchiefed on rollerblades at the side of the road a couple of miles from her parents' house. The last person to see Leo alive. This is what Thisbe has been waiting for. To talk to Noelle. Yet what was she hoping would happen? That she would tell Noelle about that night on the telephone, when she asked Leo for a separation? That she would admit it was the last time they ever spoke? And what was she hoping for in return? That Noelle would tell her whether Leo had been reckless? That she'd say if he killed himself? As if Noelle would know, Noelle, who knew little about Leo when he was alive and who knows even less about him now that he's gone. Did Leo put himself in harm's way? Of course he did. He was putting himself in harm's way from the instant he was born.

It's unseemly, Thisbe thinks, to blame herself for Leo's death. There's something tawdry about it, to give herself that kind of credit, to accept that kind of blame, to be so self-dramatic when she knows that to say "Hate me, it's all my fault" is a way, paradoxically, of not taking responsibility for everything that's happened since then. "Forget it," she says, because what difference does it make what Noelle says? There's nothing Noelle can tell her, nothing at all. She turns on her rollerblades and heads back up the hill. Noelle can follow her if she wants to, and if she doesn't, that's fine, too. Thisbe doesn't care if she ever sees her again.

When she arrives at the house, the family is dispersed, a person here, a person there, as if someone strewed them across the floor.

"How was your workout?" Lily asks.

"Okay," says Thisbe. "Terrible."

It's dark now, and the fireworks have really started to go off. They're lighting up the sky with stars and arrows and other points of light, every shape Thisbe can fathom. "I hate fireworks."

"Join the club," Lily says. "I sent my father out to buy ear plugs. I should have told him to buy nose plugs too. The whole town smells like sausage."

But David hasn't gotten far, because when Thisbe enters the living room she finds him on the couch, listlessly tapping a badminton racquet against his knee.

"Where are the kids?"

"Watching baseball," he says. "American pastime."

Sure enough, when Thisbe gets upstairs, she finds the TV playing in the boys' bedroom. The cousins are lying on the floor, their heads propped against their rolled-up sleeping bags.

"Explain baseball to me," Calder says, and Thisbe, not much of a baseball fan herself, feels suddenly remiss and strangely un-American for having failed to teach her son about baseball. She starts to tell him about the Cyclones, the Mets minor league team on Coney Island, how she and his father used to watch them play, and afterward they would stroll on the boardwalk past the amusement park, the Cyclone roller coaster plunging down its tracks, and on toward the aquarium where they had gotten married.

But Calder wants to know about the rules of baseball. "What is everyone trying to do?"

So Thisbe, sitting on the floor beside him, does her best to make things clear. "To start with," she says, "there are two teams."

The fireworks are still exploding when she reaches Wyeth. She's down in the basement, and she can feel the noise rattling the house.

"It sounds like you're in a bunker."

"I am," she says. "I've been watching the rocket's red glare. It will be coming to you soon on tape delay." She takes a quick breath. "Wyeth, please. Get me out of here."

"Has it been bad?"

"Terrible. What was I thinking? I shouldn't have come." Her shirt has come out of her shorts, and she tucks it back inside, but it emerges again. "I'm all right," she assures him.

"Are you?"

She doesn't know. Or knows in only the vaguest, most fleeting sense: a shadow on the wall of a cave. What's wrong is she's here and Wyeth's there. She should have brought him with her. He's her boyfriend; she had every right to insist that he come. The blood funnels to her head. *I will always be part of your family.* She said those words, not because she meant them but because she believed she was supposed to say them, that flying across the country for your dead husband required you to make a pronouncement. So she made one. But saying those words made her feel them. *We shall do and we shall listen.* Noelle was right. What if she dropped out of graduate school and never came back? What if she stayed in Lenox? The idea is preposterous, but the fact that she can entertain it, even as whimsy, makes her lose her breath.

"Do you want me to come get you?" Wyeth says. "I could catch the next flight to Boston."

"Oh, Wyeth, you can't do that."

"I could be at the airport in less than an hour."

He could, no doubt. Threading his way through traffic, finding seams between cars where none exist. Once, watching Wyeth drive, Thisbe thought, Who said you can't fit a camel through the eye of a needle?

But it wouldn't work. He'd cast a pall over the event, her gallant horseman come to rescue her, and, she fears, she wouldn't feel rescued. Wyeth would arrive with his cheer and good intentions and he'd be received like a burglar who's jacked open the door, a cold draft coming into the house. For an instant, she longs for an age she never knew, when you lived where you grew up and you died there too, when the world that lay beyond you was only for the imagining and you waited for a letter from the boy you loved, up late in his bedroom mooning over you, sending you flares in the middle of the night. Back in Berkeley, after Calder has gone to sleep, she likes to sit beside Wyeth while she reads a book, listening to him speak on the phone. Wyeth talking. It's the background melody to her life. "Wyeth," she says. "I want to move in with you."

"You do?"

"If you'll still have me, that is."

He laughs. "Why wouldn't I still have you?"

"I thought maybe you met someone while I was gone."

"Thisbe, you've been gone for less than seventy-two hours."

"You're a fast worker," she says. "At least you were with me."

She knows what he's thinking, and what he's good enough not to say. That she was a fast worker with him, too.

"Have you told Calder?"

"Not yet," she says, "but he'll be thrilled. He's your biggest booster."

And there he is, Calder, at the top of the stairs, looking down at her in the basement. Someone has given him a cookie. Just as likely, he's given one to himself. Though she's been known to give herself a little pre-bedtime treat, too. It's ten o'clock at night, and he has a sugar high; with any luck, he'll sleep on the plane.

"Wyeth?" she says. "Can I change my mind about tomorrow? Will you pick me up at the airport?"

"I'll be waiting at the gate," he says. "I'll be the guy in the chauffeur's hat holding the lease."

And she'll be the woman with the suitcase waiting to sign it. The woman standing next to her son. It's Calder's bedtime. It's past bedtime for them both. She can hear voices on the first floor. And he's walking toward her now, Calder, come to greet her in his footed pajamas, making his way down the stairs.

14

It's not even seven-thirty when Clarissa hears a noise outside. A door opens and shuts. She rolls over into the crook of Nathaniel's elbow.

"It's the milkman." Still asleep, and Nathaniel is already poking fun at her, playing on her credulity and hauteur. He used to try to convince her that when he was a boy there was no milk in the supermarkets of Nebraska City; it was all delivered by the milkman. No telephones either, so he was forced to communicate through a Styrofoam cup extended by string to his friend's house.

Awake now, Clarissa gets out of bed and turns on the computer.

"Checking e-mail?"

She nods. She hasn't checked e-mail the whole holiday. She needs to know what she's supposed to worry about.

"Does that mean I have to check e-mail, too?" If the world can be divided between those who check e-mail whenever they can and those who check e-mail only when forced to, Nathaniel is squarely in the latter camp. He turns on the computer with anticipatory regret. Every time he thinks, What am I going to be asked to do now? He puts on his boxers, and now out pops his head through the hole in his T-shirt. He's sitting half-clothed on the bed.

Clarissa turns off the computer and lies back down beside him. "The world hasn't ended, as far as I can tell."

Noelle, meanwhile, is already awake in the room next door. Her flight back to Israel leaves this evening, and she hasn't begun to pack. Just in time for their return, the boys' internal clocks have adjusted to the States. They lie stone cold atop their sleeping bags as Noelle traffics in and out of their room, picking up their laundry and a couple of stray toothbrushes, removing their clean clothes from the dresser drawers and depositing them in their suitcase. There's a stain on the floor (Could it possibly be jam? She told them not to eat outside the kitchen), and she goes into the bathroom and brings back a washcloth and now, on her knees, she tries to rub the stain out, but it's caked like tar to the wood.

In the bathroom, she runs the faucets in the sink and tub. The boys have dirtied them too; clumps of hair have gathered along the porcelain. Her sons are related to her, no doubt. And to her parents as well. The Frankel family: had anyone ever seen so much hair? "You guys are keeping Drano in business," Leo used to say. "And Liquid-Plumr too." Though he was one to talk. He and his sisters were clogging up the drain themselves; the whole family was keeping plumbers in business, liquid and otherwise.

Noelle folds her clothes and places them in the suitcase; at this point, she doesn't know what's dirty and what's not. She'll have to wash it all when she gets back to Jerusalem. She packs Amram's clothes as well. She's tempted to leave them here; they're not her responsibility. Though they're certainly not her parents' responsibility, either.

In the shower, she shampoos and conditions her hair, then sits down on top of the closed toilet and clips her fingernails and toenails. It's so rare that she can attend to her small bodily concerns, so rare that she can be in a bathroom at all without feeling like an egg timer is ticking on the sink, without having a husband or a son—often several of them—banging on the door and demanding that she leave.

She hears voices downstairs, so she steps out into the hallway. She leans over the banister and whispers, "Shhhh." She wants her boys to sleep as long as possible; they have a twelve-hour flight to endure. But the talking continues: a low-grade hum. She thinks she hears her mother's voice, but she can't make out what she's saying. Her hearing has failed her once more. Though before long, everyone she knows will catch up to her. Life is one long process of losing your hearing. She's read that there are cell phones now whose ring can't be heard by adults. High school students leave their phones on during class because the teacher won't hear them. Only teenagers can hear them. Teenagers, mice, and dogs.

She puts on her clothes and heads downstairs, and when she reaches the landing she sees it's not her mother, but Gretchen, her grandmother, sitting primly in the living room in the brown armchair, her feet crossed, her hair up in its signature beehive. Lily once said that she never saw Gretchen unprepared at a moment's notice to be transported to the Philharmonic. That's how she looks now, wearing pressed gray slacks and a white button-down shirt with the collar open. Around her neck hangs a string of pearls, and she has on matching pearl earrings, delicate as fish eggs. Her skin is creased like a ripened pepper; the tendons in her neck dance as she talks. She has on a little blush and a dab of lipstick, looking as if she is, in fact, expecting to attend a concert.

"Grandma," Noelle says. "What in the world are you doing here?"

"Is that how you greet me, darling?"

"Grandma." She bends down to kiss her. "It's just . . ."

"What?"

"How did you get here?"

"By car."

She looks at her watch. "It's eight in the morning, Grandma. You're saying you got up at five and drove here yourself?"

"I most certainly didn't."

"Then how did you get here?"

"I was chauffeured." Gretchen looks up as she says this, and Noelle, following her gaze, sees that it's trained on the chauffeur himself, who has walked in from the kitchen holding a glass of tea for Gretchen and a plastic cup filled with milk for himself. "Good morning, Noelle."

"Amram," she says, and she's so livid she's struck mute.

"Nice to see you," he says, and he sits down on the couch.

Amram is wearing the same jeans he had on two days ago, only they appear to have spent the whole time crumpled; they bear an uncanny resemblance to elephant skin. He had a day's growth of beard when she last saw him, and now he has three days' growth, which, Noelle knows, makes him think he looks rabbinic, but to her it makes him look like a hoodlum. He's wearing the same blue button-down shirt, but it, too, appears to have been folded over on itself, and it has a small mustard stain across the middle. Even his black velvet yarmulke, which is bobby-pinned as always to the side of his head, looks as if it's been left in the gutter.

She would like to wring his neck, and that's no figure of speech. She's tempted to put her hands around Amram's throat and tighten them in a vise grip. She's not a violent person—she can't remember having hit anyone since she was a child—but it's all she can do not to punch him in the face.

He's sitting across from her with his cup of milk on his lap, looking in his own soiled, slovenly way as if the world owes him no explanation for what has come to pass and he owes no explanation in return. Noelle, standing above him on her parents' Persian rug, clenches her fists, and the nails cut into her palms. "Amram," she says, feeling a line of spit come out from between her front teeth, "you look like a bum from the Bowery. Is that where you just came from?"

"Actually, I just came from the Upper East Side. It's where Gretchen lives. On Fifth Avenue."

"I know where she lives."

"It's where I spent the last couple of nights."

"You what?" Gretchen doesn't like having guests in her apartment; she finds them an invasion of her privacy. The only exception was her grandchildren, whom she used to let stay over, and even in their case she would tire of their company after a day and insist on packing them up. Noelle has an image of Gretchen's apartment, the vast open space of the living room, her gaze traveling past Indonesian rugs, past coffee tables and side tables and end tables, the sheer expanse of surface, those lovely walnuts, cherries, mahoganies, and oaks whose job was to sustain lamps and little glass figurines, in some cases serving no function at all, meant to do nothing besides be there, entire forests cleared for Gretchen's sumptuousness. "You didn't sleep in my grandmother's apartment."

"I most certainly did."

Gretchen, still sitting primly in the armchair, says nothing to contradict him. She's simply drinking her tea, looking ahead expressionlessly toward the porch, where a blue jay is pecking at the feeder.

And Noelle realizes it doesn't matter where Amram slept. He could have slept in Gracie Mansion, for all she cares. He could have spent the last two nights at the White House itself, installed in the Lincoln Bedroom as President Bush's personal guest, and it wouldn't make a difference to her. "Excuse me, Grandma, but I need to talk to my husband alone." She takes a step toward Amram and now she has grabbed him by the arm and yanked him up from the chair. She has him by the shirtsleeve and he's following her, out through the porch door and into the garden, where the clouds are heavy and it has started to mist, and where, standing beside her mother's azaleas, she gets up in his face, standing so close she can smell his breath, a revolting combination of pizza and spearmint. She's actually poking him in the chest.

"Would you get off me?" he says, stepping back from her.

"No," she says, "I won't get off you." She takes another step toward him and is poking him once more. "Do you have any idea how long you were gone?"

"I'll tell you one thing, Noelle. I didn't come back here for a lecture."

"Well, you're going to get one whether you came back for it or not."

Amram retreats another step and almost trips over the garden hose. He's staring at her irately.

"You've been gone for two days, Amram. Forty-three hours, to be precise. That's long enough for me to file a missing persons report if I'd been foolish enough to file one."

"Is that all you can say?"

"What else would you like me to say?"

"How about 'Thank you'?"

"Thank you? Thank you for what?"

"For bringing Gretchen back with me. Because if you think it was easy, you have no idea."

But Noelle doesn't care if it was easy. She doesn't care if Amram slung Gretchen over his back and carried her the hundred miles up the Taconic Parkway. "Where in the world have you been?"

"I told you," he says. "New York."

"Our flight leaves this evening, Amram. I was prepared to fly home alone."

"And I was prepared to let you."

A hoe is toppled in the garden soil, and she picks it up and leans against it. Though now, too agitated just to stand there, she grabs the hoe and starts to dig some dirt, going at it violently, piling it into a pyramid next to her mother's rosebushes. She could take the hoe to Amram, she really could. She understands for once the logic of gun control, how it's dangerous to have a weapon in the house, though in

Israel all the men serve in the army reserves and there are guns every-where you walk on the street. She's glad she doesn't have a gun right now.

She jams the hoe into the ground. "You missed my brother's memo-rial, Amram. You were supposed to say kaddish. That was your one job, and you screwed up. I had to say it for you. And don't tell me a woman isn't supposed to say kaddish."

Amram just stands there, his arms folded across his chest, as if to make the point that he hasn't said anything.

The tree branches in the garden bulge in front of her. Above her, the clouds crack and break apart. "Why didn't you call?"

Amram is silent.

"Did you even consider it? I was afraid you might have been killed."

"Well, I wasn't."

"I almost wanted you to be killed. At least that would have explained why you were missing."

"Noelle—"

"Just stop."

Again he tries to speak, but she won't let him. "And it's not just me who was worried. The boys were scared sick. I had to lie to them—tell them you were calling and you were coming back. The rest of the fam-ily was scared, too. My parents, my sisters."

"Your parents and sisters couldn't have cared less."

"Amram," she says, "tell me where you were."

"Jesus, Noelle. How many times do I have to say it? I was in New York. Would you like an actual zip code?"

She glares at him.

"What difference does it make where I was? I'm here now, and I brought your grandmother back with me. I convinced her to come, which is what everyone wanted. The whole family together one last time. Because it's not going to happen again, don't you understand?"

"Why did you go there in the first place?" And the thought occurs to her: Amram drove down to the city to plead for money. "Did you ask Gretchen for help?"

"What?"

"Did you request money, Amram?"

"And if I did?"

"If you did, I'll kill you."

Amram laughs. "Since when did you become so pure? You're always talking about how when Gretchen dies—"

"Amram, did you?"

Sweat beads on Amram's forehead. His throat pulses, like a toad's. "I told you, Noelle. The only reason I went down there was to bring your grandmother back with me. So you could have your last hurrah."

"Hurrah?" she says. "Is that what you think this is? Hurrah? *Hurrah?*" She claps her hands hard, once, twice, and the sound reverberates through the garden. "You wanted a hero's welcome, is that it?" That's the problem, she thinks. Amram wants to be a hero, and what she's trying to tell him, what she's been trying to tell him for years now, is that if she wanted a hero she'd have married one.

But before she can say anything more, she can see through the porch window the rest of her family come downstairs and discover Gretchen in the living room. They're hugging her, telling her how glad they are she's here, and now the boys have come out into the garden and are embracing their father, saying, "Abba, we missed you, we missed you so much!"

Now Noelle's sisters and parents have emerged into the garden, too, and are greeting Amram with an enthusiasm Noelle isn't accustomed to and can't abide. They're thanking him for having driven Gretchen up to Lenox. "How in the world did you pull it off?" David says, and Amram, putting on a show of mock sheepishness, simply shrugs.

Now even Nathaniel has walked over and is pumping Amram's fist, the fact of which clearly pleases Amram—he has on, Noelle thinks, an enormous and stupid grin—and he's saying, "It looks like Gretchen has met her match," and Lily is saying, "I never thought anyone could convince Grandma to do anything," and Gretchen, throughout it all, is sitting in the living room sipping her tea, calmly observing the ruckus.

But Noelle isn't through with Amram. "Everyone back inside," she tells the boys, though she means the command for her whole family. Now it's just her and Amram alone again next to the pile of dirt she's dug.

Amram takes off, around the bend of the house.

"Where are you going?"

He reaches the garage, where the electric door is up, and he steps inside and retrieves a tennis racquet.

"That's my mother's, you know."

"So what, Noelle. I'm not stealing it." He drags out a bucket of balls and pushes the button so the garage door closes.

"What in the world do you think you're doing?"

"I'm hitting tennis balls." He removes a couple of balls from the bucket and swats them in succession against the garage door, making a dull thudding sound, over and over.

"You're going to break that door, and then what will you do?"

"I'll worry about it when it happens."

But that's the problem, Noelle thinks. Amram always worries about things when they happen; if he worried about them before they happened, maybe they wouldn't happen in the first place. And the words come to her: *You break it, you own it.* Wasn't that what Colin Powell said about Iraq? The Pottery Barn rule? Amram is drum-chested and strong—back in college his roommates used to call him Moose—and now, as he continues to hit the tennis ball against the garage door, Noelle can feel the strength in his swing and follow-through. "You'll wake the neighbors."

"What neighbors?"

"The ones right over the hedge. The Simmonses? They've lived here as long as my parents have."

"From the looks of it," Amram says, glancing over the bushes, "they've been awake for hours." Mrs. Simmons is on her knees in her own garden patch, and when she catches sight of Noelle and Amram she waves.

Amram bounces the ball and catches it, then bounces it again. "This isn't some apartment building, Noelle. It's the country. If I want to play tennis, I'll play tennis."

A car passes on the road below them, the sounds of "You're a Grand Old Flag" coming from the radio. Amram stops bouncing the ball. "It's July fifth," he says. "Haven't they had enough?"

Noelle doesn't answer him.

"You've got to love it," he says. "The country that celebrates Memorial Day by going to the beach."

"It's July Fourth," she tells him, "not Memorial Day."

"Same difference." He starts to hit the ball again, but Noelle presses the button inside the garage and the electric door rises and disappears.

"Fine," he says. "I'll play some real tennis." He grabs the bucket of balls and heads straight for the tennis court, and Noelle follows him.

Standing on the baseline, he starts to serve while Noelle, outside the fence, watches him with revulsion. He puts a couple of serves into the net, but then he places his next two serves squarely in the service box. The serve after that he hits so hard it slams into the fence, just inches from where Noelle is standing. She feels the chain links vibrate against her face, and she flinches.

"You're playing great," she says. "You're really socking it to your invisible opponent."

Amram places his racquet at his feet. "I'm happy to sock it to whatever opponent wants to play me. Including you, Noelle."

"Is that right?" Noelle hasn't played tennis seriously in years, but then neither has Amram; in fact, Amram has never played tennis seriously. He has a weekly game of racquetball back in Jerusalem, a game that's suited to him, Noelle thinks, since mostly it requires a modicum of coordination and a willingness to whack the hell out of the ball. She, on the other hand, used to play tennis with her mother when she was growing up, and with her sisters, too, at the club in Larchmont; she's a natural athlete, besides. She's still standing outside the fence with her nose pressed to it, watching Amram take his serves, but she's thinking, Don't challenge me, Amram. You'll regret it.

"There's another racquet right there." Amram points to the chair across from the net, where one of Marilyn's racquets lies.

Noelle knows what he's thinking. Anything to shut you up. She knows it because she's thinking it, too.

She has on a long skirt above her sneakers, which puts Amram at an advantage; he's wearing a T-shirt and shorts. But she doesn't care. The skirt is loose, and by now she's used to maneuvering around in it. It's what she wears when she goes running and she manages just fine.

"We better get this match in before it rains." Amram licks his forefinger and raises it above him. He's merely testing the wind, but it appears as if he's saluting.

He measures the net, one length of the racquet plus the width of the head; he nods as if to say it looks right to him. On the baseline now, he sits on the clay, legs straight in front of him, leaning over to touch the soles of his sneakers. Presently, he stands up and stretches his calves and hamstrings; he grasps his left ankle and pulls it toward his back, then does the same with the other ankle.

Meanwhile, Noelle is just standing there.

Amram's yarmulke is bobby-pinned to his head, but it escapes its clasps and hops up and down with him. His dungaree cutoffs strain beneath his thighs. "You think you're going to beat me?"

She certainly plans to. Because what she wants from him, finally, is a simple apology. For disappearing for the last two days. For terrifying and humiliating her. For being how he's been for the past few months, for even longer than that if she thinks about it. And because he won't apologize, because he's pigheaded and obtuse, because he's Amram, she will wrangle that apology from him the only way she knows how to. She will humiliate him just as he's humiliated her. She will beat him into submission. She's slapping her racquet against her sneakers, hitting them so hard her feet start to sting.

Amram's ground strokes are topspin-heavy, whereas Noelle hits a straighter, flatter ball, which skims over the top of the net, occasionally hitting the tape and popping up to land short of the service line. This gets Amram running. They're not keeping score yet, but they're taking the ball on a single bounce.

Amram is overweight, but he's quick nonetheless, bearing down on the ball with a relentlessness that's accompanied by heavy breathing; saliva goes flying as he exhales. When he's up at net, he stands practically on top of it; Noelle, on the other hand, stays further back at net, and when Amram hits what appears to be a passing shot, she manages to return it to his court.

"Are you loosened up?" he says.

"I'm as loose as I'm ever going to be." She grabs her ankle and pulls it up to her rear.

"In that case, up or down?" He spins the racquet at his feet.

"Up," she says.

"Down it is. I'll serve first." He places his yarmulke in his dungarees pocket.

Just minutes ago, in their rallies, there was a methodical discipline to Amram's game that impressed Noelle. In sports, she has found, there are few surprises: you play the way you are. With squash, and especially racquetball, she can always tell the batterers and smashers, the ones who wish to pulverize the ball. So she was surprised to discover that Amram was more self-contained than she expected. Except for a few exuberant overheads, he seemed happy to play between the lines.

Now, though, as they begin their set, she detects a shift in Amram. It happens with a lot of players; tennis is the most psychological of games. But the change is starker in Amram. He was landing his practice serves in the box, but now that they're actually keeping score, his first serve rockets past her ear. His second serve sails long, too. He taps his racquet against his ankles and begins what will be an ongoing conversation with himself. "Calm down, my man. Concentrate. Put the ball where it's supposed to go."

His exhortations appear to work, because at love-fifteen he aces his first serve, then aces her again at fifteen-all. Then come two more double faults, accompanied by further rebuke—"Amram, you idiot, bear down!"—followed by another ace. Noelle is essentially an onlooker to this spectacle. When Amram aces her there's nothing she can do, and when he double-faults there's nothing she can do either, except get out of the way.

Noelle's own serve is efficient and well placed, and Amram responds by chipping at it. He hits his backhand with underspin, and his forehand too, talking to himself as he does so, which distracts Noelle, and she considers asking him to quiet down, but she decides not to. A couple of times she hits what appears to be a winner, but Amram calls the shot out. Are you sure? she wants to say, but again she remains silent.

Sometimes Amram will lob the ball so high Noelle loses it in the shadows. Then—randomly, it seems—he will try to hit a winner, as if he's decided it's time to assert himself, and the ball will go sailing over the fence, which seems to give him a perverse pleasure. But then he's back to chipping at the ball, forcing her to rush the net for another in a series of drop shots, followed by another in a series of lobs. Then he's back to trying to hit winners again.

There's no rhythm to the set other than the score itself, which was tied at one and at two and again at three, and which is tied now once more at five. "We might have to go to a tiebreaker," Amram says. They're between games, and he's banging his racquet against the tape, as if hoping to lower the net. "Too bad we're not playing total points. It wouldn't even be close."

"That's just how the game works," Noelle says, growing impatient with his excuses.

The clouds have thickened. A thatch of cumulus obscures the sky. Amram kneels on the ground to tie his sneakers; he's out of breath, Noelle can see, his back moving up and down like a piston. "Do you need a break?" she says. Her own breath, she observes silently, is even.

"I'm fine," Amram says. Soon, though, he reconsiders. It's his BlackBerry he blames it on, which rests on the chair beside the court and which, he tells Noelle, has been beeping incessantly. He sits on the ground near the net, which, in the growing shadows, segments him. As he punches the keys on his BlackBerry, sweat trails down his face. His roommates in college may have called him Moose but Noelle recalls hearing that when he would come back from the gym after a game of pickup basketball, his shirt so drenched he would wring it out the window onto the heads of unsuspecting passersby, they would call him other things, such as Pig.

"I'll be with you in a second," he says. He punches more keys. A minute passes, then another. "Okay, that should do it." He rises from the ground. Clay is caked to his shorts; it looks as if he sat in cookie dough.

Rejuvenated, he unleashes a serve that flies past Noelle's ear and crashes into the fence. He hits his second serve, and as he does, it starts to rain. A shard of lightning pierces the cloud cover, followed immediately by thunder: the storm is close by. It has gotten dark as well. It's as if night has ambushed them, though it's only nine in the morning. "Let's get out of here," Noelle says. She wishes she hadn't challenged Amram to a match; she doesn't know what she was hoping for.

But Amram remains where he is, and Noelle recalls his rabbi back in yeshiva, who used to invite the students over for Friday night dinner, after which he would deliver a talk. One time, the lights went off while he was still speaking—it was the Sabbath, and the lamps must have been on timers—but he went on talking in the dark, not even acknowledging that anything had happened. That's how Amram is with the rain. He's the tennis-playing version of his rabbi: stupid, principled about things there's no need to be principled about, always trying to make a point. Amram delivers his second serve, and Noelle barely gets a racquet on it, sending the ball flying over the fence.

It's raining harder, and the clay, which when dry doesn't provide much bounce, provides even less of it now; the ball simply stops when it hits the ground, as if it's been dropped into a marsh. The rain comes at Noelle sideways, bludgeoning her like an assailant. She should just walk off the court. But Amram doesn't even acknowledge the storm except to wipe the water from his face. He continues to chip away at the ball, delivering his underspin forehands, hitting drop shot after drop shot, all of which die when they hit the clay. It's thirty-fifteen, then forty-fifteen, then game for Amram.

"You win," Noelle says. "Good for you."

"It's six to five," Amram says. "Win by two—I have to get to seven. We could end up in a tiebreaker."

"There will be no tiebreaker," Noelle says. "I withdraw."

"You can't withdraw."

"Watch me."

"How about this? If I take this game, the set's over, I win, and if you take the game, we're tied at six and we finish up tomorrow."

"Not a chance." Noelle is determined to lose as quickly as possible. What, she wonders, was she trying to prove? And what good will beating Amram do? It won't make her feel any better.

But the prospect of losing to him makes her feel even worse. And she fears that if she doesn't complete the set she'll be treated to a plane ride home of postmortems, twelve hours of how Amram really would have won had it not been for the weather, the rehashing of a match she regrets having played in the first place.

The rain feels firmer—is it possible it's hail?—and from behind her comes a rapping on the window: wiser souls than she are urging her inside. She can hear her father's voice from years ago, telling the kids to come in. *You silly geese. You don't even know to get out of the rain.* Akiva calls to her, but she can't hear what he's saying. She hits her first serve long, and as she picks up the ball for her second serve she gets a whiff of it, damp and mangy as a dog's coat.

Her second serve sails long, too. Double fault: love-fifteen.

"Don't throw the set!" Amram calls out.

On her next serve, Amram rushes the net. She lobs the ball over him, and though she can't tell whether it's in or out, Amram calls it out. Love-thirty: two more points and they can go inside.

Amram rushes the net on her next serve, too, and seeing him bear down on her, moving like a lunatic through the rain, she hits the ball straight at him and he volleys it back. It lands at her feet, and as she pivots to swing at it, as she keeps her racquet even, moving it across the plane of her body, extending herself on her follow-through, Amram's sneakers catch in the clay. He's sinking, she realizes, plunging into the mud, while she herself has lost sight of the ball. She sees nothing for a moment, until she hears it, the smack of rubber against his face, the taste of wool—she can practically taste it herself—the sense that something has gone through him, and his neck snaps forward and recoils.

He lies facedown in the mud, utterly silent; everything seems to have gone black. When he finally calls out, his voice is so piercing she doesn't realize it's coming from him. He screams like a wild boar.

She leaps over the net, her skirt nearly catching on it. She's crouching next to him now. "Shit!" she says. "What happened?"

"What do you mean what happened? You hit me in the face, you sick fuck!" With one hand Amram is protecting his eye—it's as if he's expecting her to hit him again—and with the other he's gently poking at his cheekbone, making sure it's intact.

"Are you all right?"

"No, I'm not all right."

"The rain," she says. "I couldn't see you."

"Just get me inside!"

She tries to drape him over her back, but she can't hoist him up. "I'll go get help," she says, but she simply stands there in the rain. Amram removes his shirt, which he holds above his head, and they walk slowly, side by side, Amram in nothing but his dungaree shorts and prayer fringes.

Clarissa gets to them first, followed by Lily and David. Soon Marilyn arrives with ice packs.

"Leave him alone," Noelle says.

"What happened?" says Nathaniel.

"I hit him," she admits.

"With a racquet?"

"With a ball," she says impatiently.

"I just need to lie down," Amram says. He climbs the stairs to their bedroom, and Noelle follows. When he slumps across the bed, he still has his sneakers on. She puts a cold compress to his face, but he winces. "Leave me alone, will you?"

She hands him an ice pack. "This should help stop the swelling."

He's sitting up now, drinking from a glass of water. The color has drained from his face.

"You've gotten yourself quite a shiner," she says.

"*I've* gotten myself quite a shiner?"

"Okay," she says. "I have."

"You hit me on purpose, didn't you, Noelle?"

She doesn't even know. She hit the ball straight at him, hit it with purpose, with force, hit it the way she was hitting it all set, hit it to shut him up. But did she mean to hit him in the face? She has no idea. All she knows is that something has been taken from her, and now, as she apologizes to Amram, she feels that everything she has endured these past three days, everything she has endured these last months with Amram, has been blotted out with one lousy black eye. "I'm sorry," she says, and she kisses him on the forehead, and when she goes downstairs she makes a plate of their kosher food and brings it up to him, and seeing that he's fallen asleep, she leaves it on the nightstand beside his bed. She *is* sorry. She wishes she hadn't hit him in the face. But she's sorrier still for what she's lost, the feeling that she's in the right and nothing can change what's happened, sorry to see her parents and her sisters and her own children looking at her askance as she returns to the kitchen, as if she's the bad guy here, and her husband, who has earned no praise from them, no love, is now, battered as he is, transporter of Gretchen, the family matriarch, back to their country house, somehow, perversely, the hero.

In the kitchen, surrounded by her family, Noelle remains wound up. She stands silently, still in her sneakers and long skirt, her nose smudged with dirt from a ball she dove after, while Lily sets the table for breakfast. Gretchen has taken her post by the oven, watching Marilyn prepare scrambled eggs.

"How are you, Grandma?" Clarissa asks.

"I'm fine." As if to prove it, Gretchen removes the spatula from Marilyn's hand and tends to the eggs herself. She looks at Marilyn with silent determination, her every gesture saying, I was making scrambled eggs before you were born. Watching this, Thisbe feels a small, secret pleasure: even Marilyn has a mother-in-law.

And Lily, watching as well, makes a mental note to tell Malcolm, who's in the living room playing cards with the boys. Thank God he seems to have found a backer for his restaurant. If Gretchen were to contribute so much as a penny to the cause, she'd rename the place Gretchen's Gourmet.

Gretchen, still at the stove, turns her attention to Noelle. "How's your husband doing?"

"He'll be okay, Grandma."

"You certainly beat him up."

"Grandma, he'll be fine," Noelle says, her voice clipped, her arms folded across her chest, making clear through her carriage as she walks to the fridge to remove some butter and milk that she doesn't wish to discuss this further.

But now Dov has come downstairs, having just visited his father, and as he walks into the kitchen he announces, "Abba's eye is black and blue."

"Abba's eye's not black and blue," Akiva says. "It's going to *be* black and blue, but it's not black and blue *yet*."

"Bruises take time," Yoni agrees.

"Don't you know how the human body works?" Akiva says to Dov.

Apropos of nothing, Calder says, "My daddy's dead. They buried him yesterday. I was there."

"Actually," Thisbe says, crouching beside him, "they buried him last year. Yesterday was just the memorial."

"They buried him again," Calder says.

David brings out the Monopoly set and tries to explain to the boys how you amass as many hotels as you can, the fact of which the older cousins already know and the younger cousins aren't interested in.

"Eema broke Abba's face," Ari says, and he starts to cry.

"I didn't break Abba's face," Noelle says. She takes him in a hug, but then she says, "That's enough." Because it *is* enough. But when he persists, wanting to know what went wrong, she's forced to address the issue once more. "It happens in sports," she says. "People get injured, and eventually they heal." Then she says the words *the blessing of the skinned knee*, a phrase that's always being uttered by the Anglo-Saxons in her Jerusalem neighborhood, coming from a book she hasn't read and doesn't care to—she hates parenting advice books—knowing as she says this that the analogy is imprecise, that when people say *the blessing of the skinned knee* they don't have in mind hitting your husband in the face with a tennis ball. But she's said it, and now, she makes clear, the discussion is over. She goes into the living room and sits down in the rocking chair and, finding nothing else with which to occupy herself, she picks up one of her mother's medical journals and pretends to read it.

When her mother calls everyone in for breakfast, she reluctantly joins them. She'd rather not eat, rather not be here at all, but she doesn't want to be upstairs with Amram either, his eye slowly turning colors, so she deposits herself in the dining room and takes out the last of their kosher food.

She realizes she forgot to introduce the boys to Gretchen. Gretchen has met them before, of course, but she hasn't seen them in a year. "This is Akiva," she says. "Amram's and my eldest."

"Nice to see you again, Akiva."

She introduces the other boys, too, but it's Akiva Gretchen is most interested in. "Are you in school?" she asks him.

"It's summer vacation," he says.

"I mean in general."

This perplexes Akiva. He's eight years old. Is there anyone who's eight who isn't in school?

"What do you study?"

But his answers either bore Gretchen (math, reading, social studies) or confuse her (*chumash, navi, dikduk*), and so she moves on to other topics, such as the weather, which, rainy as it is in July, confounds her.

Noelle goes upstairs to check on Amram, but he remains asleep. She inches the food closer to him—cream cheese on a bagel, white-fish, some orange juice—thinking the smell of it might wake him. She recalls that concussion victims need to be kept awake. Though what is she thinking? Amram doesn't have a concussion; he didn't injure his head. In a week people will look at him and they won't even know anything happened.

"How's he doing?" Marilyn asks when she comes downstairs.

"He's fine," she says, her voice clipped again, feeling her family's stares on her, the stain of their collective accusation. "Can we talk about something else?"

"What would you like to talk about?" Clarissa says.

"How's Israel?" asks Gretchen.

"It's fine," Noelle says, not wanting to talk about that either, not wanting to talk about anything at all.

"I read about Israel in the *Times*," Gretchen says. "For a little country, you make a lot of news."

"I know," Noelle says ruefully. She could give Gretchen an earful about the Western press. All the distortions and falsehoods.

On a platter beside the coffee cake, Marilyn has arranged little square sandwiches with the crusts cut off, toothpicks piercing them, the red tassels at the top like tufts of hair. Cucumber and cream cheese. Egg salad. Smoked salmon. Gretchen helps herself to a sandwich, and as she does so, she lets the bracelets around her wrist clank against each other, as if she's ringing for a dog. She holds a teacup to the light, examining it for blemishes. Gretchen's famous hands, Noelle thinks. They've grown spotted over the years, but beneath the mottled hues they're as lovely as ever. Once, taking Amtrak down to Baltimore with her fiancé, the man who if he'd lived would have become Noelle's grandfather, Gretchen was approached by someone in their train berth who told her he was in advertising. A modeling agent, he called him-self, and he told Gretchen she had the loveliest hands he'd ever seen; he wanted to make her into a hand model. A hand model! She was almost offended. What was a hand model, anyway? They put you on billboards advertising bracelets and wedding rings? They took photos of you pouring milk? They wanted your body parts, Gretchen told her grandchildren, took your limbs and did what they wished with them. Not that she was suited for modeling of any kind. All that preening and primping: she wasn't good at sitting still. Though she kept the man's address. For all Noelle knows she still has it somewhere; she's never been one to discard a compliment.

Gretchen excuses herself to go to the bathroom, and when Marilyn asks if she needs help, she refuses it. She ferries herself past the refrigerator and into the other room.

When she returns, she looks down at the boys clustered around the table.

"Those are your great-grandchildren, Grandma," Clarissa says.

"I know who they are."

"Of course you do."

"Then why did you say it?"

"I was just reminding you," Clarissa says. "Sometimes you step back and take note."

"I don't need reminders," Gretchen says.

The scrambled eggs get passed around, moving from plate to plate until they're finished, and now Nathaniel rises to get some more, but at the sight of this Gretchen says, "Please sit down."

Nathaniel looks at her quizzically.

Clarissa says, "Grandma thinks the women should serve." Years ago, she explains, when Gretchen had the grandchildren over for dinner, it was always the girls she made clear the table and place the dishes in the sink. "Leo can clear the table, too," Clarissa said. "You're being sexist, Grandma." But Gretchen looked nothing so much as amused. The very word *sexist*, if it meant anything to her, she took as a compliment. She had read about women's lib, and she'd learned all she wanted to know about it. She had three husbands, and not one of them ever washed a dish, ever boiled an egg, ever folded laundry, ever touched an iron. It was for the help to do, and when the help wasn't available, it was her job. The world may have been embarking on a time when men would do women's work and women would do men's, but she wasn't coming along on that expedition.

Nathaniel, smiling, promises Gretchen he won't assist in her kitchen, but in his mother-in-law's kitchen he'd like to help. Soon he's back with the plate of eggs, and it seems Gretchen has capitulated because now she's letting him serve her.

"How are you, Mom?" David asks.

"I'm just fine," Gretchen says, and she proceeds to tell a story about one of the workers in her building who came in to replace a lightbulb and dragged the ladder clear across the floor. "I had to put down a rug to hide the scuff marks. Compassion alone prevented me from saddling him with the bill."

Noelle smiles. Compassion, she thinks, isn't the first word she associates with Gretchen, but then she will surprise you. She can be extraordinarily kindhearted, except for when she's not being kindhearted. And she's loyal to her family. In her worldview, there's her family and there's everyone else. In this regard, at least, she's like President Bush: you're either with the Frankels or you're against them. David, in particular, can do no wrong. Gretchen was similarly devoted to Leo. She favored him unabashedly, and when this was pointed out to her she simply shrugged. She's never made any bones about it: she prefers boys.

"I'm not hungry," Calder says, and soon he and his cousins have gotten up from the table and gone into the other room. Akiva, ever the dutiful eldest child, passes out decks of cards and sets everyone up to play solitaire. He seats himself next to Calder and Ari, who are too young to know how to play solitaire, and he tries, vainly, to explain the rules to them.

Back in the dining room, everyone is silent. Finally, Lily says, "We're so glad you came here, Grandma. It's hard to imagine having done this without you."

"You did do this without me," Gretchen says. "The memorial was yesterday, and I wasn't there."

"Leo forgives you," Lily says. But the words, intended lightly, come out wrong, and Gretchen remains silent.

"Better late than never," Clarissa says.

"It doesn't matter when you came," Lily says. "Just as long as you're here."

But Gretchen won't be toadied to. She nods in the direction of Malcolm. "I'd like the chef to make me some French toast."

"The chef's off duty," Lily says. "There are labor laws, Grandma. Malcolm's on break."

"That's okay," Malcolm says, rising from his seat. "I can make an exception for Gretchen."

"Do you prepare it with vanilla?" Gretchen asks.

"If you'd like."

"I wouldn't," she says.

In that case, Malcolm says, he won't prepare it with vanilla.

"I bet if you ask nicely," Clarissa says, "Malcolm will even put horseradish cheddar in it."

Malcolm raises a single eyebrow, the closest he's come to registering a complaint.

"That's your favorite cheese, Grandma, isn't it?" Lily says.

But Gretchen doesn't respond. She raises a tissue to her face and dabs fastidiously at her mouth, careful not to disturb her lipstick. "You say better late than never, but I didn't want to come here at all."

"Well, we're glad you did, Mom."

"The only reason I came was because of Amram. He drove down to the city to get me."

"And we're thrilled he did," Lily says.

Hearing this, especially from Lily, sets Noelle's teeth on edge. Amram drove down to the city to ask Gretchen for money. She has no evidence of this, but she also has no doubt. Yet even as she's thinking this, she's wondering who she is to be accusing him, thinking that if he in fact managed to secure a gift from Gretchen she would be grateful. She tries to imagine how much money her grandmother has, and all she can think of are those dead CEOs. She recalls that old joke: "How do you make a small fortune in Israel? You bring a large one from abroad."

"You told me you didn't want to come here," David says. "That you'd already been through too much."

"I *have* been through too much," Gretchen says. She's sitting up straight, her napkin folded primly in her lap, but there's a vacancy to her gaze, as if she's looking through them.

Lily says, "Malcolm made French toast for you, Grandma. Normally that would cost you fourteen dollars."

"Well, I don't like it."

"Now you've offended him."

Malcolm, complying, playing along, has his hands pressed to his heart; he's looking at Gretchen in supplication.

"You haven't even tried it," Marilyn says.

Gretchen takes a compulsory bite of French toast, then stirs the eggs around her plate. "I've always hated this town."

"I know you have, Mom. You said there was nowhere to get a decent cup of coffee, much less a good bagel."

Gretchen looks at him distantly, as if being reminded of someone she's forgotten, a former version of herself.

"You'll be going home in a few hours," David says. "You won't have to come back here for a long time."

"I'm never coming back here." She deposits her fork on her plate, her napkin in a ball beside her cutlery, and asks to be excused. She traffics into the hallway, where everyone can see her straightening the art on the walls. In the living room, she nudges a pile of books on the coffee table so they're not too close to the edge.

"What's she doing?" David asks.

"Making sure the picture frames aren't off-center," Lily says.

"She just needs to get back to the city," Marilyn says. "She was forty-nine when I first met her, and even then she hated to leave New York."

"I'd like a cup of tea," Gretchen says when she returns.

David jumps up; Clarissa, Lily, and Noelle do the same. Soon Nathaniel and Malcolm join them, too, and this time Gretchen doesn't object. The cupboard is open, and they're all reaching for a glass.

"You see, Gretchen?" Nathaniel says. "You ask for a cup of tea and you get six."

"You still rule the roost, Grandma," Lily says.

"One cup is sufficient," Gretchen says. "And a biscuit, please, if you would."

"One biscuit, coming up," David says. He brings his mother a plate of cookies.

"How are they?" Lily asks.

"They're not entirely disgusting," Gretchen says.

"Look, Grandma," Clarissa says, pointing at what's left of Gretchen's cookie. "It's in the shape of Pennsylvania. Remember how we used to do that? Play 'United States of Confectionaries'?"

Gretchen gazes back at her distantly.

"We'd chant 'United States of Confectionaries,'" Lily says. "That was your signal to bring out the cake and cookies. Then the four of us would bite into them in the shapes of the states."

"One time," Clarissa says, "Leo made you buy him five packages of Oreos. He claimed he needed to complete all fifty states. He said it was for his geography homework."

"Leo was the champion, wasn't he?" Gretchen says.

"Yes, Grandma," Lily says. "He was."

For an instant it seems as if there are tears in her eyes. She lays her head on the table, her hands on either side of her.

"Do you want to lie down?" Nathaniel asks.

"I'm just resting," Gretchen murmurs.

"You can rest on the sofa," Marilyn says. "You'll be more comfortable there."

"I'd rather rest here."

Gretchen stays with her eyes closed. Her breathing has gotten slower; it seems she might have fallen asleep. A minute passes, and she looks up. "I'm sorry," she says, dabbing her eyes with a napkin. "I must have been exhausted."

"Mom, you don't need to apologize."

Gretchen presses her hands against the table, and now she's standing up. She never was tall, and she has shrunk considerably over the years, but she has a way of staring down at people from below. Poised before her chair, looking out at her family, she looms above them all. "My only grandson died last year. I said I didn't want to go through this again, and I meant it."

Everyone nods. From the living room come shouts. Somebody has won at solitaire.

"Then Amram came to fetch me, and I'm not someone who's easily fetched."

"We know you're not, Grandma," Clarissa says.

"I don't do things I don't want to do."

"We understand, Mom."

"But then Amram told me what's happening in this family, and I marched straight to the car."

"Mom—"

"Please, David, let me finish. I'm not about to be party to this—the breaking up of my family."

"Gretchen." It's Marilyn who's speaking now, but Gretchen won't let her interrupt either.

"I didn't want to come here," Gretchen says, "but I'm here now, and you're going to listen to me." She's looking at her son, at her daughter-in-law, at both of them together, and they're looking back at her, and now they're looking away. "There's no excuse for this. Don't talk to me about love, and don't talk to me about grief. Do you think I don't know about grief? My grandson died a year ago. I'm ninety-four years old. Almost everyone I know is dead, starting with my first husband, your father, David, whom I loved."

"I know you did, Mom."

"I loved all three of my husbands. I won't talk about my private life, but if you want to know whether we ever had problems, the answer is we did. But I never thought of leaving them, and none of them ever thought of leaving me. I know something about integrity, and I know something about love. And I know something about loyalty, which is the most important quality of all. You," she says, and she's pointing at Thisbe, who's so startled she shoots up in her chair. "You've been quiet the whole meal."

"I . . ."

"It's okay," Gretchen says. "Your actions are more important."

"What actions?" Thisbe says, feeling as if she's been caught at something, she has no idea what.

"How old were you when Leo died?"

"Thirty-two," she says. "I'm thirty-three now."

"I wasn't much older when David's father died. I know what that's like, to be a young widow."

The porch door is open and a breeze comes in, sending the chandelier spinning so that the bulbs shine on Thisbe. She can feel herself breaking out in a sweat.

"No one understands something like that," Gretchen says, "until they've gone through it themselves."

Thisbe agrees. No one really knows what she's endured: not her family, not her closest friends.

"You could teach your in-laws a lesson about loyalty."

A piece of scrambled eggs is impaled on Thisbe's fork, which she's holding in front of her, not sure whether to raise it to her mouth or lower it to her plate, so it just hovers in midair, like a bird. "What do you mean?"

"You flew out here, didn't you?" Gretchen says. "You traveled across the country with your son."

"He was Leo's son, too," Thisbe says. She can hear Calder now, playing with his cousins in the living room.

"But you could have declined the invitation. It would have been easy enough to find an excuse."

Thisbe looks down at the floor.

"No one likes to fly across the country with a small child. Believe me, I've done it myself. And that doesn't even take into account the cost of plane fare."

"It's okay," Thisbe says. "It wasn't a burden."

"Please, Thisbe. Learn to take a compliment."

"Okay," she says. "Thank you, Gretchen." It's true, she thinks. She's never been good at taking a compliment, certainly not from Gretchen, who always scared her and still does. She's never been good, either, at being floodlighted with attention the way she's being flood-lighted now, and she thinks if she just acts grateful and says thank you, Gretchen might cast her gaze, her reedy voice, at someone else.

"All I know," Gretchen says, "is that I'm surrounded by blood rela-tives, but it's the people who have married into this family who have shown the most character."

Noelle sits up ramrod straight. She's not sure whom to defend and whom to attack. She looks directly at Gretchen. "If Thisbe's so loyal, why does she have a new boyfriend?"

"She what?" Marilyn says.

Lily turns in her seat. "Jesus Christ, Noelle!"

"Not only that, but she's about to move in with him. I overheard them on the phone last night."

Lily says, "What happened to your vaunted hearing defect, Noelle?" And the words come back to her, *You little snoop.* Noelle always with her ear to people's doors, never able to keep a secret. The girl who couldn't keep her legs shut couldn't keep her mouth shut.

"And you," Noelle says to Lily, "saying what you did at Leo's memorial. Don't you have any shame?"

"I have nothing to be ashamed of," Lily says. "Mom and Dad are splitting up. Everyone at this table knows it's happening, and the rest of the world will know it soon, too."

"You have a new boyfriend?" Marilyn says to Thisbe.

Thisbe hears a fork fall, a single blueberry roll across the table and drop slowly to the floor. "I was going to tell you."

"She *tried* to tell you," Lily says.

"You already knew?" says Marilyn.

"I knew Thisbe had a boyfriend," Lily says. "He's an old friend of Malcolm's and mine. When we heard Wyeth was going to Berkeley, we put him and Thisbe in touch."

"You set them up?"

"She didn't set us up," Thisbe says.

"Even if I did." Lily can hear her mother's voice. *He was your brother. Where do your allegiances lie?* And she hates that question. Hates the very idea of allegiances.

"I'd have met Wyeth, anyway," Thisbe says. "Our department is tiny. A year in, and we already know each other too well."

"That's what kills me," Marilyn says. "A year in."

"What do you mean?"

"Leo was alive a year ago."

Thisbe nods. How, she thinks, can she possibly forget this when she's here, in Lenox, thousands of miles from home, returned like a package to Leo's family, to everyone, to everything, she abandoned?

"Why?" Marilyn says, and she might as well be asking this about Leo himself. It's what Thisbe herself has been asking this past year, what she continues to ask: why did this happen to him, to her, to all of them?

But Marilyn is asking her about Wyeth. "Why are you moving in with him?"

"Because I love him, Marilyn. Because I want to move in with him. Because Calder loves him, too. Because I'm thirty-three years old and . . ."

Marilyn is standing now, and Thisbe senses anything is possible; she believes Marilyn might hit her.

"You may think I'm an unreasonable person, Thisbe."

"No, Marilyn. I don't think you're unreasonable."

"I wasn't expecting you to be alone for the rest of your life."

"But you'd have liked more time?"

Marilyn nods. But now, looking down at the remains of her scrambled eggs, she says, "I don't know."

She'd have liked more time, too, Thisbe wants to say. She certainly hadn't been planning for this to happen. A friend of hers once said that it's the people with the best marriages who are the quickest to meet someone new. They *like* being in a relationship; it's actually a testament to the person who died. But Thisbe's not going to tell Marilyn this because it will sound condescending, and because she suspects it won't ring true; she's not even sure it rings true to her. She won't tell Marilyn about her and Leo's troubles. It would seem like she's trying to absolve herself, and she doesn't wish to be absolved. And why should she destroy her mother-in-law's illusions when they may not be illusions in the first place? She loved Leo; they might have worked things out if he'd come home from Iraq. And if someone said it was a blissful marriage, she wouldn't disagree. Only a year has passed, but she can't remember it any longer. "I'm sorry," she says. The words feel piddly, insufficient, a coat thrown over a corpse, but they're all she has.

And Marilyn nods, removes her plate from the table, and silently exits the room.

Holding an ice pack, Lily climbs the stairs to the second floor and knocks on the door to Amram's bedroom. "Can I come in?"

Amram, who has just woken up, groggily admits her. The tissue surrounding his right eye has started to inflate; the skin has already begun to yellow.

"How are you doing?"

He shrugs. "The oddsmakers say I'm going to live."

"I'll tell you one thing. I'd sure like to see the other guy." Lily recalls the time Malcolm got a black eye, playing pickup basketball. He'd been breaking up a fight, and a punch intended for someone else landed on him. Socked in the eye by his own teammate. Felled by friendly fire. The skin around his eye turned yellow, then purple, then orange, before settling into a dusky blue-black. Killer Malcolm, his friends began to call him, and Lily started to call him that, too. She discovered, to her surprise, that with a certain segment of the population Malcolm's injury conferred on him a kind of status, and one time, on the Metro, a girl whistled at him and said, "Baby, you're hot!" Whatever else, getting punched in the face made you public property. She suspects Amram is in for that now.

"You did see the other guy," Amram says. "She was downstairs eating breakfast with you."

Lily steps tentatively toward him, holding out the ice pack. "Here," she says. "I thought you could use replenishment."

He could. The ice pack Noelle gave him is all melted now, sitting on the nightstand beside the bed, dripping to the floor. As he props himself up, he looks at Lily askance through his good eye. "Have I missed something, or have you become a doctor?"

"I was born to one," Lily says, shrugging. "Maybe some of it got passed down." Passed down enough, she thinks, for her to have for a time contemplated going to medical school, though a week of organic chemistry her sophomore year at Princeton ended any chance of that. It wouldn't have worked out, anyway. She gets squeamish at the sight of blood.

"So is this the pity vote?"

"What pity vote?"

"Come on. Don't pretend you ever liked me." Amram seats himself up straight so he's staring directly at her, though he needs to tilt his head to look out of his good eye.

"Since when do doctors have to like their patients?"

"Or patients their doctors."

"Exactly."

Lily's hands have gotten wet from holding the ice pack, and a little numb too. She wipes them on the back of her jeans. She's standing by the window where she can see out on the deck her father's new telescope directed at the firmament like a cannon. Astronomy's a guy thing, she thinks: point your phallus at Cassiopeia. There's something about the stars, especially in Lenox where there are so many of them, that turns a person mushy-headed. The world is so big and you're so small; it can make you start mooning. "We missed you at breakfast," she tells Amram.

"Was it a notable meal?"

"Among the most notable I've been at."

He gives her a dubious look.

"You should have heard the praise that got heaped on you. It was a veritable love fest. Some of it even came from me."

"Somehow, I doubt that."

"Just ask Noelle. She'll fill you in on what happened."

"If she ever talks to me again."

"Oh, she'll talk to you again."

"What makes you so sure?"

"She has to. You're her husband. And you have something else going for you. How angry can a person stay at someone who looks like that?"

Amram shrugs. "Noelle can be pretty stubborn." Though, he's forced to admit, he can be pretty stubborn, too.

"Just try not to let that thing heal too quickly. You're going to want to milk that injury for all it's worth. And one more thing. The next time you disappear for a couple of days, you might call your wife to let her know where you're going."

Lily means what she says. She believes Noelle and Amram will work things out. If they've been together for this long, there must be a reason. She and Malcolm have worked things out themselves, though it's true they don't fight the way Noelle and Amram do, and she certainly has never hit him in the face. Still, she knows how to fight, and Malcolm, for all his reserve, knows how to fight, too. Mr. Inward-Focused, Mr. Self-Contained, but if the black cod has been cooked five seconds too long, if the leek emulsion is too lemony, he'll take a pot to the line cook. Leo was the same way. Affable, unruffled, but you put him on the basketball court and he'd throw an elbow at you if you were in his way; he would curse out the referee and be called for a technical foul. If only, Lily thinks, she had an arena in which to do that. People think lawyers do that in the courtroom, but that's because they watch too much TV. Lawyers spend little time in the courtroom; it's all about negotiating and self-restraint.

Now, as she looks at Amram, she recalls the sabra, the Israeli fruit, come to be the nickname for Israelis themselves: hard on the outside and soft on the inside. "I want to thank you," she says.

"For what?"

"For bringing my grandmother back with you. Because you're the one who did it, and though I suspect there may be a more complicated story, I'm choosing to believe the simple one."

"What's that?"

"That you wanted the family together one last time." She takes a step toward Amram. She's sticking out her arm.

"What's that?"

"It's my hand, Amram. I'd like you to shake it."

He hesitates.

"Come on. You can't claim you're not allowed to shake a woman's hand. You shook my hand at the airport the other night. And don't tell me you've become more religious in the last few days."

"Okay," he says, and he reaches out to take it.

She's still standing there awkwardly shaking his hand, and it's only when he pulls his own hand away that she manages to extricate herself. "Get some rest," she says.

Amram looks at her impassively and nods.

She bends over the nightstand to pick up the old ice pack, and now, holding the old one in her left hand, the new one in her right, she shuts the door and heads downstairs.

15

"Closing up for winter?" Lily says.

And for fall, spring, and summer, Clarissa thinks. She has her suit-case open and she's tossing her clothes into it, and Nathaniel's clothes, too. She considers herself a light packer, but now that she's gotten to the end of the trip she hasn't worn half the things she packed. "And you?"

"I'm looting and pillaging," Lily says. "Mom and Dad are selling the house. I'm never coming back here."

"You sound just like Grandma."

"Grandma's wise." Lily is standing on the lip of the doorway, wait-ing to be invited in. "Where's Nathaniel?"

"In the driveway." Clarissa points out the window to where he's standing, refilling the bird feeder.

"Doing some last-minute son-in-law tasks?"

"And some last-minute tall-person tasks."

They could all use a tall person, Lily thinks. She and Malcolm practically have to stand on each other's shoulders just to get down supplies.

Now Malcolm has come outside with more birdfeed. He hands it to Nathaniel, who has his arms extended above his head so it looks like he's climbing a rope.

"Our men," Clarissa says. She's sitting beside Lily on her bed, her suitcase open between them. "So Thisbe has a new boyfriend."

Lily nods.

"Now I understand why you were being so protective of her. You knew all along."

"I knew," Lily says, "but I didn't realize how serious it was. Not until she told me the other day."

"Are you surprised?"

"It's a little sooner than I expected. But no."

"Have you seen them together?"

"Just once," Lily says. "They had a layover in D.C. for a couple of hours, and Malcolm and I met up with them at the terminal."

"And?"

"It was two hours sitting across from them at a Cinnabon. But looking back at it now, I guess they were in love."

"So he's a good guy?"

"He was when I knew him. He was the kind of guy women wanted to marry, at least if you were the marrying kind."

"It seems Thisbe is."

"Most people are," Lily says. "I'm the stubborn exception."

"So I shouldn't be overprotective?"

"Of Leo?"

"Of Calder."

"You're asking if Wyeth is good with him?"

Clarissa nods.

"I can't imagine Thisbe would be with someone who wasn't." The summer Lily and Malcolm knew Wyeth, he used to entertain the other waiters by juggling produce in back. Cucumbers, melons, rutabagas: he could do it all. What three-year-old, Lily thinks, wouldn't like that?

"I wonder where they'll be going," Clarissa says.

"Going?" says Lily.

"Anthropologists have to do fieldwork, Lil. And Thisbe always had wanderlust. She was married to Leo, remember?"

"Maybe she'll go back to Africa."

That's exactly what Clarissa is worried about. When she pictures Africa, she thinks of dysentery and mud huts. Why can't Thisbe fly to Scandinavia to study the Norse? "Oh, God," she says. "It's not like I haven't been to those places myself." When her boss needs someone to fly to the developing world, she's the first to raise her hand. She's sitting on her stripped bed, and she lets her arms fall dully against the mattress. "I'm becoming middle-aged."

"No," Lily says. "Just overprotective."

She's right, Clarissa thinks. But who is she to be protective of Calder when she's seen him how many times since Leo died? Two?

Maybe three? When he arrived in Lenox the other day, he didn't even recognize her.

She's in the closet now, making sure she hasn't forgotten anything. She opens and closes dresser drawers.

"And I thought *I* was compulsive."

Clarissa laughs. Nathaniel makes fun of her for doing this, but then, when he thinks she's not looking, he does the same thing. "What about you? Did you find anything good in your looting and pillaging?"

Lily removes from her bag a T-shirt with the words I DIDN'T DO IT printed across the front. "Remember this?"

How could Clarissa forget? It was Leo's T-shirt, and when he misplaced it one time, he painted the words directly across his chest, emblem of his professed innocence. The shirt is faded, and there are tiny holes along the sleeves, and a bigger one across the back. "What are you going to do with it?"

"Save it," Lily says, shrugging. "I don't know."

"You're not going to ask if anyone else wants it?"

"Why?" Lily says. "Do you?"

As a matter of fact, Clarissa does. Though she's embarrassed to say it, embarrassed even to think the words. It's an old T-shirt, worn by her brother when he was twelve. What in the world would she do with it? It wouldn't fit her; she'd stretch it until it really ripped. Besides, she hates T-shirts with words printed across them; they make her feel like a message board.

"Here," Lily says, handing her the T-shirt. "You can have it."

"Lily, come on."

"You deserve it," she says. "You were closer to him than I was." Lily can still remember Clarissa when she was six, pressing her nose to the glass of the NICU. And years later, she would send Leo care packages at summer camp, and then again at college. "Clarissa," she says. "Please. Take the T-shirt."

Reluctantly, Clarissa agrees.

Out in the garden, Lily and Malcolm can be seen kissing. At least Nathaniel can see them, and now he's saying, "Hey, kids, get a room!"

Clarissa, sitting beside him on a beach chair, agrees. "Look at those lovebirds."

"You see?" Lily says. "Absence really does make the heart grow fonder. You should try it yourselves."

"Okay," Nathaniel says, looking up at them from beneath his baseball cap. "We'll take it under advisement."

"Take it under advisement?" Malcolm says. "What's that? Neuroscientist talk?"

"It's just talk-talk," Nathaniel says, settling himself onto Clarissa's beach chair so that it nearly topples over.

Now Lily and Malcolm are at the badminton net, hitting a shuttlecock back and forth.

"Watch him slam that thing," Lily says. "Have you ever seen anyone so competitive?"

Clarissa says, "It takes one to know one, doesn't it, Lily?"

But Lily doesn't respond. She and Malcolm have a few rallies, each of which ends with Malcolm hitting the shuttlecock into the net. "Goddamn!"

"Look at that guy," Lily says. "His sous chef isn't here, so he gets to yell at me."

"Actually, it's me I get to yell at. What am I? The world's worst badminton player?"

"You're the world's worst sport, is what you are."

As if to prove her right, Malcolm slams the shuttlecock so hard and so high it goes clear across the garden and up onto the roof.

"Go get it," says Lily.

Malcolm climbs onto the beach chair beside Clarissa and Nathaniel, and now, balancing himself on the plastic strips, he steps onto the garden table. Reaching his hand out and extending his foot, he hoists himself onto the window ledge. Then he's shimmying up the side of the house.

Lily claps. "Look at that monkey go!"

He's at the top of the wall now and over onto the roof. All Lily can see are his sneakers dangling down, and then she can't see anything.

"Did you find it?" She takes a step back, and now she can make out Malcolm on top of the roof.

"There's a whole lot of junk up here. You should climb up and have a look."

"I'd rather not." There's already enough junk on the ground. She's staring at her wet towel and shorts, which lie in a ball at the porch door.

Now Malcolm is coming down again, clinging valiantly to the side of the house. He needs both hands to lower himself, so he has the shuttlecock in his mouth, and when he reaches the pavement he spits it onto the grass.

"Disgusting," Lily says. "No more badminton for me."

"Or for me either," says Malcolm.

"Or for me," says Nathaniel, who wasn't even playing badminton in the first place. "Time to go pack and shower."

"Me, too," Clarissa says, and she follows him inside.

Soon everyone is showered, their luggage ready, the suitcases deposited at the foot of the stairs. Noelle and her family have a flight to catch; Lily has to get on the road, too. Clarissa and Nathaniel will drive Gretchen to the city; everyone needs to head home.

Now, though, the sisters are out in the garden, the three of them beside each other on beach chairs, lying in the emerging sun. Noelle is drinking a glass of iced tea, and Lily reaches over to take a sip.

"It's from a mix," Noelle says.

"That's okay," says Lily.

Clarissa leans over and takes a sip, too.

"July fifth," Lily says, "and we've finally gotten some good weather."

Clarissa rolls over onto her stomach, and then rolls over again. "Maybe we'll do better next year."

"There won't be a next year," Lily says.

"Sure, there will," says Clarissa. "We can still get together without Mom and Dad."

"In that case," Lily says, "to good weather." She takes the iced tea from Noelle and raises her glass in a toast.

"Here's to hoping," Noelle says.

"Look at you," Lily says. "You've gotten a sunburn. You're starting to peel."

On her arms, no less. Because that, Noelle thinks, is the only part exposed. She's wearing her kerchief and a long cotton skirt, so that really it's her clothes she's sunning. "I have the world's tannest forearms."

Lily says, "The arms that used to set the boys' hearts aflutter."

"That was just the beginning of things," Clarissa says. "Noelle's arms were the least of it."

"Okay," Noelle says, laughing, "you're embarrassing me."

The sun beats down on them, and now they're rolling over again, like chickens on a rotisserie.

"Remember when we got sunburnt," Lily says, "and we would sit out on the grass and peel each other?"

"I would slough you two like snakes," Clarissa says.

"Ah, for the days before skin cancer," says Lily.

"I used to want to get sunburnt," Noelle says, "just so you would peel me."

"It was our favorite summer pastime," Clarissa says.

"We were disgusting," says Lily. She recalls a summer afternoon, lying sprawled in the sun, and afterward in the den watching *The Dukes of Hazzard*, the three of them still with their bathing suits on, eating s'mores, peeling the dead skin off each other's backs.

"So this is it," Clarissa says. "Ready for takeoff."

"Till next time," Lily says. "Many happy returns."

The sun is hiding behind the trees, which mottle them in shadow. Then it comes out again, lighting them up as if they're onstage.

"I want to apologize," Noelle says.

"For what?" says Lily.

"What I said at breakfast. I've already apologized to Thisbe, and I wanted to apologize to you too. I made quite a scene."

"It's okay, Noelle," Lily says. The fact is, she's already forgotten about it. Noelle has made so many scenes over the years she's become inured to them.

Noelle says, "There's still more apologizing to do."

"To Amram?" Clarissa says.

"To Amram and from Amram. I suspect there will be a lot more apologizing when we get home."

Her sisters flip over and Noelle does, too. Clarissa is lying on her stomach, and Noelle reaches out to touch her. "I'm glad you're trying to have a baby."

"Oh, Noelle."

"Seriously," she says. "I think you'll make a wonderful mother."

Still lying on her stomach, her face pressed against the slats of the beach chair, Clarissa says, "I'm not even sure it's going to happen."

"What do you mean," Noelle says.

"I got some more tests back, and it looks like I'm going to have trouble. I mean, I'm already having trouble, obviously, but now we'll have to intervene, and even with intervention it might not work."

"But that's what you're going to do, right?" Lily says. "Intervene?"

"I don't know," Clarissa says. "Now Nathaniel is saying he doesn't want to go through with it. It seems we're at an impasse." Maybe, she thinks, it's not such a bad thing. It's been an awful year. It's probably not the best time to be making big decisions. It's better to wait and let cooler heads prevail.

"So you're okay if it doesn't happen?" Lily says.

Clarissa shrugs. For a long time she thought she didn't want children, and then she decided she did. All that changing your mind does things to a person. It would be hard to go back to feeling how she did. "I suspect Nathaniel may still come around."

"And if he doesn't?" Lily says.

"Then I guess I'll have to adjust to that, too."

"And there I was," Noelle says, "about to ask you to become the guardian for my children."

"The what?" Clarissa says.

"You know, in case something happens to me and Amram? I figured since you were trying to have children yourself . . ."

"I could use four more?"

"I could understand why that wouldn't sound appealing. I just figured there's no substitute for family."

Clarissa can already see it. Noelle and Amram will get themselves killed on the West Bank, and their kids will be on the next plane to the States. Unable to conceive, she'll be given Noelle's children as consolation. "Let me think it over," she says. "I'll need to talk to Nathaniel."

"I've been thinking about something else," Noelle says. "I want to come back here for a while."

Clarissa and Lily sit up. They're poised beside each other in their shorts and tank tops. "What do you mean?" Lily says.

"I was thinking the boys and I could spend the summer in Lenox."

"What about Amram?" Clarissa says.

"He could come, too, if he wants. Though I don't know if he'll be able to once he finds a job. He probably won't get much vacation."

"I thought you hated the States," Lily says.

"I do," Noelle says. "At least I thought I did. I don't know. . . ." She takes another sip of iced tea. "It would be good to spend some time here. This house has history. It's where we grew up."

"But Mom and Dad are selling the house," Lily says.

"It will take time," says Noelle. "It's hard to find a buyer in this market."

The sun passes behind a tree, and now it's shining on their mother's azaleas. In the shadows the leaves are darkening, deepening into an inky hue. "Don't you care about our relationship?" Noelle says.

"What do you mean?" says Lily.

Clarissa says, "Is that why you want to come back here?"

"We could try to work things out."

Lily nods, not knowing if she wants to, not even sure what it would mean to work things out with Noelle. She could try to be nicer to her. She *will* try to be nicer to her. But being nice to Noelle won't make them close, and Lily doesn't see how they can ever be close no matter how nice they are to each other.

Noelle says, "Wasn't Leo's death supposed to bring us together?"

That's what Lily thought, too. Her brother died, and they would all become closer, even Noelle. But they're like dogs at mealtime, everyone with her bowl, alone. Even Clarissa is moving slowly out of her orbit. (As girls, Lily recalls, they used to walk on the beach with twine tied between their wrists because they didn't want to be separated.) Is it simply because she's been trying to get pregnant? Because she never told Lily, when for years she told Lily everything? Lily can't be surprised that Clarissa wants a baby. But Clarissa never mentioned it, and in her silence Lily allowed herself to believe that Clarissa was like her, happy to be an aunt to five faraway nephews, boys they could send birthday cards to and then get on with their lives. Lily thinks of her parents' old next-door neighbors, two sisters who were sixty-five years old, living together as they always had. Was that what she'd been hoping for? She and Clarissa living together like those sisters did, the Frankel sisters growing old together, no men to take their place, no Nathaniel, no Malcolm, no Amram; no children, certainly; no deaths, no divorces, nothing at all?

"Remember when Leo was born?" Clarissa says. "Those weeks and weeks at the NICU and we wondered if he was going to make it?"

Lily and Noelle nod.

"And even once Mom and Dad brought him home, I was always going over to his crib to make sure he was still breathing."

"I was scared, too," Noelle says. "How old was I? Four? I didn't really understand what was happening."

"We all just knew to be afraid," Lily says.

"But I had this idea," Noelle says, "that the three of us were in this together. Our brother had been born premature, and it was our job to take care of him. It was something no one else could understand."

Lily nods: she felt the same way.

"And then he got bigger," Noelle says, "and you wouldn't have known anything had ever been wrong."

"But it stayed with me," Lily says. "For years I still thought of him as he'd been those first few months."

"When he was only weeks old," Clarissa says, "I took pictures of him with my Polaroid camera. I wanted to have them in case he died."

"And once he was fine," Noelle says, "I started to think, what if he *had* died. Because if that had happened, we'd have forever been known as the tragic family. I had this idea that it would cement us, because how could you not be close when something had happened like that?"

"It would have changed everything," Clarissa agrees.

"And then he did die," Noelle says, "and, sure, we were older and we had our own lives, but I believed it was going to make a difference.

And now Mom and Dad are splitting up, and even that, I can tell, isn't going to make us close."

"We can try," Clarissa says. "I'm not against that."

"Our brother *died*," Noelle says, "and if it's not going to make us close, what good was it?"

"It wasn't good," Lily says. "It was just bad. All of it."

"Leo would have wanted us to be closer," Noelle says.

Maybe, Lily thinks, but she's not so sure. She suspects Leo would have been fine if they'd been close, and that he'd have been equally fine if they hadn't been close. His mind, his heart, was on other things.

"Your speech at the memorial?" Noelle tells Lily. "You were right. Leo was the most conflict-averse person I've ever known."

"Yet he died in Iraq," Clarissa says. "He spent his whole life seeking out conflict." Though she thinks at bottom that Noelle is right.

"So what I want to know," Noelle says, "is if I return to the States with the boys, if we decide to pitch tent in Lenox for a while, will you at least come visit for an occasional weekend?"

Clarissa and Lily nod.

"Will you give things another shot?"

"We can try," Clarissa says, though she, too, doesn't know what trying would mean, and her words come out faltering.

Now the porch door has opened. Amram is holding a suitcase in each hand, and he puts one down long enough to look at his watch. The boys are holding bags, too, even Ari, who has a small suitcase on wheels, which he's pushing back and forth beside his father.

"Okay," Noelle says. "My guys are waiting for me." She leans over her sisters still lying on their beach chairs and kisses them goodbye.

"You're leaving so soon?" David says.

"The holiday's over," Thisbe says. "Everyone has a plane to catch."

They're out behind the house, where David's telescope is mounted. He's peering into it now.

"Are you taking that back to the city with you?"

"If they don't stop me at the border. Marilyn used to say I was transporting heavy machinery across state lines."

"Is that not allowed?"

"She claimed telescopes weren't permitted in New York City apartments. Who was she kidding? People keep zoo animals in New York City apartments. Last year, a lion cub got loose on the Upper East Side."

"Where will you set it up?"

"On the balcony, I imagine."

"And you'll stand out there and peer into it?"

"I'll point it toward New Jersey. I hear they have some good constellations there." It's a hot morning, and David's hair forms curlicues, growing out to the sides. The better to attract mosquitoes, Leo used to say.

"How are you, David?"

"I'm okay, I guess."

Thisbe's glad she has found him alone. Even when Leo was alive, she always felt more comfortable with him than with Marilyn. He has the gentler personality. Or maybe it's that she prefers men to women; her closest friends have always been guys. She's not sure why, and it shames her in a way, but women make her anxious, most of them, at least. She has a few close female friends, but the stakes feel higher with them, as if there's something precarious in the relationship, a slight waiting to happen that she won't be able to repair, a loss she's always trying to preempt. "Men are simpler," Leo said to her once, but he was probably just trying to keep her off some scent, and she, in any case, didn't agree. "So Marilyn will be moving into a new apartment."

David nods. "In a couple of weeks the trucks will come." He does his best to make light of it. "Calder will have two vacation homes. And he'll have to do double-time back east. Neither of us will want to get short shrift." He presses an eye to the telescope, covering the other eye with his hand. He's wearing blue jeans and a white gingham shirt with the sleeves rolled up, and he's humming an old Frankie Valli tune. Thisbe hears Leo's voice. *No, Dad, please stop!* Their first summer together, she and Leo would turn on the car radio, and they would always know when David had been the last one in the car.

"Where's Calder?" he asks.

"Inside," she says. "Playing with his cousins."

It's as if the boys have heard her, because now they all come running out. Calder is crying, and he's trailed by Yoni and Ari, each of whom is claiming he didn't do anything wrong. Those little Israelis, Thisbe thinks. Six and three, and they've already been trained to interrogate and be interrogated. Though Calder is no different. Whenever anyone near him starts to cry, he's the first to proclaim his innocence. Just last week, he accidentally hit Wyeth with a paper airplane, and when Thisbe said, "Calder, what do you say?" he immediately responded, "Thank you." *Thank you, please, you're welcome, excuse me.* It's the social code she's drummed into him and that he spits out at her command. It surprises her how much parenting feels like domestication. It's no different from raising a dog, or a cow; it just takes more time. What a long period of maturing humans go through, so dependent are they on their parents. Calder will be four next February. If he were a dog, he'd be an adult already. He'd be in graduate school now; he'd have left her. "Come here, you. Say goodbye to your cousins."

"Goodbye!" Calder says. "Goodbye, goodbye!"

"Tell them you hope to see them soon."

Dutifully, he mimics her.

"When does your flight leave?" David asks now.

"Not for a few hours. But it will take us a while to get to the airport."

"I could drive you there."

"It's okay," she says. "I have the rental car." She pictures her flight home, the screen in front of her mapping out the route, letting her know the barometric pressure and the temperature change. The higher you go, the colder it gets; eject her from an airplane at thirty-five thousand feet and, among other problems, she'd freeze to death. Why, she doesn't know: she always thought hot air rises. There's probably an easy answer to this, something she learned in earth science. But earth science was years ago, and she, the aspiring professor, has her head in the proverbial clouds; the real clouds, on the other hand, she knows nothing about.

David straightens his shirtsleeves, then rolls them up again. He kicks some stray pebbles from his path. "Come here," he says, staring into the telescope. "Have a look."

Thisbe laughs. "Leo warned me this day would come. He said you'd insist on giving me a tutorial."

"You can't see constellations in the daytime, but if you're lucky you can see Venus and Jupiter."

She approaches the telescope. He looms over her: a mother hen.

"So what does it look like?"

"It looks like nothing." It's a swirl of white and yellow, the sunlight coming headlong at her.

"Do you see airplanes?"

"No."

"Think of it as a Rorschach test. You see whatever comes to you."

A crow flies overhead, casting them briefly in silhouette. She presses her eye to the lens.

"So when's your next trip east?"

"I don't know."

"Listen to me. I sound just like those doctors Marilyn's always complaining about. The physicians cum entrepreneurs. They won't let you leave their office until you've scheduled your next appointment."

Thisbe stares into the telescope, but all she can see is diffuse light. "In a few years, Calder will be ready to visit on his own."

"You think?"

"If I armed him with the proper snacks, he'd do it right now. Give that kid a bag of chips and he'd fly to Neptune."

David sticks a blade of grass between his incisors, where it bobs like a compass needle. "So what happens next?"

"I go back to my routine."

"And what's that?"

"Another year of classes. With any luck, I'll take my orals. With even more luck, I might pass them."

"And after that?"

"Then there's my dissertation and the wilds of the job market. I could end up with a four-four load in Dubuque."

"Will you be getting married?"

Thisbe laughs. "I've been with Wyeth for less than a year. I'm only just moving in with him."

"But it could happen."

She doesn't respond.

David remembers what Clarissa told him when she moved in

with Nathaniel. How she couldn't imagine living with someone she didn't think she could marry. Breaking up was hard enough, she said, without having to divide possessions. He tells this to Thisbe. "What about you?"

"Do *I* think breaking up is hard enough?"

"Would you live with someone . . ."

". . . I couldn't see a future with?"

He nods.

"No," she says. "I wouldn't." She takes a few steps this way, a few steps that, trying to avoid David's gaze. But he's still staring at her. "If Wyeth and I ever get married, he'll probably end up adopting Calder."

David's quiet.

"Is that all you're going to say? Nothing?"

"I didn't realize it was up to me to grant permission."

"It isn't."

David's back at the telescope, his eye pressed to the lens. "A boy should have a father, don't you think?"

"In an ideal world, he'd have had one all along."

"So, yes," he says, "I'm okay with it."

"And Marilyn?"

He gives her a mournful smile. "You're not dumb, Thisbe. I assume there's a reason you spoke to me."

She reaches into her pocket and hands him a check.

"Two hundred and five thousand dollars!" he says. "I didn't realize anthropologists were paid so well!"

"We're not."

"What have you been doing? Spending your spring break in Reno?"

"If only."

And David's just standing there, waiting for her to explain.

"The money's from Gretchen," she says.

"I figured as much."

"After Leo died, she gave me a check for two hundred thousand dollars."

"And the extra five thousand?"

"That's my paltry interest rate. Good thing I didn't go to business school."

David turns the check over in his hand. "What were you planning to do with it?"

"I figured it would go to Calder's education."

"Sounds like he's going to be a very well-educated young man."

"Except now I'm giving it back to you."

"Why?" he says. "It's not for *my* education."

"It doesn't belong to me, or to Calder either."

"Who do you think it belongs to?" David gives her back the check, and when she refuses to take it, he tears it in half.

And now he has returned to his telescope.

Men and their implements, Thisbe thinks. Though Marilyn, she realizes, is the same way. Leo used to say that's why his parents played the piano, so they could move their hands and feet at the same time. And Leo, it turned out, was no different. "Do you always have to be in motion?" she asked him once. "Apparently so," he said. "I'm a Frankel."

So it's with hands aflutter, going up and down the telescope, that David says, "You won't have an easy time cutting ties."

"Is that what you think I'm trying to do?"

"Isn't that why you returned the money? So you wouldn't be beholden to us anymore?"

"Oh, David. That's not true."

"I'm still Calder's grandfather," he says. "Unless you're planning to have Wyeth's parents adopt him, too."

Thisbe laughs. "I barely even know Wyeth's parents."

"Well, you better get to it, don't you think?"

She touches him on the sleeve. "Don't worry," she says. "I'm not cutting ties. Calder will be back soon. I promise."

"And I'll come out to visit as well. As long as you'll have me, I'll be on the next flight."

"Of course I'll have you."

"Well, I'm glad that's settled." And he folds up his telescope and goes inside.

Now, in the driveway, Clarissa sits behind the wheel of her car. Gretchen is next to her; Nathaniel has his legs extended across the backseat. Marilyn and David stand beside the open window.

"Look at that guy," Clarissa says, thrusting her thumb toward Nathaniel. "How tall is he? Six-eight?"

"Try six-two," Nathaniel says.

"I volunteered to sit in back, but he wouldn't let me."

"Chivalry isn't dead," Nathaniel says.

"Neither, apparently, is discomfort."

"I'll be all right," Nathaniel says, and now Gretchen, who's been silent through this all, inches her seat forward. She's sitting with her pocketbook on her lap, and she reaches inside it and removes some lipstick. She's putting it on now, examining herself in the rearview mirror.

"You want to look good for the tollbooth collector, Grandma?"

"You'll do the same thing when you're turning ninety-five."

"I can only hope."

"Wait a minute," Marilyn says. "I forgot something." She trots back to the house, and when she returns she's holding a Tupperware of leftover food. "A doggie bag," she says. "Reward for your travels."

Though the reward, Clarissa thinks, will probably go to their actual dog, to Gwendolyn, whose idea of travel is to migrate from the couch to the armchair and back again. "That dog could have gone to college with me," Leo used to say. To Wesleyan, where the students' idea of exercise was to walk to the store to buy cigarettes.

As Clarissa turns on the engine, Marilyn presses her nose to the window, the better to say goodbye. It's what she and David used to do when the children left for school, pressing their noses against various panes of glass: the living room window looking down at the bus stop, the elevator window through which she and David would make funny faces as the children dropped out of sight.

Now everyone has departed, and it's just Marilyn and David alone. It's lunchtime and Marilyn is hungry, and David has offered to make her an omelet. She sits behind him on the breakfast stool while he cuts peppers and onions and grates cheddar cheese. "You're chopping vegetables again."

"Use it or lose it, isn't that what they say?"

"And you're wearing goggles."

"Onions," he explains. "I'm the culinary Kareem Abdul-Jabbar." He gets onioneye, and now that he has started to play racquetball again, he brings out his goggles when there are onions to be chopped.

"Who?"

"Lew Alcindor," he says. "Basketball reference. He got poked in the eye, so for the rest of his career he wore goggles."

"I see."

In the dining room, she clears the last of the breakfast dishes. She better take care of those before there are lunch dishes, too.

Back in the kitchen, on the butcher-block table, she finds a copy of the memorial program that someone must have left. She leafs through it while David butters the pan.

"I'm sorry," he says, looking up at her.

"What?"

"You asked me to change the font on the program, and I never did. You said it was too blocky."

"That's okay."

"I meant to," he says, "and I plumb forgot."

She finds a few Styrofoam peanuts beneath the breakfast table, left over from the packing materials, the boxes of new dishes they bought for Noelle. She sweeps them into the dustpan, then removes a pair of nail scissors lying on top of the toaster oven and a child's yo-yo secreted beneath a chair.

On the counter sits a photo of Clarissa, taken when she must have been twelve. "She was a beautiful girl," Marilyn says.

"She's still beautiful," says David.

"All the girls are. Leo was beautiful, too."

"He was, wasn't he?" It's not something one usually says about a boy, but in this case, David thinks, it's true.

Marilyn washes a few more dishes, then sets them out to dry.

"I remember when he had the chickenpox," David says. "How old was he? Five? Maybe six? Every morning, he would stand naked in his bedroom and the girls would count his chickenpox. Lily would take the front and Noelle would take the back and Clarissa would stand there with her pad and pencil."

"He was utterly unself-conscious, wasn't he?" Marilyn says.

"And he wanted to win. He was determined to set the world chick-enpox record."

"He could always turn a bad thing into a good thing." The world, Marilyn thinks, is filled with people turning good things into bad things, and then there was Leo.

Again she glances at the photo of Clarissa. She's holding a lacrosse stick, running through some field, and the thing is, she can't remember Clarissa's ever having played lacrosse, and David can't, either.

"I guess she's not going to have a baby, after all."

"Are you disappointed?" he says.

"For her, I am. I liked having babies. I'd do it again if I could."

"It might still work out for them."

"You never know."

"You would be a good grandmother."

"*Would* be?"

"Are."

"But you're saying with Clarissa it would be different?"

"Don't you think?"

She does. In many ways, she still feels like a grandparent in waiting. It's as if Noelle's children have been taken from her, these alien boys with their yarmulkes and prayer fringes, speaking a language she doesn't understand. She sees them only a couple of times a year, and when she does, there are countless rules she must follow, the very structure of Judaism designed, it seems to her, to impede her relationship with her grandchildren, the way Noelle's living in Israel seems similarly designed. And Calder, darling Calder, carries with him his own attendant complications, and not just geographic ones.

She's in the girls' bedroom now, where Noelle's wedding dress is laid out, the one from when she was engaged the first time, years before Amram. It seemed to Marilyn at the time that Noelle barely knew the boy she was going to marry. They had dinner with Noelle and her fiancé, at which point they were already fighting, and soon the engagement was called off. Although she never told Noelle this, Marilyn delayed ordering the wedding invitations because she suspected the marriage wouldn't take place. Though Noelle waited to call it off until she got her wedding dress. She looked beautiful in that dress. She must have spent hours examining herself up in Lenox, where if you opened the adjoining closets the mirrors would line up: Noelle after Noelle after Noelle after Noelle, an endless row of brides.

"Do you even remember his name?" Marilyn says. "That boy she was planning to marry?" And he *was* a boy, she thinks: he and Noelle had been only twenty-one.

"Tom?" David says. "Something plain like that?"

"Plain?" she says, laughing. "Like David?" Though she's thinking Noelle would have done well to marry someone like David. But there's no point in wishing for that, in going down paths that might have been taken, when with Noelle any path was as likely as the rest. "At least he wasn't Orthodox." In fact, she recalls, he wasn't even Jewish.

"No," David says, "but he was other things. I seem to remember he couldn't keep a job."

Though the same could be said about Amram. But this path, too, she doesn't wish to take. Noelle has been with Amram for over a decade now. It's time, she suspects, to make peace with that.

Five years later, when Noelle was engaged to Amram, Marilyn suggested she wear her original wedding dress—she'd looked so lovely in it—and it was left to Leo, who generally didn't pay attention to such things, to say, "No way Noelle is going to wear that dress. She'll think it's bad luck."

Though bad luck was the least of it. Noelle was Orthodox now; the dress was too low-cut.

Earlier today, as Noelle and Amram were preparing to leave, Marilyn said, "You should take that dress back to Israel with you."

"What for?"

"You could give it to a friend."

"My friends are already married," Noelle said. "And even if they weren't, they wouldn't wear that dress."

"Then how about taking these?" Marilyn handed Noelle a stack of books with Hebrew handwriting inside the covers. How peculiar, Marilyn thought, when for most of her life Noelle hadn't been interested in books. And now Noelle was staking claim to their books, writing Hebrew inside them. "What do those words say?"

Noelle read the Hebrew back to her. "Actually, it's Amram who wrote that. It's his handwriting, not mine."

"Proselytizing from afar?"

"Could be."

Though in her own quieter way, Noelle had become a proselytizer, too. One time visiting Lenox, she lamented that there were no mezuzahs on her parents' doorposts, and feeling fragile, eager to please, grateful to have their daughter home if only for a visit, Marilyn and David allowed her to bolt a mezuzah to their front doorpost. But the following summer it was gone, removed by the renters, and the next time she visited she'd moved on to other things, to a stealth campaign against their books. Though apparently it was Amram who did that.

Noelle had been four when Marilyn got pregnant again, and everyone assumed it was a mistake, the girls already older, Marilyn getting older herself. But it hadn't been a mistake. In an abstract, hypothetical way she and David had talked about having a fourth child, but at thirty-six, she was convinced she wasn't going to get pregnant, and so, in having intercourse without protection, she saw herself as engaged in a scientific experiment whose results she knew in advance. When the doctor told her the news, she made him repeat the pregnancy test. As her body began to thicken, she and David grew to realize how intimately their decision to have a baby was tied to Noelle. They never said as much, but they each thought it. *In case something happens to her.*

They'd had Leo as an insurance policy against Noelle, but soon they came to believe the reverse was true. Stormy, reckless Noelle would protect Leo, whose recklessness was of a more affable sort. Even when he left for Iraq, they weren't worried. Iraq was dangerous, but Leo wasn't in the military; he was reporting for a good newspaper. The person they worried about was Noelle, who was in the Middle East, too, but she lived there—for a time she'd been living on the West Bank—with her temperamental husband, with her four small children and her part-time job.

In their old bedroom, Marilyn sits down to the computer. She's idly surfing the Web, looking for what, she has no idea, but David assumes she's writing another op-ed (she has published twenty-four of them over the past year, nearly one every two weeks), so he's surprised when she says, "That's it for me."

"What do you mean?"

"I'm officially retiring from the opinion business. The world has heard enough from me. I've heard enough from myself. If I ever publish anything again it will be filled with medical jargon. I'm going to make sure it's completely unreadable." She reaches into the desk drawer and removes a stack of letters. "Now I can finally get rid of this hate mail."

"What hate mail?"

"There are even a couple of death threats mixed in with the rest, just to keep me on my toes."

"Hate mail?" he says. "*Death threats?*"

"There are a lot of nuts out there."

"Why in the world didn't you tell me?"

"Because I didn't want you to be worried." She holds the pile in her palm as if to weigh it. Then she drops the letters into the trash.

At the washing machine, she piles the clean clothes, but now she's confused them with the dirty ones, and she finds herself gathering the same pair of jeans, folding and unfolding them like dough.

"And now," she says, "the great molting begins." She's standing with David in Leo's old bedroom, trying to figure out what to discard, and she seems to think that if she's dramatic about it, she'll find the task easier.

She goes through his desk drawers. She recalls the mounds of condolence letters, many of them unanswered, unopened, dozens upon dozens of friends to write back. And then, amidst everything else, were the people who, unaccountably, hadn't heard what had happened, and so she was forced to deliver the news all over again. A year after his death, they continue to get mail addressed to Leo: subscription offers, pledge requests, statements from a bank account with $1.22 left in it that they haven't managed to close down. Leo still gets summoned for jury duty, though he hasn't lived at their address for fifteen years; apparently, he's still registered to vote there. When Marilyn told him this, he said, "I should have given them a few addresses for me in Florida. Perpetrated a little election fraud of my own." One time, she handed him his jury summons and said, "Here, *you* deal with it," and Leo, in his idea of a joke, returned it with the word DECEASED across the envelope. But it didn't work then any more than it works now. His *Reader's Digest* still arrives faithfully every month. When he was born, Gretchen gave him a lifetime subscription, but no one seemed to understand what lifetime meant; they'll just have to wait for *Reader's Digest* to close down. Now the smell of mothballs wafts through the room, and something else, sweet and sickly, like rubbing oil and lemon, something she can't name. "I can't remember what they dressed him in for the funeral."

"I can't, either," David says.

She recalls a discussion: did the dead get buried naked or in clothes? What, she wondered, was the tradition? And what tradition, besides? The Jewish one? It was her tradition in a way, but she felt so removed from it she was loath to rely on its edicts and consolations. Thank goodness for Noelle, whose tradition it now was; maybe she would have an answer. Though even as Marilyn considered it, she found it foolish to bury Leo in clothes; it was too reminiscent of the Egyptian pharaohs. There was talk of having him buried in a jacket and tie, which was ridiculous, she thought, because when he was alive he never wore a jacket and tie. She recalls a disagreement she had with Thisbe (there were so many of them—she's always regretted that) about what clothes to bury him in, and it was decided that someone should buy him new clothes so he wouldn't have to be buried in the ones he had lived in. Though even of that she isn't sure. Everyone shielded her and David from these things, left them up to Thisbe and the girls, to the funeral people themselves, the diggers and embalmers. "I remember what Thisbe was wearing that day."

"I do, too," says David. "She had on a black pants suit."

"And a pale yellow shirt." This has stuck with her, she doesn't know why. She looks up at David. "Did you talk to her?"

He nods.

"And?"

"She's moving on, but we knew that already."

"Are they getting married?"

He shakes his head. "At least not yet."

"But eventually . . ."

"I presume."

"And if not to him, then to someone else." She's standing at the window, looking out at the elms swaying in the breeze. A sparrow has landed on the bird feeder. "Maybe she'll do us a favor and not invite us to the wedding."

"Why would she do that?"

"Retaliation for when we didn't invite her to our party."

"Oh, Marilyn, that was years ago."

"We can hope she bears a grudge." She presses her face to the window. The sparrow seems to be looking at her, but then it flies away. "You knew about him," she says, "didn't you? You knew Thisbe had a boyfriend."

David nods. It was a few months ago, and he called California to speak to Calder. A man answered the phone, and he figured it out. "It's another thing you can hold against me."

"What do you mean?"

"You could threaten to leave me, but then you've already played that card."

"David," she says, "we don't have to do this."

"Do what?"

"I could cancel the moving trucks. I'd lose my deposit, but I don't care."

"And come home with me?"

"We could at least try." They're standing in their son's bedroom, gathering what possessions remain. Marilyn sits down on the bed; David installs himself next to her. He's sitting up straight, the back of his head pressed to the wall; Marilyn is looking at him. "Aren't you going to say anything?"

"What would you like me to say?" He walks across the room to Leo's dresser. He opens drawer after drawer, all of which are empty, until he reaches the last one, where he finds Leo's San Diego Chargers pennant. "Didn't you give this to Thisbe?"

"I thought I did."

"She must have forgotten it."

"Or declined my offer."

He places the pennant back inside the drawer. "I don't get it," he says. "Was it my mother?"

"Was what your mother?"

"All it took was Gretchen coming up here to rebuke you? If I had known, I'd have driven her up here myself."

"Oh, David. It wasn't Gretchen."

"What was it, then?"

"I don't know." She's still sitting on their son's stripped bed, looking up at David. "So you're not going to give me another chance? If I don't leave you, then you'll leave me instead?"

"We'll go back to the city," he says. "We'll have to see what happens."

She steps outside to catch her breath. She replenishes the bird feeder, and pulls a few weeds from the garden. The pear tree is in bloom, and she plucks a fruit off the branch. She takes a bite of it, then leaves the rest of it on the garden table.

She goes into the garage, where she's looking for some gloves and garden shears. But she can't find them, and what she unearths instead behind the rake and the hoe and the bucket of tennis balls is one of the girls' old bicycles. Dry mud is caked across the frame, but once she wipes it off and wheels the bicycle outside, she finds it's in good shape. The tires are a little low but still inflated. Even the bell works. And in the basket is a dandelion, desiccated but intact.

She gets on the bicycle and circles around the stone path behind the garden, then pedals out to the driveway, where David is attending to something beneath the hood of the car. "Look at me!"

"Jesus," he says. "I haven't seen that thing in years."

She does another circle around the car, and when she loops back she parks in front of him. "Here," she says. "You have a go."

"You want me to ride a girl's bicycle?"

She laughs. "You think it will compromise your masculinity?"

"It very well might."

But then she remembers. The kind of bicycle is just an excuse, because David doesn't know how to ride a bicycle at all. "Wasn't I going to teach you how to ride?"

"That's what you kept threatening."

"Well, come on," she says. "Now's your chance."

He's still hidden beneath the hood of their car, attending to the oil or the antifreeze or the carburetor fluid, some liquid or another. "Are you going to humiliate me, Marilyn? After everything?"

"I'm not going to humiliate you. I'm going to teach you how to ride."

She has him on the seat now, and she's standing behind him, grabbing hold, first of his shoulders, and now, as the bicycle moves forward with him atop, just of the handlebars, which he's grasping as well. She lets go for a moment and he wobbles. He takes his feet off the pedals and rests them on the ground.

"Let's go down to the path," she says. "There's a clearing there. And if you fall, you fall on grass."

"Oh, Marilyn. I don't know."

"It's just like riding a bike."

"Exactly."

"You have to keep pedaling," she says. "If you come to an obstacle you just steer out of the way."

He's on the seat again, pedaling as she has told him to. She lets go for a second.

"Marilyn!"

"Don't worry," she says. "I won't let you fall."

He lists this way and that, like a canoe.

"Pedal, David, pedal!"

"I am!"

"Don't go out onto the road! There's traffic there!"

"What am I supposed to do?"

"You steer!"

She lets go now, and he's circling the path, making tight revolutions, teetering but staying aloft. She counts the seconds—ten, fifteen, twenty—until, finally, he keels over, toppling onto the lawn.

"Bravo!" she says. "You did it."

"Did what?" he says. "I fell." He looks up at her from beneath the bicycle. He has grass stains on his rear and on the legs of his pants.

"You fall, you get up."

He brushes off his pants, and now she's brushing them off, too. She slaps dirt off the knees and the cuffs at his ankles.

"I'm hungry," he says. "I've worked up an appetite. I'm going inside to eat your omelet."

"Okay," she says, though she hopes he'll save at least a little for her. She's worked up an appetite herself.

On the garden table, she finds the pear where she left it. She dispenses with it in a few bites and takes another pear and dispenses with it too, then deposits both cores in the compost heap. She gets down on her knees and removes more weeds from the garden, and now her pants are stained, just like David's. Only his are torn. There's a small hole in each leg; she can see the pale glint of his kneecaps, like two matching eggshells.

She walks around to the front of the house, where the hood of their car is still open. The mail has arrived early, and she goes to retrieve it. She has the weeds in one hand, the mail in the other, and it's only now, walking back to the house with her pile of letters, that she sees the return address on the top envelope. 1600 Pennsylvania Avenue. The White House. Someone must have placed her on the wrong mailing list. She opens the envelope. It's a letter from President Bush. He's sending her and David his condolences on the anniversary of Leo's death. Could it be a peace offering?

It's July fifth, she thinks. A day late and a dollar short. And an image comes to her from five years ago, she and Lily down in Florida for the recount, a Tuesday in December, waiting for the Supreme Court decision to come down. Florida, she thinks. A state that will forever in her mind be the state of shame: dimpled chads and butterfly ballots, Katherine Harris's noxious mug splattered across the TV. How different the world would be were it not for Florida. How different her own life would be, the life of her whole family. Standing in Florida with Lily, waiting for the decision to come down, then learning of it, the deflating conclusiveness of it all, she started to sob. "It's all over," she said. She was right, and she didn't even know it yet.

She can hear Lily's voice. *You should use that letter as a dartboard.* She would, she thinks, if only she had darts. And she's overcome by the strangest feeling, that she needs to go inside and tell Leo about this.

Guess who wrote me. President Bush.

You mean he's still president?

For another three years.

And here I was thinking it was just a dream.

And here she was thinking it, too. She'll think it again two years from now, out in Santa Cruz, on the Pacific Coast. She'll have flown there for Thisbe and Wyeth's wedding; David will have convinced her to go. The whole family will be there, except for Gretchen, who will have died the previous spring. A beach wedding, and she'll sit with Calder at a table in back, and Calder will say, "My daddy's dead," and she'll say, "Yes, he is," but it will be as if she hasn't heard him. Because from behind the bride and groom, a seal will have poked its head out of the water, and what Marilyn will be thinking about is Thisbe's first wedding, the one when she married her son.

"It was at the aquarium," she tells Calder.

"What was?"

But she doesn't answer him. She's thinking of the walrus pressing his nose to the glass, making his walrus noises.

"Will you take me swimming?"

"Sure," she says, and now he's leading her to the water. He's wearing a tuxedo and he has his pants legs rolled up, and she's holding the hem of her dress. They have their feet in the water, facing the wedding party up on the bluff, and now everything has blurred, and they're all just figures on a hill. Her dress is getting wet, she's taking her grandson for a swim, and then a wave is coming, and another, and another.

Now, in Lenox, she walks up the driveway with the mail in her hand. She moves purposefully along the path, holding the bills and flyers and subscription notices, the president's letter on top. She can hear David's footsteps upstairs. For a moment they stop, and she's alone. Then he's there, her husband, coming down the stairs, his shoes making their syncopated beat, and she's looking up at him, anticipating his voice, waiting to see what comes next.

ACKNOWLEDGMENTS

For help on everything from Berkshires swimming holes to legal trusts, and for assistance more essential (and time-consuming) than that, I am grateful to the following people: Marty Asher, Paul Bogaards, Michiko Clark, Maggie Carr, Shannon Donnelly, Dan Frank, Chris Gillespie, Janice Goldklang, Erica Hinsley, Linda Huang, Jenny Jackson, Altie Karper, Nicholas Latimer, Stephanie Listokin, Beth Meister, Peter Mendelsund, Brian Morton, Karen Ninnis, Miriam Nunberg, Anne-Lise Spitzer, Ian Twiss, Rosalie Wieder, and Danny Yanez. A special thank you to John Fulton for his acuity and insight, and to my agent, Lisa Bankoff, and my editor, Lexy Bloom, for their intelligence, doggedness, and great generosity.

ALSO BY JOSHUA HENKIN

"Charming. . . . Henkin keeps you reading with original characters, witty dialogue, adn a view that marriage, for all its flaws, is worth the trouble." —*People*

MATRIMONY

It's the fall of 1986, and Julian Wainwright, an aspiring writer, arrives at Graymont College in New England. Here he meets Carter Heinz, with whom he develops a strong but ambivalent friendship, and beautiful Mia Mendelsohn, with whom he falls in love. Spurred on by a family tragedy, Julian and Mia's love affair will carry them to graduation and beyond, taking them through several college towns, over the next fifteen years. Starting at the height of the Reagan era and ending in the new millennium, *Matrimony* is a stunning novel of love and friendship, money and ambition, desire and tensions of faith. It is a richly detailed portrait of what it means to share a life with someone—to do it when you're young, and to try to do it afresh on the brink of middle age.

Fiction

VINTAGE BOOKS
Available wherever books are sold.
www.randomhouse.com